ALSO BY WAYNE CALDWELL

Cataloochee

REQUIEM BY FIRE

REQUIEM BY FIRE

A Novel

Wayne Caldwell

RANDOM HOUSE

NEW YORK

Copyright © 2010 by Owlhead, Inc.

Published in the United States by Random House,
an imprint of The Random House Publishing Group,
a division of Random House, Inc., New York.

RANDOM HOUSE and colophon are registered
trademarks of Random House, Inc.

Grateful acknowledgment is made to Williamson Music o/b/o
Irving Berlin Music Company for permission to reprint an excerpt
from "Say It Isn't So" by Irving Berlin, copyright © 1932 by Irving Berlin.
Copyright © renewed. International copyright secured. All rights reserved.
Reprinted by permission of Williamson Music o/b/o
Irving Berlin Music Company.

All images copyright © iStockphoto.com

LIBRARY OF CONGRESS CATALOGING-IN-PUBLICATION DATA
Caldwell, Wayne
Requiem by fire: a novel / Wayne Caldwell
p. cm.
ISBN 978-1-4000-6344-4
eBook ISBN 978-1-5883-6972-7
1. Cataloochee (N.C.)—Fiction. 2. Rural families—North Carolina—Fiction.
3. Rural landowners—North Carolina—Fiction. 4. Mountain life—Great Smoky
Mountains Region (N.C. and Tenn.)—Fiction. 5. Great Smoky Mountains
National Park (N.C. and Tenn.)—History—Fiction. I. Title.
PS3603.A438R47 2010   813'.6—dc22   2009021562

Printed in the United States of America on acid-free paper

www.atrandom.com

2 4 6 8 9 7 5 3 1

FIRST EDITION

Book design by Dana Leigh Blanchette

For Jake

They wanted a quiet place that was dark at night, unwanted by other people, where they could grow their food or catch or find it, and be warmed by firewood burning on a hearth they made of rocks carried up from the river or the creek.

—WENDELL BERRY

A place that ever was lived in is like a fire that never goes out.

—EUDORA WELTY

Well, you really got me this time,
And the hardest part is knowing I'll survive.

—EMMYLOU HARRIS

Partial Cast of Characters

Silas Wright, farmer. Born 1850.

Jim Hawkins, warden, United States National Park Service. Born 1904.

Nell Johnson Hawkins, Jim's wife. Born in Asheville, North Carolina, 1907.

Henry Mack and Elizabeth ("Little Elizabeth") Hawkins, Jim & Nell's children. Born 1926 (Henry Mack) and 1929 (Elizabeth).

Henry and Elizabeth Johnson, Nell's parents. Born 1887.

"Aunt" Mary Carter, matriarch, widow of Hiram Carter, who died 1926. Born 1861.

Manson and Thomas Carter, farmers, Mary Carter's bachelor sons. Born 1885 (Manson) and 1886 (Thomas).

Levi Marion Carter, farmer, nephew of Mary Carter. Born 1881.

Valerie Brown Carter, Levi Marion's wife. Born 1882.

Hugh Carter, oldest son of Levi Marion and Valerie, auto mechanic. Born 1914.

James Erastus (Rass) Carter, second son of Levi Marion and Valerie, student. Born 1916.

Zeb Banks, farmer, son of the late Ezra Banks and Hannah Carter Banks. (Hannah is first cousin to Hiram Carter.) Born 1884.

Mattie Carter Banks, Zeb's wife, sister of Levi Marion Carter. Born 1884.

Jake Carter, farmer, brother of Hannah Carter Banks. Born 1871.

Rachel Thrash Carter, Jake's wife. Born 1884.

Oliver W. Babcock, Jr., attorney. Born in Currituck County, North Carolina, 1900.

Velda Parham, co-postmistress in Little Cataloochee, Billie Brown Parham's daughter. Born 1907.

Billie Brown Parham, co-postmistress in Little Cataloochee. (Probably cousin of Valerie Brown Carter.) Born 1878.

J. Harold Evans, superintendent, Great Smoky Mountains National Park. Born in Ohio, 1878.

Bud Harrogate, drifter. Born in Tennessee, 1888.

Horace Wakefield, surveyor, employee of park commission. Born 1888.

Harris "Red" Pendleton, employee of park commission. Born 1873.

Willie McPeters, pyrophiliac. Born 1883.

Rafe McPeters, farmer, Willie's father. Born ca. 1840.

Rev. Grady Noland, preacher to Little Cataloochee Baptist Church. Born 1869.

Rev. Will Smith, Methodist pastor to Big Cataloochee. Born in South Carolina, 1880.

Mack Hawkins, farmer, Jim's father. Born 1875.

Rhoda Hawkins, Mack's wife. Born 1877.

Rhoda Hawkins, Jr., Mack's daughter, Jim's sister. Born 1901.

Posey Bennett, otherwise called Old Man Bennett, farmer. Born ca. 1828.

Posey Bennett, Jr., otherwise called Old Man Bennett junior, farmer. Born 1854.

Lucius Bennett, physician, second son of Posey. Born 1856.

William Carter, brother of Hiram Carter, miller, farmer. Born 1852.

"Uncle" Andy Carter, Hiram Carter's uncle, farmer. Born 1822.

Thad Carter, ne'er-do-well, Uncle Andy's grandson. Born 1894.

Cash Davis, farmer on Little Cataloochee. Born ca. 1840.

Elijah (Lige) Howell, farmer, boardinghouse operator. Born ca. 1845.

Family names native to Cataloochee are Carter, Hawkins, Bennett, Wright, Parham, and McPeters. The rest are from various degrees of "off."

Foreword

The Great Smoky Mountains National Park, dedicated by Franklin Roosevelt in 1940 during his fourth presidential campaign, was not always inhabited solely by wild animals, tourists, and rangers. In the 1920s, North Carolina and Tennessee created park commissions to amass a half million acres of private property to give to the federal government. Much of the park used to be cut-over timberland exploited by northern companies, but, as any visitor to Cades Cove knows, some had been owned by prosperous farmers whose ancestors had dispersed the original Cherokee people and broken the first furrows early in the nineteenth century.

In Haywood County, North Carolina, the park gobbled the settlements of Big Cataloochee (postal address Nellie, North Carolina) and Little Cataloochee (Ola, North Carolina). Big Cataloochee was Methodist, Little Cataloochee Baptist. Both maintained schools, voted Democratic, and had, ironically enough, welcomed a new type of inhabitant: the tourist. All told, some eleven hundred souls lived there in the late 1920s, when the government said they had to go.

BOOK 1

The Goodliest Land

First Frost 1928–December 1928

CHAPTER 1

A Sign of the Times

Silas Wright, dreaming.

He told his compatriots, "Hardest part'll be digging up the nerve to do it." They shook hands in the dark as if to seal an infernal bargain, then bent to their work, feeling instead of seeing, pushing tinder under the little building. Silas heard the muffled click of kitchen matches in his overalls bib and the slosh of whiskey in his hip pocket. He was not unsteady—he could hold his liquor—but a twinge of either remorse or nausea struck the instant he bent his head to poke under the edge of the building. Straightening his back, he looked at the sky.

In flatlands he would have seen a fingernail moon about to set, but Cataloochee was ringed with high mountains that always hid such a rind of light. Thin clouds obscured all but first-magnitude stars and Saturn hung high in the western sky. Brothers Hiram and John Carter, his neighbors, worked on the other side, boots scraping the ground. Silas was glad no dogs barked. It would be a bitch to explain if they were caught.

None of the men had burned a school before, but they figured if they used wooden matches and no coal oil, people would not be suspicious. This time of year the teacher banked the fire in the potbellied stove against the night chill, so there would be ample coals to start a blaze should some errant bear knock over the heater, which Silas meant to do before they lit the circumference.

Fire laid, they met at the front door. Silas, a head taller than Hiram and John, and an angular man, was rarely seen without his briar pipe. He plucked it from his bib pocket and looked at his friends. "You boys ready?"

They nodded as one, but suddenly Hiram's balding head turned, owl-like, as he whispered, "What was that?" Three intakes of breath preceded perfect silence. Hiram exhaled. "Thought I heard something."

"Don't spook a man like that," said Silas. "I ain't ready to see Jesus just yet." They listened for a half minute. "Okay, boys, let's get to it," he said, and opened the door to the smell of warm cast iron and generations of chalk dust. A dull red glow outlined the seams in the stove. Donning a pair of gloves fetched from his back pocket, he breathed deeply and muttered, "Well, son, here we go."

A good shove broke the stovepipe away from the heater. Downdraft made fire leap immediately from the nipple. He pitched the stove the rest of the way over, scattering burning coals on the puncheon floor. Outside, on their knees, John and Hiram fanned tinder.

Within a minute they had a decent fire. They were maybe twenty yards from the school's bell, which was elevated on a post on the other side of the recess field, and Silas meant to ring it when the fire was advanced enough to ensure no possibility of saving the building.

As Silas lit his pipe, a sudden wind swept the valley, rushing, like word from crazed mountaintop prophets or perhaps a gale from the mouth of God Almighty, who had seen their crime and made fair to blow them all to kingdom come. The fire devoured the schoolhouse like a living beast, leaping from yellow to orange, roaring in a noticeable rhythm, content to feed upon itself long past the existence of the puny structure it consumed.

Silas had not figured a small building to sound so sinister in its dying.

Where did them damn Carters get off to? He had to think fast. Ride home and pretend he'd been asleep? Ring the bell like they had planned? Get the hell out for a few days?

He started running toward the bell, but the post seemed to get no closer. His chest felt like he had run uphill two miles. Gasping, he stopped and grabbed for his pipe. Gone. Fallen out somewhere, damn it all, perfect evidence he had burned a schoolhouse. Cursing and wheeling toward the fire, he began to run. He again made no progress, but . . .

A bony hand grabbed his shoulder. Carl, his niece Ethel's husband, yelled in his ear. "Get up, Silas. The damn chimbley's on fire!" Silas shook himself awake. Behind his bedroom mantel something malevolent rushed and retreated, each cycle in deeper breaths, and Silas looked out the window to see if the yard might have caught fire. He and Carl raced downstairs, Carl in flannel nightshirt and Silas in long johns, like two half-naked refugees from an asylum. Harrogate passed them carrying two blankets dripping with creek water.

Bud Harrogate had boarded with Silas for some time. His habit was to stay a year or two, then go on what he called a pilgrimage, and Silas called damned foolishness, for six months or more. Then he would return, happy as a vagabond hound. Despite his ways, he was good help, and in Silas's kindly moods he thought of Bud as the son he and his dead wife, Rhetta, had never had.

Harrogate's plaid coat sleeves were soaked, and he wore wet leather gloves to shield arms and hands from the fire while he stuffed the blankets into the chimney throat to make a damper. Within ten seconds the fire in the shaft starved, and the coals still in the fireplace smoldered.

Harrogate joined Carl and Silas in the yard to watch the chimney fire's death in a succession of yellow, orange, and ruby sparks that finally turned into ashes descending over the roof peak and floating down onto the cedar shakes.

"Guess the house ain't going to burn," said Silas. His father, Jonathan, had built a cabin beside the creek in 1861, which Silas had framed nineteen years later, and then he'd added a two-story central-chimney wing. The building's footprint was a *T* whose top faced east. The men stood underneath a tall cedar, pointing to the roof and shaking their heads in the graying dawn. "A man needs a chimney fire ever now and then, but only when he sets it hisself," said Silas. "Let's make some coffee."

Carl nodded and went inside to poke up the kitchen fire. Harrogate and Silas walked the perimeter of the house to make sure no stray embers lurked among skittering dry leaves. They watched Carl—his light brown hair nearly gone on top—fuss with the kitchen stove. Harrogate shucked his gloves and jacket. "Silas, that was close."

"Yep, have to admit, my legs are still shaking. That'll scare any man. Specially one dreaming about a fire to begin with." He pronounced "fire" to rhyme with "car."

"What fire was that?"

He grinned and looked at the ground. "It was an awful long time ago." He scratched his head. "First tend to that front room fire, then maybe we can have breakfast. Then I reckon I can tell it."

Harrogate's flat face and high cheekbones led some to speculate he had Melungeon blood, others Cherokee. He was the only unmarried male in Cataloochee who wore a ring, and he absently turned it on his left pinky as he went inside to remove the blankets and throw them into the yard. He opened windows and poked the fireplace coals with hope of slow revival. Carl breezed through the front room on his way upstairs for clothes. "I'll have breakfast on in a minute," he said. Silas followed him upstairs for his own overalls and shirt.

Ethel was visiting her sister in South Carolina, so once breakfast was on the table, the three men dispensed with manners, slurping and sopping and grunting their way through coffee, bacon and eggs, biscuits and gravy, and applesauce, followed by molasses and butter. "Nothing like damn near dying to get a man's appetite going," Harrogate said. They left the wreckage in the kitchen and padded slowly to the front room, as if not to wake the giant in the chimney.

Harrogate shut the windows. "Going to be a nice day," he said. "Bids fair despite this frost." He sat in Rhetta's old chair, a privilege Silas allowed no one but him.

"Well, Bud," said Silas as they sat before the fire, "you wanted to know what I was dreaming about when I got woke up." He lit his pipe, a small smile at the other corner of his mouth. "Neither of you remembers the old schoolhouse."

"Where was it?" asked Harrogate.

"Across the creek from the one we got now, just off the valley road, where Indian Creek comes into Cataloochee Creek. I remember when we called it the new school, because the first one was down past Lucky Bottom on the left. It was built way before the Civil War. That first one was took apart for firewood, best I remember, when the second school, the old schoolhouse in my dream, got built. That was about 1875, after the war anyhow.

"This schoolhouse—where your wife went to school, Carl, wasn't but one room—was fine for twenty-five or thirty young'uns, but by the turn of the century they had fifty or more in there, setting on top of each other. It's a wonder any teacher worked there more'n a week, or a pupil ever learned a fool thing.

"You all remember Hiram Carter. A fine man, even though he did sometimes think he was a little better'n the rest of us. See, he'd been off, with his hauling business. Traveled real regular into South Carolina. Didn't have any better education than the rest of us, but he read books besides the Bible and magazines besides seed catalogs, and I admit he could hold his own talking with anybody, even Preacher Smith or Doc Bennett.

"Anyhow, Hiram took this schoolhouse problem on hisself. He wrote to the commissioners to ask for a new building. They didn't answer. So he kept at it, and finally they wrote and said they wasn't any money. You know, boys, it still smells right smoky in here. You reckon we could stand it on the porch?"

They opened all the windows, picked up their jackets, and went outside. Harrogate and Carl sat on the porch rail like kids at a ball game, while Silas settled in the rocker and relit his pipe. "Well, sir, that word from Waynesville just fried Hiram's eggs. I reckon he fumed for a month, saying how every time we turned around they stuck their hands out for taxes, and still said they didn't have no money."

As Silas rocked, he rubbed the back of his neck. "Shoot, he should have lived long enough to see the tax collector in Haywood. You know,

Carl, that Sutton with a steel hook in place of a right hand. It's a sign of the times, let me tell you. Them tax collectors in the Bible got nothing on him.

"Anyhow, Hiram stewed and got agitated, finally come over. I just had put up the mule—we'd been snaking deadfall firewood. Hiram come up on that bay mare, just huffing and puffing. Started saying how we'll all go to Waynesville, hats in hand, make them commissioners understand how bad we need a school building.

"Well, I lit my pipe and listened. He finally asked what I thought. 'Hiram, you know something?' I said. 'What?' he said. Looked at me with that turn of head, you remember, that reminded you of them parakeets that used to be everywhere. I said, 'Ain't it a law that a school's got to have a building?' He nodded. 'Well,' I said, just as slow, 'if we didn't *have* one all of a sudden, then they'd be obliged to build us one, wouldn't they?'

"The damnedest look crept up on his face, like he was staring at the Wild Man of Borneo. 'What are you suggesting?' he said. I just shook my head and kind of smiled. 'If it just cotched fire . . . ,' I said, just as innocent as a lamb.

"You'd've thought I'd said let's kill President Coolidge. It got him on his high horse, sure enough. I'd not heard such a speech in a long time. 'You mean,' he said, 'to tell me you'd set fire to a school? Why, a school is next thing to a church, Silas. It's no different than lighting a match to the Statue of Liberty, by God. I'll not hear of such a thing in Cataloochee. This's the finest place I know of. You couldn't slip such a serpent into this Eden. You can't be serious.' That kind of thing. I just let him go on.

"After he wound down, he looked at me real serious like. Said, 'I don't know anybody low down enough to burn a school, except old Rafe's boy, Willie McPeters—or do I?' Looked at me like I was a coiled-up rattlesnake.

"I said, 'No, Hiram, you don't. But for the sake of argument, let's say you and me was to light a match to that little old building. Provided, of course, that they wasn't nobody in it, and provided too that we didn't get caught. The county'd *have* to build a new one, wouldn't they?' See, that was back before income tax. We still thought government might accidentally help a fellow every now and then.

"Well, sir, he fussed about destroying public property, or some foolishness, then looked at me again. 'Besides,' he said, 'and, Silas Wright, this is, like you said, for the sake of argument, where would the young'uns go to school? The county can't build one overnight. You can't teach school in a cornfield.'

"I kind of smiled. 'Brother, you just finished building that fine frame house.' And he had, too. It was pretty as a bag of nickels. Nine rooms and two stories for him and Aunt Mary and them two bachelor sons. He meant to fill the rest with boarders. I said, 'That cabin you moved out of would do fine.' It was like one of them lightbulbs coming on over Skeezix's head in the funny papers. He paced around, cogitating, studying it every which way.

" 'Say we was to do it,' he finally said. 'We'd need one of them pacts. Couldn't nobody tell about it, unless he was the last of us left.'

"Well, we planned it that afternoon. Said his brother John ought to be in on this. I didn't know why, but I said okay. We'd leave early of a morning like we was going to Waynesville, but instead stop at the gap and "loafer" the day away. Start back at dusky dark and hide desks and chalkboard and such truck in a laurel slick. Then we'd light it and ring the bell, like we'd just come from Waynesville and found it burning. Nobody'd be the wiser.

"I still wasn't convinced he was serious, so I told him to sleep on it, talk to John, and we'd palaver the next day. He and John come back and we shook on it. I asked if we ought to cut our fingers like we made blood brothers as young'uns, but they figured folks our age shouldn't mess with that.

"The next time the commissioners was to meet, we woke about three that morning and headed out of the valley. Spent the day laying up under a big poplar past the gap, counting squirrels, listening to the Lord God birds drum, drinking a little liquor. Come back at dark and did it."

"Silas, how did folks take it?" asked Carl.

"Well, I'll never forget the look on that twerpy teacher's face. See, he didn't know the desks were safe—he had a box, too, with knives and slingshots he'd confiscated and papers that looked a mite personal—and he seemed like he'd bust out crying if you said 'boo.' I took him aside and told him to show up for school at Hiram's place in the morning.

"Everybody was wringing their hands, 'cause once it started, that little old building went pretty quick, and them that brought buckets didn't have nothing to do except turn them upside down and set on them.

"But old Hiram, I had to hand it to him, he quieted everybody down, put his hat in his hands, and gave a speech. I still remember his forehead shining in the light of them embers. He got all solemn, told how we'd been to the meeting. Said the county allowed as how we weren't worth a school building over here, that they laughed at us. We were on our way home, he told it, trying to figure how to break the news to our neighbors and friends, when God Hisself—that's exactly the way he put it, 'God Hisself'—struck that little building so the boys and girls of Cataloochee could have a new school. It was a mighty fine oration."

Carl peered at his wife's uncle. "But you said you hadn't been to no meeting."

Silas looked at Carl, not for the first time, like the boy should either clean out his ears or apply for a new brain. "We hadn't. But they didn't know that, and after such a speech I wasn't about to say different. Somebody asked what next, and Hiram put his hat back on and said we'd have school in his old cabin until the commissioners built a new one. Somebody asked about desks and such, and Hiram didn't miss a beat. 'God will provide,' he said, 'just like He provided this here fire. Mark my words.' And he got a huzzah, and a few amens. Next morning, Hiram said he'd had a dream about them desks, and took that crowd there like Moses leading the children of Israel. By that afternoon they'd cleaned up that old cabin and was having school." He knocked his pipe into the yard. "And, boys, that's the truth."

Carl slid off the railing. "How long did it take to build the new one?"

Silas chuckled. "Took forever, it seemed like. Hiram didn't get them kids out of his cabin for two or three years."

"Anybody ever suspect you?" asked Harrogate.

"If they did, they didn't say. I expect them commissioners scratched their heads a little, but there wasn't no investigation."

"You couldn't get away with it now, I bet," said Carl.

"Times was different then," Silas said. "When something needed doing, it got done—one way or another." He scratched his chin. "Even government was different. You didn't have an inquisition ever time somebody farted like they do now. They mostly let you alone except when they wanted your vote. Now it's the damnedest mess you ever seen. And look what they want to do now—take your land for some cockeyed national park. Old Hiram would spin in his grave."

Silas stood as if to dismiss their meeting. "Boys, park or no park, we got a farm to tend to. Let's start by cleaning that cockeyed kitchen up."

CHAPTER 2

Pea Soup

A fly half as big as a bumblebee droned from one side of the bedroom to the other as the sun rose. A young man lay atop the bedcovers, in suit trousers, suspenders, and a white shirt. The only indications he was other than a corpse ready to view were an open mouth and half-mast necktie. Oliver W. Babcock, Jr., attorney at law, at six forty-five A.M. on Wednesday, October 10, 1928, in Ola, North Carolina, did not quite know it yet, but he was victim of a king-hell hangover.

He lay like a dead man, light dancing a tarantella on his head and providing appreciable lift to the fly, which buzzed his head like a dirigible. He opened his eyes. No memory of going to bed. His stomach tightened as he rose slowly and put head in hands. When he closed his eyes, something behind and between them spun like a top. His eyelids sprang open like roller shades. "Jesus, Mary, and Joseph," he muttered.

Oliver had graduated from law school at Chapel Hill the previous spring. He knew nothing of the mountains but had applied for a position with the North Carolina Park Commission because its chairman, Senator Mark Squires, could further Oliver's political ambitions, which included the governor's mansion. Squires had recommended him to Red Pendleton, soon to be head of the Waynesville office, who'd hired Oliver sight unseen, along with a young man from South Carolina, to negotiate with landowners, to search titles, and to draw deeds.

Oliver had grown up in Currituck County, a flat, windy land of tides and crab pots, oyster tongs and marsh grass, country that could hardly be more different from the high peaks and spruce forests of Haywood County. Since moving, he had had to master a mess of things, including a new dialect. In Cataloochee, "far" was something kept in a fireplace behind a hearth. "Sprang" could be a season, the past tense of a verb, a metal coil, or a source of drinking water. Oliver's sandlapper brogue was equally exotic to Cataloochans. When they first asked where he hailed from, he said "Sput," meaning Spot, the settlement he called home. They smiled as if he were a none-too-bright cousin. Then he tried "Moyock," the only nearby town, which came out "Muck." So he came to say "from the coast," and that sufficed, even if "coast" sounded like the past tense of "cuss."

He had to learn a whole new vocabulary. Groundhogs became whistle-pigs. Trumpet vine became cow-itch. Strawberry bushes were hearts-a'-busting. A saddleback caterpillar was a packsaddle in Cataloochee, and was equally to be avoided. And about the only similarity between speckled trout in Currituck and in Haywood was that both fish were scaleless.

It helped to have a sense of humor and the born politician's gift of never knowingly offending anyone. Oliver might show up to appraise a farm, dressed in a good suit, wearing a pocket handkerchief and shiny shoes, and the owner, sporting a slouch hat and an innocent smile, would say they had to walk every square inch. Before Oliver knew it, he'd be shoe-mouth deep in a hog pen. Despite this he did not complain. Oliver was tolerated by most, praised by some, and tittered about by girls, who thought him dashing.

Then came the killing. On the first of October 1928, Zeb Banks, eldest son of the largest landowner in Little Cataloochee, was mending a fence behind his house with his wife, Mattie. His father, Ezra, rode onto his property, drunk, angry, and dangerous. Zeb shooed Mattie inside and walked into the front yard. With no hesitation, Ezra shot Zeb's hat from his head with his owlhead pistol. As they struggled, more shots were fired. Zeb ended up charged with murder.

Oliver asked Pendleton for time off. "What in the world for?" Red said.

"If I can represent Mr. Banks successfully, we will have no trouble negotiating. An acquittal would be a big 'feather in our cap,' as you like to say."

So Pendleton grudgingly gave Oliver leave, with warning he'd better have his sorry ass at work the morning after the verdict or he'd be fired. The trial began Monday, October 8. The state presented a weak case, and Oliver moved for dismissal Tuesday morning. The judge granted his motion.

All Cataloochee turned out for the party at Jake and Rachel Carter's place. That night Jake, an oval-faced man with round spectacles—and the younger brother of Ezra's widow, Hannah—kept everyone's glasses full. Oliver knew he needed to be in Waynesville at nine the next morning, but Cataloochans toasted him repeatedly, and the postmistress, Velda Parham, fresh-faced, fetching, and single, was happy to dance with him when he wasn't being lauded.

Toward midnight Oliver said he didn't feel a bit drunk, and started telling Velda about playing in a three-week bridge game at his fraternity. Halfway through the tale he stood, limber-legged, and asked how many windows were in the kitchen. Velda giggled, there being only one. He stumbled, caught the table with his free hand, and raised his glass with the other. "There's a Carolina man for you," he said. "Didn't spill a drop."

Now, in a guest bedroom at six forty-five A.M., he tottered to the chair, dusted his shoes, and slapped at the fly with his socks. The previous night's hearth fire was dead. In the mirror over the nightstand his eyes looked like a road map of hell, and his hair belonged atop a character in "Maud the Mule." He dipped his comb into the pitcher, parted his hair exactly in the middle, and smoothed his long sideburns. Rubbing his teeth with a wet finger until they squeaked, he figured his boss was likely on his way to the office, grinning like Simon Legree.

In the kitchen, Rachel stirred a pot of applesauce and tended a skillet of bacon. A bowl of eggs sat on the counter, and Oliver smelled biscuits in the oven. In place of last night's whiskey jar was a salt and pepper set and a sugar bowl. Jake grinned. "Honey, get this poor man some coffee but don't make much racket. Mr. Counselor, you don't look too peart."

Rachel brought him a cup. "I don't know, Jake. He doesn't look too awful bad for a man who thought we had four or five windows in here last night."

Oliver's coffee was as black and oily as the lower Pigeon River. "Got any sugar?"

Jake pushed the bowl toward Oliver. "You want your eggs fried or scrambled?"

"Just coffee, thanks. I couldn't eat a thing."

"Don't be silly," said Rachel. "In this house, I cook and folks eat. Jake, maybe he needs a hangover tonic."

Oliver looked dully at Jake, who said, "Something my daddy swore by. Morning after the night before, you got to do either the hair of the dog, or tomato juice with raw egg."

"I'll try the latter, without the egg."

Jake came back from the can shed shaking a quart of red fluid. "Here's the heat of summer in a jar. It'll do you right."

Rachel served eggs, bacon, and biscuits as Oliver guzzled juice.

"Want some aspirin?" asked Rachel.

Oliver nodded as vigorously as he dared. Rachel popped the back corner of a tin of Bayer's and shook out two tablets beside Oliver's plate.

By seven-thirty he was on his way, belly full. He drove by the clapboard church where raw dirt arched over Ezra's grave, then down through Ola, happy to see no sign of Velda. He didn't want her to see him unshaven, and he couldn't remember what he might have said late last night. He drove out of Little Cataloochee onto the main road, the car twisting and turning with the switchbacks, rocking him like a county fair ride.

Halfway up, he threw the car out of gear, ratcheted the brake lever, jumped out, and vomited in the huckleberry bushes. Leaning over the ditch, he retched until tears streamed his cheeks. He slowly unbent until he could breathe. A squirrel on a sourwood limb seemed the only witness. Oliver wiped his mouth and forehead. A quarter to nine. He would be lucky to arrive by early afternoon. Pendleton would cashier him for sure.

The auto made it up the grade to Turkey Cove, mountain fast to his left, curves too narrow to meet more than a mule's width of traffic. This high up, sourwood leaves were scarlet, and yellows showed in the tulip trees. At Cove Creek Gap sat a wagon, the teamster in the bushes for a morning errand. Oliver slowed so as not to spook the man's mules, then shoved the Ford into second. Now he had mountain on the right, bathed in sunshine, and a perfect view of Utah Mountain, past which rows of peaks stood bathed in blue mist.

Each mile increased both hunger and anxiety. Red Pendleton usually meant what he said, except when he didn't. A tall, fussy man of fifty-five, he was quickly losing the reason for his nickname. Before Pendleton's employment with the park commission, he'd been a local manager for a Pennsylvania lumber company. But as early as 1924 a Knoxville paper reported that, while Pendleton's firm had offered to sell eighty thousand acres of virgin Tennessee timberland to the park, it kept slashing the tract's lumber as fast as a Duesenberg at Indianapolis, thereby profiting twice, not to mention defrauding the government. Pendleton resigned soon after, moved to North Carolina, and changed from buying timberland for scandalous profits to acquiring farmland to make a national park. Oliver doubted that altruism had been Pendleton's motive.

Nor did Pendleton endear himself to Horace Wakefield. A trim, freckle-faced man of forty, Wakefield was a South Carolinian who had fallen in love with the mountains as a youth on a camping adventure. After a surveyor's apprenticeship, he'd started a land office in Waynesville. The park commission's Asheville headquarters had hired him to survey in Cataloochee, which he had done for some months on pretense of county business—and when they'd found they needed a Haywood County branch, they'd used Horace as interim manager.

Cataloochee landowners by and large trusted Horace, and their young sons clamored to help him find calls, carry chains, and hold rods.

He had not liked the idea of the park at first, but had slowly come to think it would protect the area from rapacious timber operations.

The commission's three small offices and reception area took up a back corner of the first story of the county courthouse. The morning Pendleton first showed up, Horace had been going over some papers with Mae Shook, their secretary. Pendleton walked in like a big dog, Horace later told Oliver, and looked things over like he was deciding whether the place was worthy of his attention. Pendleton let the door slam, announced his name, and produced a letter from Senator Squires. Horace introduced himself and Mae, and read the letter. Pendleton said, "By the way, Mr. Wakefield, I have hired two field agents. I'm not sure there's room for them here."

Wakefield gave Pendleton a wry smile. "Mr. Pendleton," he said, as smooth as butter, "if Senator Squires wants you here, it's fine with me. And if you and he want to hire so-called field agents, that's peachy. But I'll have no one undermine the confidence I have built in Cataloochee. Who have you all hired?"

"Two young men, one an Oliver Babcock from the coast, and the other a South Carolinian named Ashley Cooper Blackwell, both highly recommended by Senator Squires."

"Does either know mountain people?"

"Mr. Wakefield, people are people."

"I don't know so well about that, Mr. Pendleton. These highlanders are spooky. Make them mad, and we might have to condemn their land. Eminent domain would be a nightmare."

"May I ask why?"

"Mr. Pendleton, Governors Peay and Horton in Tennessee have spent a lot of political capital assuring citizens there will be no eminent domain. So has Governor McLean. To condemn hundreds of parcels would be a scandal. We'd never put the land together. I hope for the park's sake that you and Mr. Squires have hired well."

So Pendleton ran the office—at least Mae let him think he did— while Wakefield continued to survey and advise. Oliver avoided Pendleton as best he could but really liked Wakefield. At their first meeting, Oliver asked, "Do you have a sport?"

Wakefield turned. "It used to be baseball, young man. Third base. The hot corner. If I do say so, I was a fair fielder and not a bad hitter."

"Where'd you play?"

"In high school, in Greenville. Then two seasons at Carolina until I had to tend to my sick father. Could have played in the big time, I think, if I'd been a little faster."

"When were you at Chapel Hill?"

Wakefield threw back his head and laughed. "Good Lord, son, are you another benighted devil who thinks 'Carolina' is *North* Carolina? Will we ever have fun working together!" He slapped Oliver on the back. "I was at Columbia in '06 and '07. After my father died, I played for Greenville one season—then tore my knee up."

"Golly. Did you know Shoeless Joe?"

"We were together the year before he went to Philly. I never saw a soul better at hitting, as good a base runner as Cobb but not nearly as nasty. As modest a man as you could find."

"Then you don't think he threw the Series?"

Wakefield snorted. "Anyone who's around Joe Jackson ten seconds knows he didn't. Judge Landis is a pure-tee fool."

So Oliver got along with Horace from the first. His other colleague, Ashley Cooper Blackwell, started with three strikes against him. In the first place, he used all three names. Moreover, he was a tall, flat-faced boy with a stiff neck, which made him appear to look down on most folks. And he said he was from Charleston, although when he walked to town on Saturday it was merely to Wando. Blackwell had worked two days when Pendleton's phone rang.

"Mr. Pendleton?" scratched a reedy voice.

"Yes, what is it?"

"This here's Hub Carter. The Cataloochee mailman. You working a tall old boy with three names?"

"Yes, why?"

"Well, sir, you know what I seen at the post office?"

Pendleton leaned close to the Bakelite mouthpiece. "Mr. Carter, I'm a busy man. Get to the point."

"Well, sir, this beanpole had been to see Silas Wright about his property. Now, if I was you, I wouldn't have sent such a scarecrow to see Silas.
You know him, Mr. Pendleton?"

"Of course. I hired him."

"No, I mean Silas Wright."

"No, I don't."

"Well, he's as stubborn a man as I ever knowed, unless you count
Moses arguing with the Lord Jehovah. You know them big old wooden
barrels they ship flour in?" Pendleton said nothing. "You there, sir?"

Pendleton sighed. "Yes, Mr. Carter, go on."

"Well, one of them barrels was setting outside the post office. No idea
what it was doing over here to start with. Maybe somebody brung it
from one of the town ho-tels to catch rainwater in. Anyhow, it had a
bright yellow label stuck on it that said 'National Park, Warshington,
D.C.' And you know what? Your boy Blackwell was stuffed in there like
a plumb sardine. Somebody'd bored air holes and give him a paper poke·
with a hunk of cornbread and half a sweet tater and a little bitty jug of
water. Postmaster Nelse said they was regulations against mailing people
but, on the other hand, he couldn't open nobody else's mail, so he let the
barrel set in the sun and holler awhile. Me and Nelse talked it over considerable. We finally figured since it didn't have no stamps, and it wasn't
in the door yet, it wasn't active mail, so we let him out."

Blackwell knew better than to show back up to give Pendleton the
satisfaction of firing him. That preyed on Oliver's mind shortly after
noon on the day after Zeb Banks's trial, as he crossed the Richland Creek
bridge and headed through Frog Level. The roadster chugged by the
depot and up the hill. He parked in the gravel lot behind the courthouse,
disturbing a yellow tomcat.

Oliver entered the basement and walked deliberately to the first floor.
Echoing footfalls reminded him of the climb at the redbrick Corolla
lighthouse. He stopped at the commission office, straightened his tie,
and turned the doorknob.

"Well, if it isn't the triumphant counselor." The secretary beamed.
"Welcome back."

All the office doors were shut. "Thanks, Mae. Where's Mr. Pendleton?"

"Mr. Wakefield and he had a conference, then went to the café." She glanced at the wall clock. "They've only been gone ten minutes. You want to meet them there?"

"No, no. But I'm hungry as a springtime bear. You have anything to eat?"

She fetched three winesaps and a shaker of salt from her desk drawer. Oliver thanked her and picked two apples. He understood salting tomatoes and melons, but not apples. He started peeling one with his pocketknife. "Am I about to get canned?"

"I would have said so first thing, but they've had word from Mr. Squires that seemed more important than you, if you'll pardon that way of putting it."

Oliver finished the first apple, dropped its core into the trash can, and peeled the second. "You're a lifesaver. I got drunk last night and then sick coming up the mountain. About Dellwood I was hungry. Almost stopped at the Railroad Café but figured Mr. Pendleton'd be mad as hops."

"I knew you hadn't attended a Sunday school picnic. Wash up good."

Oliver closed his door and finished the second apple. Wishing for a razor, he washed his hands and face. Straightening trouser creases and adjusting his collar, he waited.

Two sets of footsteps echoed in the hallway. Oliver cleared his throat and smoothed his tie. Horace opened Oliver's door. "Good day, Counselor. Congratulations. Come to Red's office right away."

Behind Wakefield's greeting Pendleton walked briskly, a clicking thumbtack lodged in his left heel. "Thanks," said Oliver. "Someday I'll tell you about the trial."

"Certainly. But this afternoon we three need to put our heads together." They pulled chairs close to Pendleton's desk. At first Pendleton paid no more attention to Oliver than he would the spots on a ladybug.

"Gentlemen, we need to agree on things this afternoon," Pendleton began. "First, Senator Squires perceives we lag behind our Tennessee counterparts. That is a black eye. He wants us wrapped up by spring, if not sooner. There are about a hundred parcels. That would average five per week. Ten a week would finish it by Christmas. That would be a feather in our cap."

Oliver and Horace nodded. "I see no reason we can't meet that goal," Horace said.

"Good. Now, second, people are given a choice: sell outright for a certain sum and move immediately, or sell at a reduced price, reserving a lifetime lease, and stay." He plucked a cigar from his pocket. "Gentlemen, we need to carefully soft-pedal this life lease business."

"What do you mean, Mr. Pendleton?" asked Oliver.

Pendleton fished for a knife, cut the end of his cigar, and reached for the lighter on his desk. Blue-white smoke soon clouded the room. "There will be no lifetime leases."

Oliver looked ready to throw up again. "Mr. Pendleton, we have told people they can stay the remainder of their lives. It's the only reason we haven't been strung up by our heels. Is the commission going back on its word?"

"Of course not, you simpleton." Pendleton exhaled toward the ceiling. "What I mean is, we need to be careful with our terminology. We will still call these arrangements lifetime leases. But in legal fact, they will be one-year leases with option to renew for another year—as long as restrictions are not violated."

Wakefield frowned through the haze. "These restrictions—why don't we go over them? Not to harm the land is one. What else?"

Pendleton blew four concentric circles toward the ceiling. "They may not cut trees."

Oliver grinned until he realized Pendleton was serious. "Mr. Pendleton, please explain how a man can heat his home without firewood."

"He will pick up deadfall, or he can fell dead trees with a Park Service Special Use Permit. There's coal. But no more green timber will be cut. We mean for this to be wilderness."

"Sir," Oliver said, "I don't mean to be argumentative, but how—and where—can someone who uses ten or twenty cords a winter find that much deadfall?"

Pendleton shaped the cigar ash on the side of the ashtray. "That is not our concern."

Wakefield shifted in his chair, then stood and opened the window. "Mr. Pendleton, these people will not take kindly to that. What about fishing and hunting?"

"There will be seasons and limits, as on all public game lands."

"So you expect us to tell a man he can hunt squirrels, say, only a month a year? Or use only artificial bait for trout, that sort of thing?"

Pendleton waved the question away. "Listen, gentlemen. Our job is not to explain, wheedle, or cajole. It is to sell. Whatever it takes to get these yokels to sign on the dotted line is fine. If not mentioning specific restrictions helps the process, so much the better."

Wakefield sat and scratched his head. "Mr. Pendleton, how would you like it if I knew it would be impossible for you to pasture your cattle on the balds—by the way, Mr. Babcock, another restriction—but I didn't tell you. You sell your land, then discover you cannot pasture your cattle there. How angry would you be with me? Or say you don't know, take your cattle up, and lose your lease? Would you not be ready to kill me?"

Pendleton fiddled with his cigar. "Mr. Wakefield, you have read Mr. Squires's letter. Ethical niceties are past. If we produce no results, he will find someone else who will."

Wakefield sat back down. "Let me take a new tack. How does the park service mean to police these restrictions? How many wardens for Cataloochee, for example?"

"No more than two or three, I would expect."

"Aha, a game! That's it. You see, it would take an extraordinary man to be in fifty-leven places at once. Because that's where he would have to be to police each mile of stream, count all the downed limbs, and, while he's at it, squirrels and fish. Mr. Pendleton, these yokels, as you call them, know the service won't be able to catch them any easier than revenue officers can find their stills. In fact, many will enjoy the challenge. So I don't know that we need to soft-pedal restrictions. Unless some are really outrageous."

"The service wants this land to revert to wilderness, so they could not break new ground. They couldn't build new buildings without a Park Service Special Use Permit. No hunting and fishing except in season.

They couldn't make or possess liquor, which we know will be honored only in the breach. I would expect more trouble over one PSSUP"—Pendleton pronounced it "pea soup"—"condition than these you have mentioned. One would have to obtain a PSSUP to bury one's family in the park."

Horace nodded. "Would such a request ever be denied?"

"I can't see why. Who would deny access to a family cemetery?"

They nodded in silence. Pendleton spoke first. "That's about it, gentlemen. I want you men in Big Cataloochee tonight. I'll tend to Little Cataloochee. Remember that feather in our cap."

Wakefield looked at him. "Mr. Pendleton, a dollar to a donut says Oliver and I can close them more quickly. Use your administrative skills here."

Pendleton eyed Horace. "Are you telling me I don't know my job?"

"Not at all. But Oliver here has built trust, as I have. And the people over there who know you—well, I don't know how to say it except bluntly—they don't care for you."

"Maybe you have a point. I *would* have to establish myself."

Pendleton and Wakefield shook hands, but when Oliver put his out, he received only a glare from his boss. "That will be all, Mr. Babcock. There *will* be a next time."

CHAPTER 3

Blood and Flesh and Bone

The Wednesday when Oliver and Horace started to Cataloochee, exhaust from Horace's green Chevrolet hung in the air like cigar smoke. Horace meant to leave Oliver at Zeb Banks's place in Little Cataloochee, then pick him up Friday evening to return to Waynesville. Horace, meantime, would visit Big Cataloochee. The sooner they wrapped up the commission's business, he figured, the sooner they removed Red Pendleton from their hair.

North of Waynesville, misty wood smoke lay in people's front yards. "See that?" Horace asked. "A sure sign of falling weather."

"You know," Oliver said, "I can't remember noticing that as a boy. First time I remember smoke lying like this was at the university. The sward between South Building and that library they're constructing looked covered with cotton batting a yard thick. Two days later came a foot of snow. Cry mercy, I'm glad I brought an umbrella."

Oliver wore a black chesterfield coat over his suit, and had swapped his long-cuffed driving gloves for a short kidskin pair. His hat, of silk-lined beaver felt, perched rakishly on his head. Horace wore army duck trousers, a denim jacket over a flannel shirt, and a striped cotton cap such as railroad men wear. "I think you're the only person I know who owns an umbrella," Horace said, and laughed.

Gabbing starlings festooned power lines, and waxwings and robins migrating from northern haunts tore berries from bittersweet vines and scattered orange droppings behind. Hay shocks stood in the middle of cut fields to feed what cattle had not been sold or beefed. Dogwood berries shone red ripe, roadside asters winked blue, and spiny sweet gum balls littered the road. Oliver smiled. "You know, I love the change of seasons. Almost makes you want to get your luggage and follow the birds, doesn't it?"

"Cataloochee folks will love being migratory, won't they?" said Horace. "They might as well. The surveys are finished, they all know the park is coming, and we're about to close this out."

"Actually, people in Little Cataloochee are mostly ready to move. They figure they can't fight it. Jake Carter, for example, is angry about the park but figures what can he do? And the sooner he leaves, the sooner his hurting will heal. Will lots of people in Big Cataloochee stay?"

"You couldn't move Silas Wright with dynamite. Most of the Carters will stay. I just hope there aren't many soreheads. That McPeters bunch was downright nasty at the community meeting."

"I wouldn't put it past them to kill over this," said Oliver. "The way I heard it, the old man—Rafe—was threatening to shoot any government employee who sets foot on his land."

"Did you hear about the revenue man?"

"No, what about him?"

"A man named Moody came into Cataloochee a dozen years ago looking for whiskey stills. Worked for the T-men, as they say in the moving pictures. The first day he made some folks mad. The second, he disappeared. Nobody found even a whisker."

"Was McPeters a suspect?"

"Not the old man. It's hard to prove murder without a body. But revenue men carry folding money to reward 'tips,' and Willie McPeters bought himself a nice rifle that winter—with cash."

Oliver nodded. "Where there's smoke, there's fire. Is Willie still around?"

"He's a strange one. I've only seen him once, and when he realized I'd spotted him, he faded into the woods like an old bear. They say he never speaks. Kind of a wild man, famous in this country for setting fires. Yes, I'd say he's around, but you likely won't see him."

Horace left Oliver at Zeb and Mattie Banks's place and headed to Big Cataloochee. Oliver carried an overnight bag in his left hand, sandwiched a briefcase under that arm, and twirled a Chaplinesque umbrella with his right as Jake greeted him.

"Afternoon, Counselor. You look a sight better'n you did this morning."

They shook hands after rearranging Oliver's baggage. "Much improved, thank you."

"Come in the house. We'll have everybody gather here tomorrow, so you won't have to do this sixty times. Rachel and Mattie'll fix dinner."

Next day, at least two dozen people milled in Zeb's front room. Zeb's mother, Hannah, occupied the upholstered chair, her clustered grandchildren reminding Oliver of a picture of Queen Victoria's family. She wore a black dress with a silver brooch pinning a foam-green kerchief. Oliver took Hannah's outstretched hand.

"Mrs. Banks, how perfectly delightful."

Hannah beamed at him. "Young man, you are a sight for sore eyes yourself. Tell me, do you have a steady?"

Oliver smiled as his eyes met Velda Parham's. "No, ma'am. Not enough time." He bowed slightly in Velda's direction.

"You should make time," said Hannah, as Jake picked up a stick of kindling and rapped on the mantel. "Neighbors," he said, "Oliver Babcock is back, this time on official business. Oliver, how long do you expect to take?"

"It depends on the number of questions—no more than an hour, I would guess."

"How hungry are you?"

"I can always eat."

"Then let's put on the feed bag, if dinner's ready." He lifted eyebrows to his wife, Rachel, who nodded. "Let's bless it. Everybody stand and hold hands."

The line of people snaked from the front room into the kitchen and back. Most were related, but even the hands of such outsiders as Neil LeClerc, a Canadian logging foreman working over the mountain at Crestmont, made a link in the family chain. Children looked up at parents, who gestured for them to close their eyes. Jake waited for dead quiet. "Lord, look down on us poor people. Jesus said whenever two or three are gathered in His name, He'd be there. We need a lot of Jesus in this hour. Bless us with His presence, bless this food to the nourishment of our bodies, and bless the hands that prepared it. Forgive us our many sins. In Jesus' name, amen."

They ate wherever they could find a place to set a plate or sit with dish on knee. The kitchen table held great quantities of pork and, it being fall, roasted beef and stewed beef, along with several kinds of beans, corn, potatoes—mashed, fried, and scalloped—deviled eggs, and cornbread. Mattie opened a jar of her special okra pickles, seasoned with cayenne peppers, which men sampled but women and children carefully passed to their neighbors. Oliver sat beside Velda, eschewing onions but otherwise spooning out great helpings. Dessert was apple stack cake and green Jell-O with fruit cocktail.

After dinner Oliver stacked papers on the mantel in the front room. After taking off his jacket, he fingered his paisley suspenders and gathered his audience. He carefully explained the alternatives—a landowner could sell and leave at one price, or sell and stay at another. Despite Oliver's oratory, Cash Davis soon snored softly.

Staying meant changing habits, Oliver explained. "There will be restrictions. For example, one could not break new ground. One would have to abide by hunting and fishing regulations. Seasons, bag limits, bait restrictions, that kind of thing. One— Why are you laughing, Jake?"

"Tell me who's going to enforce this—pardon my French—bull feathers?"

"There will be wardens, Jake, but no one knows how many."

"Derned if I don't think I'll stay. I'd love to match wits with some tin-pot warden."

Rachel elbowed his ribs. "Let the poor man finish, Jake."

Oliver ran his finger between collar and neck and straightened his tie. "Where were we? Oh, yes, one could not possess, make, or sell alcoholic beverages."

Cash Davis stopped snoring and looked around. "They God, I never heard such mutton-headed rot in my life. Now I *know* I'm leaving."

All laughed, some more nervously than others. "Uncle Cash, the whole country's been dry for years, and that's never put a crimp in your style," said Zeb.

Cash stretched and looked at Zeb squarely with his right eye. The other seemed to focus about ten feet away. "Son, that's true enough. But I'm too old to risk getting put out of my home because of it." He looked at Oliver. "Ain't that right, young man? They'd kick me out?"

"Yes, Mr. Davis, you would lose your lease, plus incur any legal penalties appertaining to the case."

"Ain't going to chance it, then," Cash said, folding his arms across his chest. "I'm leaving."

"Other restrictions," Oliver went on, "include a prohibition on cutting live trees, whether for fence posts or firewood."

"How in tarnation are we supposed to heat our houses?" yelled George Banks, Zeb's younger brother, a man whose normal expression was as happy as a mole in daylight.

"The simple answer is—the best way you can. Collect deadfall. Switch to coal. Truck in firewood. But the park service will not sanction harvesting live trees. It's the same principle as that against breaking new ground. They mean for the land to return to wilderness." Oliver looked outside, where sunshine promised a dry end to the day. "There are two more restrictions. One, you may no longer range cattle on the balds."

"So there goes your income from beef cattle," said Jake. "Let's sum this up. You can't make money off cattle. You'll freeze to death of a winter with no wood to burn. You'll starve to death because you can't kill game. About all that's left is die and leave it."

"That's another restriction. One may not bury in the cemeteries without a permit."

"Even if we stay here?" asked Mattie, springing to her feet.

"Yes, I'm afraid so."

"Listen here." Despite four children and forty-four years, Mattie Banks, standing straight and proud, could still turn a man's head. "Zeb and I had already decided to take their price—if it's fair—and leave. But now you say Zeb might couldn't lay me to rest beside Mama and Papa? Because if that's true, I'll stay and caretake that graveyard. Come to think of it, if they want this to be wilderness, how can we know they won't get shed of the cemeteries once we leave? Or what if in thirty years it's so growed up we couldn't find them? And could they turn a body down for one of those permits?"

Oliver shoved his hands deep into his pockets. "Mattie, they tell me the cemeteries will be protected. And I cannot think why they would prohibit a family from burying a loved one as long as there is room."

Mattie's reddened eyes watered. "Mr. Babcock, I—we—can't give up our dead like that. We have to know we can come back to tend to their graves. We got to be able to rest beside them when it's our time." Oliver noticed many heads nodding.

Mattie plucked a handkerchief from her apron pocket and wiped her eyes. "You see, leaving our dead ain't like leaving a barn, or even the house where we was raised, hard though that is. Either one is abandoning a part of yourself, same as if you left a leg or an arm. But deserting your dead? That's sacrilege. The children of Israel toted Joseph's bones all over creation until they came to the promised land. Is that what we'll have to do? Dig them up and bury them somewhere else?" Mattie put away the handkerchief. "Our parents gave us life. Along with kinfolk and neighbors they raised us to fear God and help our fellow man. They are our blood and flesh and bone—and when we die, we want to lay beside them so at the last trumpet we can rise together and meet our Jesus." She got more amens than Brother Noland normally received during an hour's sermon.

Oliver nodded. "Mattie, I will clarify all that. I can't imagine burial in the park would be denied, even to a miscreant with a lost lease. But I will ferret that out."

"Get it from somebody besides that dern Pendleton," said Jake. "That man's a liar. While you're at it, get it in writing."

"I will. Any other questions?"

Cash Davis unfolded himself and stood. "That little lady's speech makes me think to make one, too. Mr. Babcock, bear with a man nearer ninety than he likes to think about."

"Of course, Mr. Davis."

Cash slowly scanned the crowd. "Folks, I fought under Colonel Love in the Sixteenth North Carolina. From Seven Pines to Antietam, we was going to win that war. Then they sent us over the mountain yonder, to Strawberry Plains, and made us defend a front that really didn't exist. It was plain stupid. It was like government said, 'Well, sir, instead of fighting and winning, we'll set around and lose this war.' After that came reconstruction, flatland Republicans ever dern where. You never seen the like of stupidity. Then we had that Spanish War. I never did see any need to fight them people, and then, aye Godfrey, we had us a world war, and mark my words there'll be another'n before long.

"But this park beats any of that. We've minded our own business for a hundred years, living quiet and peaceful, like democracy says to do. That's a big word, 'democracy,' a word they said that Great War made the world safe for. Democracy? Did they let the first one of us vote on this park? What in heaven's name kind of democracy is that?"

He sighed. "But I'm old. If they offer something reasonable, I'll go over the mountain—for the last time. I won't come back. Because when government gets through ruining this here paradise, I won't *want* to see it, not even if I'm dead. They can bury me wherever I fall."

"Anybody else?" asked Oliver. No one said anything. "Okay, folks. Your farms have been surveyed and appraised. I have the offers. I'll meet with you privately at that table. You can decide today, but you don't have to. I *would* appreciate hearing from you all by the end of next week. And I will report on burial regulations."

Within twenty minutes folks shook their heads or privately congratulated themselves. Neil LeClerc was happy at a five-hundred-dollar offer for land for which he had paid Ezra Banks two dollars. Jake and Rachel's seventy-five acres appraised for five thousand, and Hannah's inheritance from Ezra, the largest parcel in Little Cataloochee, thirty-five thousand. The only man lingering at Oliver's table was George Banks, whose arrogant swagger not even his father, Ezra, had managed to beat out of him. George's greasy, pointing finger smeared Oliver's paper. "What if I don't like that figure?"

"You think it's too low?" asked Oliver.

"No, Mister Fancy-Pants lawyer. I think I'll buy myself eight or ten aeroplanes with it. 'Too low.' What the hell did you think I meant?"

"There's no cause for profanity, Mr. Banks. You can go to court over the price. That would involve a lawyer. You'd have no guarantee a court would agree with you, although historically courts tend to favor plaintiffs in such matters."

"That's all?"

"Yes, Mr. Banks. That's all."

"Why don't you and me negotiate it man-to-man?"

"That is not what I'm here for, Mr. Banks. Any changes have to be decided by a court."

"And you damn lawyers work on shares?"

"An attorney would get a certain portion of the settlement."

"Bullshit."

"Excuse me, Mr. Banks?"

"You heard what I said." George stomped out of his brother's house.

As Oliver gathered papers, Velda appeared at his side. "Oliver, did he threaten you?"

"No, Velda. He's just upset over the price."

"He's been what you call 'upset' ever since I've known him. Be careful. His temper's as bad as his late lamented father's."

Oliver smiled. "Don't worry your pretty head about that." He looked her over. She had intrigued him when they'd met, as he was preparing for Zeb's defense, and had positively fascinated him at the party after the trial. "May I visit this afternoon?"

"If you didn't, I'd feel slighted."

He picked up his briefcase. "Then 'Let me not to the marriage of true minds/Admit impediments,' as the poet says."

"Marriage, Oliver? Is that on your mind?"

"Miss Velda, I'm only quoting Shakespeare."

CHAPTER 4

Don't Know What You're Talking About

Horace Wakefield usually stayed with Lige and Penny Howell at their boardinghouse in Big Cataloochee. He left Oliver in Little Cataloochee on Wednesday afternoon and drove the twisty road to Big Cataloochee. Coming down the hill past the Bennett house, he forded the creek, and a left turn soon brought him to Lige's, where several fishermen vied for trout behind the house. Penny had sent a card saying his usual room would be ready, so he parked, reached for his bag, and crossed into the dogtrot.

In the downstairs left-hand bedroom something gleamed in the corner. He picked up an ivory-colored tooth sporting a golden banner with BPOE in raised letters, and walked to the porch, where Lige sat whittling, in the exact spot Horace had last seen him.

Lige Howell was a large man with a shock of long white hair and a beard reaching his waist. His prominent nose and sapphire-blue eyes made both men and women take notice. Preachers who met him remembered prophets such as Elijah, his namesake, or Moses. Southern romantics thought of an aged Robert E. Lee.

"Afternoon, Horace. Have a good ride?"

Horace pulled up a chair. "Fine, Lige. Good day to travel. This was in the corner of my room."

Lige squinted at it. "Ain't that Pendleton's elk tooth?"

"Could be. He hasn't worn his in some time. I'll be happy to take it to him."

Lige laughed. "It's a dern sight safer'n asking him to come get it. The way local folks took a dislike to that man, they might bring him some tar and feathers."

Horace put the pin into his pocket. "I dread going to see Silas Wright, but if I have a pile of different jobs to do, I like to do the worst first. Then the rest seem easier."

Lige nodded. "I'm the same way. Or used to be. Now I take it all easy. Like this park. Getting too old for the boardinghouse business. Give us enough money to buy a one-story bungalow, with central heat, we'd be set. Do my children right and that'd be copacetic."

Horace smiled. "I wish everyone had that attitude."

"Son, anymore, things go through me like a dose of salts through Sherman. I'm an old man, born in 1845. Fought in the war. Wounded, got over it, they put me back in. Somehow came home in one piece. Hard times after that, Lord. But we managed to make a good life. Raised ten young'uns, didn't have but two die on us. We're just running this house to do something till the Lord takes us, and if He comes today, I'm ready. They're going to have this park in spite of what a doddering old man thinks."

"What *do* you think about the park, Lige?"

Lige scrutinized the piece of cherry, trying to figure what manner of creature lurked inside. "I haven't told anybody this, and if you tell it, I'll deny it to my last breath, you hear?"

Horace nodded. Lige motioned Horace to lean in closer. The old man smelled like a dog in a pile of leaves.

"You folks are doing us a favor."

Horace looked around to make sure the world wasn't about to end. "Really?"

"Look around, Mr. Wakefield. Only people doing any good is folks like Silas who have enough land. Everybody else either struggles on too few acres or hires themselves out. And another thing. Young men is running out of women to marry. Everybody's practically first cousins. Won't be long before Cataloochee young'uns'll be so cross-eyed, when they cry, the tears'll roll down their backs. But if you tell I said this, I'll call you a liar. I got to live here a little while yet."

"It's safe. I'm honored you spoke frankly." He watched Manson Carter's automobile chug by the house. "Well, I got to get going. Silas won't be as friendly as you are."

"Let Silas puff and blow. He talks mean but he likes you. He told me so one time. But I'll deny saying that, too. Matter of fact, so would he."

Silas Wright farmed the last place on the western end of the valley, hundreds of acres of pasture, fields, and, on the higher slopes, virgin forest. His gruffness was appreciated by those who liked to know where they stood with him.

He and his late wife, Rhetta, could hardly have been more opposite. Silas was quiet, but Rhetta would talk to a fence post. She had the idea to keep boarders, which he tolerated to preserve peace. After Rhetta died, only a few regulars remained. His niece Ethel and her husband, Carl, kept the boarders happy, while he and Harrogate minded the farm.

Horace drove slowly, rehearsing his speech. At the last turn the barn loomed on the left, along with a full corncrib and woodshed. Horace wondered how a man would fill such a shed with deadfall. Behind the barn several head of Hereford steers picked grass, and a fine black mare snorted in a separate enclosure. Fifty yards from the west-facing barn a two-story frame house with a three-columned porch across the western half faced the road. Close by stood a springhouse, a smokehouse full of curing hams, and an apple house. He cut the Chevrolet off and heard roosters crow and guinea hens holler. He waved at Silas, who emerged from the barn with a shovel. Silas propped it against the barn and walked to the house. On the porch they shook hands. "Mr. Wright, it's good to see you again," said Horace.

Silas pulled two cane-bottomed chairs from the wall and sat in one. "Mr. Wright was my daddy. My name's Silas. Have a seat, young fellow."

"Thank you, sir."

"I imagine you're here for that damn park."

"Yes, sir, if you have time this afternoon."

"Don't know as I'll ever 'have time' for such foolishness."

"Silas, let me put it straight. My job is to lay out your choices and explain the rules. If you'll let me do mine, then I'll let you do yours, which is figure what you want to do."

The old man's eyes were wary. "Fair enough."

Horace explained choices and restrictions. He took a deep breath. "Now, Silas, here's the commission's offer for your property: twenty thousand five hundred dollars."

Silas's eyes widened like he was in a revival meeting hearing someone rip a sloppy fart. "Horace, I know I agreed I wouldn't tell you how to do your job, but I *do* think you looked at that figure wrong. I own near about three hundred acres."

"Silas, this property surveyed at two hundred and four acres. That price is a good one, a little over a hundred dollars an acre. Have you ever had the property surveyed?"

"Why would I spend money for that when I got deeds?"

"Silas, your deeds are like all others over here. The metes and bounds are often vague—if they're there at all. One corner refers to a tree that became firewood fifty years ago. So you make judgments about the corners."

"That won't make us disagree ninety acres' worth."

"No, Silas, it won't. But surveying it will. A deed based on a proper survey will show less acreage in the mountains than one based on just walking the property, you know."

"I don't know any such thing. Land's land, straight up or flat. Fifty foot's fifty foot whether it goes up the side of the hill or sets off down the road."

"In a sense it is, but in another it isn't. You studied geometry, didn't you?"

Silas fished in his overalls for pipe and tobacco. "Yep. But I've slept since then."

"Let's say this table is your property. May I?" Horace pulled a small stick-built table between them. Silas generally kept a flyswatter and a pack of matches on it. This morning there was also an apple.

"When we draw it up, it's on a piece of paper, flat like this table, right?"

Silas hooded his pipe with his left hand and lit it, nodding almost imperceptibly.

"That's how the surveyor looks at it, too, except he has to render elevation onto it. Just across the creek there, there's about enough level ground for a man to stand, then the mountain goes straight up for fifty feet. That's like the relation between this tabletop and this apple. If you could walk from the spot across the creek to the top of the rise—or from here on the table to the top of the apple—you've gone up fifty feet, sure, but you haven't gone forward but four inches."

Silas shook his head quickly. "That don't make a damn bit of sense. Listen here. Since you're taking this table as my land, and this apple as the mountainside, don't it make sense that if I peeled that peel off the side of that apple and laid it flat, that'd be my fifty foot instead of your four inches?" Silas looked like he'd laid down a full house to Wakefield's three fours.

"No, Silas." Taking a notepad and pencil from his breast pocket, he drew a straight line. "Let me try again.

"Let's say this inch represents a hundred feet, and it's perfectly flat, like on the coast. Okay?"

Horace drew another line. "Now, this is the same inch, the same hundred feet, but at a twenty-degree angle. Now I'm going to drop a line perpendicular to the first hundred feet, and you can see we haven't gone but eighty feet in a straight line even though we've walked a hundred up the hill.

"I don't know how to explain it any clearer than that. Everyone's acreage is less than old deeds call for." A nuthatch perched upside down on the juniper trunk in the front yard.

Silas looked a hole through Wakefield. "Is that shit-fired figure based on my going or staying?"

"Going."

"I ain't going."

"Then they reduce the amount ten percent. Eighteen thousand four hundred and fifty."

"I get to stay until I die?"

"Yes, sir. As long as the stipulations are met."

"And that's all that foolishness you talked about—firewood and fishing and such?"

"Yes, sir."

Silas stood. "Sir, I reckon this talk is over. If I didn't like you, I'd throw you off the porch. This land's worth double that, and if I have to get a damn lawyer to prove it, I will."

Horace gave Silas a straight sale agreement and a lease contract. "If you want a lawsuit, Silas, that's your right." He handed Silas a card. "Here's where you can reach me in Waynesville. Or I'll be at Lige's place weekday evenings."

"Much obliged."

Horace stepped into the yard, stopped, and turned. "Silas?"

Silas had taken off his hat, showing a bald, gullied forehead. He said nothing.

"Did you put the Blackwell boy in that barrel?"

Silas put his hat back on. "Don't know what you're talking about."

CHAPTER 5

Luck and Happiness

Velda Parham grew up tall and thin, quite unlike anyone else in her family. Nonetheless her apple did not fall far from the tree. Equal portions of Parham hair-trigger temper and Cagle stubbornness, mixed with her grandmother Brown's sunny disposition and her grandmother Sutton's head for figures, created a woman easy to get along with, at least if one decided to let her have her way.

Velda did not inherit the meanness that nipped the heels of her particular branch of Parhams. That trait skipped erratically among her father's siblings. Her father became a faithful Baptist, even in time eschewing strong drink except on Saturday, but his brother Tine never trod a church floor after he grew too big for his father to beat him into attendance.

Valentine "Red" Parham—he was a February baby—abused his wife, Ruby, when he drank, which was often. He came by his ways honestly. His father, a choleric one-eyed rounder, used to knock cats senseless, tie their tails together, and drape them over a clothesline for the fun of watching them wake and fight. To put beans on the table Tine ran a log skidder. One Monday, after a violent weekend, an outsize log hung up. Instead of slacking and trying again, Tine impatiently jerked the rig. A snapped, recoiling cable crushed his head like a watermelon.

Velda's mother, born Amanda Brown, was called Bill by everyone except her husband, Ernest, who called her Billie. A four-year-old Mandy Brown changed her name because she wanted to be a boy, and "Bill" stuck because it was better than her brothers' corruption of "Mandy" into "Mangy." Billie Brown Parham, a good-tempered woman, perpetually carried the smell and feel of white flour and brown sugar with her.

Billie worried that her twenty-one-year-old daughter might end up an old maid, but Velda had simply not known anyone interesting enough with whom to spend one night, much less a lifetime. Boys paid court, but she was distant to most and rude to some, so none persisted. Oliver was the first to mesh with her desires and dreams, none of which included birthing a houseful of mountain children and growing old at forty-five.

Velda's aunt Ruby had been postmistress at Ola for three years when Tine was killed. After Velda's father died, Billie, Velda, and Ruby banded together as postmistresses and storekeepers. "Sisters," they called themselves, "building a family business."

The afternoon when Oliver had first stopped in Little Cataloochee, the week before Zeb's trial, Velda had been alone in the post office. She'd perked her ears upon hearing his Ford and had decided to looksee out back on a trip for firewood instead of aping through the window. She watched a tall, thin, well-dressed man a little older than she fuss with a pair of long-cuffed driving gloves. After he came in the keeperless front, she made an entrance at the back. Smiling, she dropped firewood into the box, removed her denim jacket, and arched her back. Running a hand through her dark straw-colored hair and tossing her head, she said, "Welcome, stranger," holding out her hand. "I'm Velda Parham." He seemed to appreciate the performance.

His handshake said he was neither acquainted with hard labor nor afraid to touch a woman. He didn't stay five minutes, but when she hinted he might visit, he beamed. After he left, she watched him from the window, putting those silly gloves back on and whistling some tune she couldn't hear.

Her mind raced. They would fit together nicely. He was close to handsome, with a crooked smile just this side of mischievous. It didn't hurt that lawyers were smart and made money. He didn't sound like he hailed from Cataloochee, nor would stay long. Her mother could go with them, leaving Ruby to run the family business. Settled, except for how long it might take to seal the bargain.

"Velda, that young man was nice," said Billie Parham, "but I didn't understand half of what he said. Where's he from?" Velda and Billie were home after Oliver's presentation, Billie to sweep, dust, and wonder how to spend the nine hundred dollars the commission had offered for their property. She had never seen fifty dollars in one place, so she fairly tingled with delight at the offer. Velda had more than money on her mind as she brushed her hair at the bedroom dresser.

"Way down east, Mama. Near about at the ocean."

"Wonder if they all talk like that." She wore a full-length apron over the Sunday dress she had worn to the meeting.

Velda kept brushing. The sun emerged, highlighting her dark hair and reflecting off the japanned hairbrush.

"You looked like you could eat him up. I hope folks don't talk. Girl, what do you know about him?"

"Just what people say, Mama. That he's smart, and rich, too. They say Mrs. Banks gave him a lot of money for getting Zeb off."

"Pshaw. Hannah needn't have bothered. No jury in the world would've sent Zeb to the chair. I could have got him off myself."

"Mama, you aren't a lawyer."

"It don't take a paper from Chapel Hill to know right from wrong." She walked into the bedroom and laid hands on Velda's shoulders. "Even if I did make it, that dress looks good on you." It was dark green with a high collar and a little flounce to the sleeves. She watched her daughter in the mirror. "Don't believe you've looked this happy in a while."

"It's not so much happy, Mama, as it is dreamy."

"What do you mean?"

"I've dreamed of something for a long time, and now I see how it can happen. Like God's shown me the way."

"You mean that young man."

Velda nodded.

"Child, a good-looking man his age is likely spoken for. And if not, he's played the field so long he's not worth having. You're barking up the heartbreak tree."

Velda stopped brushing. "Mama, it isn't that way with him."

"How do you know?"

"I can feel it." She patted Billie's hand. "Can't you, Mama?"

"I'd like to. And I believe I hear the door."

Velda jumped like a jack-in-the-box. "Mama, wish me luck."

Billie took the hairbrush and hugged her daughter. "Luck and happiness is all I've ever wished for you."

Velda fairly skipped into the front room and opened the door. Oliver proffered a bouquet of asters and zinnias from Mattie's hothouse. "For you, Miss Velda."

"You shouldn't have," said Velda, sniffing them. "Mama, where can we put these?"

Billie arranged the flowers in a fluted green vase and set it on the mantel. "Mr. Babcock, these are beautiful. Thank you so much."

"My pleasure, Mrs. Parham. I hope you are well."

"I'm able to sit up and take nourishment, young man. Will you stay for supper?"

Velda nodded to Oliver.

"I would be honored."

"I'll get it ready while you two visit." As Billie headed to the kitchen, Velda gestured for Oliver to sit in one of the upholstered chairs before the fireplace. They sat edgily, as if awaiting a starter's gun.

Oliver cleared his throat and asked Velda's favorite color, and when she said blue, he allowed that was his, too. A half hour later they had established compatibilities galore. But when Oliver waxed poetic about oysters, she paused.

"Velda, is something wrong?"

"I've never seen an oyster—least not the kind you're talking about."

"Oh, they're simply divine. You eat them raw, and as cold as you can get them. They taste of salt spray and sunshine. I admit, they look strange—Swift said the first to eat an oyster was a bold man—but once you get past the look and feel, it's good to eat a bucketful. Now you said, I think, there's another kind of oyster?"

She blushed and looked at the floor. "Well, I've never eaten one, but men talk about—mountain oysters."

"Tell me about them."

"I shouldn't."

"Why not?"

"They come from the he cattle—you know . . ."

After being puzzled for a second, Oliver grinned. "You mean when they make steers out of bulls?"

"We should change the subject."

Oliver did so, and enthralled her for an hour as he told of boyhood, travels, and good times at the university. Billie brought a stoneware pitcher of cider and a matching plate stacked with sugar cookies, and sat with the couple as Oliver told about a professor.

"He knew everything, not only British history, but also mathematics and philosophy and law. Wore tweeds, used a cane for a pointer. English accent. I always wondered where he was born. One day he was telling about Richard the Third, the king who killed the princes, when he suddenly paused, like he'd lost his memory. We looked up in consternation. Suddenly he remembered the word he was looking for, finished his sentence, then said 'Even a blind hog'll find an acorn ever now and then,' as country as you please. After the lecture he told me he was from Rockingham County! I never would have guessed it in a hundred years."

Billie chuckled. "That's a funny story, Mr. Babcock."

"Please, ma'am, call me Oliver."

She hesitated, then smiled. "All right, Oliver. Have I missed your telling Velda about your church?"

"No, ma'am. I haven't mentioned it. Would you like to know about my religious life?"

They nodded as one. "Yes indeed," said Billie.

"I belong to the Presbyterian church, U.S., which, as you know, is the southern branch, formed in 1861 as the War of Northern Aggression began. I keep membership in the little congregation in my hometown, although I attended the university church in Chapel Hill."

"What do Presbyterians believe in?" asked Billie. "All we have around here is Baptists and Methodists."

"It's probably very similar to your beliefs," said Oliver. "We sprinkle for baptism, like Methodists, and most believe in predestination and election, but otherwise it's pretty similar."

"What's that? Reverend Noland's never preached about predestination."

"It says certain of mankind have been elected by God to be saved or damned—and there's nothing one can do to change that. No, excuse me, ma'am, that's *election,* but predestination is similar. If you get up in the morning and stub your toe, predestination says you were meant to do that from the beginning of time."

"That's nonsense," said Billie. "All that means is you stub your toe."

"I agree, ma'am, but a strict Calvinist will say he's glad he got *that* over with."

Billie and Velda missed the joke entirely. "But you believe in Jesus?" Billie asked.

"Absolutely, ma'am. As the gospel says, 'without Him was not anything made that was made.'"

Velda smiled. "Oliver, do you believe people are predestined to meet?"

He nodded to Velda. "A myriad of words could describe that, Miss Velda. People are predestined, foreordained, star-crossed, fated, determined, however you might put it. But I also, as I said, believe in free will, which some think makes predestination look awfully like happenstance, or serendipity, simply random occurrences. But I will say this. But for my birth, my journey to the university, and my acquaintance with Senator Squires, I would not be in this room with you lovely ladies this afternoon. Either it just happened that way, which I tend to doubt, or it was meant to be. For whatever reason, I'm very happy to be here."

Were it not for Billie's presence, he would have held his hand out to Velda, whose expression hovered somewhere between swoony and ecstatic.

Billie stood. "I'm going to finish up supper."

"Do you need any help?" asked Velda.

"No, you two get some fresh air. I'll call you when it's ready."

The couple put on their jackets and went outside. Billie watched from the kitchen window as her daughter wrapped her arms around Oliver's arm as they walked toward the road. "Jesus," she prayed quietly, "stay near us all."

CHAPTER 6

You Might Have to
Trust Them

Hiram Carter had built his new house away from the main road because that road followed the creek, and he would not clutter adjacent bottomland with a thing as unproductive as shelter. For like reason the family cemetery lay notched into a mountainside. The view from the footbridge that crossed the creek was of a house crouched against Nellie Ridge like it might welcome a laurel slick to veil its face from the passing world.

The house's most striking feature was an asymmetrical roof, a marriage of gable, hip, and valley, like a person stacking several hats on her head, the uppermost a tiny overseas cap. A gable at the end of the otherwise linear north side lent an air of a girl arching a left eyebrow. A porch began four feet from the east corner, made an ell in the west, and ended at the south. The front door opened into a central hall stocked with a mirror, a half dozen coat hooks, and a cherry case clock.

Hiram had made the clock in 1880, a present for his new wife Mary's nineteenth birthday. They had been married four months, and about all they'd owned was a sizeable debt on a good-size farm, and love. But Hiram had swapped two hams for the works; had milled, planed, and polished the case; and had decorated it with two hand-carved flowers that, given some imagination, were rosebuds. Aunt Mary had presided over family meetings backgrounded by its tick and chime since Hiram's death two years before.

They opened the house to company Friday, a day that dawned foggy after a circle had surrounded the moon the night before. Horace Wakefield brought briefcase and hat, and the Carters carried covered dishes. Any time the family gathered, whether for wedding, funeral, or lesser occasion, food appeared according to an unarticulated formula that somehow resulted in the proper ratio of deviled eggs to biscuits, ham to applesauce cake.

Aunt Mary's older son, Manson, forty-three, resembled his father, Hiram, with a high bald forehead surrounded by thick black hair. A droopy mustache counterpointed his usually dour expression. His brother, Thomas, seventeen months his junior, had Mary's people's abundant brown hair and prominent ears. Neither son was interested in romance, preferring the music of baying coon dogs to that of fiddles at dances. They treated their mother as if she were the queen of Sheba because they loved her, and, as Manson said, "If we didn't, Papa'd haunt hell out of us."

They welcomed Hiram's nephew Levi Marion Carter, and his family, a little after three o'clock. Levi Marion was a man with a reputation for hard work in a place where all worked themselves nearly to death every day. He was blue-eyed and prolific—his and Valerie's seven children ranged from teenagers to a knee baby.

Valerie's maiden name was Brown. Her father said the Good Lord hadn't thought enough of the Browns to make but one set, so she had to be a cousin of Billie Brown Parham. She and Levi Marion were forty-six—he was about six months her senior—but she looked a decade older. She had strong brown eyes and wielded a wicked hickory switch.

Perhaps twenty folks milled in the front room, smoking, conversing of weather—last night's moon brought talk of cold rain and early winter—and the upcoming feast, in tones more funereal than festive. Horace, wearing a red and blue plaid flannel shirt, laid out papers on the long table in two unequal stacks, while Aunt Mary gathered the family by ringing a small silver bell, a present Hiram had traded for on a produce run to South Carolina.

Her hair had been dark with red highlights in the former century, but she was now sixty-seven, and it shone as white as bleached muslin, in a bun secured by a tortoiseshell pin that formerly might have sported a bright ribbon or flower. After Hiram's death, she had worn black from head to toe.

"Listen," she said, setting the bell on the mantel, "we're here to see what Mr. Wakefield has to say. No matter who he works for, he deserves a fair hearing." She fingered a brooch at her throat. "Mr. Wakefield, the room is yours."

"Thank you, Mrs. Carter." He cleared his throat and looked at the crowd, dressed for solemn occasion. *My shirt is too gay*, he thought, *but there is no help for it.* "I won't waste your time," he continued. "I will answer questions and help your decisions. Nobody in this process wants misunderstanding or ill feelings."

He smiled and passed hands, priest-like, over the table. "Here are two sets of papers. On the left is the stack to sign if you choose to sell and leave. Here are those to use if you stay—more paper because it's more complicated. That's your choice—sell and leave within a short time, or take a lifetime lease at a lower figure. Are there questions?"

Levi Marion's faded blue eyes floated over dark semicircles. "Tell us about the lifetime thing."

"You sell to the commission. They convey the land to the government, which leases it back for your lifetime, which one would hope is long. Then the government assumes full title."

"Just me, or both of us?"

Horace looked through his papers. "It's deeded jointly, so yes, both of you."

"So if I died, she could stay on?"

"Until her death, yes, sir."

"We could farm like always?"

Horace pushed a strand of hair off his forehead. "With restrictions, of course."

"Could we keep our summer pasture on the balds?"

"No, sir, that is one of the restrictions, I'm afraid."

The clock struck the quarter hour as Levi Marion scowled at Horace. "Then we might as well go out of the cattle business. Keeping them year-round down here, we wouldn't have room to grow nothing."

Manson and Thomas had penned their dogs, mostly Plotts but also a few Walkers and black-and-tans, for the meeting's duration. They did not bark at familiar company, but they suddenly started to raise hell. Thomas glanced outside but saw no reason for their excitement.

Valerie rubbed the corner of her eye. "What if we get too old to work?"

"Your children could farm until you both pass. Then they would have to leave. Immediately."

Thomas, still worried about the dogs, went to the window. He saw nothing out of the ordinary but decided to walk outside. On the porch he found muddy boot prints he was pretty sure had not been made by anyone inside. Whoever this was had walked from the woodlot and slouched briefly on the edge of the porch, perhaps to spy.

Thomas looked around. The dogs had not stopped barking but were less urgent. He surveyed this side of the property and saw nothing strange except the boot prints. In the yard he realized who had made them and why the dogs were upset.

"McPeters," he muttered.

The center of the left heel print sported an *X*, a mark that Willie McPeters had worn since a youth. No one knew if such decoration was meant to ward off bad luck, or whether, as some said, the devil himself had studded that boot with crossed nails.

"Where'd he go?" Thomas asked the hounds, by this time quiet enough but still with raised hackles. That the tracks went close to the dog pen meant McPeters had been unafraid of them. "Wonder if he was carrying that rifle gun," Thomas said.

Two or three spent match stems littered the ground in front of the pen door. "My Lord," he muttered. "Was he trying to set these dogs on fire?" Sure enough, the top of the door was freshly singed. "Least it was dampish out here. What kind of man would do that?"

The dogs were of no help with his question. He decided to stay outside awhile, just in case. He had no relish for what was going on inside anyway.

In the front room Horace looked around. "Now, then, are there more questions?"

"Can we talk money?" asked Levi Marion.

"Only generally, unless everybody agrees to be specific."

"We're all family. How much for our farm?" asked Levi Marion.

"At straight sale, the commission is prepared to pay"—he shuffled in the left-hand pile—"eleven thousand five hundred dollars. Surveyed at 134.35 acres, more or less."

"Dad jim it, my deeds call for a hundred fifty-two. Mr. Wakefield, you did Silas Wright the same way. It's like our land drawed up."

"Mr. Carter, we based this on an accurate, up-to-date survey. May I explain that?"

Levi Marion waved him off. "Silas told us about the lines and angles. He's going to get a lawyer to see about that. Now, how much is that an acre?"

"Eighty-five dollars and sixty cents."

"What if we take the other?"

Horace turned the second document in the right-hand pile toward Levi Marion. "Ten thousand three hundred fifty dollars. Seventy-seven dollars and three cents per acre."

"So it's worth less with us on it." Reddening, he turned to Valerie. "Makes a man proud, don't it?"

"Mr. Carter, that's a standard real estate calculation. A life interest makes property less valuable to a potential buyer."

"Who in the fire else is going to buy it? I thought it was to be the government's forever."

"You are right, of course."

Valerie raised her hand. "How do we know this ain't a land grab? Government puts the land together, then gives it to the Vanderbilts or some-body?"

"The law says forever, Mrs. Carter."

Levi Marion's face approached the hue of a spring radish. "I can't get over this. A man works his whole life, and his property ain't worth hardly nothing, and if he wants to live on it awhile longer, it's even less." He stood and grabbed Valerie's hand. "Honey, let's go home, before I pop a mainspring."

"Levi, what about supper?"

"We can come back. I just need to get out of here awhile."

"Mr. Carter, I'm sorry this upsets you," said Horace.

"Mr. Wakefield, it ain't nothing personal. Me and her got to pray over this. I'd been of a mind to stay. Now I don't know if we can afford to."

Horace offered the papers to Levi Marion. "No offense taken, sir. Keep these copies. I will call on you in a few days."

Valerie looked pointedly at her oldest sons, who began putting jack-ets and caps on siblings. "I thought we were going to have a good time here," Ruth Elizabeth, six, complained.

"Hush, Miss Priss," said Rass. "We'll come back for supper."

On the porch Levi Marion asked Thomas about the dogs. "Let's just say you folks need to be careful going home," said Thomas. "That was Willie McPeters them dogs was hollering about."

"God, that's all we need," said Levi Marion. "Thanks for the warn-ing."

Thomas shook hands and went inside, where his mother spoke to Horace. "Mr. Wakefield," she asked, turning her better ear to him, "best I can tell you're offering us eighty dollars an acre. What might a farm in, say, Maggie or Dellwood cost?"

"These values, Mrs. Carter, are based on fair market value. If you find a comparable place, the commission's offer will certainly pay for it."

Manson set his coffee cup on the table. "Mr. Wakefield, do you think there's land in Haywood for sale that's half as fine as this?"

Wakefield shook his head. "You have a point, Mr. Carter. The only properties I know that approach this one are not for sale. But outside

Haywood County you could double your acreage. Land is cheap in Clay County, for example."

Manson looked to be within a hair of an apoplexy. "Mr. Wakefield, we ain't worrying over money or property. We're talking about right and wrong."

Aunt Mary opened her mouth to speak, but Manson put up his hand.

"Mama, let me finish. He says 'fair market value,' but there ain't a thing fair about this." He pointed a bony finger at Horace. "Take it or leave it ain't choices, Mr. Wakefield. It's you all saying what we're going to do. And all so some dern Florida tourist can sleep in a fancy tent. . . ." He faced the front window, hands clenched behind his back in red and white knots.

"Mr. Carter, my job is to make this as easy as possible."

Manson turned suddenly. "Nothing's easy about this. My daddy used to say there's only two things worth fighting over—family and land. Nothing else, God and mammon included. I guarantee you he's having a conniption over this." He shook his head at his mother. "And if Mama won't ask you to leave, I'm going to get out before I do something I might be sorry about." He left and stomped down the hall. They heard the back door slam, resonating the chimes.

Aunt Mary, sighing, offered coffee, but there were no takers. "Mr. Wakefield, I apologize for my son's manners. I can say I don't much blame him, though. I'd fight it if I was younger." She examined the backs of her hands. "We're going to stay, Mr. Wakefield, or at least try. So you better tell about those restrictions."

"I can boil that down easily."

The clock struck the half hour. Aunt Mary pointed toward the hall. "Mr. Wakefield, did you hear that?"

"It's very pleasant, Mrs. Carter."

"Clock and creek, Mr. Wakefield, soothing music, clock and creek, the same except you don't need to wind the creek. Creek's outside, clock's inside, that's all the difference. They've been what you might call background music to me and Hiram's life, our babies and sickness and sorrow, happiness and love. I don't know if I could stand to leave. These boys have a say, of course, but I want to be buried beside Hiram. When

I die, they'll carry me across the creek and up to the cemetery, then they'll take this old clock to its next home."

Horace hesitated a second. "I'm afraid that will require a Park Service Special Use Permit as well, Mrs. Carter."

"To carry out a clock?"

"To be buried in the cemetery."

"A body has to have a government paper to be laid in the ground beside her husband?"

"I'm afraid so, Mrs. Carter."

"That settles it, Thomas. I'm not moving any farther from your papa. If I did, they might change their minds and not let you bring me back." She sat heavily, found a handkerchief, and dabbed at her eyes. "Mr. Wakefield, Preacher Smith says the good Lord don't put anything on a person she can't bear. I have to trust that's true. I'm going to lay down awhile. The rest of you hear about those restrictions and visit before supper."

As she slowly climbed the creaking stairs, Thomas grabbed Wakefield by the arm and headed toward the front porch. "Let's make sure Manson's okay," he said. "Mama's right, the preacher does say that. But you know something? He don't own no farm over here."

CHAPTER 7

Lemonade Springs

Late in 1928 Jim Hawkins was hired as interim warden for the North Carolina side of the coming national park. All Cataloochee was relieved at that news, for Jim was a local boy.

Everyone knew Mack and Rhoda Hawkins raised decent children despite the fact that every one had started life with colic. Fred, the first, born in 1895, cost his parents nearly six months' sleep. Troy, born two years later in June, put them through the same ordeal. This time Mack bedded in the barn, where all that might spoil rest were distant baby squalls and nearby livestock farts.

They had a Christmas baby in 1901. "I'll name her Rhoda," said Rhoda, hair matted on her forehead after a night's labor.

"Now, woman, you're a little tuckered. Let's think about that later," said Mack.

"If you men can name babies after your own selves, so can I," Rhoda decreed.

"Well, then, can I call her Junior?"

If she had possessed enough strength, she would have thrown the nearest object at him.

This baby was no less prone to howl bloody murder than her brothers. Mack again slept in the barn, Fred spooning beside him for warmth, glad to be away from sister's constant caterwauling.

Rhoda carried her around the house, singing silly songs in a vain attempt to quiet her. "Mama's little Ro-Ro, gonna get a yo-yo, from an old mean so-and-so, yelling out a 'yo-ho-ho.'" Mack fondly wished for a bottle of rum. Another went "Keep me up a little later, gonna plant a big toe-mater, name it after my Ro-tater." Mack started calling the baby Tater Bug, which stuck like rosin. Little Rhoda grew up to hate sobriquet, Christian name, and, half the time, the parents who had afflicted her with both.

Her little brother, Jim, emerged the morning of the great Baltimore fire, which destroyed seventy blocks of that downtown—February 7, 1904. The baby slept quietly for a month, then burst into a fit of full-blown colic until the first of June. Mack and Rhoda decided to have no more offspring if they could help it.

Jim the boy became intensely interested in both nature and music. He built cages for all manner of creatures. No good at taming possums or raccoons, he domesticated flying squirrels instead, and kept frogs, snakes, cooters, and, to the horror of both Rhodas, a bat in a box on the back porch.

Mack put a fiddle in Jim's hands early, and by age twelve the boy played hundreds of tunes, learned from relatives, church, and Carter Fork's only battery-powered radio. He particularly loved "Sally Ann," for which he named his mule, a creature that, unlike most of her kind, willingly slogged through water and mud.

Jim's early notoriety stemmed from his being the second person in Cataloochee to see a dead mule. Henry Sutton's Old Sal had been killed in her stall during the cloudburst of 1916. Jim, after sawing her legs off so they could drag her out of the barn, had helped Henry bury his old friend. Jim got as much mileage from retelling that story as Tom Sawyer got after showing up for his own funeral. People pointed him out to newcomers: "That's the boy sawed them legs off that dead mule."

The little school on Carter Fork stopped instruction after seven grades, so he'd boarded with relatives in Waynesville to finish high school. In 1922 he entered the Normal and Industrial School at Cullowhee. The little school boasted seven buildings, two of which were, respectively, if not mutually respectful, Baptist and Methodist churches. The school teetered on the verge of the twentieth century. When a rich man gave them a field, the chief campus sport became watching the football coach argue with the agriculture professor over whether it would become gridiron or stay sown in crops.

All subjects interested Jim except an ironclad requirement, English grammar, which he refused to study. But he stayed in the library or under a tree, reading about anything from Einstein to eugenics. On weekends he fiddled at a dance club. Sunday evenings usually found him alone, walking in the woods, homesick. He left in 1924 without a degree, but with a job.

A forest service recruiter had brought news of an experimental forest near the Vanderbilt estate in Buncombe County. Jim hated pushing a pencil, so he figured he could do a sight worse than work outdoors. His application landed him a job late in 1924. On a sunny December morning he strolled into the parking lot of the new facility, whistling a tune, jacket over his shoulder, looking forward to whatever one did in an experimental forest.

He knew he was in trouble when he walked inside. "I'm Jim Hawkins," he said. The room smelled of raw pine and linseed oil. His supervisor, wearing a brass badge engraved with the name Thomas, dangled a Camel from one corner of his mouth and looked the new man over. "Clayton Thomas, son. My friends call me Wolf. You're a tall drink of water, ain't you?"

"I guess so, sir. What do you want me to do?"

"Get used to this." Thomas pointed to a desk, upon which a black Remington typewriter sat like an outsize toad. "You type?"

"No, sir."

"Learn. We make lots of reports."

After a month Jim wondered if their experiments would ever result in additional tonnage sufficient to provide extra wood to produce an additional quantity of chips with which to manufacture enough paper upon which to create the triplicate reports he typed with two fingers.

In the summer of 1925 he began boarding with Sid Crook's family, who lived within a half mile of a Methodist church on a hill above Sardis Road. But Sundays the Crooks loaded the jalopy and drove a mile and a half beyond it to the brick Presbyterian church at Sand Hill.

"How come you all don't go to the Methodist church?" asked Jim.

"You don't better yourself in a Methodist church," Sid said.

The male Presbyterians wore suits and ties, and their women sported fancy dresses and hats with veils. One woman, a banker's wife, wore a stole year-round. Whether mink, otter, or polecat no one could tell, but she loved to arrive late and sashay down the aisle, critter tail dangling from her shoulder.

On his first Sunday with Crook, Jim donned his best overalls, a white shirt, and a pair of spiffed square-toed black shoes.

"Is that really what you plan to wear to church?" asked Sid, straightening his necktie.

"Sure thing," said Jim.

Sid put on a gabardine jacket. "You don't own a suit?"

"No, sir."

Sid shrugged. "You'll see your mistake."

At the church Jim got down from the truck bed, brushed dust from his clothes, and ran a comb through his hair. Sid took him by the elbow. "Jim, you have to meet some of these people," he said, and walked to the front of the wooden building.

A tall seersucker-suited man with a mustache out of fashion since Teddy Roosevelt had died greeted Sid. "Mr. Crook, I believe," he said. "How are you, sir?"

They shook hands. "Fine, Mr. Queen. I want you to meet my new boarder, Jim Hawkins. He works with the forest at Bent Creek. Jim, this is Mr. A. R. Queen. He lives in Malvern Hills."

Jim put out his hand. "Mr. Queen, a pleasure," he said, while Queen looked him over.

"Mr. Hawkins," Queen said, finally shaking Jim's hand. "I thought someone told me you were a university man." He fluffed his brightly patterned silk bow tie, no made-up affair.

"Well, sir, no. I spent a couple of years at the state Normal."

"Is this what a young man wears to church there?"

"Yes, sir."

"My word," said Queen, nodding to Jim. "That would never do in Chapel Hill. Mr. Crook, you would do well to advise your young man to dress properly," he said, and lumbered inside.

"Who does he think he is?" asked Jim.

Sid, smiling, indicated Jim should lower his voice. "He's made a very lot of money—in real estate."

"Sure didn't help his manners."

Sid put his arm around Jim and walked him out of earshot. "Now, you must take advice if you're going to better yourself."

"I can get along with anybody, Mr. Crook. And I don't know I need bettering. In fact, I might better haul off to the Methodist church."

"Give it a chance, Jim. Here. This is our classroom."

The men's Bible class consisted of fifteen men plus the teacher, a round-faced electrician, who droned on about Matthew's gospel while nervously glancing outside as if someone were stalking him. Chancing on the story of the demoniac and the pigs, he spoke of demons with animation and familiarity. Jim wondered what in the world he had gotten himself into.

After Sunday school they walked to the chapel, where Jim determined he in fact wore the only pair of overalls. He was stubbornly proud of that until a tall, bosomy young woman strolled toward the chapel, flanked by her parents. Eighteen or nineteen, she wore no wedding band, and was, he judged, as pretty as a speckled pup. Only sexier.

Jim eased in with the Crooks on the right side penultimate pew. The girl sat four rows forward on the left, fanning herself slowly with a landscape-print fan. "Who is she?" he whispered to Sid.

"Nell Johnson. Her father's Henry and her mother's Elizabeth. Henry's in sales with Sawyer Motors downtown. Elizabeth's—well, she's interesting."

Nell Johnson covered her short dark hair with a Clara Bow hat showcasing an escaped curl at each cheek. The nape of her neck reminded Jim of his mother's pale pink Christmas mints. He heard nothing of Dr. Brotherton's sermon, nor did he speak to Nell afterward, for her parents protected her like linemen do a quarterback.

Sid lent him twenty dollars for a suit and tie, which he proudly wore to church two weeks later. Jim was tall and angular—nothing much on him was round, at least nothing that showed—and the suit softened him somehow. Nell gave him a coy smile half-hidden behind her fan. The next week her parents were distracted, so he asked if he might visit. Through sheer persistence he was invited to Sunday dinner.

Elizabeth Johnson had not been born a Queen, but aspired to the Queens' society, despite being a Crump from South Carolina. When Nell first brought it up, Elizabeth refused to entertain Jim Hawkins. "We don't know *any*thing about him, do we, dear?" she purred. "He doesn't appear well-bred. You *do* remember those horrid overalls?"

"But, Mother, he's so dreamy. He reminds me of Dick Tracy in the comics. It's his jaw."

"You shouldn't read such *lowbrow* material," said Elizabeth.

"I don't like the idea," said Henry Johnson to his wife later that afternoon. "I know what boys that age think. Used to be one myself." He rustled the sports section.

"Now, Henry, Nell's far too refined to have an *affaire de cœur* with such a bumpkin. It's a passing fancy, believe me."

Hominy Creek was named by the first whites who rode into the valley, who surprised Cherokees making hominy on its banks. When the Cherokees fled, they threw corn and lye into the stream. Very close to where this allegedly happened, in the bottomland half a mile downhill from the church, the Sand Hill congregation built a rude structure from locust uprights and joists roofed with oak shakes. They called it Calvin's Destination, and determined once a summer month to hike there to picnic after worship.

One such Sunday, after the meal, Jim waded into the sparkling creek.

After a dry summer it was shallow, exposing enough rocks upon which Nell could walk with his assistance. The pair made their way slowly upstream, Nell falling against him, sometimes on purpose. Jim loved the feel of her hand in his, and the proximity of her body and perfume made him a little giddy.

They stopped mid-creek while he squatted to turn up rocks like a twelve-year-old. Actually he needed to smooth the bulge in his pants, but meantime flung a crawdad at Nell, who screamed, but not too loudly. They went on, he wading, she following on the rocks, until the playing children's uproar was totally muffled by creek noise. They got out on the opposite bank, and, after Jim determined that no one had followed them, ensconced themselves behind a large boulder.

Fire in her eyes, she leaned back and sighed. "Jim, dear, it's surely hot."

When Jim put his arms around her, something speared her abdomen. "My," she said, "what's that?"

He kissed her. "It's all yours," he said, as they fumbled for openings in clothing. Quickly, in postlapsarian daylight, Nell enjoyed things about Jim that were not angular.

Elizabeth took to her bed for a week when she discovered Nell was pregnant. Then mother and daughter confronted Henry with the news. Henry bit a cigar in two. "You're what?" he yelled.

"Now, Henry," said Elizabeth, "you might as well calm down and make the best of this."

"By God, I'll shoot him for this."

"Daddy, he's my man," said Nell.

"He done you wrong," said Henry. "I'm a mind to—"

"Daddy, you're going to have the finest grandson in the world," she cooed, and after a few days Henry agreed maybe a son-in-law with a job and a little education might be, if not all right, at least bearable.

Elizabeth had emerged from what she called her boudoir with a plan. She invited Jim for dinner, shined the silver plate, polished the semi-porcelain, and folded her best cloth napkins into Lady Windermere's fans. She served a standing rib roast garnished with rosemary. Nell baked potatoes and peppers stuffed with ham and bread crumbs, and took credit for yeast rolls, although Elizabeth had done most of that preparation.

"We're *dying* to find out about you," said Elizabeth to Jim over a bite of potatoes. "Tell us of your ancestors."

Jim thought a second. "Ma'am, my daddy's Mack Hawkins from Carter Fork. His daddy was Henry, died when I was a baby, on a hunting trip. I have no idea about his daddy's name."

Elizabeth laid fork on plate. "How about your mother?"

"She was Rhoda Mooney, from over in Cosby. Her daddy made liquor, they say. I never knew him. Killed in a wreck. Car left the road and plowed grille-first into a tree. That's as far back as I can go on that side."

Elizabeth arched her eyebrows. "I *see*," she said, then smiled and swept the air with her hand. "We're going to have to *invent* your family tree. Hawkins sounds like a *lovely* English name. So does Mooney, although maybe it was spelled Mauney in the old country. *Oh, my,* it can't be *Irish.* No, certainly *not.* Surely you have knights in your pedigree."

"Ma'am, if it'll make you feel better, we can make some up."

By dinner's end Jim descended distaff-side from Welsh royalty and sword-side from King Henry the Fifth. A radiant Elizabeth poured coffee, which pleased Henry enough to ask Jim to retire to the porch for a cigar. Next day Elizabeth launched into wedding plans. It forever galled Elizabeth Johnson to announce her daughter's engagement to a mere forester from Cataloochee, but Nell was "in trouble," and there was no help for it.

The wedding was a simple affair in the chapel, bare save for one candle on the communion table and sprigs of boxwood in the windows. They had the reception, replete with a two-layer coconut cake, green punch, and fancy nuts, in the Sunday school building. No Queens attended. Elizabeth kept her head up until she came home, then took to her bed.

Just off the east-west highway north of an enormous bottom one hill west of Calvin's Destination sat a settlement called Scratch Ankle, consisting of a general store, a two-story boardinghouse, and a Baptist church. Other than the fact that it was a flat spot about halfway between Asheville and Canton, there seemed no reason for it.

Jim hoped the name had nothing to do with biting insects. He and his bride settled into a two-room apartment in the boardinghouse. Jim worked with the forest service, and Nell, sharing Jim's worry about fleas, scrubbed floors and walls. They enjoyed getting to know each other, and spent a merry Christmas Day with Nell's parents in West Asheville.

In May of 1926, what Elizabeth called "the blessed event" and what Nell termed the product of the most hellish night of her life, arrived. They named him Henry Mack after his grandfathers. Elizabeth and Nell called him His Majesty. Remembering his mother's jingles, Jim called him Little Mack Truck, but the boy did not inherit his father's colicky disposition.

Jim received a postcard from his father in the summer of 1927. "Come see us," it said, in a shaky scrawl. "Mama's not herself." Jim was as surprised at his father's writing two sentences as he was to get the card. Back in Cataloochee, he found his mother wandering in their woodlot, not entirely with all her wits.

"Mama, it's me," he said.

She looked up toward her son's face, recognition rising in her eyes like steam off a winter pond. "You home from school, Son?"

"Mama, I'm married now, remember? With a son?"

She nodded passively as he led her back to the house. Both his brothers were gone from home, but his sister, Rhoda, lived in Big Cataloochee, working in Lige and Penny Howell's tourist business. Jim sat with both Rhodas and his father in the kitchen that weekend, and they decided little Rhoda would move home to take care of big Rhoda, who by then had decided she didn't need anybody to take care of her.

"Jim," said his sister in a private moment on the porch, "if she gets to wandering off all the time, I don't know what I'll do. I have my own life, you know."

"I know, Tater Bug. But I can't do it. We're counting on you."

"Damn you, don't call me Tater Bug."

Jim left on Sunday full of no particular optimism.

When the park came in the fall of 1928, it was, as they say, "a blessing." Jim helped his parents settle with the park commission and move to Maggie Valley. Rhoda Senior soon had a four-room one-story house veneered to the windowsills with creek rocks. Jim bought her a Sears vacuum cleaner, two dollars down, three dollars a month. Fascinated with it, she cleaned house every day, forgetting to wander. Mack, who had a little money for the first time in his life, paid a neighbor girl to stay with Rhoda while he "loafered" at the barber shop, telling tall tales. His favorite was about a prodigious night of coon hunting, during which they treed so many they had to go for a mule and sled to dray them home.

Having settled Mack and Rhoda, Jim visited the park commission, in those days upstairs in Asheville's brand-new 1928-model city hall. Everything in Asheville looked too new to him—the green and pink tiled cafeteria, the skinny, fragile Jackson Building, and the Baptist church's outlandish Florentine dome. The old courthouse—built in 1903 and, to Jim's eye, perfectly fine—had not yet been torn down in favor of the new gray classical courthouse, beside which a brand-new city hall sat like a painted woman. He walked inside its cavernous entrance and looked into the gloom. A black man in a white uniform materialized. "Going up, sir?"

Except for some hands at the feed and seed, Jim had never talked to a black man. But this person seemed friendly and cordial. "Park commission," said Jim.

"Fifth floor, sir. Watch your step."

Jim rode his first elevator behind the brass scissor-fold doors. The receptionist took his application and gave him a written test and some encouragement. A month later Jim heard from Red Pendleton, telling him to report for an interview for a position as Cataloochee interim warden. He was so far the only applicant, and, since he knew the territory, he was an attractive candidate. Assuming he landed the job, when the park superintendent was named, Jim would be in the running for a permanent position.

Nell had seldom been outside Buncombe County except on occasional trips to Spartanburg, the ancestral seat of the Crumps. She had never been to Haywood County. When Jim showed her the letter, she hugged him. "Congratulations, honey," she said. "Are we going to be happy there?"

"You bet," he said. "It'll be a fine place to raise the kids. Away from all this infernal construction."

"Kids?"

He grinned. "I thought we were talking about another one." He rubbed her shoulder.

"Is there a school?"

"Right now, yes. Teacher and everything."

"Where will we live?"

"I'd guess in Lige Howell's old house. It's really big, a fine place. You'll see."

"What's it *really* like there?"

"Paradise, honey. Pure paradise. You'll love it." He patted her on the bottom.

She giggled, cleared her throat, and sang: " 'At the lemonade springs where the bluebird sings, in the Big Rock Candy Mountains!' That it?"

"Pretty close, darling. Pretty close." He took down his fiddle and played an intro. They harmonized Haywire Mac's version, ending with "I'll see you all this coming fall in the Big Rock Candy Mountains!" When he hung up the fiddle, she danced her beau into the bedroom.

CHAPTER 8

Bird in the Hand

"Old gal, you ready?" As Silas smoothed Maude's glossy mane, she snorted and stamped her rear off hoof. "I'll take that for yes," he said, tightening the cinch. "We got a fur piece to go."

Silas wore a black suit, a broad-brimmed hat to match, and a collarless white shirt buttoned at the throat. Although he owned one necktie, he never wore it. His late wife had made it when they were newlyweds. He had thanked her, told her he was not prone to such frippery, and tucked it into a dresser drawer. They had never spoken of it again.

He led Maude from the barn and mounted. "Saddle's been so long between me and you it don't squeak anymore," he said, and smiled. They journeyed early enough to pass Mary Carter's darkened farmhouse without being hailed. Likewise, no wood smoke ascended from the schoolhouse chimney—and the churchyard was quiet in the gray late October morning. Seeing Nellie's general store's door yawning open, he stopped. He tied his horse and climbed the two creaking steps. "Nelse, what are you doing this early?"

Nelse, Lige Howell's first cousin, a widower, was a saturnine man. "Couldn't sleep. Might as well come over and dust the shelves. You know, I could ask you the same."

"I'm off to town. Thinking about suing the park."

"I'd sue the britches off them, except I don't own but just that patch I make a garden on. Take them to the cleaners."

Silas looked around the store. Between a bolt of cotton chintz and a row of Borax boxes lay a tray of small, round lightbulbs. "What's these for?" he asked, examining one as if it came from Madagascar.

"Auto bulb, Silas. There's enough cars in the valley now to stock some. You ever going to buy an automobile?"

"Hell, no. If I can't get there by foot or on Maude, I don't need to go." He put the bulb down. "It's not that I've got anything against them— I just got no use for them." He wandered to a pile of blankets with eyelets stitched in their corners. "What about these?"

"Camp blankets. When the park comes, we'll have a bunch of campers."

"Nelse," said Silas, "I haven't left a perfectly good, warm bed to sleep outside in years. Now you're telling me people are stupid enough to sleep outside when they don't have to. I guess I don't belong in this modern world."

"Sometimes I don't think I do, either. In fact, I know I don't."

Silas looked over his neighbor, a paunchy man of seventy-odd years, as though for the first time. "Nelse, how come you made a storekeep?"

He laughed. "Too old to go to the war. Didn't want to be a preacher. Too lazy to be a ditchdigger. Never was handy at anything. My daddy always said if he locked me in a room with nothing in it but an anvil, I'd find a way to break it. So when this came along, I stepped into it, and I been here ever since."

Silas chuckled. "Well, give me two tins of sardines and a pack of crackers before you bust them, or your head, one. I'll need a snack this morning."

Past the Bennett turn Silas gently coaxed Maude into a faster pace. "Come on, gal, or we'll never get there." From the valley floor to the top of the mountain, farms were smaller and more numerous. Most houses were set back from the big road. He saw one farmer turning rye under for the winter, another snaking a firewood tree, a woman harvesting greens. Getting ready for what Old Man Winter would bring. Judging from the size of people's woodpiles, he meant it to be a hard one.

At the gap Silas rested the mare and ate his snack. This high, leaves had cascaded. Bare limbs featured angles and notches and boles invisible in midsummer. A bear had rooted the base of a fair-size oak, trying to topple it in search of underground grubs. Silas finished one tin of sardines, wiped the oil out with a leaf, stomped the tin flat, and laid it in a saddlebag. They made fine roof patches. He lit his pipe. "Old gal, we better get going."

Up Jonathan's Creek, motorcars were as thick as mites on a banty rooster, and Maude became skittish. Silas had never seen so many cars in one place as in Dellwood, so he led her through the intersection. Horns blew, and several times he was jeered by young drivers, one of whom yelled "Go back to the county home." At Barberville he led the horse into the parking lot of a dry goods store. A man wearing sleeve garters swept the porch. "Friend, where are you headed?"

"Town," said Silas. "But she don't much want to go."

"Don't blame her. Tell you what. There's a stable behind the store. She can stay there if you want to catch a ride. Take her to town, you're liable to get a ticket."

"For what?"

"They don't cotton to manure in the street."

Ten minutes later he put out his thumb for the first time in his life, and quickly caught a ride to Main Street. He said little, preferring to concentrate on how to exit the vehicle if the driver, who seemed bent on making a land speed record, slowed enough to allow it.

He didn't know any lawyers save Oliver Babcock, who, he had to admit, had somewhat changed his inherited opinions. Silas's father had maintained that attorneys at their best were but carrion crows out to pick every bit of flesh from their clients. Silas saw a shingle on the left-hand side of the street advertising James Smathers, Esq. An old family name in Haywood and, for the most part, respected.

He tried the doorknob and walked into the reception area. *How many cattle gave their lives to cover this furniture?* A bookcase with glass doors held leather-bound volumes, and dull brass spittoons, ashtrays, and umbrella stands littered the floor. The room smelled of something Silas could not quite put a finger on—wealth and revenge, fear and outrage, tempered by very little mercy and justice.

"Sir, may we help you?" sang a pleasant voice from behind a partition. Silas looked over the black counter at a young woman, pretty enough to win a county fair ribbon. "Yes, ma'am," he said, and removed his hat. "I'd like to see Lawyer Smathers."

"What is your name, sir?"

"Wright. Silas Wright."

"Mr. Wright, I'll tell Mr. Smathers you're here. Would you like some coffee?"

"No, ma'am. I'm fine."

Alone, he looked over Smathers's certificate of admission to the bar. Below it hung framed pictures, one of Chapel Hill's Old Well, another of some fancy building sprouting corn, wheat, and he didn't know what all from its columns.

Smathers, a short curly-haired man with bushy eyebrows and rolled-up sleeves, appeared, hand extended. "Mr. Wright, a pleasure. You like the photos, sir?"

Silas shook Smathers's hand. "Yep. I've seen the well before, but what's this? The agriculture school?"

Smathers laughed. "Playmaker's Theatre. I was an actor there. Those columns, by the way, are wooden."

"Could have fooled me. I bet being an actor comes in handy in court."

"It does, sir. Come in and have a seat."

Silas sat before a desk with so many layers of paper obscuring its top it could have been made of acacia for all anyone could tell. Its side panels were cherry, its hardware was shiny brass, and its owner was a man who liked a good cigar. "Smoke?" asked Smathers, opening a humidor in Silas's direction.

Silas plucked his pipe from his pocket. "Thanks, but I'll stick with this."

Smathers lit a cigar and sat back. "Mr. Wright, it's a pleasure to meet you. I believe my father and you went hunting one time."

Silas noticed a patch of weeping bumps on the lawyer's left forearm, evidence he'd brushed poison oak recently. "Then you must be Joe Smathers's boy. Me and him had us a time one weekend. You couldn't have been much more than a pup."

"I was four. I was scared to death when they took me to the hospital to see Daddy."

"Well, he sure didn't bargain for that old boar to run him over. Them things' tushes are like razors."

"How did it happen?"

"Your father came to Cataloochee to boar hunt. He'd killed bear and deer and even been out West for caribou and elk. But he'd never killed a wild hog. We hunted the better part of a Saturday, saw sign but no hogs anywhere. About halfway up toward Davidson Gap, where the springs seep the switchbacks, the dogs raised something in a big old laurel hell.

"First thing we knew, here come a boar with dogs hanging on it like they was stitched to its neck. Your daddy fired at that hog. I thought he'd hit it between the eyes, but it kept coming. For a better shot, he dropped to one knee, but the damn thing run him over and liked to have ripped his jaw off. The second it was far enough away that I could shoot without killing your daddy, it fell dead. I expect after that your daddy quit hunting."

"Actually, after he retired, he journeyed West again, several times. Hung several trophies on the wall. He always spoke fondly of you."

"I'm glad. He could have figured me for the cause of that scar."

"He wore it proudly. Like a *schmiss* on a German officer. Now, Mr. Wright, how can I help you?"

"I'm thinking about suing the government."

"I take it over the national park?"

"Yep. I figure I'm about to be took advantage of."

Smathers opened a window to let out the tobacco smoke. "Do you have the papers they gave you?"

Silas twisted a piece of paper from his inside pocket. "No, but I wrote

the money down, and here's the deeds. Three hundred acres. They're offering twenty thousand five hundred dollars. Less than seventy dollars an
acre."

Smathers took the deeds and with raised eyebrows smoked and read.
"How many total acres according to Mr. Wakefield's survey?"

Silas snorted. "Two hundred and four."

"Mr. Wright, I have to say Mr. Wakefield is likely right. Many metes
and bounds are ancient and unfindable. I have gone to trial with Mr.
Wakefield on my side, and implicitly trust his work. So I doubt you have
a case based on these deeds. I'm sorry. Let me return these before they get
lost on my desk."

"Then I've made a trip for nothing?"

"I didn't say that. Let's see—two hundred four acres for twenty thousand five hundred dollars amounts to about a hundred dollars an acre. I
take it, Mr. Wright, your acreage is mostly level—or as level as it gets over
there?"

"Yes, sir. I run as pretty a farm as you'd want to see."

"Unfortunately, pretty has nothing to do with it. But I recently com-
pleted a sale comparable to your acreage for twice that money per acre. I
would be happy to represent you."

"Now we're getting somewhere. What is your fee?"

"In land matters, thirty percent."

Silas laughed. "Good one, Mr. Smathers. Real good. Now, let's be serious."

"Sir, I am quite serious."

Silas rested his hands on his knees. "Mr. Smathers, I'm a poor old
man, never been a thing but a dirt farmer. I came here because I thought
you would treat me fair. Even a cussed miller don't get but a sixteenth."

"Mr. Wright, land cases take considerable preparation. The percent-
age is calculated to make sure that over the long haul this office makes
money. It is, after all, possible that the state will win, in which case this
office would receive nothing."

Silas stood and fingered his hat brim. "Is that thirty percent of all of
it, or just of anything over their offer?"

"Thirty percent of whatever additional settlement we receive. You get twenty thousand five hundred regardless. I think a jury would easily award you twice that."

"What's thirty percent amount to if we got that much?"

Smathers scribbled on the back of an envelope. "Six thousand one hundred and fifty."

"Son, rich folks might afford to pay that kind of money, but I can't. On the other hand, I know you need to get paid, like anybody that works for a living. Why not work by the hour?"

"Mr. Wright, I admire your determination. How about we agree to twenty-five percent?"

Silas sat and put his hat on his knee. "Make it ten and it's a deal."

In a few minutes they settled for twenty. "I'll need to think about this," Silas said, rising from his chair. "How about I let you know next week?"

"That will be fine, Mr. Wright. By the way, there's something else."

Silas stared at Smathers, saying nothing. The lawyer scratched his arm absently. "Say we win. Or, say we lose. Either way, there will be tax consequences."

"What does that mean?"

"The government will assess capital gains taxes on your profit."

"Pardon my French, Mr. Smathers, but just how damn much taxes?"

"Federal capital gains amount to twelve and a half percent. How did you come about this land, Mr. Wright?"

"Inherited most of it."

"So you purchased some of it?"

"I bought out my sisters. Didn't have to give them too much."

"Okay, Mr. Wright. The worst they can do is twelve and a half percent of your whole settlement. That would be a little over five thousand dollars if we win our case. I can probably reduce that substantially if we can prove how much you paid for the portion you purchased."

"Mr. Smathers, it'll be a cold day in hell before I'll give the bloodsuckers that kind of money."

"Mr. Wright, please think about it before you dismiss it out of hand. You would still have a lot of money. You could buy a nice farm, or travel, or . . ."

Silas jammed his hat onto his head. "Mr. Smathers, my daddy told me there was hardly nothing lower than a lawyer. I'm starting to think he was right. You're in cahoots with the damn government."

Smathers put out his hands. "Mr. Wright, I assure you that is not the case. I'm merely trying to keep your eyes open, so, whether you sue or not, you will not go afoul of the law."

"Wait a minute. Do you mean even if I don't sue I'll have to pay them taxes—what'd you call them? Capital gains?"

"Yes. I could help minimize them, of course, but you would have gains. I'm sorry, but that's the way it is."

"Then I'll go home, Mr. Smathers. What do I owe you?"

"Nothing, sir. I simply ask you to think about this. I could see that you end up with more money than if you do nothing."

"What I think right now is you and the government ain't getting ten thousand or more of my money. If I change my mind, I'll let you know."

Silas left the lawyer with a handshake, and the outer office with a glance of appreciation at the receptionist.

He had plenty of time coming home to mull over Smathers's offer. He retrieved Maude at Barberville and made his way to Cove Creek, where he sat on the same rock wall where, years ago, his best friend, Hiram, had met Mary. He cracked his other tin of sardines and chewed meditatively. *If that boy gets me double the state's figure, he'd pocket over four thousand of my dollars. That's sure better than sixty-one hundred and fifty, but, God, I hate to think about a damn lawyer skimming that cream.*

Oh, I'd still have plenty of money. Least I'd have it if he wasn't just blowing his horn. My daddy said never trust a lawyer or a preacher. There's the God's truth in that.

So the rub is whether I trust this boy—the son of a man didn't have no better sense than to drop to one knee in front of a charging boar hog—to get me a better settlement. Who knows if he was playacting me?

Then he thinks I'd pay five thousand, maybe more, to the goddamn same government fixing to steal my land in the first goddamn place. I ain't going to do it, I'll say that. I can be mighty stubborn. I've outlasted most everything. Maybe this park thing, too. Craziest mess I ever heard about.

So, do I sue or not? Bird in the hand, a bird in the hand. Plus if I was to get the extra I'd have to give part of it to the government. I ain't going to do that. I just ain't.

He stomped the tin and filed it beside the other in his saddlebag. A glance at the sky told him it would be way past dark before they arrived home. "Get up, gal. We'll sleep in our own stalls tonight," he said, and clucked the horse up the mountain.

CHAPTER 9

All Manner of Flowers

Reverend Grady Noland led his horse, Priscilla, into Little Cataloochee one November afternoon because she threw a shoe atop Cove Creek Gap, exactly where Bishop Francis Asbury, his Methodist forerunner, had crossed a hundred and eighteen years before. Noland, Baptist to his toenails, knew nothing of that, nor would he have cared had he known. He often declared that when God Almighty created the world, there were two things He never made nor intended to be—mules and Methodists.

One of the last circuit preachers to ride a horse, Noland said motor vehicles were the devil's handiwork. "Is 'automobile' in the Book?' he would ask, wrinkling his forehead. "In the last days, the prophet says, God will take the 'round tires like the moon' from the whoring daughters of Zion. Besides, did Jesus ever ride in anything but a boat? And he didn't even *need* that!"

Except for white shirts, all his clothes were black. He wore a broad-brimmed hat in all weather to protect his scalp, no longer adequately shaded by thinning reddish-white hair. Although he had preached nearly every month at Ola Baptist Church in Little Cataloochee for four decades, old members such as Polly Rogers still sometimes referred to him as "the new preacher." In 1888, at nineteen, he had replaced William Goff, a saturnine stump of a man who'd affected a white neck ruff, for what reason no one ever knew. He had been quick to scare hell out of anyone. "Will you spend eternity in the smoking car?" was a sermon Polly heard as a girl, and four decades later she was still scared to set foot in a train.

Noland never wrote out a sermon, but meditated for hours on a text, pulled from neither psalter nor lectionary but his own head, a vessel filled with the Bible. That afternoon at the gap he should have heard the steady clink from Priscilla's off front hoof, but he'd been thinking about Moses striking the rock in Horeb, Exodus seventeen, verse six. The prophet's staff reminded him of the spear that pierced Jesus' side. Water poured forth from the wilderness rock. From Jesus' side came water and blood, John nineteen, verse thirty-four. God yanked a rib from a dead-asleep Adam to form Eve in the second chapter of Genesis, verses twenty-one and -two. Just so did God pull the water of baptism and the blood of the Lord's supper from Jesus. That was ready to lead to a diatribe against sin in general when Priscilla laid her ears back, raised her head, and snorted.

He dismounted, examined her hoof, and patted her neck. Prowling in his saddlebag, he shook his head. "Sister Priscilla, I left my shoeing kit at home." Backtracking a short distance, he found no shoe. "Sister, I'll lead you the rest of the way. It's only six or seven miles. We'll have a little talk with Jesus on the way." The horse seemed indifferent to that prospect but on that switchback journey heard Noland practice his Sunday sermon twice.

He stopped at the store, where Jake Carter whittled on the porch. Jake could carve an old man's face from a peach pit in nothing flat. His round-lensed black-rimmed eyeglasses put Noland in mind of an owl.

"Preacher, how in the world are you?" asked Jake. "You and Priscilla decide to be yoke-fellows?"

Noland beat road dust from his coat and smiled. "That's a good way to put it, Brother Jake. We've been that for a long time. She threw a shoe at the gap."

"I'll take care of that," said Cash Davis, Jake's whittling companion. He put his knife away and led the horse up the lane. Despite the imminent national park, and the preference lately for horsepower derived from gasoline instead of oats, Cash's cousin Lonnie still kept a forge.

The screen door screaked open to reveal Velda Parham in a gingham apron. Noland doffed his hat and grinned. "Sister Velda, what a pleasure. I do believe you've grown prettier."

She fairly hopped down the steps and hugged the preacher. "Reverend Noland, guess what?" She held up her left hand.

"Oh, my, a diamond, I believe. Who is the lucky man?"

"Oliver Babcock, Reverend. Will you marry us tomorrow?"

"That lawyer fellow?"

She nodded eagerly.

"Pretty sudden, isn't it?"

"Oh, Reverend, it's only been a month, but it feels like we've loved each other all our lives."

"Well, child, sure I'll marry you. I can tell you think this is the berries. You're glowing like a lightning bug. What does your mama think?"

Velda's hazel eyes danced. "Reverend Noland, she thinks it's fine. When Oliver said he'd take me to Raleigh, I said he could, if he'd marry me, and Mama comes with us. Scared me to put it that way, 'cause what if he'd have said no? But two days later he had this ring. We're going to be a family, the three of us."

"Then it's settled. Where and when?"

"Right before dinner, at Jake and Rachel's place."

Noland enjoyed his calling immensely. Aside from works of the spirit, he loved tasty food he did not have to cook, and the privilege of touching females with impunity. He hugged Velda and patted her back. "Child, are you packed for a honeymoon?"

"Yes, sir. We're leaving Sunday."

· · ·

None of Velda's father's siblings were still alive, and their progeny shied from ceremonies, so none had been invited. Various other relatives, however, Suttons and Cagles and Browns, had taken up residence in local homes for the weekend, eagerly anticipating a ceremony bringing an honest-to-God lawyer into the fold. Oliver's family, thin and scattered, would have disapproved of his marrying a mountain woman, so none knew of the impending marriage.

Saturday morning broke bright and clear, a November Indian summer day, when a fellow could almost think cold weather would not return. Rachel had forced jonquils for Velda's bouquet, and earthen pots of yellow and white chrysanthemums carefully hidden from frost sat on the porch rails. Jake had garlanded the front porch with spruce boughs. Rachel caused cakes and pies to go in one direction, chicken and ham in another. They brought the last of their ice from the barn to help make ice cream. She herded musicians to the north corner of the porch, where they uncased guitars, a banjo, and an upright bass. Cash Davis brought a mandolin he used to play before "Old Arthur-itis" set in, figuring some youngster would pick it.

Jake put chairs in the yard for old people, and chastened three children who wanted to play lion tamer with one. Jake's nephew was in charge of parking, but in spite of his efforts, wagons and automobiles sat snaggletoothed. Children ran, played hide-and-seek, and threw balls down the hill for dogs to fetch. Chickens not yet stewed or fried hid in odd corners.

The musicians warmed up with "Wayfaring Stranger," then tried "Just a Closer Walk with Thee," and moved smoothly into a chorus or two of "On Jordan's Stormy Banks," which Preacher Noland appreciated because the line "I am bound for the promised land" afforded him a chance to kid Oliver about his wedding night. When the band grew silent, Rachel cued Noland and Oliver to walk from behind the house. Oliver sported a dark brown worsted suit with a hint of green. A silk handkerchief the color of well-creamed coffee puffed in his jacket pocket. Women smiled, while men searched Oliver's face for signs of panic. A mockingbird landed in Jake's yard maple, trilled like a warbler, yelled "thief" like a jaybird, then left in a gray and white flash.

After some argument the band had settled on bass and mandolin as suitable to play the Wagnerian march, which they started while Rachel held the screen door open. Velda's older brother Samuel readied his arm for her. She emerged beaming in a white wool outfit from the mail order. It showed entirely too much of her to suit the older women, although it was only a peek of calf and a hint of shoulder. Men old and young nodded approval. Her hair was secured in the back with her grandmother Cagle's mother-of-pearl pin and a dangling yellow ribbon.

Samuel and Velda walked slowly down the steps. "Who giveth this woman?" asked Noland, to which Samuel replied, "Her brother," and handed her to Oliver, whose grin said he was enjoying this even more than his victory at Zeb's trial.

Bride and groom vowed with clear voices, but by the time Preacher Noland pronounced them man and wife, Velda had practically destroyed her bouquet from sheer nervousness. Reaching to kiss her new husband, she scattered white and yellow petals on his shoes. The band broke into a reel as the crowd huzzahed and clapped, and folks started lining up—women to congratulate the couple, men to eat.

Loads of lemonade, milk, and, for those close to the Banks family, elderberry wine that Hannah served discreetly in teacups, washed down great quantities of food. Men visited their cars through the afternoon for a pull or two. The younger men would have chased a native bridegroom into the barn to pull down his pants and paint his privates with gentian violet, but they spared Oliver, outsider and Zeb's savior, that indignity. They were content to cuff him on the head and joke leeringly.

As dark crept down the mountain, the musicians packed instruments and folks pretended to leave. Anxiety began to gnaw at Oliver. Velda's mother's house was very small—three rooms, kitchen in the rear, front room, and small bedroom—and he wondered if he and his bride might have to wait until Raleigh to consummate their marriage.

But Billie insisted the newlyweds take the bedroom, while she would sleep on the front room sofa. A joyful Oliver went to the bedroom and stripped to his skivvies. He shivered, whether from the growing chill or anticipation he could not tell.

Suddenly a commotion from gunshots, dozens of cowbells, and dish-pans beaten by wooden spoons practically lifted him from the floor. Up-ward of fifty folks swarmed into the living room. The men yelled "Where's he at?" Velda grinned and pointed to the bedroom.

They found him struggling to get his trousers back on, hooted, and carried him outside. Borne by half-drunken and more than mildly ob-scene enthusiasm, Oliver was carried around the yard fast enough to dizzy him. When they deposited him back in the front room, the table was laden with presents, and women were saying good-bye. As the party left, men fired weapons and yelled for Oliver not to do anything they wouldn't.

"What in the world?" he asked.

"Shivaree," giggled Velda. "Happens to newlyweds hereabouts."

The party left quilts and pillowcases, jars of honey and beans and sausage, multitudes of dried fruits, bags of nuts and flour and cornmeal. There was a cross-stitched sampler reading "God Bless Our Home" in pink and blue. Oliver discreetly picked up a quart of straw-colored whiskey to take to the bedroom for a swig. Mother and daughter ad-mired the gifts, then Billie patted Velda's shoulder. "Honey, it's time we were asleep." They hugged, and Velda came to the bedroom and shut the door.

Oliver cut a fine figure as an attorney and a dancer, but his sexual ex-periences were limited to dates with his hand—he joked about squiring Minnie Fingers—plus one Saturday night in a Durham hotel where women of indeterminable ages serviced soldiers, college boys, and other strays for money. So he stood before his wife wearing shorts and a coun-tenance fluttering somewhere between joy and trepidation.

Velda smiled. "It's cold, dear. I'm going to slip into bed."

He watched her remove dress and slip, then unpin her hair. She shook it loose, turned to him, and stretched her arms over her head, a pose that liked to have killed him. She blew out the lamp, shucked in under the covers, and purred, "Get under here and hold me, Oliver."

She was altogether soft and warm and smelled like all manner of flow-ers. He looked at the bottom of the door to make sure her mother's light had been extinguished, then laid hands on his bride to begin as discreet a frenzy as they could manage. They enjoyed it so much they dared try it again after a short respite.

Next morning Velda woke, dressed, and left the bedroom. Oliver listened to the women awhile, wondered why all the laughter, and got up to the smell of perking coffee and frying pork.

Oliver really wanted to get on the road, and Velda had made an argument for leaving at dawn. It was at best a two-day journey to Raleigh, and four, more likely, because tire troubles were certain, but Billie made them wait. "I'm plenty ready to find out what this new life will be," she said, "but I'm not leaving anywhere until I worship the Lord. Why tempt fate?" So they dressed, ate breakfast, and walked to the clapboard sanctuary.

Preacher Noland shifted his text to the second chapter of Genesis, verse twenty-four: "Therefore shall a man leave his father and his mother, and shall cleave unto his wife: and they shall be one flesh." Considerable throat clearing and shuffling of feet commenced when he threatened to talk in detail about cleaving, but soon he wandered three verses prior, where God caused a deep sleep to come upon Adam, and before long the sermon led to Moses striking the rock at Horeb, the soldier's spear and Jesus' side, and blood and water. He ended, as always, by calling for sinners to repair to the foot of the cross, where there is always plenty of room.

That was certainly not the case with Oliver's Ford. It was a young man's car, a brand-new Model A roadster, marriage and mother-in-law having been far from his mind when he bought it. Nor had he thought of fall and winter driving, for its only glass to speak of was a windshield. Dark green with black fenders, it was so shiny a man could have safely shaved in its reflection. He didn't seem to care that some wags had tied old shoes and tin cans to his bumper.

A fair-size trunk was strapped to the rear platform—Jake would ship the rest by rail. Inside was a tin tobacco container with charcoal from Billie's fireplace, to help start their first fire in their new home. He said good-byes and ushered his mother-in-law into the passenger side. Velda meant to ride in the rumble seat, at least until they were out of sight.

After seeing how much of the seat Billie required, he wondered if he would have room to change gears when Velda squeezed in. "I'm ready, Son. Take us to Raleigh," Billie said proudly.

Velda hugged the preacher one more time. "Reverend Noland, we appreciate you marrying us. If you ever get down east, come visit," she said.

He smiled. "Child, I'll never get that far from the house. But thanks. Here's a little something for you." He handed her a daintily filigreed pin.

"Reverend Noland, it's beautiful."

"It belonged to my wife. It's laid in my saddlebag ever since she died. I reckon I kept it for good luck, or to give to a pretty gal like you."

"I couldn't, Reverend Noland. What about your family?" Velda dabbed at her eyes with a white handkerchief.

"We never had girls, and this is too old-fashioned to suit my daughters-in-law. Take this before you make an old man mad."

They hugged, and Velda handed the pin to her mother. Oliver helped his wife into the rumble seat, an operation more to be contemplated than done with grace and ease. Once seated against the rolled leather, Velda waved like she was on a parade float. Oliver shut the door, stepped on the starter, put the car in gear, and headed off, shoes and cans bouncing and clattering. Cataloochans and wedding guests waved them out of sight, wondering if they would see them again.

BOOK 2

Thy Feet upon the Mountains

December 1928–March 1931

CHAPTER 10

Greenland's Icy Mountains

Nell Hawkins had been nauseated mornings for a couple of weeks, and although sunny days usually made her bouncy, this one in December of 1928 sapped her energy. Tying her blue terry cloth robe closed, she shuffled from the bedroom to find Jim reading a letter. "What now?" she asked, rubbing sleep from her eyes.

Jim sat at the kitchen table drinking from a mug of coffee. "It's from Red Pendleton. Says to see him Monday week before we head for Cataloochee."

She sat across the table twisting a strand of hair around her middle finger. "Darling, don't slurp so loudly. Would you serve me a cup, the way I like it? Where is he, anyway?"

Jim poured a mug half full, then stirred in two lumps of sugar and a lot of cream. He loved the smell of black coffee, and always grimaced at how Nell took hers. "He's still at the Asheville office. I won't have to go to Haywood."

"You said Monday?"

"Yep."

"How are you going to get there?" Their recently purchased second-hand Ford was in the shop.

"Reckon I'll borrow Wolf's car. Or I'll hitch a ride."

"Daddy always says walking isn't crowded."

"He's right about that." He saw Nell shudder and shake her head slightly. "What's the matter, honey?"

She sipped, hugged herself, and looked out the window. "I'm feeling like I could just die."

"Honey, I'm sorry. Anything I can do?"

"Jim, I think I might be—you know—going to have another baby."

"Really? That's wonderful." He held out his hand. "Care to dance?"

She looked at him like he was insane. "I'd throw up on you."

He took his fiddle down and, playing "Fly Around My Pretty Little Miss," danced around the kitchen, grinning. "Maybe this'n'll be a girl. Sweet thing like her momma."

She shrugged. "Right now I don't feel sweet."

"I'll have to bring my girls a present." He stood behind her chair and rubbed her shoulders. "We'll be fine, honey. I'll find you a pot of gold at the end of a rainbow."

"That only happens in fairy tales, Jim."

"It's our story, honey. It's better'n a fairy tale. You'll see."

Jim stood in Pendleton's office Monday morning, hat in hands. "You wanted to see me, sir?"

Pendleton rummaged in his desk drawer for a package of cigarettes. "Care for a smoke, Hawkins?"

"No, sir. I never took it up."

Pendleton lit it with a thin brass lighter and blew smoke toward the ceiling. "Have a seat, Hawkins. I suppose you're wondering why I asked you to come here today."

Jim sat on a wooden bench that didn't sit square with the desk. "Yes, sir, it had occurred to me."

"I wanted a look at you. Since you applied, there have been more people interested. I want to make sure I'm hiring the right person."

"Yes, sir. What can I tell you?"

"I'll get to the heart of this, Mr. Hawkins. We need an interim warden until the park service formally assumes jurisdiction. Maybe a year from now, maybe longer. Meantime someone will have to keep order over there." Pendleton stood, walked to the front of his desk, and looked down at Jim. "To be perfectly honest, Hawkins, I sent that letter based solely on you being familiar with the territory. No consideration of education, training, that kind of thing. Now I have applicants who look better than you on paper. You only went to a normal school, did not take a degree, and that is suspect, in my book."

"Mr. Pendleton, if I may ask, what does a degree have to do with this job?"

Pendleton half sat on the desk and flicked at his glass ashtray. "Everything, Mr. Hawkins. A degree from a well-connected university means everything."

"Will it help you find your way from Deadfall to Long Bunk?"

"It will help you read a map."

"I've never seen a map of Cataloochee, sir, but I know the place like the back of my hand. I was born there, and I'd love to die there. And work in between. I'm your man."

"I'm not so certain. It seems to me a man who shirks his requirements—your transcript indicates you failed English—might also shirk his duties in the field."

Jim smiled. "You have a recommendation from my forest service supervisor?"

Pendleton nodded.

"Does it say I'm a goldbrick?"

"No. In fact, it says you're quite a good worker."

"Then what's the problem?"

"I am, sir, quite a judge of character. People will, despite glowing recommendations, occasionally want to get rid of an employee badly enough to lie about them. So I thought it best to interview you personally."

"Fair enough, sir. Just tell me what you want to know."

"I want you to talk about something that's dear to your heart."

"Person? Place? Thing?"

"Your choice, Mr. Hawkins."

"Then I'll talk about a place. Cataloochee. I love it. I was born there, back when it was what they call a thriving community. I know it's not that way now, and the plans are for it to change into wilderness. But as long as I live, I'll remember where people used to live, where the cemeteries are, where the springs are, where a man can find anything from healing herbs to snakes. I'll be able to tell people about that. When folks come back after they move away—or their children come years from now—I can show them where they came from. I'll remember.

"Part of my heart is there, Mr. Pendleton. It always will be. That's not anything a man can take from me. And I would hope that part of this job is to protect it. To keep it safe. I would consider that an honor."

Pendleton stubbed his cigarette. "Very impressive, Mr. Hawkins." He turned and looked at Jim. "Are you really as big a sap as that answer would indicate?"

"I meant it, sir."

Pendleton seemed to consider this with high seriousness. "Hawkins, you're not even close to the kind of man I would hire for this job if I had my way. But I don't, and I have to consider the fact that we could not get a candidate with a better knowledge of the terrain. So I think we'll get along fine. Are you ready to take the oath?"

Jim straightened his hair with his right hand. "Yes, sir. But let me make sure about what you said in your letter. I get a horse and a place to stay, right?"

"You will live in the Elijah Howell house. You know it, I assume."

"Yes, sir, that's a fine house, right big for my little family."

"Well, fill it up, then. Keep her barefoot and pregnant, eh, heh-heh?"

Jim made a halfhearted smile. "When do I report for duty?"

"Can you be in Cataloochee tomorrow?"

"I can move in Friday week." Jim stood and breathed deeply. "I'm ready for that oath."

Pendleton fetched a Bible from his desk drawer. "Place your right hand on the book and raise your left hand. Repeat after me: 'I will support and defend the Constitution of the United States against all enemies, foreign and domestic; I will bear true faith and allegiance to the same; I take this obligation freely without any mental reservation or purpose of evasion; I will well and faithfully discharge the duties of the office on which I am about to enter, so help me God.' Welcome aboard, Hawkins. You are a park commission employee. There will be a uniform and manual ready here in a day or two. I assume you own a sidearm?"

Jim nodded.

"Then I wish you the best of luck."

In the fall of 1928 a Dutch corporation, doing business as American Enka, had begun to build a sprawling redbrick rayon plant on two thousand acres of bottomland adjacent to Scratch Ankle. Anyone nearby with extra land built as large a boardinghouse as possible, anticipating thousands of workers. Jim and Nell soon became the only folks in their boardinghouse having nothing to do with the plant. And they were leaving.

The morning they moved to Cataloochee a low gray sky threatened snow. They had the yard and house mostly to themselves. Henry Johnson, wearing a brand-new pair of denim jeans with a matching jacket, had borrowed a black beat-up half-ton Chevrolet truck. The back left corner of the bed looked like rusty lace, but the vehicle had a solid-sounding drive train. Elizabeth wore a wool frock with a tailored rose on the left shoulder. It came in two colors, ashes of roses and cocoa brown, and she had finally decided that matching her brown eyes was just as important as picking a conservative winter color. Her felt hat had almost a masculine look to the brim, which, she had been assured at Bon Marché, was perfect for travel.

At first Nell and Elizabeth supervised Henry and Jim's packing, but Henry soon joined the women while Jim both toted and arranged. It wasn't all that much to reckon with. A kitchen table with a white baked enamel top and three chairs. Two beds and mattresses. A washstand, bowl, and pitcher. Two rocking chairs, one with a split cane seat and the other with wood. Boxes of dishes and kitchen utensils. A crib. A box of towels, dishrags, and diapers. Three cardboard suitcases full of Nell's clothes and a duffel bag for Jim's. A churn, a washtub, a board. An ironing board and flatiron. Jim's toolbox and shotgun. Odds and ends collected since they'd married in 1926.

When Jim brought out a wooden box holding bits of pipe, old nails, half a pair of pliers, a maple bobbin from the rayon plant, a half skein of pink yarn, two rusty mousetraps, dull scissors, and a screwdriver without a handle, Nell frowned, but Jim grinned. "You never know when you'll need something, honey." Jim filled spaces in the load with firewood and two bags of Kentucky anthracite.

Jim thought they were finished about nine, and stood in the yard wondering where everyone would ride. His mother-in-law emerged from the entrance holding a wooden box big enough to contain a large medicine ball. "Dear, you need to make room for this," she trilled.

"What is it, Mother?" asked Jim.

"A housewarming gift, silly boy. For entertaining."

The box held a green pressed glass punch bowl and a dozen cups. "Thanks, Mother." Jim tried to remember who was left in Cataloochee. Maybe, he thought, Aunt Mary and Nell could host a soirée. "Just the ticket," he said.

"Pack it safe and snug," Elizabeth said.

Jim nestled it between a box of towels and a suitcase.

Henry drove the Chevrolet, Elizabeth in the middle, Nell and the baby next to the door. "Thank God this thing has a decent heater," Henry said, and lit a King Edward cigar. Nell cracked the wing window a half inch to let out the smoke. Jim led in the Ford, the dog his happy companion.

For the first part of the journey, through Canton, Clyde, and Waynesville, Henry flashed his headlights often so Jim would stop for the women to stretch their legs. They shared a lunch of cold ham, cheese, and sliced bread inside the general store at Frog Level. The proprietor wanted them to eat on the porch, but Elizabeth charmed him with a promise Henry would buy sodas. "Jim, where in the *world* are you taking us?" asked Elizabeth. "I had no idea such a place existed."

"This is Waynesville, Mother. It's civilization, and I don't have a lot of use for it. Wait until you see the valley. It's the prettiest place in the world." His mother-in-law rolled her eyes at her husband.

Halfway toward Cove Creek Gap any appreciable width of road was eaten by serious switchbacks. Jim was glad not to be in the Chevrolet. He got along with his in-laws, but he preferred small doses and could barely stomach his father-in-law's cigars. This way he enjoyed the sights. A gray snow patch beside a laurel thicket. A hint of winter warbler in the periphery. A branch freshly broken from a huge hemlock, white wood dangling over the road like a sword. A stalk of Joe Pye weed bent but unbroken by wind and weather. Brown oak leaves clattering in the breeze, refusing to fall. A buzzard soaring in lazy arcs above the valley.

The Chevrolet flashed its lights and stopped suddenly. Nell and Mack stumbled out, followed hurriedly by Elizabeth, overcome with motion sickness. Jim chose not to embarrass his mother-in-law by watching her retch into the roadside bushes. "How's little Mack?" he asked, but Nell simply gave Jim the boy's hand and walked down the road.

"Honey, what's the matter?" Jim yelled.

She turned, pouting. "Where in creation are you taking us?"

He looked at Mack, who grinned at his father. "Home," Jim said.

Henry dipped a sizeable handkerchief in a roadside spring and handed it to his wife. "This is the worst road I have ever tried to drive."

"Least there isn't much traffic," Jim said, as all clustered around him.

Elizabeth, as pale as dried pine rosin, looked up at her son-in-law. "Are you sure there are houses there?"

"Trust me, Mother. We didn't grow up in mud huts. You'll love it."

Elizabeth straightened her hat, found a compact, and refreshed her lipstick. She took Mack by the hand. "Well, we simply *have* to make the best of it, don't we?" she said, and piled them back into the cab.

They crossed the gap and started down by the deserted Sutton farm at Turkey Cove. Black silhouettes of thistles thrust three feet high in their pasture. Poison oak, honeysuckle, and bittersweet grew on fence posts. A crow perched on the point of the barn roof like a weathervane.

Toward the bottom of the mountain things looked more normal, because Old Man Bennett junior—the son of the original Old Man Bennett, whose house was burned during the Civil War and rebuilt by his namesake son—had so far been too stubborn to leave. His place in the curve of the road was kempt.

They forded the creek around four in the afternoon and turned sharply left. In a quarter mile Jim pulled beside a darkened house and parked. The Chevrolet backfired and dieseled to a stop. Doors creaked as the passengers emerged. The metallic thud of closing doors echoed off the barn.

Jim had never seen Lige Howell's house without occupants or chimney smoke. The right-hand wing had been a stand-alone cabin, converted to a kitchen for Lige and Penny's boarding business. In the gloom it looked tiny and cold. Across the dogtrot the squat two-story frame addition paled against the drooping sky. Elizabeth, raised a Baptist, thought it as cold as that hymn about Greenland's icy mountains. She laid the back of her wrist to her forehead, said "Lord save us," and fainted. Nell, having seen her mother swoon many a time, had to smile despite her own misgivings. Henry sat his wife on the edge of the truck seat and fanned with his handkerchief. "Son, what in the world?"

"It's fine," he said. "I'll just go in and build a fire or two."

A stack of stove wood and a box of kindling waited in the kitchen wing. He fired the cookstove and two coal oil lamps, and gathered his family into the room. Mack thought this a great adventure, and his face glowed in the lamplight. His mother and grandparents hovered in doubtful shadows. "It'll be fine in a few minutes," Jim said. "Meantime I'll build the bedroom fires."

As he started out the door, Henry grabbed his arm. "Do you mean we're sleeping here?"

Jim looked at his father-in-law's hand like it was a small, gnawing animal. "Yes, sir. It'll be fine when we get some fire."

"If you think Elizabeth will spend a night here, you have another think coming. This place doesn't have electricity."

Elizabeth, recovered from her swoon, paced like a trapped cat. Jim started toward the dogtrot, but she intervened. "You are *crazy*, Jim Hawkins. My daughter won't stand for this." She grabbed Henry's sleeve. "Take us back. I *demand* it."

"Elizabeth, calm down. I will get you all back home, but I have to have something to eat."

Jim raised his hands. "If you'll let me get us heat and light, this place will be snug in less than an hour. We can eat, unload the truck, and it'll look a lot better in the morning."

A mouse, flushed out of a nest in the oven, skittered along a baseboard and under the back door. Elizabeth shrieked loudly enough to break window glass. "Kill that THING," she cried into Henry's jacket. Her hat crashed to the floor.

"Dear, it's gone."

"I'm not spending another minute here! Next thing, we'll see a snake."

"Snakes are underground this time of year," said Jim.

This only gave Elizabeth visions of snake heads peeking through floorboards. "Henry, pick up my hat. Nell Marie Johnson, get that little boy's coat on. You and Henry Mack are coming home, where you belong."

"Now, just a minute," started Jim.

"Son," said Henry, "she's right. We're going back."

"Will you at least help me unload the truck?"

Henry said nothing as Nell looked out the window, choking back tears. Jim put his hand on her shoulder. "Honey, what do you say?"

She wept on his shoulder. Mack started crying because of his mother's tears, and Elizabeth followed suit. Jim held Nell, wondering if this night might be the end of his marriage. "What do you *want* me to say?" she asked. "You said it would be perfect, but it isn't, Jim. It *really* isn't."

"We can make it perfect," he said quietly. "We have to. For Mack and our new one."

"What's that?" shouted Elizabeth. *"New one?"*

Nell hugged her mother. "I wasn't going to tell yet. It's too early. But, yes, I'm expecting."

"*That* settles it. Nell Marie, you were foolish to even have *thought* of coming here." She pointed a bony finger at Jim. "I am surprised at you, putting yourself ahead of the welfare of these sweet people, one of which is *unborn*. To think!"

Nell clutched Jim's arm. "Mother, we made this decision together."

"Nonsense. He surely browbeat you into this."

"No, Mother. It wasn't like that at all." She dried her eyes and smiled at Jim. "We are going to be fine." She took a deep breath and faced her father. "Daddy, help us get our things off the truck. Mack and I belong with Jim." She hugged her husband.

"Well, I never," said Elizabeth. "We'll see how long *this* lasts. Henry, help them, quickly. I *have* to go home, and I don't care if it's dawn when we return. I will not sleep in a pigsty." She looked at her feet as if a boa constrictor were about to engulf her.

Unloading took a scant ten minutes. They didn't even break the punch set. Jim, Nell, and Mack stood on the porch beside their worldly goods and waved at Henry and Elizabeth as they backed into the road. Henry shoved in the clutch as Elizabeth rolled the window down. "Nell, please come home!"

"I *am* home, Mother," she said. "At least for now. I'm sorry you feel this way."

Jim's heart felt as heavy as a glass paperweight as he watched Elizabeth roll up the window and gesture to Henry, who slammed the truck into granny gear and headed toward the ford. Jim and Nell watched their taillights, put Mack to bed, and then turned into the kitchen to heat ham and beans and hope they had chosen well.

CHAPTER 11

Flying Squirrel

Nell's children were napping, so Nell sat at the kitchen table, left leg crossed under the right, and opened her mother's envelope with a pewter letter opener. It was the only manufactured letter opener in Cataloochee—pocketknives, tenpenny nails, and fingers having always been sufficient. She liked both its heft and delicate engraving, reminiscent of muscadine vines. It was a going-away present from her mother, who had made Nell promise to write often and answer each of her letters.

Her mother wrote every Sunday. The letters usually arrived Wednesday morning, and Jim brought them home at dinnertime when he was working in the valley, that night or the next day when he was not. Nell's mother perfumed her stationery box with a lavender sachet. When she remembered something after she had sealed a letter, she wrote it in pig latin on the flap, but there was no message there today.

Nell slit the envelope and removed the letter, written in her mother's perfect penmanship. Elizabeth used vellum or onionskin under which she laid ruled paper so her lines did not slant or vary in spacing. A scan told Nell how her mother was feeling. Normally there would be several words in all capitals, some in italics, some underlined once and occasionally twice. If she were down, there would be fewer flourishes, but if manic, every other word might shout.

November 17, 1929

My Dearest Nell,

I DO hope you are well and that awful climate there is not WEIGHING you down. You know, you are like me, of a <u>delicate sensibility</u>, so be very conscientious to always feed that with pretty flowers, nice stories, and good companions. We must stick together, we <u>women</u> of <u>refinement</u>.

How are our precious children? It was so good to see them when you last brought them over. I think Little Elizabeth looks exactly like me when I was that age. She has my coloration and, I might add, temperament— treat her gently, Nell, do not chastise her with a <u>switch</u> or any awful and barbaric punishments. Henry Mack, I'm afraid, is the image of his father, but with time should OUTGROW that. Your brother Charles looked like his father for the longest time, but he finally (and happily) came to look like—Charles.

*Church was simply horrible this morning. Pastor King has taken it upon himself to smugly speak about politics, but my opinion is that the <u>church</u> should stay out of such matters. What happens in New York, or in Washington, seems to me to have **nothing** to do with our little Presbyterian church. We have enough trouble keeping our own little church house in order.*

Mrs. Queen, Mrs. Arrowood, and Mrs. Hughey will be here tomorrow for bridge. You don't remember when Monday was washday. My mother washed clothes, by hand, every Monday, come—as they say—the <u>D—l</u> or high water. Delicate though I was, I would have to help, but now I am glad I play bridge Mondays. We are fortunate to have an automatic washing machine. I wish you would come back so you won't have to bear such a "COUNTRY" schedule. Your hands were always so pretty and soft, like mine are now.

THANKSGIVING will be the 28th. I must insist you and James bring my Grandchildren *home so I can see them. I intend to cook a feast, and you and I can finish the kitchen preparations while your father and James play with the children. We girls can TALK.*

*I will close. Let me repeat what I said when your father and I left you in that horrible place. YOU MUST FIND A WAY OUT OF THERE SOON. No good can come from living in such a primitive backwater. I know you Love your Husband and want to stay with him. He will, as they all do, bring up your **DUTY** to him. But it seems to your poor mother your **DUTY** is to your **Children** (and me). There are WAYS, my dear, to really make him come around, to get him to clearly realize your happiness is more important than his silly job. If you know what I mean. If nothing else, I cannot continue to cruelly be deprived of seeing my grandchildren as I alas currently am.*

Your Affectionate Mother

P.S. This silly situation with the stock market should blow over in a few days so do not worry about it.
P.P.S. Kiss my little ones and remind them they have a
GRANDMOTHER!!!!

Nell looked at her hands. The tops of her knuckles were red and cracked, and her palms were callused from mop and broom. Nell had a tin of Watkins red clover salve, but her hands seemed endless in their capacity to soak it up. She rubbed the back of her left with her right and pursed her lips. Little Elizabeth cried.

Nell carried the letter into the pantry and put it into her stationery box, promising herself to answer it soon. She nearly slipped on Mack's wooden truck in the front room, sending it crashing into the wall. Little Elizabeth stood squalling in her crib in the next room.

"Honey, here I am." Her daughter was not yet a year old and was thoroughly wet. Nell comforted her and changed her diaper, wrinkling her nose as she dropped it into the bucket. "Now, then," she said, "let's go see what we can do this afternoon."

They played awhile with a set of wooden blocks painted with letters and numbers, then Nell put Little Elizabeth in her crib and swept the floor in that room. They moved to the kitchen, where Nell laid paper and kindling in the cookstove. She had not yet mastered the art of keeping fire. She was hot-natured, so did not like a daytime fire, and because her parents had gotten electricity when she was seven or eight, she had never learned to keep a fire all day. She was not given to talking to herself or swearing, but the cookstove could trigger a bout of both.

She lit the fire and put the eye back in the cooktop. She opened the vent to let air into the chamber and was happy to see good fire and to hear kindling pop. It had taken Jim several sessions to show her which wood species to use when. They had inherited several winters' worth of firewood from Lige Howell, and she had learned to tell rich pine from poplar, and actually admired the way dead locust bark made tinder. Poplar bark felt smooth, sourwood was rough and pitted, and she had found the hard way not to handle hairy vines of mature poison oak. But she still had trouble sorting green wood from dry.

Her fire began to warm the cooktop, so with a lifter she opened the lid and threw in a piece of poplar, which would have been fine had it been split last year. It was, however, what Jim called "greener'n a gourd," a week ago part of a large limb that had crashed in a storm. Her object was to warm a bottle for Little Elizabeth, but the fire went out without even putting much char on the poplar billet.

"Phooey," she muttered. To Little Elizabeth, happy on a blanket on the floor with two of her blocks, she said "Honey, your bottle will be warm in a minute." When she lifted the lid, smoke curled into the room like an unwanted relative. With a glove she gingerly picked out the green wood, trotted it to the porch, and threw it into the yard.

An hour later Mack was up playing with his truck, Nell had a fire in the stove, and Little Elizabeth sucked from her bottle. The females sat in the kitchen rocker, Little Elizabeth pulling hard on the nipple and Nell fanning them with a magazine. "Wonder when Daddy'll be home," Nell said. "He's at Mount Sterling but said he might be through early. We hope so, don't we, darling?"

Something thrashed around in the pantry. Nell quit rocking and fanning and listened. She had almost gotten used to hearing creatures in the walls, but would still have a fit if one showed itself in daylight. "If that's a mousie, it's a pretty darn big mousie," she said, and hugged Little Elizabeth. "Mommy won't let it get her baby."

They rocked until Little Elizabeth had drained the bottle, and her half-shut eyes made Nell hope she might take another nap. Carefully Nell laid her in her crib, and rubbed her daughter's forehead with the back of her hand. Little Elizabeth seemed content to sleep.

Nell went back across the dogtrot to the kitchen and stood still. She checked her cookfire and, hoping to keep it until supper, added a piece of locust. She asked Mack to fetch potatoes from the basket on the back porch. Jim would eat potatoes seven days a week, and it was good, she thought, because they had God's plenty of them. She began to peel and slice, thinking she had some hoop cheese, and scalloped potatoes would be good for a change. She heard Jim's horse heading to the barn, and smiled.

From the corner of her eye she saw a brownish gray creature scuttle across the baseboard. Screaming, she threw potatoes, knife, skins, and bowl toward the ceiling, jumped onto a kitchen chair, and held on.

Jim knocked his hat off on the door frame as he rushed into the kitchen. "What is it?" he yelled. Nell pointed to the corner and continued to scream, now backed up by Mack and Little Elizabeth.

The creature jumped to the counter and aimed for the window over the sink. Jim put on his work gloves. Its tail was furry, its eyes were too big, and it wasn't quite the color of a rat. The animal scraped its claws on the window glass like it was trying to tunnel out. When Jim caught it, he saw whitish pockets on its side. "It's only a flying squirrel," he yelled, but Nell still shrieked.

It turned and gnawed the back of his glove furiously. He hoped to make the back porch before the thing ate to the quick. Outside, he hurled squirrel and glove, which hit in the yard as one. The glove stayed but the skirted squirrel tumbled, jumped, soared to the smokehouse porch, and disappeared inside.

Back inside, Nell held Little Elizabeth. Both females were blubbery. Mack still looked out the kitchen window. "It was a flying squirrel," Jim said. "They won't hurt you. One of the Carters made a pet out of one when I was a boy."

"Jim Hawkins, I don't care. That thing was nasty and doesn't belong in a proper house. You must promise me there aren't any more. What if it had bit Little Elizabeth?"

He put his arm around his women. "Honey, it just crawled in somehow. Sometimes they come down the chimney. It was scareder of you than you were of it."

"I have to lie down with Little Elizabeth now. If you want supper, you'll have to fix it." She went to their bedroom and shut the door.

He and Mack trotted to the barn to finish stabling the horse. "Daddy, Daddy, guess what?"

Jim hoisted his son with both hands. "What, big man?"

"Chicken squat," yelled the boy.

Jim laughed, walked his son over to the chopping block, and made to turn him over his knee. "I'm a good mind to tan your hide for saying that," he said, still chuckling. He let Mack rise and pointed a bony finger at him. "Son, don't ever say that—in front of your mother."

" 'Kay, Daddy. I won't."

"Good. Now we got work to do."

They stabled the horse, cleaned up the kitchen, and then made what passed for supper, boiled potatoes, cold ham, cornbread, pickled beets. Jim brought in two armloads of firewood for each fireplace, while Mack made six trips for stove wood for the morning's kitchen fire. Nell and Jim dressed the children for bed at the hearth, then kissed them good night. Nell put Little Elizabeth to bed, and Jim, Mack. After the children were down, Nell sighed.

"What's the matter, honey?"

"Oh, Jim, I just don't know if I'll ever get used to living here."

"Give it a chance, Nell. I've told you how great it was growing up. It will be that way for us, too. Especially for Mack and Lizzy. They won't have all those city problems."

"Like electricity? Or running water?"

"No, I'm talking about booze. Auto accidents. Getting pregnant before they're married. Breathing car fumes. That kind of thing. And I'm working on both water and electricity. We should have our gravity system ready in the spring, and when they build the fire tower, it'll have electricity we can use."

"I received a letter from Mother today."

"What did she say?"

"The usual. She wants us to move back to West Asheville."

"Nell, I work for the park service. I *have* to live here."

"Couldn't you find another job?"

He laughed. "Nell, this is the closest to a perfect job a man could want. I'm in charge of where I grew up, and I mostly love it, except for trying to figure out who's setting these confounded fires."

"Well, I hate it. There's rats and mice and bats and snakes and I don't know what all. I don't have anywhere to go except church. And what if the kids got really sick? They could die before we got them to a doctor."

"Honey, you just need a good night's sleep. You want a dram before bed?"

"You know I don't drink that stuff."

"I don't either unless I have a cold or can't get to sleep. You sure?"

She stood. "I'm going to sit on the porch a minute before bed. Think about what I said."

He kissed her on the forehead. "I will, honey. But think about what I said, too."

She put on a sweater and went to the porch. Leaning against the column, she looked past the top of the mountain to a clear northwest sky. She made a wish on the first bright object she saw, although she neither knew its name nor cared to learn it. "Lord, I must get out of here somehow," she said softly. She heard Jim come out the back door on his way to the outhouse. When he returned and she no longer heard footsteps, she came into the kitchen for her stationery box.

After filling the Sheaffer black and pearl fountain pen her mother had given her the previous Christmas, she removed a sheet of stationery. The fires Jim had banked for the night popped gently. She bent to answer her mother's letter.

November 20, 1929

Dear Mother,

Yrs of the 17th in hand, many thanks. I'm glad to hear you are keeping up with the Queen family. As Papa says, they put their pants on the same way we do. Real estate has made them rich, but they must not get the <u>big head</u>.

 Mack is doing well, and Little Elizabeth is a good baby. I, too, hope they will live in West Asheville (where we belong). But it will not be soon, for this is Jim's dream job, and he means to impress the superintendent. I will do what I can short of leaving him, a thing I am not willing to contemplate. Your suggestion put ideas in my head to be sure. I will let you know what happens.

 Today, of all things, there was a flying squirrel in the house! In the <u>house</u>, my shelter from all this national park! I thought it was a rat. Jim, thank heavens, took it outside. Sometimes I don't know about him. He let it go, to come back another day. Entirely too much country living for me!

 There are more people here than I realized at first glance. You ride through and think no one much lives here, but on Sundays they come out of the woodwork for church, the one social event I have to look forward to. I think there were seventy-five in worship this week.

 Rest assured, dear mother, that I will do what I can to get us back to civilization.

 Your loving daughter,
Nell

CHAPTER 12

Fish for Breakfast

A crisp October Monday morning in 1930 made Silas Wright feel kindly toward both the world and his boarder, Bud Harrogate. Silas woke as usual at five, stared at the ceiling awhile, then got up and dressed. He padded to the cabinet for a swig of whiskey—and, instead of waking Bud, lit a lamp and read the Bible for an hour. Then he rapped on the ceiling with a broom handle.

Harrogate's feet usually hit the floor seconds after such racket, but this morning, nothing. Silas knocked harder, dislodging a rain of floor-bound particles. *Damn*, he thought, climbing the stairs, brushing debris from his thin crop of hair. *Hope he ain't died on me like Cousin Lucius. He passed in his sleep. Didn't smoke, drink, or cuss—one of them Christians that God can't stand. Papa figured him for a woods colt, said there never was a clean-mouthed male Wright.*

Topping the steps, Silas stopped. Silence. Harrogate snored with the best, so he was either dead and gone or simply gone. Harrogate's door opened to a made bed, shut window, clean floor. Silas held a note—

penned on a page torn from a yellowed Sunday school quarterly—at arm's length. "Visiting Sis. Back before Christmas. Don't take no wooden nickels. Bud."

These times, I'd take any kind of nickel. Silas absently scratched his left ear. *Just like him. Ever now and again it's not "see you" or "kiss my ass," just gone. Says he gets to craving excitement. Hmp. What's better'n a cabbage harvest? I better get moving. Ethel and Carl's gone over the mountain, and work won't do itself.*

Silas fed livestock, milked, and fixed breakfast—three eggs, fried in the previous night's pork grease, a dish of applesauce, and a cup of coffee. He ate in silence, then carried a second cup to the porch. Poplar leaves, tree-bound and bright yellow a week before, lay like brown afterthoughts on the dirt yard. Ridgetop maples and sourwoods still sported yellows and reds, and oaks were beginning to show scarlet, yellow, or brown.

Silas sipped coffee, inhaled the autumn air, and lit his pipe. *When I was young, coffee and a smoke would trot me to the outhouse. Anymore, a shit hobbles along when it gets around to it, late, like a mail-order package.*

Hell to get old. Eighty. Aches and pains in places I didn't even know I had two year ago. Orta set and stare at the mountains till dinnertime.

I miss the chestnuts. Their yellow was prettier than maples or tulip trees. And big, Lordy. Them was trees, *trees God was proud of. A man could build anything out of them. Now they're gone.*

Used to see them yellow-headed parakeets. Gone. Pigeons? Flocks used to hide the sun. Gone. Me, too, soon enough. Wonder how gone'll feel? He leaned against the rail and shut his eyes.

Five minutes later he jerked awake. *What in hell am I doing? Only a Rockefeller can afford to nap away a morning.*

Harrogate had dug a trench beside the house, in which they meant to store cabbages. Silas grabbed a potato digger and loosened the trench bottom, tossing stray redworms into a mason jar. He spent the morning filling the trench with cabbages and covering them. He saved several to make a run of kraut.

His dinner was simple—bread and butter and a tin of sardines. He ate them with relish. *Good as these are, it makes me want fresh fish for supper. Rhetta was here, she'd say not to have fish twice a day, but, hell, when I was a pup, we ate fish for breakfast. I've eat it three times a day many a time.*

Later that afternoon he rode to Nellie to find no mail, which lately suited him—no meddling government that day. He took his time returning, sitting the horse halfway home to watch yellow jackets line into the roadside. He dismounted and, tiptoeing, tied a piece of shirttail to the overarching doghobble to help him find the nest hole toward dark. *Wonder if I need one of them permits to burn these things out. Damn government. The way we're headed, Warshington'll take a notion to breed the damn things. The tourists'll get stung so bad, some peckerhead bureaucrat'll say that was so good, let's restock rattlesnakes. Next thing you know they'll bring in packs of wolves. Hell, I remember my daddy talking about getting a ten-dollar bounty for a wolf pelt. They'll end up bringing back beavers. Elk. I'd not be surprised by it.*

Silas cocked his head toward a keening hawk, but the bird had outraced his hearing. His eyes lit on a crow preening on a sourwood limb, backlit by the setting sun. He tipped his hat to the bird, clucked at the mare, and headed slowly homeward.

The creek beside the road was barely six feet wide. He stopped often to read its rushing water. *I was a boy, I used to catch specks barehanded, dots and lines on their sides like God's handwriting, long as your forearm, holding in pools, waiting for whatever darted by. Rising mayflies. Falling ants. Bees. Crickets. I've found half-digested mice in their stomachs. Kinder like a bear, they'll eat about anything.*

Ain't seen such trout in years. They was fished out of this stretch of creek by the turn of the century. Now it's hatchery fish, rainbows, browns, easy catches. They think when a man shows up, food falls from the sky.

The Hawkins boy said we can't fish with worms. Hellfire. Cart me to the clink if they like. I want trout for supper.

Between house and barn Silas spied a peck-size wad of feathers pulsating in the shade. He finally focused on a hawk munching one of his pullets. It tore flesh from the fowl and glared at Silas. *Look at that. That ain't a threat. He's just saying, "What'll you do about it?"*

Silas dismounted, close enough to hear the beak rip feathers and flesh. No other creature showed itself—dog, barn cat, chicken. *Damn it all. Ain't got my rifle. But, come to think of it, here's another critter the government wants to mollycoddle, so pretty soon a man won't be able to have eggs or fried chicken neither.* The redtail finished, looked at Silas again, and lifted with a wide sweep of wings. *I could have swore that bird sneered at me. Reckon he thinks he's in one of them newfangled bird sanctuaries?*

He fed and watered the horse and figured the time to be five o'clock, time to catch and fix supper, eat, and clean the kitchen before dark. Fetching pole and jar, he headed creekside. After cutting a forked stick into a Y, he threw a number four hook baited with two redworms into a pocket of water. His third cast raised half a supper's worth of rainbow. He slipped the long end of the stick through its gill slit and out its mouth, and laid it into the water.

When Jim Hawkins stopped his horse eighty yards downstream, Silas, facing upstream, neither heard nor saw him. Jim had thought simply to visit, so whistled as if to say, "Oh, brother, I need to go," and began to turn his horse. After Silas enjoyed another strike, he nestled pole under armpit while unhooking the fish. As he reached for his stringer, he saw motion downstream.

A horse and rider. No mistaking the uniform hat. *Well, if he wants me, I'm cotched. He can leave without messing with me, which means he likely never will. If he comes on, then I'll likely get my ticket punched. Silas Wright, gone as a goose, over a damn fish supper. Hell, he's coming. Blame it all.*

Jim rode toward Silas at a funereal pace. He touched his hat brim, hitched his mount, and strode toward the creek. "Son, how in the world are you?" asked Silas.

"Fine, Mr. Wright."

"It's Silas."

"Yes, sir."

"How's the family?"

"Nell's fine, I suppose. Little Elizabeth's had the croup, but she'll be okay. All I can say about Mack is, he's all boy."

"That's good."

Jim removed his Stetson and examined the inside closely, like he might find a nest of cooties. "You haven't seen anything suspicious around lately, have you?"

Silas shook his head. "What makes you ask that?"

"Outbuilding burned back at the Howell place. I'd suspect Willie McPeters but couldn't find that boot print of his."

"Been dry lately. I ain't seen that odd bird in years."

"Well, if you do, let me know." Jim put his hat back on. "I figured if I was this far up the valley, I'd come by to say howdy."

"I appreciate it."

"Only trouble is, I'm on duty, and you're fishing."

Silas's eyes rounded and he nodded slowly. "Wouldn't dispute neither point."

Jim eyed the mason jar. "Bait?"

"See any on this here hook?"

"No, sir."

He held up the stringer, on which two trout gasped for water. "Ain't these pretty? If you want to stay for supper, I'll catch two more. Unless that puts me over the limit."

"Thanks, Silas, limit's seven. But I need to get to the house."

Jim stooped and poured the jar's contents onto the ground. If he saw more living creatures than a couple of stray sow bugs, he didn't let on.

Silas glanced from jar to Jim and grinned. "If you'd found something, would you have give me a ticket?" Jim nodded. "Guess you didn't find no evidence today. But if you had, I'd claim it to be what you call circumstantial. These trout just thought this hook was so pretty they jumped on it. No law I know of prohibits that."

Jim smiled. "Maybe the law of nature. Don't let me catch you again, hear? I'd hate to have to write you up, long as I've known you."

Silas put a fishy hand on Jim's shoulder. "Son, this old man ain't going to quit fishing because you wear that uniform. If you don't want to write me up, don't come here. 'Cause if it ain't fishing, it'll be hunting. If it ain't that, it'll be some other chickenshit rule. I ain't fighting the park, nor you neither. I just ain't paying no attention to it. Understand?"

Jim nodded. "Let's leave it at that, Silas. Fair enough?"

They shook hands. "Fair enough, young man. You sure you won't take supper?"

"I better get back. Nell's been hollering because I'm gone so much."

"Does she think you're going to take care of half a million acres by sitting in the house? By the way, how's the Howell place holding up?"

Jim looked toward the ridge. "Aw, it's all growed up, like everything else."

Silas gestured toward his house and barn. "What do you think ten more years will do to this place?"

"You tell me, Silas."

"If I get Harrogate back—by the way, he left last night—and if I live that long, it'll be the same. Until I get down in my back or lose my mind, I'm going to work God's green earth. This farm'll be an island in the middle of pure-tee chaos. The rest of Cataloochee'll look like we give it back to the Indians. I take that back. Indians care for the land. It'll be a downright Borneo jungle."

Jim chose not to remark a solitary redworm wriggling at his foot. "Well, take it easy, Silas. I better get back down the creek."

"Much obliged for the visit. Now go home. You got to keep a young wife happy."

"That's easier said than done—anymore, I stay in the doghouse."

"I remember days when Rhetta thought I was the cause of everything bad from Noah's flood to prohibition. But a man's got to keep peace."

"How long were you all married?"

"Nigh on sixty years. We had our differences, but we did all right. You know the secret?"

"Lord, Silas, spit it out."

"Talk. Don't sull up like an old sow possum because she's mad and clammed up her own self. Keep talking. In time things right themselves and you go on. But if you get to where you all don't say three words in two days, you might as well go live in that doghouse permanent-like."

"I'll keep that in mind, neighbor. Sounds like wisdom."

They shook hands. "Experience, at least. Come again, when you ain't carrying your ticket book."

Silas pulled the fish from the creek as Jim rode away. "Suppertime, gals. I'll introduce you to some bacon grease and cornmeal." He slit their bellies and raked out innards like hollowing a ripe cantaloupe. He cut off fins, heads, and tails, then headed for the house. *Sure will be good eating. After supper I'll burn some bees, and try not to set the woods on fire. Boy's got enough on his mind without a plumb conflagration.*

CHAPTER 13

Word from Raleigh

Cataloochee life for Mary Carter and her sons was mostly quiet. Thomas Carter and his brother, Manson, swung in contrary rhythms, counterbalanced by devotion to their mother. Thomas rose early, sometimes before four, fixing coffee, rushing daylight, thin brown hair skewing from under an olive-colored felt hat. Manson hated opening his eyes before daylight because he kept owl hours, reading almanac or Bible, or sketching out the upcoming season's kitchen garden, scratching his bald head with a pencil end. Thomas cooked breakfast, hot cereal, sausage, eggs, and biscuits—some said his biscuits were better than his mother's, but never to her face. When breakfast was cleared, she began to prepare the noon meal, chicken and dumplings with butter beans and cabbage, or ham with green beans and tomatoes and corn, or, in the fall, beef with turnips and kale. Manson warmed leftovers for supper, soon after which Thomas made for bed.

After lunch Mary's custom was to nap, then read her mail. Her sons alternated days walking to the post office. Having no word from the outside world made her fuss and fidget—abundant mail days made her as happy as a pig in mud.

It seemed to Thomas, returning from the post office on an exceptionally warm day in October 1930, that lately their box's contents had dwindled in both number and importance. Still, he dreaded seeing a park service envelope, which meant not greetings but the salutation of a lost lease. They were not brazen violators, but all Carters figured rules were made if not to be broken at least to be bent until they screeched. It was a matter of time, he figured.

He laid the mail on the wicker table beside his mother's porch rocker. Aunt Mary picked up her glasses, fanned through the pile, and picked out a letter postmarked Raleigh. "Oh, goody. It's from Velda." She found no sharp instrument in her apron pockets so reached to the bottom shelf for a blunt-ended kitchen knife, a nineteenth-century relic Hiram had rehandled when they'd moved into their new frame house. She slit the envelope and shook out a dozen folded sheets of pale blue paper. "Yep, it's her handwriting," she said. "Fancier since she left. Oliver sent her to one of those colleges down there, you know, to finish her education. And here's a picture!"

Thomas brought his mother a glass of tea. "Who's that?"

"Little Mary Babcock, thank you very much." Mary beamed. "Ain't she the cutest thing? I wish they'd bring her up here. One year old and I've never laid eyes on her. Look at that hair, would you?"

He held the photo to the light as if it were a negative. "Wonder if they have one of them Brownies? Takes a good picture, don't it?" He handed the photo back. "We could go see her if you wanted to."

"Pshaw, Son. It ain't that easy. That's three hundred miles."

"Trains run that far."

She fanned herself with the envelope. "Don't think I could stand such a trip, Son. Maybe this'll say they're coming." She drank some tea. "That hits the spot. Listen, Son. There's lots of news, so why don't you and Manson see if anybody wants word from Raleigh. I could read this out loud for everybody."

"Yes, ma'am."

By four the porch was crowded. Levi Marion and Valerie, who held little Ned, sat on the steps. Their children Ada, George, Ruth Elizabeth, and Little Mary, ranging from eleven to five, sat on the railing swinging legs, the sound like washing hung in a brisk wind. Manson slouched against the column while his brother paced, porch to kitchen, offering tea, cake, and cookies. Thomas had enticed Silas Wright from his place up the valley, and he and Carl and Ethel rocked opposite Aunt Mary, who noticed Ethel had grown broader across the beam than a single ax handle could accurately measure.

"Thomas," said Aunt Mary, "keep that tea coming. Folks, here goes."

Dear Aunt Mary,

Yrs of the 29th in hand, for which thanks. It doesn't seem two years since we left our beloved Cataloochee. I like it here except for summer, which is too blooming hot. A sizeable number of Yankees work for the government; you wouldn't think the State of North Carolina would have that many in the first place, then turn around and put them to doing "official" work to boot, but . . .

We are getting ready for politics, as I am sure you are in Cataloochee. Do you still vote before the other precincts? As a girl I was so proud when our votes (all Democratic) were counted a few minutes after midnight and couriered to Waynesville to be certified at six A.M. Fayetteville Street is awash in gay red, white, and blue banners and patriotic posters. Oliver is running for mayor. He says anyone demonstrating physical responsibility in this day and age will be elected. Then he'd love to be governor if things work out right.

"I'd like to see him mayor of a big city," said Silas, "even if he did work for them varmints."

"Can you imagine if he made a governor?" asked Manson.

"Mayor's one thing. Governor's a whole 'nother," said Levi Marion, glancing toward his children, two of whom suddenly seemed too sleepy to sit on a porch railing. "They've been few and far between from the mountains."

"Let's see," said Silas. "Swain was before my time, but he was from

Asheville. Vance during the war. Locke Craig about twenty years ago. Anybody else?"

"Wasn't there a Caldwell right after the war?" asked Manson.

"Hell," snorted Silas, "he was a no-count Republican." He tamped his pipe and laughed softly. "You know, it's funny, but we all plumb forgot Oliver's a sandlapper. He just married a mountaineer. And I think Mary wants our attention. Beg pardon, Mary."

Thomas refilled her glass as she cleared her throat and started her namesake's photo around the porch.

> Our little Mary just turned one, and a sweeter dispositioned child you'd never want to meet. She slept nights from two months. Brown curls and blue eyes (her eyelashes are longer than mine!) guarantee she will make friends everywhere. I will never cease to pray she will survive to adulthood. So many babies in Cataloochee never did.
>
> Aunt Mary, I remember you saying when you go to heaven you want to rock the little babies that die. If there ever was comfort in such a death it would be to know women like you stand by at the celestial gates. Still, I hope it will be years and years before you join them.

"I give that a hearty Amen," said Thomas. The crowd echoed that and raised their glasses to Aunt Mary. Ruth Elizabeth jerked awake on the railing and glanced sheepishly to see if anyone noticed she'd been asleep.

"Thank you, you all," said Aunt Mary. "I ain't planning to leave here anytime soon."

> I bet it's different there these days, isn't it? I know the Bankses are gone. I keep up with Mattie, and they seem settled in Saunook. Mattie and Hannah and Rachel sell quilts to tourists, not a living exactly, but it puts "butter and egg money" in their pockets. Seems not all that long ago we were such a cozy little community. Then the park shattered the calm.
>
> Then the crash. There are people here who lost everything. As Oliver says, we didn't have much to lose, so we haven't suffered extremely. He

thinks things will be normal next year at the latest, especially if the Democrats regain the White House.

I know Cataloochee folks are at least eating well. It isn't like down here, where you need money every time you turn around. Up there you could go forever without spending much of it. I've told Oliver that if times get really hard, we'll move home, make a garden, and raise some hogs. I miss the homeplace, such a scene of good times, something fierce. I'd love to see Mama's daffodils bloom once more.

"Wouldn't Oliver Babcock raising hogs be a sight?" asked Silas, lighting his pipe.

Levi Marion laughed. "The boy nearly fell into my hog pen one time, shiny shoes, suit, and all. For a fact, I'd like to see him plow behind a mule."

"Necessity drives us," said Mary. "I'd not make fun if I were you. No telling what God will visit on us in His good time."

"But, Aunt Mary, admit it—Oliver laying a furrow would be worth standing in line to watch," said Silas.

"It's a fact, but I bet he could if he put his mind to it."

"He'd need some down-east plow stock. A homegrown Haywood County mule couldn't understand him," Manson said, and laughed.

Ruth Elizabeth had fallen back asleep, and her brother had followed suit. Aunt Mary crinkled the letter by way of reclaiming the adults' attention.

Is anybody left on Little Cataloochee? I heard Uncle Cash Davis moved in with his niece in Dellwood and died not a month after. I never knew man or woman who loved Cataloochee more than him, except maybe my mother, and the same thing happened to her. The doctor said it was a stroke, but I know it was a broken heart. Stay as long as you can, Aunt Mary.

Mary coughed and nearly choked on a swig of tea.

Manson had been dozing but sprang toward her rocker. "You all right, Mama?"

"Of course, Son. I just had a frog in my throat. Now let me finish."

Do you still sew with your old Burdick? Hannah uses hers every day.
I'd hate to see how many miles of thread has wound through those shut-
tles. Who is left on Big Cataloochee? Does Uncle Silas still live at "the head
of the holler"? Give my love to him (and everybody else).

Did Mr. Harrogate come back? Last I heard he was in Tennessee. A
mystery, that man was, coming and going like a streetcar. He'd stop and
say howdy on his way to and from Cosby, first with that big chow dog,
then by himself. I blush to say he flirted with me once, but I figured a
woman couldn't trust him.

Valerie yelled "Ruth Elizabeth" as her eight-year-old fell backward
into a boxwood. The girl hit like a stiff rag doll, breaking a limb off the
evergreen. "Baby, are you all right?"

Thomas leapt the railing and picked Ruth Elizabeth up. She rubbed
dirt from her elbow but suffered more from embarrassment than trauma.
"Cousin Manson, I'm dandy," she said as he set her on her feet.

He picked sticks and leaves from her cotton pinafore. "Honey, it's a
fact, you *are* dandy, and you smell like Christmas, too," he said.

"She looks like the dickens," said Valerie. "Honey, sit with Mama. I
don't want you falling again. Sorry about your bushes, Aunt Mary."

"These things happen, child. I'm just glad she didn't break anything
of hers." She winked at Ruth Elizabeth, who settled between her parents.
"Least you didn't name her Eutychus. You'd have needed Saint Paul instead of my Thomas."

"Who's that, Aunt Mary?" asked Ruth Elizabeth.

"A boy who fell out a third-story window when Paul was preaching.
Liked to have killed him, but you're in good shape, dear. Now, then, back
to the letter."

Oh, I was going to tell you something of our life here. When we left,
I hadn't any idea what to expect, just a Cataloochee girl, hardly ever out
of Mother's sight. Imagine my big-eyed wonder at this area. Nearly three
hundred thousand people live within thirty or forty miles. Raleigh, Dur-
ham, and Chapel Hill all have universities—Mr. Duke's is brand-new
and kind of raw-looking, the other two are old and stately—and libraries

and concert halls. You could go to a play, a concert, or an art exhibition
every weekend.

"Bet they don't have turkey shoots," said Levi Marion.

"Is that where Rass wants to go?" piped Ruth Elizabeth. Her hair
curled, promising rain soon.

"Yes, dear," said Valerie, picking a boxwood leaf from her daughter's
hair. "He plans to go to the university in Chapel Hill after he finishes
high school. He could eat with Oliver and Velda every now and then.
Keep him from being homesick," said Valerie.

"Not to mention starving to death," said Levi Marion.

"I don't want Rass to die," said Ruth Elizabeth.

"Honey, Daddy didn't mean it like that. It's a figure of speech."

"What's that?"

"Child, hush and let Aunt Mary finish," said Valerie.

The best is the state fair in October. Lordy, what a place! They moved
it to a brand-new fairground in 1928, so modern and beautiful. There's
every kind of chicken you could imagine, jams and jellies, cattle and
horses, tractors and combines, rides like the Tilt-A-Whirl and Ferris
wheel and merry-go-round. If you ate just a bite of everything they sell,
you'd have the bellyache for a week. The Raleigh churches, too, all have
"eating booths," where you can find the most divine things, all homemade
and so good. Toward the end of the midway are some risky shows that
Oliver and I wouldn't go to for love nor money. (Least I best not catch him
slipping in there!)

"Mama, what does Cousin Velda mean by risky?" asked Ruth Elizabeth.

Valerie smoothed the left side of Ruth Elizabeth's hair. "It means—
well, it means some shows aren't nice."

"What does that mean?"

"Tell her about the hootchy-kootchy, Mama." Levi Marion chuckled.
"There's figures there, by Nellie, but maybe not figures of speech."

"I'll do no such thing," she said, and slapped her husband's shoulder. "Ruth Elizabeth, you ask too many questions. Aunt Velda is talking about women dancing on a stage, that's all."

"Then they're not Baptists," the girl said, nodding her head with conviction.

"Who?"

"The women. If they're dancing, they're not Baptists!"

"I reckon you could say that," Levi Marion said, laughing. "Now let Aunt Mary finish. I'd like to hear the rest before milking time."

Mary glanced at Ruth Elizabeth. "See, child, it never hurts to ask questions."

We don't go out much—he's too busy with his law practice and politics—but we always go to the fair.

We live in a nice apartment between State College and the fairgrounds, just off Hillsborough Street, not country but not city, either. When the market crashed, Oliver thought we might lose the apartment, but lawyers seem to do all right no matter what. My wringer washing machine almost makes it fun to do diapers—sure beats boiling them in a kettle outside—and our radio picks up the farthest stations at night. We both like WWVA in West Virginia. Do you have electricity in Cataloochee yet? When you do, get a plug-in radio—it's the most comfort on a lonesome night, and you don't worry about nursing a battery.

I suppose you will think me spoiled, but a woman cleans our apartment every two weeks. Bessie is such a dear. Negroes here aren't like those in the mountains, at least any I ever heard about—not that I ever knew any. When money got tight, Oliver wanted to let her go, but I said Bessie was so fine we simply couldn't. It's a struggle, but she has four children and a layabout husband. She might be black as the ace of spades but we're both women in God's eyes, and I refuse to be a party to making children hungry.

Aunt Mary looked over the tops of her eyeglasses at her audience. "Well," she said, slowly shaking her head. "It's a different world, isn't it?"

Silas relit his pipe. "Lots of things is. Everybody's got problems, black and white. Just because there ain't niggers here don't mean they ain't people, like some want you to believe."

"Why, Silas, you sound like the Yankees that used to board here," said Aunt Mary.

He peered through a halo of tobacco smoke. "I ain't no damn Yankee. It's just that hard times make you realize people is people. One was to come through here, I'd share my table with him, and you all would, too. But that don't mean I want him marrying my daughter."

"Amen, brother," said Levi Marion. "Read on, Aunt Mary."

Oliver says politicians need to be either Presbyterians or Baptists, and loads more Baptists vote, so we joined the big Baptist church downtown. It has the prettiest steeple, and you could put everybody in both Cataloochees in the front corner and still have room to seat a circus.

I miss the church at Ola, though. You always knew everybody, and Preacher Noland was on the same level with you. Down here the pulpit is in a tower. I remember Preacher Noland's sermon the Sunday after Ezra was buried, about transplanting people to new ground. He said some would thrive—but some wouldn't survive—(remember how he used to rhyme when he'd get going?) and he was right. Mama's soul did not take root in this red clay ground. I miss her daily.

She's been gone a year now. Doesn't seem possible. Take a good whiff of mountain air, Aunt Mary. Mama would sigh in this heat and say she'd give a fortune for one breath of cool Cataloochee air.

Oliver used to be a string bean, but he's getting some meat on his bones. If I could just tame that hoi toide accent—sometimes even I can't understand him when he gets worked up about something. He's right now excited about the Carolina football team. Last year they lost but one game, and he has high hopes for an undefeated season this year. No matter what folks say, he says Carolina means football and always will. The basketball team—they don't even call them Tar Heels, but "White Phantoms"—look silly running around in their little shorts.

Come see us in October, Aunt Mary. We'll take you to the fair. I can see you oohing and aahing over every chicken. I'm serious. We'll meet you at the train station and put you up—we have a small but lovely guest room—and show you the town!

Give my love to all. And wish Oliver luck in the election!

"Can we go to the fair?" asked Ruth Elizabeth.

"Honey, we don't have the money," said Valerie. "Besides, it's a long way."

"But Cousin Velda wants us to," she protested.

"Maybe someday," her mother said. "Meantime it's getting toward suppertime. Thank Aunt Mary for reading to us."

Ruth Elizabeth hugged Aunt Mary. "Thank you," she said. "I 'specially liked the part about the hootchy-kootch."

Aunt Mary handed her four hard candies wrapped in cellophane. "There's one for each of you. Save these until after supper, young lady. Promise me."

Ruth Elizabeth put them into her apron pocket and raised her hand like a Boy Scout. "I promise, Aunt Mary. I love you." She ran to catch up with her family.

"Bless her little heart," said Aunt Mary. "I hate for the young ones to learn about life. But I reckon they have to. Manson, what's for supper?"

CHAPTER 14

Vast Outdoor Playground

Cataloochans who moved were generally of two kinds—older folks who bought farms with their settlement money, and younger people who purchased modest homes and worked at the paper mill in Canton, or learned a trade. The farmers tried to replicate the old life, and were as successful as soil and energy would allow. The others missed farming enough to grow enormous kitchen gardens at the back of the house and to fool with a few head of cattle on a leased pasture.

Some, like Zeb Banks and Jake Carter, started in one direction and finished in another. They had gone together to buy an orchard west of Hazelwood, near Saunook, a settlement with electric lights, telephones, and stores. It was sold to them as an "established" concern, but its former owners had fallen on hard times even before the nation had, and the orchard needed a lot of work. The fall of 1929 and the following spring the Bankses and Carters worked hard, grafting, fertilizing, and budding the old trees, and actually made a decent crop in the fall of 1930.

Zeb had settled with the commission before Oliver had left for

Raleigh—in fact, his money made the down payment on the orchard, while Jake guaranteed the balance with a note, while he held out for a better offer. To Jake's mind, his gravity system, with its reservoir of sweet water, had made his property worth an extra ten dollars an acre. But Horace Wakefield had shown him the evaluation form, where, on the line marked "water," he could only check yes or no. He'd sent Jake a postcard from the Asheville office in mid-November saying his settlement was ready. Jake had written that he would pick it up Friday the twentieth.

Zeb's mother, Hannah, had inherited Ezra Banks's Model T Ford when Ezra was killed, and had tried to give the car to Zeb, who would have none of it. So she gave it to Jake. He figured to trade it on a new automobile after his settlement, but until then it was walk, catch the bus, ride a horse, or drive the old flivver. Jake and Zeb decided on one last road trip to Asheville.

They left Saunook about four Friday morning. Patched a tire in Hazelwood, and took on some store-bought coffee to go with their bag of fried apple pies. The rest of their journey was, except for seven stray hogs in the road at Turnpike, uneventful. They crossed the French Broad about eight, drove up Clingman Avenue, and chugged to the middle of town via Patton Avenue, marveling at the changes.

They drove on the right, careful not to encroach on the bricked middle, where streetcar tracks ran like arrows. They passed Efird's, and the Man Store at the corner of Lexington, across the street from the shiny new Kress building, five overblown stories faced with gleaming terracotta. Streetcars clanked and buzzed their way to and from the square, disgorging and gobbling passengers like noisy robots. People scurried everywhere. Jake thought himself lucky not to have to put on collar and tie every morning and go to town and count whatever these poor devils were paid to count.

At the square they turned left in front of the Vance Monument, bouncing over streetcar tracks onto Broadway, and parked in front of a furniture store just past the six-story Langren Hotel. Zeb emerged from the car and stamped his foot. "Dern thing went to sleep on me."

"Looks like furniture row," Jake said, surveying the block. Stores named Susquehanna, Sluder's, Kincaid-Swain, Donald & Donald, and—

behind brand-new terra-cotta—J. L. Smathers & Sons promised everything a man could need for a home. He pointed to Tingle's Café. "I wouldn't mind tingling a little."

A short man in a gray suit and fedora walked up the sidewalk, smiling, key in his right hand and bag of lunch in his left. "Top of the morning, gentlemen," he lilted. "Sir, you wouldn't ever have that foot problem if you owned one of my chairs. Just the ticket for people with circulatory problems." He put the key into his pocket, pulled out a card, and handed it to Zeb. "Chas. L. Sluder & Co.," it read. "Dealer in Round Oak Ranges, Dutch Kitchenettes, Brunswick Phonographs, 22 Broadway, phone 1509." Zeb had no idea what a "Dutch Kitchenette" might be. He tried to hand the card back, but the man refused. "Let me open up, gentlemen. Then you must try out a chair. Sluder's the name, Charlie Sluder."

"Thank you kindly, sir, but we live in Haywood."

"No barrier to commerce, sir. I can put it in your fine auto, or I can ship it by train."

"Thank you, Mr. Sluder, but we have business this morning."

Sluder brightened. "When you come back for your auto, I'll show you the most comfortable chair you ever sat in. A steal at forty dollars."

Jake and Zeb ambled up the street. "Forty dern dollars for a chair? Don't he know they got a depression?" Several drummers stood in the door of the Langren, ready to convince shopkeepers to stock their wares. At College Street, Jake gave a boy a nickel for a newspaper and they lit on a bench. Zeb took a deep breath. "Can't figure out why a man would want to live in a city. Air stinks, nothing but racket."

Jake chuckled. "This ain't so bad. Look at these headlines. They had thirteen killed in Oklahoma and Kansas by a tornado yesterday. More'n five hundred stranded on an ocean liner, but they were rescued. Oh, here's a good one. This was in California. Listen. 'Mr. & Mrs. Joe Davis were happily married today after an engagement of forty-two years. Joe popped the question in 1888 but Miss Virlinda Seaward's parents objected. Neither Joe nor Virlinda wanted to antagonize the parents so they waited. Recently the parents died. So last night Joe and Virlinda were married.'"

"I'd a run off, myself. What kind of fool would do without for forty-two years?"

"Ain't that the truth? They'd be my age, and that's nearly too damn old for it. I'll be sixty my next birthday."

"I heard you say 'nearly,'" Zeb said with a grin.

"Mind your own business," Jake said, and laughed. "Says here George Iseley was elected Raleigh mayor. I guess old Oliver Babcock will have to try again."

"That's a shame. What's that headline there?"

"'Smoky Park Will Draw Crowds, Hotel Man Says.'" Jake rustled the paper. "'When Horace M. Albright, director of the National Parks, announced in Asheville recently that the number of motor roads into the Great Smoky Mountains National Park would be restricted and decided preference given to the use of saddle horses, he created in New York City and other sections of the country a greater interest in the vast outdoor playground in Southern Appalachia, according to Walter Baker, prominent hotel man of New York, Los Angeles, and Palm Springs, who arrived here yesterday on a brief business trip.' Did you know we used to live in a vast outdoor playground?"

"Could have fooled me. Looked more like a section of farms about to go all to hell. Them first folks that left wasn't gone three weeks before pigweed started taking over."

"Man says that with the economic times, not as many folks is traveling to the Mediterranean as usual. You know where he says they'll come to? Right here."

"God, Jake, maybe it's best we left after all. A Yankee with more money than sense is something I don't care to look at or listen to. Hey, look yonder." Zeb pointed to an older man dressed in black except for a white shirt and panama hat. His string tie blew in the breeze. He wielded a large walking stick, with which he tapped his way up the south side of the square, heading toward the courthouse. "Blind, ain't he?" asked Zeb.

Jake nodded. "Reckon so. I'd hate to have to make my way blinder'n a bat in these crowds. Wonder somebody don't trip and rob him."

They stood and stretched. The wide vista to the west was of the mountains from which they had journeyed that morning. They walked downstairs to the public toilet behind the monument, then headed east toward the new municipal buildings.

To the south two new skinny buildings shot skyward, one with candy cane columns upstairs, the other a Gothic creation of a dozen stories, with gargoyles and a penthouse. "Wasn't there a monument shop there?" asked Zeb.

"Yeah, he had an angel in the window."

The City Building, of pink marble and brick and topped with a bell tower and pink and green tile, sat beside a gray, sober-looking new courthouse. "How did they think they were going to pay for all this?" asked Zeb.

Jake shook his head. "They'll end up chicken houses. Damned expensive poultry palaces."

Zeb pointed to the frieze, undecorated except for chiseled letters: CITY BVILDING OF ASHEVILLE. "You'd think with all the money they spent, they could have spelled it right."

Jake tucked his newspaper under his arm as they walked through the revolving door and removed their hats. A smiling black woman stood outside the elevator. "What floor, gentlemen?"

"Third," said Zeb. "Just show us where the steps is at and we won't trouble you."

"Y'all come in and I'll take you right up. Watch your step."

As she folded the round seat against the wall, Zeb hesitated, but Jake pushed him inside. She closed the exterior door, then the brass cage, and pushed the handle to the rear. The car bounced slightly when they stopped. "When you ready, push the button and I'll come for you, hear?"

Zeb barged out first. "Much obliged, ma'am," he said. "They's got to be steps somewhere," he said to Jake.

"Rather walk than ride?"

"Jake, I been in jail. Damn right I'm finding steps when we get through."

When they entered, Horace Wakefield was rooting through the top drawer of a file cabinet. "Well, look what the cat drug in," he said, and left off his search. "How are you two?"

"Fair to middling," said Jake. They shook hands. "I came for my money."

"Of course. Come on back. Sorry it couldn't be more, but they wouldn't let me count your springwater."

They caught up over cups of bitter coffee. Horace told of closing the Haywood office, and Jake and Zeb related family news.

"What ever happened to that other man—what was his name? Pendleton?" asked Zeb.

"Nothing good," said Wakefield. "He died, you know."

"Yeah, we heard, but there's different stories of how. Did he nasty away?"

"Not in so many words. He was up at Sunburst, where they were still logging. Somehow, something slipped. Coroner ruled it an accident, but they say there was bad blood between him and one of the skidders. Anyway, he was crushed between two logs. Said there wasn't hardly enough of him left to bury."

"Damn," said Jake. "I didn't like him, but I wouldn't wish that on anybody."

"Well, you might say he kind of died like he lived, I guess," said Wakefield.

"So you're the head snake now?" asked Zeb.

"I'd hardly say that. I'm chief until they close it, which won't be far in the future. Maybe a year. Then I'll be back in the business, if there's any more call for surveyors."

"What about that museum you were talking up?"

Wakefield stood, rammed his hands into his pockets, and stared out the window. "I'm growing less and less optimistic. For starters, there's no money. And it looks like the government is determined to get rid of all structures except those housing wardens. I'm very disappointed." He turned from the window. "I have written everyone from the president on down about it, but no one seems interested. It wouldn't be the case if you had been easterners."

"Mr. Wakefield, if we was easterners, they'd have left us alone," said Zeb.

"That's a fact. Here, Jake, is your check. Bank it today. Anymore you don't know."

They found the staircase. When they walked by the elevator on the ground floor, they tipped their hats to the operator, who nodded, then grinned as they went outside.

"Ready to go home?" asked Jake. "Or you want to try that Tingle place?"

Zeb shrugged. "I'd just as soon go home," he said, and led off toward the monument. They were about to turn down Broadway when Jake stopped his nephew. "Zeb, I wonder what's wrong."

Crammed between the Legal Building and the Pack Library, the Central Bank and Trust Company boasted a fancy door in the chamfer under a blue awning. It was shut. A crowd milled. Folks emerged from streetcars, hesitated, and then ran toward the bank. Three or four hundred people stood in clumps, gesturing with hats and newspapers. Zeb and Jake made their way closer, among snatches of conversation. "Can't believe it . . . I knew it . . . God, we're rurint." A hastily written sign on the bank's door: CLOSED BY ORDER OF THE BOARD OF DIRECTORS FOR LIQUIDATION AND CONSERVATION OF ASSETS FOR PROTECTION OF THE DEPOSITORS.

"Son, let's get back to Haywood before something else happens," said Jake. "This keeps up, nobody'll be cooking anyhow. Wait. Ain't this where Levi Marion put his settlement money?" They looked at each other.

"I think it was. God, I hope he moved it. Let's go," said Zeb.

At the edge of the square the white-haired man brandished his cane at the bank. "Bastards," he yelled. "Bastards, I told you!" He repeated it with a ghoulish smile. A man next to Jake laughed.

"What's so funny, brother?" asked Jake.

"He's perdicted this crash for years. I reckon now he'll say he told us so the rest of our lives."

"Who is he?"

"Judge Bland. A lawyer. The syph made him blind."

On their way to the car Mr. Sluder stood outside the A&P with his nephew and Gay Green, a partner in the Langren. Sluder broke away and hurried to Zeb and Jake. "Gentlemen, can I interest you in a chair before you return to Haywood County? I could sell it on time." He rocked on his heels and fingered his suspenders.

"No, Mr. Sluder, we need to get back. Besides, after this morning, nobody's got cash money. I reckon you heard about the bank."

"We will weather this storm, gentlemen. We must hold a steady course, not lose our heads. Next Thursday will be Thanksgiving. I truly hope we all will have something to give thanks about, and over. Have a good day."

When Hannah gave Jake the Model T, her younger sons refused to visit with or speak to her. That suited Zeb and Mattie fine, and, after a short time of feeling sorry for herself, Hannah had to admit life rolled more sweetly without that bunch of arguing rascals. She lived two Christmases after Zeb's trial, and, as Mattie said, "wore the spots off" several decks of cards. She died in her sleep, and Zeb applied for a "pea soup" to bury her in the Carter family cemetery, about as far from Ezra's grave as a body could get and still be in Cataloochee.

Mattie met Zeb with a kiss and hug that knocked his hat off. "Jake get his money?"

"He did, but I was mighty worried about it. Central Bank crashed this morning like that New York panic. We stopped at First National in Waynesville. They didn't much want to cash it, but he gave me my part and it's in the bank."

"Didn't Levi Marion have his money in Central?"

"Jake asked me that. We thought it might have been."

"God, that'll kill him for sure. Want a glass of cider?"

"No, thanks. What's this?" He lifted an envelope, addressed to his mother in Oliver Babcock's flourishing hand.

"He sent a Christmas letter every year. We didn't think to tell him she died."

"She sure liked him. One of us ought to write."

"I will after supper."

Zeb had offered to buy Mattie an electric range, but she'd said no, so the children came in from their chores carrying armloads of stove wood.

After supper they all either drew pictures or wrote notes to Oliver and Velda.

When the children were upstairs, Zeb and Mattie put on jackets and went outside. Warm for November. Sitting on the porch edge, they listened to late crickets, smelled wood smoke, saw stars. A truck shifted into a lower gear to make the Balsam Mountain grade.

"Sure is noisy here," Mattie said.

"You'll get used to it. It don't keep me up of a night anymore."

Mattie gave a little shudder and grabbed her husband's arm.

"You all right, honey?"

She nodded and leaned her head to his shoulder. He smelled the sweet smoke of apple wood in her hair. A screech owl started up across the road. "Hear that?" she asked. "When I was a young'un, I thought they was haints."

"Ain't no such thing."

"I don't know about that. You know them nightmares I used to have after your daddy died? I had one last night. We'd moved back home to Catalooch. We was setting up a bed and I looked out the window. Know what I saw?"

"A warthog?"

"A warthog from hell, maybe. Your daddy, standing at the barn, holding a pitchfork, saying 'Now, it's mine' over and over. I was scared to death."

"Honey, we covered his sorry carcass in the churchyard. He won't ever bother us again."

"Can we go back to Catalooch, maybe next spring? I'd like to see Mama's yellow bells blooming. Maybe root some of it."

"They won't let you."

"My mama's mama planted them. I'll get some if I want to."

"We'll see. I wouldn't mind some fishing. If we find Jim Hawkins's back turned, we could get a few plants. Let's go in. I bet the fire needs another stick of wood."

After they made love, Zeb went straight to sleep. Mattie lay on her back awhile, thinking about heaven, and how much it would look like the Cataloochee she had known as a girl.

CHAPTER 15

This Time It'll Be
Done Right

The first time J. Harold Evans sat in a saddle, he was eight. It was strapped onto his neighbor's Shetland pony, an ill-tempered beast with no particular affection for humans. But Evans wanted to ride, and its owner pledged to keep a close eye on the equine, a known biter.

When Evans mounted, the pony promptly bucked, the distracted owner dropped the reins, and the pony galloped away, hell-bent to use the fence to dislodge its burden. Evans slid smoothly from the saddle on the other side, however, and would not have been hurt except that his right foot hung in the stirrup. After what seemed hours to the screaming upside-down child, the pony tired of dragging him around the lot, stopped, and began to kick. Evans vowed never to find himself on horseback again.

At fifty, he had fulfilled that promise, despite working for the park service. Most service employees and all backcountry wardens rode horses. Their high boots and bloused trousers proclaimed descent from horse cavalry. Evans proudly wore the uniform, despite his nearly life-long equinophobia.

His wife had presented him with the perfect accessory: an antique English riding crop with a silver top shaped like a fox's head. Why such a thing had been in Helena, Montana—his former duty post had been Glacier National Park—was anybody's guess, but after his fortieth birthday, the crop rarely left his hand. Some underlings whispered he bathed with it, and others sniggered, suggesting he might never go near a horse but rode his wife with vigor.

Evans had been a halfback—he'd gone out for fullback but the staff had said five feet five was too small—at Northwestern, and might have made All-American but for an injury prior to his junior season. The day publicity photos were shot, he ran, cradling pigskin in his right arm, stiff-arming with the left, planting his right foot before the camera for an abrupt turn. The fierce grimace in the photo meant his knee had given way. He never played again.

He loved a good cigar, but was known to whop employees for spitting in the grass, and if he caught a smoker tossing a butt, he made the poor soul police a square mile. The other weakness he admitted to was gin, which he enjoyed, two drinks with tonic water, just before bed. "Can't be too careful about malaria." Good gin was abundant at Glacier, next door to Canada. In the winter of 1930–31 he crated many gallons to move to Tennessee. Until they arrived intact, in January, he was as nervous as a cat birthing kittens with barbwire tails.

Ray Bradley, an east Tennesseean, was hired as much for polishing his boss's brass and leather as for his talents at filing and typing. He had played basketball at Tusculum College. Never in danger of becoming an All-American, he nonetheless had enjoyed the game enough to consider a coaching career. He was a head and a half taller than his boss, so when Evans whacked him with the crop, it hit belt buckle, if Ray was lucky.

In their new building at Sugarlands, Ray worked in a spacious anteroom with a window overlooking the hemlock-ringed parking lot. One passed through it into Evans's generous office, which featured a large picture window oriented toward Gatlinburg. On a March Monday in 1931 Ray fed a triplicate report into his black Remington, typed the date, and heard Evans call. When he walked into the office, the boss was staring out the window, absently tapping his leg. "Yes, sir?"

Evans turned with a self-satisfied smile. "I've decided to visit the people." A lit Henry Clay lay in the crystal ashtray on his otherwise uncluttered desk.

Ray cocked his head wryly. "Yes, sir. Incognito?"

"What in hell's that supposed to mean?"

"Nothing, sir. Your language reminded me of a folktale."

"Now you *really* need to explain yourself." He slapped his palm with the crop's cane.

"Kings used to go disguised among their subjects, to find out what they really thought."

"That's damned medieval, Bradley, not to mention risky. I'm going because they want to meet their new landlord, so to speak."

"Yes, sir."

"We'll leave after lunch."

"Very good, sir. You *have* cleared this with Mrs. Evans?"

He picked up the cigar and puffed until he could blow smoke rings. "Of course. What kind of damn fool do you take me for?"

"No kind, sir. I'll round up tents and bedrolls."

"Won't people put us up? That famous mountain hospitality?"

Ray coughed into his hand. "Excuse me. Yes, sir. Tell me where we are off to."

Evans walked to the map on the east wall. His crop outlined a trip along the northern border, from Sugarlands to Cosby, then to Big Creek and up to Mount Sterling, where Evans figured to spend the night. Cataloochee beckoned next, then to Ravensford, over Newfound Gap, and back to Sugarlands. A trip, depending on hospitality, weather, and their vehicle's temperament, of four to six days. "I really want to see Cataloochee. You've been there?" Evans asked.

"Once, sir, when we were lost on a family outing. It was farmland—nothing like the crags around Chimney Tops. Pretty, but in its own way."

"Well, finish that damned report and get ready."

That afternoon they headed east in the black Model A, the trunk holding a leather bag, a cloth satchel, tents, and bedrolls. At a Gatlinburg roadside stand Evans bought apples and a jar of cloudy fluid the proprietor called sourwood honey. At first they drove with windows cranked down, but a breeze soon dropped the temperature. Ray counseled they find beds in Cosby, but Evans wanted to sleep in high mountains. Shadows lengthening, clouds gathering, Ray worrying, they set out for Mount Sterling.

Halfway to the gap, a roadside cabin appeared. Full clothesline, wispy wood smoke hugging the ground. "Damn it all, Ray, pull in here."

"This won't help, sir," said Ray, braking the car and shoving in the clutch, but Evans seemed not to hear. He plucked a jar from the backseat, adjusted his hat, and headed for the porch. Ray shook his head, killed the motor, and followed. Evans knocked.

A young woman opened the door slightly. "Don't believe I know you."

Evans removed his hat with a flourish worthy of Valentino. "Miss, I'm J. Harold Evans, superintendent of the Great Smoky Mountains National Park. This is Mr. Bradley, my right-hand man. We're traveling through the park to become acquainted with people, and perhaps partake of your hospitality."

"That so." Dim afternoon light accented a sharp jawline.

"Yes, miss," said Evans. "May we come in?" He held the jar up. "We brought you this."

Her piercing gray eyes shot from one interloper to the other. "What makes you'uns think I'm a miss? Or, for that matter, taking in boarders for one sorry jar of apple butter?"

"Madam, it's honey."

She laughed. "That mess is too dark to be any good except to bait a bear with. Look here. You want drink, the well's yonder. You want vittles, I'll set out a pan of cornbread. But you won't come in, nor sleep here." Her left leg was suddenly encircled by a toddler's dirty arm.

"Sorry to have put you out," Ray said, tipping his hat brim. "We best go. Much obliged."

She looked over Evans to acknowledge Ray with the briefest glance, then closed the door.

"I'm sorry, sir. I read the clothesline right but should have warned you," Ray said as they headed to the car.

"What do you mean?"

"Nothing but diapers and a frock."

"So there's no man."

"Not now. Maybe not ever, at least not the marrying kind. She sure as shooting isn't going to let two men in her house."

Twice more they struck out. One house seemed to hold only girls giggling at their uniforms. At the other a man slowly eyeballed them and spat. "So you want to get to know us." He pulled a knife and stick from his bib pocket. "To do that you'd have to run them furrows yonder," he said, whittling a groove toward the end. "Kill or grow what you eat. Lay your old woman in the ground one day and go back to plowing the next. Look your boys in the eye and tell them the government's taking this land." He'd turned the end of his stick into a rudimentary acorn—which he lopped like an executioner. "Misters, I'd get to hell gone if I was you."

They saw houses recently abandoned, and one burned to the ground, either by the prior owners or by firebugs. They climbed toward the gap through cut-over timberland that reminded Ray of pictures of the western front. A deserted church looked as lonely as its cemetery. A chilly wind, turning southwest, smelled of moisture.

At the gap, a rude lean-to built by a prior generation's herdsmen sat by the roadside. Ray looked at his boss. "We can bunk here against whatever's coming."

Evans cranked the window halfway down. "You're nuts. We can't sleep here."

"Why not, sir?"

"It's . . . it's . . ."

"Had you rather pitch a tent?"

Evans emerged, muttering. "Hellfire. Let's look."

They were obliged to duck their heads to enter. Dirt floor littered with the bones of animals campers had eaten, and scat and tracks of smaller creatures those meals had attracted. "Bradley, we can't stay in this shit hole."

"Give me ten minutes, sir. I'll build a fire and sweep. I have bedrolls. Weather's coming, and no one's between here and Cataloochee except the fire watch, who has no room."

Evans stopped complaining after a smoke and a slug of gin from a silver-capped hip flask. Two more made him agreeable enough to crawl into his covers. In the night both wind and fire died, and by morning the snoring men's covers were dusted with snow. Six inches on the ground. Not even a songbird flitted among the balsams. After Ray rebuilt the fire and made coffee, they broke camp and headed down the mountain.

A slip had them heading over a precipice before Ray steered into the slide. Evans cursed Ray up one side and down the other, then praised Jesus they were not stove against a tree seven hundred feet down. Ray put the car in granny gear and was happy a scary mile later to escape the snow line.

They pulled beside the Carter barn at about eleven. Across the road, the house, snug against Nellie Ridge, seemed an oasis of normalcy amid abandoned farmland and boarded-up houses. Smoke drifted from the chimneys, and there seemed also to be a backyard fire.

A man appeared on the porch, shading his eyes. Evans waved, spoke to Ray, and started across the road.

"Hellfire," muttered Thomas Carter from the porch. "Park brass. And us canning bear meat." He bolted toward the backyard.

After a mild winter, bears were active. Two of their shoats had been purloined, so on Monday, Manson and Thomas had hied out with their dogs, which had raised chase early. By noon they'd bagged a sow of some two hundred and fifty pounds up Shanty Branch. The dressed carcass had hung in their backyard at dusk. The night had promised cold, so Tuesday morning they'd begun to process the miscreant. Bear roast had soon graced the cast-iron pot on the range top.

"Mama, we're done for!" yelled Thomas now.

"What do you mean?" asked Mary, sterilizing mason jars in the black kettle.

"They's park service coming. With brass all over them."

"Here, mind these jars." She went inside, hung her jacket beside the hall clock, and primped by her reflection in its face. From the front door she saw Jim Hawkins ride up and intercept the men. She hoped Jim would make them go away, but when they all started walking, she smiled resignedly. "It's worth a try." She chopped half a dozen rat-tail peppers and scattered seeds and all over the meat.

Jim knew two things were askew: a Tuesday backyard fire, and a park service vehicle. He suspected Evans did not need to nose around the Carter place. Then it hit him—neither did he. The Carters never postponed washing clothes, so likely were violating some regulation. By noon both his family and the Carters might be headed out of the valley.

"Morning, sir," he said to Evans, saluting as he dismounted. "Ray, how are you? What brings you all to Cataloochee?"

"Just a friendly visit to the natives," said Evans.

"Meaning no disrespect, sir, but don't call them that to their faces," said Jim.

"Oh, I wouldn't. Who lives here?"

"That's Mary Carter's place. They look busy. Maybe we could see Silas Wright instead."

"No, of course not—I like to observe people plying their native trades."

Jim shook his head at Ray, who winked before following Evans. Jim's heart raced. He caught up as Mary walked onto the porch. "Mrs. Carter," he said, "this is Superintendent Evans and his assistant, Mr. Bradley. Gentlemen, meet Mary Carter."

They shook hands. After considerable small talk Mary shivered. "Lands sakes, come inside. I got hot in the kitchen, but that's done worn off. We'll have a fine dinner, a beef roast I put on this morning."

Jim smiled. "You kill a beef this time of year?"

"Steer broke a leg. Wish we could have fattened him, but you do what you got to do."

"May I observe your work site?" asked Evans.

"Why sure. Thomas and Manson's out back. I'll check on dinner."

Jim walked around the house with Ray and Evans. The boys had hidden all but essentials: boiling water, jars, lids, rings, and meat. *When you get down to it*, Jim thought, *bear doesn't look much different from beef. But it sure don't taste the same. Hope she can pull this off.*

The boys answered Evans's questions, but discouraged him from prowling in outbuildings. Jim was nonetheless nervous. *If Evans finds a fresh bear hide hanging in a stall, he might as well stick my badge and hat on it.*

Mary invited them on a house tour. She pointed lovingly to Hiram's case clock, and the variety of woods paneling the hall—pine beaded ceiling imported from Waynesville, tulipwood and white pine cut from the place.

"How long have you lived here?" asked Evans.

"Nearly thirty years, but see the cabin up the road? I first moved there in 1880, when me and Hiram married. Fifty-one years ago. Don't seem possible."

"Boy, it smells great in here," said Ray.

"Wait till I fry ramps," Mary said. "We got our first mess yesterday."

"Ramps? I've never had any," said Evans.

"Why, don't tell me that," said Mary, laughing. "You like onions?"

"Yes, ma'am."

"You'll love ramps, then. Best spring tonic there is."

They sat to a feast. In the table's center sat the bear roast, surrounded by baked sweet potatoes and onions. Platters of kraut, green beans, pickled beets, and cornbread. A basket of cathead biscuits strategically stationed between a dish of apple butter and a boat of bear gravy. A plate of fried ramps and Irish potatoes. Manson doled out meat as they passed their plates. The Carters, usually no folks to stand on ceremony, held back until Evans took a bite.

"Best roast beef I've ever eaten," he said. "How did you get it so moist?"

Mary pretended to blush. "Oh, Mr. Evans, it's nothing. It's all in the spices. This one's had some red pepper laid to it."

"I want the recipe for my wife."

"Mr. Evans, I never use a recipe. I just cook it till it's done."

"If I lived with you people, I'd weigh a ton. Man, those ramps are good. Where do you get them?" Sweat beaded above his upper lip.

"In the woods."

"Here?"

Everyone stopped eating. "Sir, I don't know that they grow anywhere else," said Thomas.

"I don't remember if this is on our protected plant list." Evans's forehead reddened.

"You mean we might not be able to harvest them no more?"

"No visitors may remove plants from the park, but perhaps there could be a PSSUP."

"Long as we can have a mess in the spring," said Mary. "We've always taken care to leave some for seed, you know. Honoring the garden God gives us."

Evans sweated like a man at hard labor. From the end of his nose dangled a bead of clear snot, to which he applied a white handkerchief. "Excuse me, but I love hot pepper. Good for the sinuses." He blew his nose and nodded at Mary. "I applaud your comment about gardens. This valley will eventually have poplars big as silos, trout the size of handsaws. It'll be a veritable Garden of Eden. But you know what? This time it'll be done right." He drank deeply from a glass of sweet milk.

Everyone stared at him. "What did I say?" he asked.

"Mr. Evans, it sounded like you might misdoubt the Lord's work," said Thomas.

"Mr. Carter, I certainly meant no aspersions against the Almighty. I merely remarked that the first Eden was spoiled quickly—by people. This time—"

"Mr. Evans, put the quietus on this before—" said Manson.

Mary stood. "You all stop. This isn't a debating society." She stared at Evans. "My daddy never talked politics or religion over dinner. Nor should you men."

"Exactly, Mrs. Carter. And let me reiterate, this is the finest roast I have ever eaten. May I have more?"

The Carters waved good-bye to the uniformed men as they set out for Silas Wright's place. Jim left his horse at the Carter's barn in favor of the backseat, although he felt ill at ease in motorcars. He suppressed a grin as Evans lit a cigar and waxed poetic about roast, and silently offered thanks to whoever was in charge.

"Whose place was that?" asked Evans, as they bounced and rattled past a forlorn farm.

"Andy Carter's, sir," said Jim, leaning forward. "Andy was Hiram Carter's uncle, a brother to old Levi, the first settler."

"Stop a minute, Bradley. How long since it's been inhabited?"

"Uncle Andy died in the nineties. His widow stayed till she died, then her son took over. I reckon he's been gone five or six years. Got work at the paper mill," said Jim.

An emaciated dog with matted reddish fur emerged from the barn, dugs nearly scraping the ground. She glanced at the automobile and headed behind the structure as if on some shameful mission.

"Whose dog?" asked Evans.

"Never saw her before," said Jim.

"Excellent example," said Evans.

"Of what, sir?"

"That dog isn't the only creature holing up in these structures. Rats, mice, all carrying fleas, ticks, mites. Snakes. The vermin birds carry. Fugitives. Firebugs, too. Look at that corner—cracked wide enough to toss a cat through. Chimney shedding rocks. Dangerous for human habitation. All these buildings need to be destroyed."

"Do you mean tear them down?"

"Burning is more efficient. You will receive a directive about it soon. Move on, Bradley."

"Yes, sir." Ray put the car in gear and began crawling up the road. Jim sat back and stared out the window at his future. Burning his boyhood.

He sensed as much as saw a lurking presence behind a roadside poplar. Who or whatever it was kept the tree between itself and the car as skillfully as a woodpecker will. Jim wondered if that was Willie McPeters but decided not to ask Ray to stop the car.

Roads in the valley normally followed the creek, but this stretch of water meandered enough to force them to ford it several times. At the last crossing, the road was barely wide enough for the car. The men emerged and stretched beside a hitching post. The screen door banged shut, and Silas, head cocked, hands in overall pockets, peered at them as if they were exotic—if suspicious—birds.

Jim put up his hand. "Howdy, Silas. Brought a couple of visitors."

Silas nodded, smile as thin as a hoe blade. "Afternoon, gents," he said.

Evans walked to the porch with his hand extended. "J. Harold Evans, park superintendent."

Brass on Evans's jacket glinted in the sunshine. "Don't let a gang of crows see that coat," Silas said. "They'll up and carry you off. I'm Silas Wright."

"Pleased to meet you, Mr. Wright. This is my assistant, Mr. Bradley."

Silas nodded to Ray. "Meaning no offense, Mr. Evans, but you boys ate some powerful ramps for dinner."

"Oh, sorry," Evans said.

"Don't be. Wouldn't have noticed if I'd had some myself. Here. I've taken to carrying jawbreakers."

They unwrapped the peppermints. "Thanks very much," said Evans.

Silas lit his pipe. "You're welcome. Now, what can an old man do for you jaybirds?"

Evans put candy in his mouth and looked around. "You sure live away from everything."

"My daddy settled this far back because he didn't want every Tom, Dick, and Harry traipsing in the front yard, and I don't neither." Silas smoked and eyed Evans's riding crop, which was beginning a tattoo on his boot.

"May I ask how old you are, sir?"

"You can ask. Don't mean I'll answer."

"Fair enough," said Evans. "Mind if we look around?"

"Nothing here to hide." They walked to the barn.

"This farm is trim and neat," said Bradley. "You work it all by yourself?"

"It's gone to hell next to what it used to be," said Silas. "A man my age—eighty-one, by the way"—the aside spoken to the top of Evans's head—"can't do it all. Ten years ago you wouldn't find a weed. Now it's all I can do to keep poison oak grubbed out."

At the woodshed Evans fingered gray, checked ends on splits. "Can't accuse you of illegal firewood. This's been stacked awhile."

Silas did not mention the red oak he was working up to mix with his cured pieces. "When we heard about the park, we cut enough wood to last for years," said Silas.

"Prudent," said Evans. "This represents a lot of work."

"Hard work makes a farm, and I can lay my head down nights knowing I've made the place a little better. Not every man can say that."

The boss smiled. "Well, Mr. Wright, we'll let you get back to your chores. It was a pleasure meeting you. I hope we become friends."

"Don't hold your breath till that happens. I'm civil when Jim's around, because I kind of like the boy. But I was you, I wouldn't come here by myself."

"Is that a threat, Mr. Wright?"

"Nope. I wouldn't hurt a man. But I can sure as hell ignore him."

Once they were back in the car, Ray pulled the choke and stepped on the starter. Nothing. "Shoot, sir. It won't start."

"What the hell do you mean?"

"Pretty much what I said, sir."

Ray peered under the hood. Silas bent toward the passenger side. Evans's sleeve displayed three embroidered gold service stars like spring dandelions. "Mr. Superintendent, I got a spare horse."

"That won't be necessary." Evans pointed to Ray, who disappeared with a wrench beneath the running board. "My man will take care of it."

"Wouldn't have one of these infernal things," Silas said, refilling his pipe. "A man ought to get where he needs to go on foot or atop a horse. You got one at home, Mr. Superintendent?"

Evans pursed his lips, shook his head, and listened to Ray bang hell out of something.

"That's a shame. People say dogs is your best friend, but mine's Maude. She ain't never refused to take me anywhere, and ain't left me in strange country, like this seems to want to do."

Ray popped into the seat. "Had to get underneath far enough to whack the starter. Let's see if it works." The automobile cranked like it was on the showroom floor.

"Home, Bradley. Good day, Mr. Wright," said Evans, his riding crop tapping the door. "I hope to see you soon."

Silas watched them drive away. "I'll bet you do, you sawed-off banty rooster. I'll bet you do."

CHAPTER 16

Scrap Iron

Bud Harrogate acted like he had no cares at all, whistling, kicking leaves, fooling around under the beech grove near the new schoolhouse. On a sunny March day in 1931 his plaid flannel shirt, by female standards a rag, felt smooth and as warm as aged bourbon. At a distance he appeared a schoolboy, but closer, forty-three years showed like rust on a weathered trawler.

He had left Cataloochee when the leaves had turned the previous fall, and had shown back up like a stray cat this dogwood winter, just in time to help Silas plant the kitchen garden.

That morning he had walked to Nellie for a cold cola dope and a Moon Pie, as much to aggravate Silas as to enjoy food "with some damn taste to it." On the way back he had succumbed to a fit of what his aunt used to call "pure trifling."

But his dance stopped as his foot struck an intractable object. "What the hell?" He knelt beside an ornate cast-iron piece about three feet long, half-buried beside an emergent root. He pulled it from the ground, knocked dirt from its interstices, and wiped rust and soil with his bandana. As he rubbed, "Peabody Desk Works" slowly appeared in a central medallion.

Harrogate studied it like it might be an artifact from ancient Troy. He'd seen such things, but long ago, far away. He stared at it from every angle, then nodded. *Oh. Sure. It's one side of a school desk. Wonder where the rest of it's at. There'd be another side and a stretcher or two. Plus a wooden top that's rotted away, I reckon.*

He made several turns, each wider, sliding boots over dry grass but finding nothing save pebbles and beechnut hulls. The maker had striven for a lacy look, but the piece felt as heavy as a yearling sheep. *Ain't no way I'll carry this bastard a mile and a half.* He replaced and re-covered it for safekeeping.

The rest of the way he tossed rocks into the creek and lit cigarettes one off another. A couple of puny gray squirrels eating nuts on a pine branch seemed the only furry creatures besides cattle left in Cataloochee. Songbirds twittered, but he didn't try to spot them. *Never was good at birds. If they're littler than a jaybird, I can't much tell one from another. The old women, though, can tell them apart, even perdict weather by them. My aunt, though, she never said a word about them.*

Harrogate was country born—two miles from Providence, in Blount County, Tennessee—but wasn't raised listening to birdcalls. His father, who turned over new leaves more often than a maple, had found work at the Knoxville Woolen Mills when Bud was two and his sister Doll was nine, of six children the survivors.

They found a room in a Mule Hollow warren, two miles across the river. To and from work Bud's old man passed plenty of taverns and breweries, so kept his high-paying job only a fortnight before waking inside a big city drunk tank.

He found work in a tanyard. About four in the morning after his first payday, he dragged in, cursing, overturning furniture. A bloody left ear dangled and flapped. When his wife shushed him, he yelled he'd do what he goddamn pleased in his own goddamn house. The children hunkered behind the kitchen table.

After teetering over a splayfooted chair, he caught himself on the mantel, found the poker, and lunged at their mother, barely missing her chin, knocking a hole in the wall. Doll dashed for the broom and whacked her father on the back of the head. Her mother grabbed the shotgun. Doll swept little Bud up and ran outside, screaming. The gun went off. The double snick of breakdown and reload. A bright flash in the doorway, almost simultaneous with another blast.

Their mother hollered to get packing. Soon they headed to Providence, jumping over a dead man. No one had paid a bit of attention to their arrival in Knoxville—nor did anyone remark their departure.

Their mother died of pneumonia when Doll was sixteen and Bud was barely nine. His aunt, a fat sourpuss of a Mule Hollow Holiness woman, took him in. She preached on occasion, and was fiercely partial to church, food, and family. Her husband raised beans, squash, corn, and tomatoes beside the Holston, up toward Mascot. He sold produce, along with fish, mussels, turtle meat, and whatever he yanked from the river— tires, saw logs, pieces of houses. Bud blended with their six children like a red drop helps a pint of white paint.

Harrogate rounded the last bend of roadbed to see Silas splitting stove wood. When Bud appeared in the woodlot, Silas stopped to wipe his forehead. "About time you got back," he said. "Thought you went clean to Waynesville to get that mess."

"I took my time. Here." He handed Silas a tin of sardines. The label pictured a sailboat heading toward a full moon.

"Thanks, Bud. I love these things." He set it on the smokehouse porch. "Think we can work up this stove wood before supper?" He nodded at a pile of billets.

"Take a rest. I'll bust these up."

Harrogate picked up the hatchet. "Silas, I found a humdinger next to the schoolhouse."

"What, son?"

"Part of a desk, half-buried in leaves. Real fancy, cast iron, all ropy looking. Couldn't find the rest of it."

Silas chuckled. "We must've missed it after we burned the schoolhouse. I don't know what a man does with half a desk."

"Oh, it's worth something."

"How so?"

"Scrap iron. My uncle paid for many a thing with it. Had him an old barrel sawed in half lengthwise, so it made two what you might call tubs, sectioned off for brass, iron, tin, steel, what have you. Kept a magnet hanging next to it. Tanned me good if he caught me fooling with it."

Harrogate had settled into a rhythm that littered splits to the right of the chopping block. Between whacks Silas bent to pick up stove wood. "Who'd he sell it to?"

"Oh, any number of scrap mongers worked in Knoxville. The big yards took metal, cloth, paper. Sold it to Yankees. They'd stack bales of rags at the train yard like cotton back in slave days."

Silas carried the wood inside while Harrogate fetched more. Silas returned, brushing splinters from his overalls. "You know, Bud, I never thought I'd hear of folks selling scrap. I keep my stuff till I wear it slap out, and so does everybody I know."

Harrogate started another pile. "It's a different world, Silas. You know, I been thinking."

"Never a good sign."

Bud never paid attention to sarcasm. "You know folks is moving out. . . ."

"Yeah, I've noticed."

"Well, there's not a one of them but abandons metal—a bucket with a hole in it, if nothing else. A man could follow and glean some money."

"They don't miss nothing big enough to mess with."

"Don't be too sure. I heard them Hoglens up Carter Fork left a broke-down mowing machine. Didn't have room, nor want to make an extra trip. That's a start, and there's any number of fence steeples and tin cans and old nails laying around—they add up. A man could sell a bunch of scrap."

"Where at?"

"Folks along the French Broad in Asheville trade in it. I can ask Sis. Likely Jews."

"Why Jews?"

"In Europe, what a body does is handed from father to son. Jews do most everything, including doctoring and lawyering, but almost all scrap men are Jews. They keep at it over here. Good people, honest, hard workers. I'm ever on trial for something I didn't do, I'd rather have a twelve-Jew jury than a key to the jailhouse."

"To be devil's advocate, the Bible's pretty hard on them."

"You're right, at least about that bunch Moses put up with. I'd been him, I'd left them wandering till they rotted."

"Kluxers say they killed Jesus."

"Never knew a Kluxer smart enough to pour piss out of a boot in the direction of the heel."

Silas lit his pipe. "You saying you don't believe the Bible?"

Harrogate fished a Camel from his shirt pocket. "I believe what I need to. I'm not like my aunt. She thought them floating ax heads was just as true as the Resurrection. She said Jesus would be back—before she died, mind you—to snatch folks to heaven." He lit the cigarette and inhaled deeply. "Are you about finished meddling?"

"Nearly. Did them Holiness baptize you?"

"Yeah. I was twelve. I'd a been fourteen, they wouldn't have caught me. You wondering if I've been saved?"

"Well, you never go to church."

Bud dropped the hatchet and gathered an armload of wood. "Silas, church people do mighty low-down things. If that's 'saved,' they can keep it. I enjoy a good sunset, a pretty woman, and a stiff drink, and if that means I'll fry in hell, so be it. Wouldn't want to fly around forever with a damn harp anyhow. Now quit worrying about my soul and tell me when we can filch that mowing machine."

Next morning they hitched mule to wagon and headed toward the settlement. Nelse Howell emerged to sweep the little porch as they stopped. "Morning, gents. You'uns all right?" he asked.

"Fair to middling, Nelse," said Silas. "Any mail?"

"Yep. Bud, how about another Moon Pie?"

"Yes, sir, and a grape drink."

Nelse lumbered inside, handed Silas an automobile circular, and Harrogate his sweet confection. Bud laid a dime on the counter and fished in the drink box for a grape soda. Body and blood for Harrogate. Silas eye-balled the little store, the shelves of which were more than half empty. He was about to comment on that when he noticed the storekeeper's face. "Nelse, did a haint drag you around half the night? Your eyes look red as a fox's ass in a pokeberry patch."

"Ain't sleeping good," he admitted. "I don't know what I'm going to do, neighbor. Everybody leaves, I'd be so worthless I might as well shoot myself."

"I'd not give that any consideration," said Silas. "You could storekeep somewhere else."

"Might have to. Shoot, I'd retire, but I can't afford to. Where you'uns off to?"

"Going on a little scrap drive."

Nelse laughed. "If you get active cash money, spend it here. Where do you plan to sell it?"

"Bud knows some people, don't you?"

Harrogate nodded, his mouth full.

"Nelse, would you take a gander at this? I'd not put that in my body," said Silas. "Anything looks that awful can't be food."

"Neighbor, let him alone. That might be the only dime I take in today."

The road into Carter Fork was as rough as a cob, so Silas had to leave off smoking for fear a bounce might cause him to break his pipe stem or bite his tongue in two. They lurched and swayed for a mile and a half. They tied their cloth tool bag to a strut to keep it in the wagon bed, so pry bar, hammer, and pliers made a first-class racket. Silas's full bladder and aching head made him contemplate walking back.

Harrogate grinned like a Chessy cat eating gravel when he spied the weed-choked turnoff. Beside the barn sat a mowing machine. The Hoglens had raptured seat and sickle, grinder and teeth, but had left behind wheels, axle, levers, and frame. Iron and steel in pounds, not ounces.

Harrogate braked the wagon and found an oat bag for the mule while Silas relieved himself. The Hoglen house had never been a palace, but three months' absence had not helped. Part of the front porch had been pried up for kindling, and no pane of glass survived intact. The front door was locked, but the back door splayed from rusty hinges. In the kitchen they found liquor bottles scattered on the floor and stove neck-first into the wallboard. "Lordy," said Silas. "Looks like they had a go-away party. At least they thought they was having a good time."

"Yeah, but they're long gone. Mice done ate the candle wax out of this slut."

In the west bedroom a coil spring covered with a rotten safety-pinned sheet sat catercorner beside a rusty metal colander. "Looky, Silas. More loot."

They surveyed the rest of the house, noting locks, the possibility of cast-iron sash weights, a soap dish, some ratty kitchen utensils, a dozen or more brass .22 casings. "Silas, there's a little money here. You know, I just remembered something one of them scrap men said when I was a lad. Stuck with me better'n most stuff I had in school."

"What's that?"

"He said we've been making metal since time began, and all of it is still here, just in a different something or another. This shell casing might have been part of an Egyptian spear."

"How do you reckon it got to Cataloochee? No, I don't have time for you to answer that. I got another question. Exactly who does this belong to?"

Harrogate turned, surprised. "The government grabbed it, right?"

Silas nodded and lit his pipe.

"And America's a government of the people, by the people, and for the people, right?"

Silas grinned. "Yep."

Harrogate lit a Camel. "And we're Americans, right? So it belongs to us. Fair and square."

"I hope nobody argues that point."

"You don't need to worry, Silas. What'll they do with this stuff any-how? Put it in a museum?"

By dinner they had untwisted honeysuckle and bittersweet from the mower and loaded the machine, and harvested metal from the house and miscellaneous stuff from the barn: a broken bale hook, a rusted chick brooder, a snaggletoothed currycomb, broken plow points. They ripped galvanized roofs from corncrib and outhouse. A half-covered pile beside the corncrib yielded flattened cans that once had held anything from peaches to sardines.

Near the chicken house Harrogate spotted large square nail heads in a six-foot poplar bole on the ground. "Wonder if we can get them big nails. Why are they there, anyhow?"

Silas knelt. "Learn something. This is a mink trap. Drill you a hole in the side of the log a little bigger than the critter's head, then sharpen hell out of some nails, drive them in at an angle. He can stick his head in, but can't pull it out without killing hisself."

"What do you bait it with?"

"Anything that stinks to high heaven. Pop used to leave fish guts in a bottle on the windowsill. After it ages, it just takes a drop or two. Soak a dough ball with it for catfish bait."

They stood and stretched. "Silas," said Harrogate, "you wouldn't let me tell you how that brass came here from Egypt, so here's another deep thought. There ain't no more mink. Otters is gone. So's elk, buffalo, pigeons, wolves. Foxes ate the rabbits and moved on. Ain't but a handful of deer. We've about killed out the turkeys, and I can't remember when I saw an eagle. And soon people will be gone. You want to make a bet?"

"On what?"

"The government being right about something?"

"What in hell might that be?"

"When people leave, they'll all come back."

"What, all the critters?"

"Think about it. Who killed off the pigeons and elk? And, for that matter, who killed enough rabbits that the foxes could eat the rest? Take out people, you'll leave a few bear, and little bastards—squirrels, mice, moles, tweety birds—but pretty soon here'll come rabbits and foxes and so on until it's back like God made it to be."

"You're addled, son. We hadn't killed them rabbits, we wouldn't have raised a single vegetable. And you know what was first in the Bible— a garden tended by man."

"Yeah, and look how quick we messed that up."

"Hell, a man can't argue with you a-tall. Let's get out of here."

So they secured the load and headed back. Silas and Bud sat in front of a bizarre mixture of castoffs, at the apex of which the bar of the mower swayed like a schooner's mast in a summer squall. They had to stop every few hundred feet to throw something back in, and the load creaked and clanked like a muffled cowbell.

Nelse heard them five minutes before they arrived at the settlement. In his apron, he emerged waving from the post office. Silas, however, had another headache and stared straight ahead, his hat jammed onto his forehead. Harrogate whistled and headed down the road, determined to add to their collection. Had they been in a cartoon, his eyeballs would have been dollar signs.

They turned beside the schoolhouse and parked. Harrogate ran to the desk side and wrestled it upright. "Ain't it a beaut?"

Having lit his pipe, Silas ambled over. "Yep. Wonder where in the world the other piece is. I don't remember any missing desks."

Harrogate hefted it with both hands, bringing it about three inches off the ground. "Move over, Silas," he grunted. "Here it comes." He waddled it to the back of the wagon and rested the weight on the ground. "I might need a little help with this," he panted.

"Maybe this here warden can help," said Silas.

Harrogate had not heard Jim's horse, upon which he sat, grinning. "You look like castaways from *Don Quixote*. Where do you think you're going?"

"The scrap yard," said Harrogate.

"I suppose you think this belongs to you?"

Harrogate wiped his brow. "Well, my uncle always said possession was nine tenths of the law, and he didn't give a hoot for the other tenth. I reckon you're about to figure it different?"

Jim sat a little higher in the saddle. "Bud, think about it. This belongs to the American people. Horace Wakefield's planning a museum."

Silas blew a cloud of smoke into the air. "Jim Hawkins, how long's it been since he talked about that? For that matter, how long since he's even been over here? They don't think enough of us to build an outhouse, much less a museum. And, for God's sake, nothing here's quality enough for a museum. It ain't but a bunch of rusty old plunder. Kind of like me."

Jim looked around and laughed softly. "I'm surprised you didn't roll up the fence wire."

Silas and Harrogate looked at each other like they were a pair of motley fools. "Well, we *did* try the chicken wire, but it was so bad rusted it fell apart," said Harrogate, lighting a Camel.

Jim smiled. "Listen, boys, I'll look the other way, like I do a lot with you two. I could, after all, have been over Sterling and seen nothing. But if I see another load, I'll cite you. Evans won't grant a permit to scrounge scrap metal."

"We appreciate it, Jim Hawkins," said Silas. "We could cut you a share."

"Sounds like a bribe to me. You boys be careful."

Harrogate clicked his heels and saluted. "Yes, sir. I just need some help getting this up in the wagon."

"If that's what I think it is, I'll help you walk it to the schoolhouse. Where'd you get that?"

Harrogate pointed over his shoulder. "It was half-buried over yonder."

"Well, it's going to school. You aren't selling that." Jim dismounted and handed Silas his horse's reins. He and Harrogate humped it inside the door and stood it against the wall.

Silas and Harrogate walked the mule home, leaving their wagon beside the school. Late that night Harrogate snuck out and headed down the road in the moonlight. Silas watched him from the upstairs bedroom, wondering how they'd explain how that piece of a desk had hopped back onto that wagon.

CHAPTER 17

The Beginning of Leaving

Before the park, bracing for a Cataloochee winter began with a long-standing ritual—in two summer weeks men cut trees and distributed them to all households. In 1928 they had decided this might be their final harvest, so they felled every hardwood on the upper slopes except the huge old poplars. Levi Marion's wood stack promised to keep them warm six winters.

His woodlot ran on gravity. From the pile of logs—"firewood on the hoof," he called it—to the three-bay woodshed was eighty downhill feet. He and his sons sawed logs into eight-inch lengths for the cookstove, ten inches longer for fireplaces. They tossed those rounds to a pile beside a chopping block. Levi Marion enjoyed splitting most of them himself.

He worked with a deliberate pace. Smaller billets, first stroke; halves, second whack; fourths, done. Larger rounds split into eighths or sixteenths. When he was one with his job, passersby admired both rhythm and results. Steady, unhurried, prayer-like work.

His woodshed had bulged to begin the winter, which had not been particularly cold or wet. But on a cold morning in March 1931, he woke at four and stared at the ceiling, above which his brood slept. Coals settled at the bedroom hearth, a southwesterly wind made him think of snow, and his right big toe hurt.

It wasn't much of a toe. In his twenties—"when you're young, you ain't got no sense," his grandfather Levi had been fond of saying—he had hacked most of it off while working firewood barefooted. Some folks preserved amputated limbs or digits, to be buried with the amputee. They reasoned if folks weren't whole at the last trumpet, when Jesus took to separating sheep from goats, they'd be thrown into the left-hand pile. Levi Marion, however, figured to stand proudly Judgment Day. If toes were so important, Jesus would give him a new one.

With enough light to distinguish ceiling joints, he dressed, stood, and scratched everything reachable without bending over. The house smelled of warm iron and yesterday's fried pork. He quietly rekindled fireplaces.

Outside, gray clouds threatened to grace the ground. He headed to the barn, collar raised against a southwestern breeze. Hugh and Rass's pair of young hounds, Mutt and Jeff, nosed the air from under the porch.

When he returned, the kitchen range fairly sang as Valerie cooked. Hearthstones radiated enough heat to rouse the children. Levi Marion laid his hand on his wife's shoulder. "If it snows," he said, "me and Rass will hunt rabbits."

"I never figured you for playing in the snow."

"Hunting ain't playing. We ain't got a pot to piss in anymore. Land ain't ours. Lost our money. We need the food."

Three weeks before, his oldest son, Hugh, had moved to Waynesville to work at Boyd's filling station. His next boy, Rass, would turn fifteen that coming summer. Rass boarded in Waynesville while he finished high school but was home because school had closed while a furnace was being replaced. He trudged from the loft, clothes mostly in his hands. Over his long johns went a denim shirt and overalls.

"Son," said Levi Marion, "hurry every chance you get. You and me need to clean out the barn stalls."

"Okay, Papa. But do we have to do them *all*?"

"Depends. If it snows shoe-mouth deep, we'll hunt rabbits."

The rest of the tribe popped from the loft looking like they had haunted back corners of Noah's ark. Ada's snaky hair shot every which way. George, going on eleven, coughed as croupy as a barn cat hocking a hair ball. Ruth Elizabeth, nearly nine, carried a rooster-shaped rag doll half-hidden in her clothes. Mary, six, dragging a tattered blanket and a stuffed bear, tromped to the chimney corner to check on little brother Ned's crib.

Rass followed his father to the porch. "What do you think, Papa?"

"After breakfast, we'll see." He went out back for some quiet. Emerging from the outhouse, he spied one substantial snowflake settling slowly downward.

After the meal Rass started to work, but burst back inside. "Papa, it's snowing, *hard*!"

"It's dry in the barn."

"Papa, the ground's white."

"All right," he grumbled, "I'll see about it." But his eyes smiled.

Flakes as big as milkweed seeds clung to flat surfaces. The hemlock beside the springhouse looked like a Christmas tree awaiting candles.

"Rass, fetch a day's stove wood for your mama and stack splits by the hearth. These young'uns won't go to school this day. Me and you are going hunting."

They dressed against the weather, sweaters and britches under overalls, leggings over boots. Rass found his double-barreled .410 and a box of shells, kissed his mother, and gave his siblings the razz. Levi Marion hugged Valerie, took his shotgun from over the door, and went outside.

Across the road, weed heads bowed under snowy hats. Sound was muffled, even the flittering peeps of a solitary cardinal. They could see no farther than the middle of the big field and barely made out the edge of the orchard.

They meant to hunt to the schoolhouse, then up Indian Creek. Rass called his dogs and started ahead of his father. When Levi Marion stopped to retie his homemade leggings, a shot sounded like a fist hitting a feather pillow. He met Rass, who held a good-size rabbit by its hind feet. "Good work, Son. Head toward the schoolhouse. I'll watch for anything backtracking." Rass started westward as the dogs sniffed creek-edge briars and weeds.

Underfoot the ground was as slick as—Levi Marion would have said in some quarters—owl shit. Snowbirds pulled orange berries off bittersweet snaking into a patch of scrub oaks. If the shots he heard were dead on, the family would not starve.

At the schoolhouse Rass carried a blood-mottled tow sack heavy with rabbits. Breath pluming, he and his father ducked into the structure, stamping snow. The dogs shook and ran under the front stoop.

Two rooms, two dozen desks, one unfired heater. Levi Marion lifted its eye and examined cold charcoal. "Son, I bet you've backed your butt to this stove many a time." Levi Marion chuckled. "I went to the old school, the one that burned down."

"That's a good story," said Rass.

Levi Marion returned the lifter. "Back then a man could get away with things. Good old days. Hell, it snowed oftener, deeper, days on end. We had woods in the valley. Standing half a field off you could count every limb. You'd think them all straight until a big snow told you otherwise." He shook his head. "Tell you what. Let's go see your uncle Will."

At the stoop the dogs had disappeared. Snowing, more powdery now, three inches deep. Two sets of paw prints headed home. "Them dogs ain't worth shooting," Levi Marion said. Next to their tracks orange and scarlet stains radiated from bittersweet hulls. "Everywhere them birds shit, a seed's tailor-made ready come spring."

"Papa, Aunt Lizzie's girls used to make baskets and wreaths from the vines."

"That's all the bastards are good for. If you'd spent half the time I have grubbing this infernal stuff, you'd hate it, too." Levi Marion checked his pocket watch. "I'm getting hungry. How about you?"

Rass nodded as they walked beside Indian Creek, heavy sack banging against his leg.

Nearly ninety years before, Levi Marion's great-uncle Fate had built a mill. A hundred yards upcreek he'd diverted water into a wooden race, which in the fall he'd closed for a day so he could clean out leaves—and scoop left-behind trout into bushel baskets for a community fish fry. The race emptied into a forebay, a wooden tank twelve feet square at the top, tapered like a funnel to shoot water onto a wheel that turned the mill-stones.

Will Carter, Fate's nephew and successor, a wiry man uphill from seventy with a wild beard covering layers of denim, flannel, and wool, opened the door and cocked his head at his nephew and grand-nephew. "You're in a heap of need if you want corn ground this day."

Levi Marion knocked snotty ice from his mustache. "Howdy, Uncle Will. We've been hunting."

Rass showed him the game.

"I'll not start the mill, then," Will said, and laughed. "Rabbit meal's too furry. Anyhow, I just wanted to build a fire and check on things." He shuffled toward the back, returning with a jar. "Here's one of them things. Have a snort, Levi Marion."

"Been so long, my heart might give way."

"Don't say I didn't offer. Quite an occasion, you hunting on a work-day. So I'll drink one for you, too. Remember that time we all went possum hunting?"

"Sure do. I was about thirteen. Did we ever tell you that story?" Levi Marion asked Rass.

Rass, nodding, grinned. "Tell it again."

"Son, it was some night. I drunk enough popskull for us all put to-gether," said Will.

"Liquor saved your uncle that evening," said Levi Marion. "Dogs treed the biggest old possum you ever seen, hissing in the second fork of a wild cherry toward the Sutton place. Nothing would suit Uncle Will except to climb after her. He squirreled up and stood on the first fork, reached back smooth as your mama's Sunday dress, grabbed that possum by the nape of her neck. He fell backasswards, cradling that critter like a sack of gold. Hadn't been liquored up, he'd broke his neck. We thought he was dead until she got tired of laying there and bit his arm."

"Eye God," said Will, "she latched on and wouldn't let go. Three shirts and a wool coat was all that kept her from taking my arm off. You boys played hell prying her loose."

"Silas worried most of an hour with them rusty old pliers."

"What did you do with her?" asked Rass.

"Beat her to death on a tree trunk. Made her tenderish. Wasn't bad eating."

Snow had nearly stopped. Levi Marion eyed the sky. "Uncle Will, you hungry? We got dinner."

"I can always eat. Then I bet you boys'll get in a half day's work?"

Levi Marion shook his head. "I haven't prowled in snowy woods since I was Rass's age."

Will looked at him hard. "Levi Marion, I never knowed you to leave a job until tomorrow."

Levi Marion studied his hands. "Uncle Will, next winter the park mightn't let us walk in snow without a pea soup."

"Go on, then, if you can slog up that slick grade. Don't drag the rabbits, though. I'll dress them for you."

"Then you'll keep some for your trouble."

They shared Valerie's fried pies and ham biscuits, then Levi Marion and his son walked into a white silence. In a snowbank a stain feathering from purple to pink spoke of pokeweed. "You never used to see this damn mess grow past salad stage," said Levi Marion. "You're in a different world, boy."

They shouldered guns and trudged toward the bend where Davidson Branch ended its switchback crawl down the mountain. Beside it a mule-width trail began a twisted rise of a thousand feet.

Doghobble and hearts-a-busting lined the roadside. No sound save branch, breath, and slow and scrunching steps. Water and trail intersected in a watery mush at every switchback. After an hour they reached the woods edge, where Rass spied fox prints. "Look, Papa."

Levi Marion bent and grabbed his overalls legs. "Yep." He gasped, coughed, and spat in the snow. "Bet it started snowing up here before it did in the valley. You usually don't see a fox in daylight." He coughed again. "Damn, that's a mean climb." Red-faced, he sat, hard, on a chestnut log. "We're close to that cherry tree we was talking about." He wiped his brow. "Go on. I'll catch up in a minute."

"Papa, are you sure?"

He waved Rass away. "I'm just winded."

"You don't look too well." Rass started to touch his father's shoulder but pulled back.

"Believe me, I've looked a lot worse than this," said Levi Marion.

"Tell you what. If you need help, shoot twice and I'll come running," said Rass.

"You bet."

The grade soon banished worry from Rass's thoughts. He negotiated the three hundred yards, falling twice. George Sutton's deserted farmyard sported a broken-down wagon with a snow-laden bed. Clusters of bayonet grass made him think of old men bent under white counterpanes.

Rass couldn't remember if Sutton had moved, but no dogs barked and no smoke rose from his chimney. Rass started to knock, when a noise intruded. Rass craned his neck, ears straining through cold and humidity. After a tense half minute, another shot.

Rass banged the door. "Mr. Sutton," he shouted, "Papa's in trouble." The door swung to reveal a wadded towel in the far corner and a moth-eaten blanket over the north window. Rass grabbed the blanket and yelled, "Hold on, I'm coming!"

He tumbled off the porch, skittered downhill, slid on his behind, scrabbled up, and found the path to the vacant log, uphill from which Levi Marion's tracks ended at a lumpy pile of clothes.

"Papa, Papa!" Rass shouted, clambering up the slope. Snow grooved away from the shotgun's barrel. Rass knelt beside his father's body, tears streaming. "Oh, God," Rass said. "Please, God." He shook his father's shoulder. It seemed a week before Levi Marion moved his head like he never wanted to wake.

"Rass, what in tarnation?"

Rass helped him to his feet and brushed snow from his coat. He draped the blanket over Levi Marion's back and wiped the gun with a corner of it. "Can you get to Sutton's house?"

"I reckon."

"Lean on me."

They bounced off each other until a slippery rhythm took over. At the porch Levi Marion flapped a hand at his son. "I'm okay now."

The frigid house seemed vacated just ahead of a hostile assault. Levi Marion, shivering, leaned on the door frame between front room and kitchen, looking over the deserted structure. "I used to visit old man Sutton," he said. "His wife died with the Spanish flu, when you was a baby. He'd talk your ear off, but he always had a fire going and coffee on."

"Hey, why don't I build a fire?"

"Wouldn't hurt my feelings a bit in the world."

Rass hefted a piece of a stool leg. It felt sound enough to knock out pantry shelves, so he went to work, blows echoing off the hard walls. In the fireplace Rass tee-peed splinters over a mouse nest and lit it with a kitchen match fished from his coat pocket. The chimney drew, so he dragged boards to the fireplace, scattering mouse turds and silverfish. Shelves popped like guns as they caught.

The fire improved Levi Marion considerably.

"Papa, what happened?"

"Rass, when you left, it got quiet. I was resting my eyes. Praying a little. After a time I heard a bull elk bugle. Boy, every hair on my body stood in ranks. I opened eyes on the biggest elk that ever walked these hills, not thirty yards off. I didn't have but a rabbit load—I didn't even think about it, shut my eyes and fired. When I looked again, there wasn't nothing—no track, no sign, no nothing. I ran up the hill lickety-split, tripped, knocked the wind out of me. Had enough sense to shoot. Then I passed out. When you woke me, I was thinking about Jesus."

"Papa, elk live out West, don't they?"

"Son, I know it don't make sense."

Rass shoved more shelves into the fire. "Maybe you were dreaming."

Levi Marion stared at the hearth. "Glad you built a fire. When I was a boy, it was peachy to come into a warm room on a king-hell cold day— your cheeks tingled. Mama fixed a cup of cocoa, if we had some. If we didn't, warm milk was mighty fine. Those were good times, Rass. We didn't have nothing, not like now. But we had each other, and thought we was rich as King Solomon." Levi Marion seemed embarrassed at such a speech, and stared into the fire, which Rass kept feeding, listening to its pop and hiss. They studied the hearth until both stopped shivering.

Levi Marion smiled. "Son, I could stay here all day, but we need to get going. Your mama will worry."

"You up to moving?"

"It's all downhill."

Rass ratted up a rusted bucket. "I'll throw snow on the fire."

Levi Marion nodded. "Yes, we don't need to burn the house down. It's been a comfort."

From the porch Spruce Mountain's top in sudden sunshine seemed chiseled from alabaster. Jaybirds stirred—a hawk keened behind the house.

"I like living in the valley," said Levi Marion, "but a man could get used to such a view."

"Our house is more comfortable," said Rass.

Levi Marion smiled and cuffed his son's shoulder. "I believe you're right." They headed down the mountain, until Levi Marion stopped. "Son, I was setting there. And yonder's that cherry tree Uncle Will fell out of. That elk stood just shy of it." The color had returned to Levi Marion's cheeks and his eyes looked normal. "You still don't think I saw nothing, do you?"

"Papa, I don't know." The snow his father pointed to was perfectly void of animal tracks.

Downhill went considerably faster than up. Will had gone home, so they turned to his house, fifty yards downcreek from the mill. Neighboring frame houses made Will's one-story log cabin seem as antique as a blunderbuss. Thick chimney smoke coursed upward. "He's put a fresh log on," Levi Marion said. They knocked.

Will invited them into a room musty with tobacco smoke and liniment. Levi Marion wanted to get home, but Aunt Mildred, a birdlike woman with a stutter, insisted they eat. Over pound cake and coffee he told about the elk. Will cocked his head in disbelief at first, then slowly leaned toward his nephews, ever closer, a look in his eye like came when he read the Bible. "Levi Marion," he said, "you seen a vision."

"What do you mean, Uncle Will?" said Rass.

"Uncle Fate told about a Cherokee who went to the woods in the old days and starved hisself. After a while he'd see all kinds of critters, elk, buffalo, bear, and, for all I know, tigers and jayroos. Uncle Fate put it down to Indian ways. But I've always said it was more'n that. They knew forest was made for something besides giving a man furniture and fire-wood."

"Uncle Will, what does it mean?"

Will stood, hands trembling more than usual. "Maybe it's the park." He paced before the hearth, canting his head first one way, then the other. "Yes, Nephew, it's the park." He snapped his fingers. "Indians killed off the elk, or if they didn't, we finished them off. Then we marched the Indians to Oklahoma." His bushy eyebrows arched. "Now we're getting run off our own selves."

"Uncle Will, what do you mean, 'we'? Our people always was friendly with Indians, even hid them in the old days."

"Levi Marion, pay attention to your elders. Look in your Bible—old men dream, young men have visions. I'm interpreting your vision. That elk you seen was the beginning of leaving. Now you're the tail end. It's come full circle."

"P-pshaw, Will Carter," said Mildred, rising from the sofa. "You're t-touched in the head. I'll give them some blackberry jelly, then they can g-get home. V-Valerie'll be on her ear."

After the children were asleep, Levi Marion cleaned his shotgun by the firelight, rag and stick pungent with gun oil. Valerie darned socks. After hanging the weapon over the door, he sat with the Bible.

"Going to read me a story?" Valerie asked.

Levi Marion turned the pages. "First I need to find something. I'm looking for 'dreaming dreams and having visions.'"

Valerie had been a sword drill champion. "Joel," she said, looking back to her darning. "Between Hosea and Amos. I always admired them words. And it's getting cold in here, honey."

"The last of the second chapter," he said. He read to himself. When Valerie looked up, he stared at the fireplace.

"Levi Marion, are you all right?"

"Yes. I'm just studying."

"And I said it's getting cold."

He put a wild cherry split on the fire, which popped and sparked. He took up the Bible and cleared his throat. " 'It shall come to pass afterward, that I will pour out my spirit upon all flesh; and your sons and your daughters shall prophesy, your old men shall dream dreams, your young men shall see visions.' " He gazed into the fire. "Valerie, we was nearly at George Sutton's old place, and I took a spell, had to sit. Rass went on up the mountain. I set real still, prayed, and I don't know, might have gone to sleep. First thing I knowed a big bull elk bugled at me. I opened my eyes and I swear, it looked at me straight on."

"What did it do?"

"Just stood there, then nodded. I don't know why, but I leveled my shotgun. Couldn't have missed nothing that big. But then it was gone. Couldn't find as much as a bird track in the snow. No blood, no nothing. Uncle Will says I seen a vision. But I'm not a young man. What you reckon is wrong with me?"

She sat on the arm of his chair and mussed his thinning hair. "I'm as worried that you played in the snow as I am over what you think you saw."

He laid his hand, palm up, atop her leg. She squeezed his hand with both of hers. "The rest of that Scripture talks about blood and fire. Maybe you were vouchsafed a sign Jesus is coming back."

"How do you get from a bull elk to Jesus?"

"Maybe we better pray about it." She kissed him, stood, stretched to what she knew was still to her advantage, and went into the bedroom. Levi Marion shook his head and banked the fires, remembering each stick's journey to and from the woodshed. When he scooted into bed beside his wife, she held him in what he wished were everlasting arms.

BOOK 3

Fire and Hearth

April 1931–June 1933

CHAPTER 18

Sweet Savor

Rafe McPeters rattled around in an enormous shack, part log, part frame, rambling over Rough Fork Mountain toward the head of Carter Fork, far enough from everyone that he did what he pleased. It had begun as a one-room cabin where he and his young wife, Matilda, a Tennessee Sutton, had set up housekeeping after the Civil War. Following each baby he added another wing in which he swore to hole up forever, away from crying and mewling. These excrescences sprouted like fungi. Some faced north, others east; some were appended to the original cabin, others to additions. The structure resembled what a disturbed child might erect with toy blocks.

Folks had known Rafe was low-down mean since the time he blinded one of his father's hound bitches with a rusty nail. When the war broke out, Rafe enlisted with the Confederates but deserted to steal horses from one side and sell them to the other. After the war he claimed to have been a captain, a lie neither believed nor challenged.

Matilda, as unlucky a Sutton as any who ever wed, died of childbed fever after her sixth delivery, in 1872. She had passed an uncelebrated twenty-third birthday. Folks figured nobody else would have Rafe, but shortly he left in a rickety wagon pulled by a mismatched team. In a fortnight he returned with a second bride, Bess, a Moore from Thickety. Women clucked disapproval—she wasn't much more than thirteen—but visited to scrutinize this, politely put, extremely homely girl. Men privately wondered how many bags Rafe had to put over her head before he could stand to top her. She soon proved fertile.

Bess was hardier than Matilda but no luckier. After six children in eight years she hid a knife under her mattress to fend Rafe off when he tried to violate her before she'd healed. Lurching into her bedroom while she nursed their sickly two-week-old daughter, he grabbed the child and dumped her into the cradle, where she whimpered. Bess reached for the knife. Rafe enveloped her wrist with his right hand and her exposed breast with his left. He nearly broke her wrist, threw the blade, raped her, and swaggered out.

She nursed and rocked the child to sleep. "You've got to do the best you can," she said, then gently laid her in the cradle. She picked up the knife, her thighs sticky with blood and semen. She sat on the bed and laid her wrists open.

Rafe reappeared in the doorway. "Goddamn you!" he shouted, and slapped her. He got his kit bag and stitched her like she was a hunting dog sliced by a bear claw. "Try that again and I'll kill you," he sneered. She outfoxed him, dying of septicemia a week later.

Next time he brought a woman, the winter of 1880, nobody visited. This one was named Bonnie, but folks learned neither maiden name nor birthplace. For all they knew, Rafe had bought her from a white slaver. But she had pluck. After three years and as many children she refused to die barefoot and pregnant. "I'm damned if you'll ever have any more of me," she said one afternoon as he headed to the porch.

He could not have looked any more slack-jawed surprised if the dog had spoken. "What'll I do for pussy?"

"Without," she said, backing away from the door. When he started to slap her, she waved her hand. "Why don't you diddle them damned worthless girls?"

A few of her stepdaughters lay about the place like feral cats. Such a thing had crossed Rafe's mind before, but when he asked if they wanted some of what made them, they laughed. If he ordered them to his bed, they ignored him. But offering to kill them was effective with those too lazy or twisted to leave. Soon he found those girls to his liking. If one conceived, he hauled her and a load of firewood to Waynesville, and traded for an abortion.

The puniest of his fifteen children died from anything from diphtheria to neglect. Survivors turned out as mean as snakes smoking lit firecrackers, or damaged beyond hope. In the late 1920s, half a dozen slept at least part-time on the ramshackle compound, two women—one a dim-witted slattern, the other lucid or as mad as a hatter, depending on which personality dominated—and four men, who killed anything from rabid coons to, it was rumored, unwanted spouses.

Bonnie, by then sixty, had walked out of Cataloochee years before and had ended up a scullery maid at the Meat Skin Hotel in Waynesville. From the rear she could be mistaken for an outsize icebox. Her wages were barely more than room and board, but, considering, she felt as lucky as Miss Astor.

Rafe, nearer ninety than eighty, spent summer days on his porch. His rheumy eyes looked over the valley, hands scratching a fetid crotch. He remembered getting his children but not their names. In winter he visited the store on Carter Fork, where men gave him all the room by the heater he wanted, no longer from fear but from disgusting odor.

In 1931, only old Rafe and Willie still lived at the compound. Born in 1883, Rafe and Bonnie's last child had bright, beady eyes that were set close like those of the wild hogs he grew up to hunt and kill. He never darkened a schoolhouse door. He took up tobacco as much to watch the smoke as to ingest nicotine, and never ventured close enough to a church to be baptized, even during revivals, when visiting preachers urged congregants to search highways and hedges for lurking miscreants.

He tended the family's various hearths, and cut and split wood simply to relish the resulting fire. He threw firewood onto porches and into the yard instead of using their decrepit woodshed. Hunters on Carter Fork took him along on damp nights, for even when very young he could coax fire from doty wood. But when he was ten, he doused a stray hound with naphtha and lit a match to her to see what would happen. Even his family began to keep distance from him.

The summer he turned twelve, in 1895, he took to laying out of a night, something every McPeters did sooner or later. He was a tad too young to tomcat in and out of women's windows but was beginning to connect flame with desire.

He made a lair in a hemlock stand halfway down the mountain. It smelled like fuel in there and needles hit like sleet on the forest floor—canopy so thick that during a thunderstorm half an hour might pass before water found his head.

He carried flint and steel in a leather bag and rediscovered that hemlock knots made torches a man could carry for an hour. He soon prowled all over the mountain, hip pockets full of knotty limbs.

Mack Hawkins's farm occupied the last bottomland before the road snaked up to Rough Fork Gap. Mack's brand-new colicky baby, Fred, had driven Mack to the porch, where he gave up sleep in favor of sitting, watching stars, and listening to his wife tend the shrieking child.

Mack sat on the porch facing the ridgeline, nearly about to doze, when a scuttling possum startled him. A light at the ridgetop—whether lantern, foxfire, or ghost he could not tell—caught his eye. Next evening it was closer to the valley.

In a rare quiet moment he mentioned it to his wife.

"Will-o'-the-wisp," she said. "My daddy used to see such in Macon County. Jacky Lantern, some call him."

"Is he wicked?"

"No more'n any ghost—some's good, some not. Old folks say he can lead you into trouble, or get you out of a jam, depending."

"Could he set a man's barn on fire?"

She scratched her chin. "I doubt it."

For a night or two the light appeared around nine and moved till dawn, ever closer to Mack's place. Wednesday night he sat on the porch with a lapful of double-barreled twelve-gauge.

At close range this was no foxfire, which he had seen, green and stationary—nor swamp gas, which he had not, for Cataloochee had no bogs. The yellow-orange light hovered head height and swung like its holder searched for objects on either side of a zigzag line. It loomed toward his outbuildings.

Mack inched toward the barn, a two-bay affair open on both ends. On the back side a front-lit man-size figure passed into an empty stall. The horse and mule whinnied nervously, the cow lowed.

Mack eased inside, pulled one hammer back, and leveled the shotgun. "Don't do nothing stupid or I'll blow your brains out."

Willie McPeters silently held up the torch.

"You're a McPeters." Mack backed one step out of the stall. "The one set fire to that dog. Get hell out of my barn before you burn it down." The shotgun stared into Willie's eyes.

He nodded and followed Mack outside, porcine face drawn into a smirk.

For a man starved for sleep, Mack kept the gun steady. "I never want you here without it's daylight and you got business." He cocked the other hammer.

McPeters started toward the woods.

"Not so fast, damn you. Head up the road. I'll make sure you get home safe or fill you full of holes, one. Get."

Rafe, his own weapon in his lap, was sitting on the porch when Mack stomped into the yard behind Willie. He shouted the dogs quiet. "Who's that?"

"Mack Hawkins, Captain McPeters. I made sure your boy come back home instead of burning my barn down. I'd take it kindly if you'd have a talk with him about other people's property."

Rafe cocked his pistol, a Civil War relic with a hefty caliber. "I don't recall this boy being any of your goddamn interest."

"If I find him in my barn again with another burning stick, I'll blow his head off."

Rafe aimed the pistol. "Get off my land or you'll not be able to blow your whore-mongering nose, mister."

By then Willie stood beside his father, and torchlight jumped eerily on the porch. Mack lowered his shotgun and tipped his hat brim. "Have a good evening," he said mildly, backed into the darkness, and headed back down the mountain. The rest of the summer Mack saw light occasionally but never on his property, and gave thanks for soaking dog-day rains.

Twenty-one years later a revenue man named Grover Cleveland Moody nosed around for a day, but was never seen again. Willie McPeters shortly thereafter bought both a fine Marlin rifle—model 94, chambered .44–40, perfect for hog and bear—and fancy boots, with cash money. Anyone who visited the McPeters place would have seen Moody's silver badge pinned to a dried squirrel hide in Willie's end of the house.

When Cataloochans began leaving, Willie McPeters, by then a man in his mid-forties who had ceased to speak to anyone but himself, and then only sparingly, rummaged their abandoned houses, sometimes finding a comb or plow point. Mostly he uncovered broken glass, rusty wire, or splintered furniture. Once, inexplicably, he discovered, hanging like a huge bat smack in the middle of Bus Bennett's smokehouse, a single ham.

Early in 1931 Willie visited the old Brooks barn, a half mile south of the McPeters compound, and heard something knock over a fair-size metal container. He readied the Marlin. Entering the barn, he immediately shot an animal streaking out the other side. The half-wild barn cat was in mid-leap when the bullet hit its left haunch and spun it like a screaming pinwheel. Torn in two, it glared at McPeters with appreciable malevolence. He stomped its head and walked beside the barn to take a piss.

His penis became a fire hose knocking hay bits and dried manure in various directions. It might have been a pen scribbling filthy words in the dirt had he known how to spell. He shook it dry, then kept at it and closed his eyes. When he opened them, he focused on a shed composed only of locust posts, roof, and rail, in which was stacked a wealth of stove wood. He shoved himself back into his pants and buttoned up.

The Brooks twins, Donald and Ronald, had farmed this place since the early 1880s, when they came from Buncombe County and bought the Elbert Carter place. Bachelors, they had not particularly cared about the inside of the house, but everything outside had had to be just so. Maple cut half a foot long by Donald had been stacked with precision the length of the woodshed under a four-foot-high rail by Ronald. The base layer was all splits, bark-side down, over which rounds and splits had been laid to create a four-foot wall of firewood. Two full cords, ripe for the plucking.

McPeters looked the building over. While impressed with the quantity of firewood, if not its precise arrangement and uniformity of species, he especially grinned at the contents of a spidery white snuff glass wedged into a roof brace—in which a piece of oilcloth swaddled a dozen white-tipped lucifer matches.

He walked home for mule and wagon, then returned to watch three crows argue with a considerable number of flies and yellow jackets over the dead cat. He destroyed the Brooks brothers' orderly labor, throwing wood haphazardly into the wagon bed. In an hour his loaded wagon swayed in the middle, the outside rear wheel appeared ready to leave its axle, and any movement made the wagon shed sticks like long ashes off cigarettes.

The can in the barn held half a gallon of coal oil. He squiggled it down each post and sloshed it ceiling-ward. He scratched a match on a dry section and lit a wet. He loved the whoosh of gasoline but was also fond of kerosene's more orderly ignition, like a speedy worm traversing the structure.

He leaned against the wagon side, scattering more firewood. He paid the uneasy mule no attention, preferring to watch an orgy of energy destroy the woodshed. It popped and cracked, orange flames ascending, a sweet savor tickling his nose, ash falling all around. A bystanding boxwood's leaves hissed but did not fall.

The mule jerked into the traces. McPeters cursed and fell, watching the wagon clatter to the road's edge. He turned to see the little building's quick death, flame to ember to ash, yellow to red to white.

McPeters stretched and drooled like a horny savage. Thirty feet away sat a corncrib, sanctuary for rats, empty save half a dozen dry cobs and a floor full of shucks. A well-tossed match provided a few minutes' smoke and excitement.

No curious passersby showed. Rubbing his swollen crotch, he headed with another match to the chicken house, a structure twelve feet wide and six feet deep, southern door and eastern windows covered in rusty wire.

The Brookses had particularly hated mites. Besides using Sears nest eggs made of insecticide and filler, they'd collected used motor oil to mop onto floor and roosts. The brothers had lined the nest boxes with excelsior. Inside McPeters knelt, breathing the rich odor of chicken manure and motor oil, to place this perfect tinder in each corner. A match lit in succession cigarette and nests, a rite performed as seriously as a celebrant ever swung thurible.

He barely lit the last before the building erupted and boiled black smoke to the high heavens. Running outside, he threw his cigarette down, unbuttoned his pants, and masturbated to the fire's increasingly insistent crackling rhythm. Seed spilled on the ground as the roof fell in. Panting, he watched ashes drift down and wiped himself with his shirt-tail.

Someone was bound to have noticed dark smoke. He carefully rewrapped his nine remaining matches and laid them in his shirt pocket. Of no mind to douse ashes, after gathering scattered firewood, he left, resembling an itinerant peddler en route to a blacksmith, to trade fuel for wheel repair. Only wet ground and no wind that evening kept a woods fire from catching.

He unceremoniously dumped stove wood beside the kitchen addition, put up and fed the mule, and walked to what the family regarded as the front porch. His father could not have helped but see and smell his son's afternoon smoke, but Rafe sat like a wooden Indian as a silent Willie passed beside him, headed to an unlit monkish candle beside his rancid bed.

CHAPTER 19

Her Husband's Absence

"Blue and yellow, Hiram dear?" Aunt Mary cocked her head at two remnants of cotton fabric. "I always thought they blended well." She laid them on the kitchen table. "Don't you think they'll make a quilt as pretty as can be?"

Blue goods slightly duskier than Carolina skies made her think of heaven, and yellow with no hint of orange reminded her of buttercups. She measured, finger to shoulder—six yards and a fraction of blue, barely five yards of yellow, but plenty for a quilt top. She cut a yard from each and put the large pieces aside. Stopping frequently to rub arthritic knuckles, she cut the yellow and blue pieces into inch-and-a-half squares. After laying out a checkerboard pattern, Mary polished her eyeglasses on her apron.

"My mother quilted circles around us girls, but she taught us good. I can see her, by the fire, piecing squares, humming hymns. I reckon she's in that sweet by and by she loved to sing about.

"Law, I used to quilt intricate stuff, double wedding ring, log cabin, fence rail, you name the pattern, remember? Piece, baste, quilt, bind, tedious work. Don't do that no more. Older I get, the better simple looks. Don't you think so, sweetheart?" She put her spectacles back on. "That's better. Helps when a gal can see."

She didn't remember exactly when she had begun talking to her husband's absence. Certainly long before this cool April morning. It had been about fifty years ago, after he'd branched from farm work into the teamster business. When he'd hauled produce or timber, she had found herself, a new bride, doubly alone—bereft of husband, marooned at home with his mother, recluse from everyone. Talking to Hiram, whether present or not, became as important to her as prayer. When he died, in 1926, she mourned in silence. She couldn't have said why—she was a Christian woman—but she felt him tug her toward death, like Cherokee people said their newly departed did, and it frightened her enough to stop. As her fear subsided, she began to talk to him again. It took about a year.

When Thomas's boots hit the back porch, Mary dismissed Hiram with a discreet wave of her left hand. As the screen door opened, her son saw her search for thread with her right.

"Who you yapping at, Mama?" Thomas darkened the door frame, turning his hat in his meaty hands.

"What do you mean, Son?"

"Looked like you was talking to somebody. We got any buttermilk?"

"In the springhouse, where it always is. And every now and again I talk to myself when it's lonesome."

He lurched from the door and put his hat on. "Long as you don't answer yourself, that's fine." Chuckling, he headed outside.

She smiled. "Hiram, stay here. We'll lay these things out just so." The hall clock Hiram had made for her birthday chimed ten, as resonant as the sound of a woodpecker working a hollow tree.

Nell Hawkins was fed up with winter, children, and her husband's job. Lately, between stringing phone lines—the fire lookouts and their house needed to communicate quickly—and chasing firebugs, one of whom certainly was Willie McPeters, Jim was gone dawn to dusk on good days but sometimes stayed half a week in the woods like an old wandering bear. In Nell's mind such time slowed far enough to touch eternity's corners. Little Elizabeth was about to turn two, thank goodness, and Mack was getting old enough to help, but they were still constantly needful. She thought in stark terms: *I am torn between my loneliness and their dependence.*

The winter had not been preternaturally cold, but she felt a constant draft suck through the house like a low-flying ghost. Kitchen and front room fires made all the heat Nell cared to maintain. When Jim left, she and the children slept in front of the living room fireplace. When Jim returned, he tended a bedroom fire, warming their room enough for lovemaking, a pleasure Nell needed like oxygen but unceasingly prayed would bring forth no issue save monthlies.

Mack had been an engaging and happy baby, but after he had started walking, Nell knew she didn't care to keep up with another. She douched sometimes with pennyroyal tea, other times with water mixed with either vinegar or Lysol, and used preparations for "women's regularity"—and had managed to avoid getting caught for three years. Morning sickness overtook her, however, in the spring of 1929, so she steeled herself for another cycle of reversed nights and days, bound to breast and bottle. *One more, but no more, as God is my promise.*

But on the cusp of spring in 1931 Nell fancied herself victim of a long, troubled season. *I don't know how to put it—neglected, that's how I feel, alone in this valley that Jim thinks is so pretty but in which no modern person should ever be expected to live,* she thought one morning.

If I hear 'Mommy, I need . . . ' anymore, I'll scream. They're wonderful little people, but I need adult company. I need something—a knight in armor? A vision of Jesus? Or just Jim home at night?

Mack slammed the back door. "Mama, where's the saw at?"

Nell stamped her foot. "That does it, Henry Mack. You're talking like them."

"Like who, Mama?"

"Oh, never mind. Just don't end your sentences with prepositions."

"What's a preppy-sitting?"

"Never mind that, either. Young man, we're getting out for a while."

"Why, Mama?"

"Because, that's why. Keep your jacket on. Mama's going to fix fires and dress your sister. We're going visiting."

"What's that?"

"It's when you go see somebody else. Talking to an adult makes you remember there's something besides . . ." She swept the room with her right hand. "It reminds you to be civilized."

"What's sivel-eye-ged?"

"What we used to be, far away and long ago. Come along, Master Hawkins."

Fires banked, they found their way down the road.

"Where are we going, Mama?" asked Little Elizabeth.

"To the store," Nell said. "Then to visit Aunt Mary Carter."

"I love Aunt Mary," said Mack.

"That's sweet. Will you tell her that?"

"Sure, if I can. She talks a lot."

Nell playfully swatted at Mack's head. "Keep that to yourself, young man."

Nelse Howell kept an unvarying routine. Open the store at seven. Build a fire, perk coffee, sweep. Extract change from a cigar box everyone in the valley knew was hidden behind the canned sardines, and feed it to the till. Pour, sit, set the steaming cup on a table, lean against the wall, nap. When Nell and her children stepped on the squeaky stoop at nine-fifteen, Nelse started awake and stood, tying an apron around his waist. There was room for a penny postcard between necktie end and apron top. He smiled at his visitors. "A pretty family's a sight for sore eyes."

"We weren't so pretty an hour ago," said Nell. "We needed some fresh air."

"Welcome, child. Sweetening for the tykes? It's on the house."

Mack and Little Elizabeth looked hopeful. "Please, Mommy?"

"If you have good manners."

Mack squared his shoulders. "Please, Mr. Nelse, may I?"

"Certainly, my boy." He handed Mack a peppermint stick. "How about your pretty sister and mother?"

Mack looked at Nell, who nodded. "Please, and thank you," said the boy.

"We're off to see Aunt Mary," said Nell. "What might she like?"

Nelse produced a box of chocolate-covered cherries. "She's uncommon fond of these."

"How much are they?"

"Pound box is fifty cents. Little one's a nickel. It's got four in it."

"We'll take that, please." She fished in her purse for a coin. "Here's a dime."

Nelse winked at the boy. "Let's see, now. An old man has to be careful with his money." He elaborately totted up the sale on a paper bag with a stub of a pencil, making a score of exasperated faces that put Mack and Little Elizabeth into a fit of giggles, then worried every piece of money in the drawer like Scrooge himself before handing Nell a nickel. "There," he said. "Hope I done that right." They left, cherries in a brown paper bag, mother and children eating peppermint sticks. Nell held hers in her left hand and daintily licked it. Little Elizabeth emulated her mother, but Mack sucked his like a felon having a last cigarette before facing a firing squad.

Times past, Nell would have met folks walking to the store, or might have stopped to pass time with women preparing a patch of early greens, but this morning she saw little evidence of human presence. The church door was shut. *Poison oak in the churchyard is, if not a bad omen, at least a sign.* The road between church and schoolhouse was likewise deserted—or she hoped so, after stopping to see whether a shadowy movement behind a tree was real or imagined. Jim never mentioned McPeters to her, but she had heard talk about him, and for a very brief moment felt vulnerable and alone in the middle of the road. The feeling soon passed.

The schoolhouse chimney suddenly poured white smoke, a sign the teacher had laid a fresh stick of wood in the cast-iron heater. Nell strained for the sound of lessons, but the breeze fought against hearing.

As the road bent gently right, they crossed the creek on upended rocks and lifted the lid from the spring Old Jimmie Carter had discovered nearly a century before. His son Levi had enclosed it in a stone reservoir for the community to share. Nell dipped a handkerchief and wiped her son's mouth, then took a small metal cup from her handbag, gave Mack a drink, then had one herself. *One thing I'll say, this water is cold and sweet. And look at the size of that crayfish. Jim says they won't live in bad water.* Back on the road, they hugged themselves against the cold, and soon made the edge of Thomas and Manson's fields. *You can sure tell where the Carter place begins.* She shook her head. *No, not really theirs— it belongs to the government. Like where I live. It's not* my house, *just where I stay with Jim and the children, a place that will never be* mine *but only something to keep weather off our heads until I figure how to return to civilization.*

Mack's mittened hand knocked on Aunt Mary's front door. "Try again, honey," Nell encouraged. Mary finally appeared at the door, all smiles. "Lord have mercy, children, let me see you. Growing up, little Mack, and *look* at this little girl! Nell, how are you?"

"I'm fine, Aunt Mary."

"Come out of the cold. It's mighty fine to see you this morning."

When they came into the front room, Mary fussed over the children. "I baked tea cakes this morning," she said, "didn't even know why. Mack, Elizabeth, you like tea cakes, don't you?"

"Yes, ma'am," they said. Nell handed Mary the paper bag.

"What's this, Nell?"

"Just a little something."

Mary peeked inside. "Lord have mercy. I'd not let you do this except I love these things." She set the bag on the table. "I believe you two have already had some candy."

Nell knelt to clean Little Elizabeth's mouth. "Mr. Nelse gave them some, Aunt Mary. I thought I'd wiped it all away."

"Nell, I believe it's cold enough to make our own peppermints. You know how, don't you?"

"No, ma'am, we always bought it."

"Then we are going to have fun this day. My boys couldn't care less about learning to make butter mints, but this morning you'll be the daughter I never had a chance to show how."

In the pantry she found sugar, food coloring, and a vial of peppermint oil. "You young'uns sit at the table and be good. Nell, fetch a print of butter from the springhouse," she said, and laid rich pine in the firebox. She carried two pots to the back porch, dipped a measuring cup of water from the cedar bucket into one, and filled the other. Bringing the first back to the kitchen, she set it on the stove and added a stick of dry locust to the fire. Nell came inside. "Where do you want the butter, Aunt Mary?"

"In that saucer. Then measure out two cups of sugar. When the water boils, stir it in." She kept a stone slab by the kitchen window so it would stay cold. "This is the secret. Candy won't harden right if you drop it on anything else." She cut some butter with which to grease the slab.

"Is it marble?"

"The best. Pure white with them little bitty green streaks."

"Where did you get it?"

"Law, Nell, my Hiram used to leave Catalooch with a wagonload of firewood or cabbages or apples, depending on the season—some of it was ours and some of it he hauled for other people. He'd go as far as South Carolina, delivering what he got paid to carry, and trading our stuff on the way there and back. He'd be gone sometimes two or three weeks at a time.

"One day he left with a load of locust fence posts heading to South Carolina, I think around Honea Path. Found a man needed fence but didn't have cash money. Hiram traded him fence posts for his poor wife's marble slab, sewing machine tools, and cream separator. Ain't that just like a man, trade off everything of his wife's, but never shotgun or fish pole? Oh, look, it's boiling. Stir in the sugar with this wooden spoon."

"Seems like a lot," Nell said.

"Two of sugar to one of water, no more or less. See them crystals forming inside the pot? If they fall into the candy they'll make it grainy." She wiped the inside of the pot with a damp rag. "Keep stirring. I'll wipe it out every now and then. In a minute we'll give it some butter. Mack, want to help?"

"Yes, ma'am!"

"Then cut this butter into little chunks with that table knife, please sir. I'll get a little picture book for your sister to look at in the front room."

Mary laid a stick of locust in the firebox and threw the butter into the pot when the mixture looked right. "Now that it's melted, quit stirring. Just cook until it's ready."

"How do you know when?"

"That's what our pan of cold water outside's for. You need to let the candy come to a hard ball. Drop a piece into cold water. If it balls up so you can't pinch it flat without straining, it's ready. Grease the scissors with butter."

"Where did you learn this, Aunt Mary?"

"From my mama, rest her soul. She learnt it from hers, I reckon. Like she used to say, cooking is common sense. You don't start out with butter and eggs and expect bean soup, now do you?"

Nell laughed. "I guess not, Aunt Mary." She looked into the front room, where little Elizabeth slept, her arms curled around her book. "Little angel," she said.

Aunt Mary hadn't missed a beat.

"My mama, her name was Louise, taught me to make cornbread. I was just little, I don't know how old. Anyhow, she said *some* folks put *sugar* in cornbread. She made a face, like that was plumb outrageous. 'Now, Louise'—she used to talk about herself like she wasn't even in the room—'wouldn't no more put sugar in cornbread than she'd lay a cupful of rock salt into whipping cream. Sugar goes in *cake,* not bread.' Never forgot that."

When it balled, they laid the wad of candy on the slab. "Now for color and flavor," Mary said. "Just a drop or two of mint oil will go all the way through it. And I like mints to be green." She added four drops of McCormick's food coloring. "When it cools a little, then's the fun part."

They greased their hands, separated the candy into three portions— one small for Mack—and pulled it until it glistened. "It'll give you muscles, that's for sure." They pulled about fifteen minutes. Mack worried his until he sat beside the table. "Mommy, I'm tired."

"That's fine, Son. Just rest." Nell melded Mack's glob with hers.

"This looks creamy now, so get the scissors," said Aunt Mary.

They cut candy strips into pieces the size of the first joint of Mary's index finger, and dropped them onto the slab.

"Aunt Mary, can I have some?" asked Mack.

"You don't want to burn that sweet little mouth. It'll be a few minutes yet."

They began to put the kitchen back together. "Not long after Hiram got this marble," Mary said, "his mother—Granny Lib we called her— might go for two months without saying a single thing. Anyway. I forgot what I was going to say—oh, yes, one Christmas, must have been 1883, I was going to make butter mints. I didn't have no oil of peppermint, but figured to use dried mint—we still grow spearmint by the springhouse. Well, I pulled what I thought was dried mint out of a pantry jar. I didn't smell it, just threw it in and made the candy. I gave one to Granny Lib, and she gummed it a minute, spit it into her lap, and said 'This tastes like hog manure.' I'd put parsley in the candy! We had a big laugh over that. Here, Mack, it's ready. They're really chewy, so be careful. That candy pulls out a tooth, your mama won't let you come see me again."

Mack, mouthing a wad of candy, asked Nell something. "Son, when you talk with your mouth full, you sound like you don't have good sense. Do you need to go out back?"

Mack nodded. His mother put his coat on him, and Mary opened the door and shooed Mack outside. "Nell, take these mints home with you. How's Jim, by the way? I see him ride up the road but he doesn't stop often enough to suit me."

"He's busy, Aunt Mary. Says he has to string all that telephone line from down here to the Sterling fire lookout before the trees put out." She sighed. "Don't know what good it is. We can only use it in an emergency."

Mack came back inside. "Son, be a good boy. Go in the front room and tend to your sister, please."

Nell sighed as Mack left the room. "Aunt Mary, may I ask you something?"

"Of course you can."

"Didn't it drive you out of your mind having your husband gone so much?"

Mary cut her eyes to Nell. "That's been fifty years, so it's hard to remember. But yes. You keep busy. If work fills your day, it's easier." She went to the pantry for two pint mason jars. "Also—and I ain't ever told nobody this—you talk to him."

"You mean when he's home."

Mary filled the jars with mints. "Well, then, too, but you talk to him when he's gone, like he's there with you. It helps." She looked at Nell. "I take it you're not as happy as you ought to be. Or at least not as happy as you thought you'd be."

"Well, Jim's gone so much. Some days I don't see him at all. And I don't—except for the children—have that much to do around the house."

Mary pulled a chair beside Nell. "Child, it might ruffle your feathers, but I'm going to be blunt. You're a town girl. There ain't no sidewalks here for you to walk on, to the store or the moving pictures or the library. There's just Cataloochee, church, and work." She stared into Nell's eyes. "I'd bet your mother didn't teach you nothing about a garden, did she?"

Nell shook her head.

"Canning food?"

"No, ma'am."

"Sewing?"

"I embroider a little."

She took Nell's free hand. "I got an idea. Jim makes a garden, right?"

Nell nodded.

"But he tends to it?"

"Yes'm."

"Know which end of a hoe is the business end?"

She nodded.

"Know jimsonweed from a corn plant?"

Nell bit her lower lip. "I never had to learn."

"Don't cry, dear. Tell you what. Come every week this spring. I'll learn you about a garden."

Nell nodded. "Thank you, Aunt Mary."

"Say no more about it. It'll give me something to do besides sit here and quilt. We women got to stick together, don't we?"

Nell and her brood headed homeward, Mack and Little Elizabeth skipping, Nell thinking, *I'll help Aunt Mary garden, but I still have to get out of here. That's creepy to talk to somebody who's not there. How in the world can I convince Jim to leave?*

CHAPTER 20

My Heart's True Love

The maple trunk, lined with red cedar, held bedclothes, lacework, mementos. Some quilts had been pieced by Hiram's paternal grandmother, whose first name had become a matter of dispute. Some remembered Elsie, others Elsa, still others Elspeth. In Aunt Mary's view, the last was preposterous—a woman not rich enough to possess a middle name would never have been saddled with such as that.

Elsie had been a daughter of a tribe of Browns, whites who'd intermarried with Cherokees, which explained her son Levi's and grandson Hiram's cheekbones. Anyone who knew Elsie's family agreed she had "married up" when she'd latched on to Old Jimmie, patriarch of the Cataloochee Carters.

The Carters claimed English ancestry, but Aunt Mary, Howell on her father's side, Davis on the distaff, knew Scotch Irish when she saw it. She married Hiram Carter anyway, despite—or perhaps because of—his quick temper and ability to squeeze the buffalo off a nickel.

Elsie's son Levi had built the trunk before the Civil War, and her

grandson Hiram had lined it the year he'd married Mary. A simple box
with a beveled top, as deep as a coffin and half as long. Two bradded
leather straps had long since dry-rotted from its ends. The top had been
smoothed first by Levi's plane, then, after it was hauled upstairs, by children, rainbound indoors, sitting on the trunk and pretending to drive a
stagecoach full of treasure.

News, after being read and discussed, usually papered bedroom walls,
but sections saved in the trunk announced such events as the archduke's
assassination and the World Series scandal. The trunk also held heir-
looms—letters from long dead family, Hiram's seventh-grade certificate,
a china cup Mary had scrimped to buy for her first, stillborn, child.

Aunt Mary had asked Manson and Thomas to carry the trunk down
to the hall last week, with a mind to clean it out or at least see what lay
therein. A pack rat, Mary for years had had the luxury of a large room in
which odd stuff could be stowed. She was, near the beginning of her
eighth decade, taking inventory. Not that she wanted to get rid of anything, but she saw the writing on the wall—the park would prevail, despite everything. Besides, Hiram said they ought to move.

He visited often these days, which both delighted and confused her.
She loved seeing him, but her faith said no one had risen from the dead
except Lazarus for a while, and Jesus for all time. She believed at the last
day Christ would call the quick and the dead—everyone, not a solitary
Haywood County Carter. But staring faith in the eye was Hiram's presence, as solid to her as a chinquapin.

Perhaps he was preparing her to step into the next life, for which she
was ready. On the other hand, maybe she was as crazy as a bedbug. She
could not say which. But if keeping her wits meant Hiram would return
to wherever he had been, she didn't want to get better.

She had not told her sons, who were solidly at home in this world of
cantaloupes, crows, and cow manure. If they ever prayed outside of
church or table grace, it was a farmer's simple plea for rain—or for it to
stop. They would be quite happy for Hiram to stay in his grave.

She pulled two kitchen chairs in front of the trunk. Sitting in one, its
familiar creak merging with the sound of the hall clock, she checked the
time: one-ten. Almost three hours before beginning supper.

The topmost item was a log cabin quilt Elsie Brown Carter had pieced. Mary, thinking to ease Hiram's departure, had brought it down to cover him when he lay dying. *So five years ago was the last time this trunk was opened,* she thought, as she unfolded the bedcover on the floor. Next came a red and white crazy quilt inherited from Hiram's mother, one edge mouse-gnawed years ago. Then a layer of newspaper, some full sections, others just a couple of pages. Between two papers—one declaring that an electoral commission had favored Hayes over Tilden, the other trumpeting McKinley being shot by a foreigner with an owlhead pistol—lay a red scarf.

She took a sharp breath. "Oh, would you look at that?"

"Mary Belle, you wore that when first we met."

She smiled at her husband in the other chair. "Oh, do you remember that day?"

"Tell it again."

"Mama'd started cleaning Cove Creek church Wednesdays before prayer meeting, right after Papa died, in 1879. Mama swept and dusted. They didn't pay her, but she took satisfaction from it and I guess it kept her mind off her grief. Summers, and when school was out, I went with her. Church wasn't big, we cleaned it top to bottom in an afternoon. Soon as I spied you starting up the mountain in that wagon, your coal-black eyes shining, I can't describe the feeling inside me—but then and there I meant to have you.

"Didn't know how old you were, but I was sixteen going on twenty-five and didn't care. A body could set a clock by you. Every Wednesday you drove by at three. 'Well,' I said to myself, 'I'm going to meet that pretty man,' so I brought *this very* red scarf, and snuck away from Mama, and wore it just so." She folded it into a triangle and tied it under her chin.

Hiram grinned. "Redbird in the sun."

"When you stopped, my heart liked to jumped clean up in my throat, because you was older than my married brothers, and I was scared you'd think me nothing but a silly girl. You asked if your mules might drink, and I said there was water enough in the creek. You laughed like that was the funniest thing. Asked my name, you did, and repeated 'Mary Amelia

Howell' seven times, like a poem. Looked me up and down, like your eyes were licking stripes off a stick of barber-pole candy.

"Well, I was scared, because I didn't think Mama would let an older man come courting. I didn't know a thing about you, so I started asking questions."

He laughed. "The green wood smiled."

"I said you better go before Mama catches us. Talk about slap full of contraries—I didn't want you ever to leave, but didn't want you to stay, either. I thought you'd never tell them mules to get up.

"I skipped back to the church, where Mama was trying to look busy, but I caught her wiping her cheek with the back of her hand. I asked what was the matter, and she said, 'You know good and well what,' and I played dumb, but she wheeled and let me have it. 'What do you mean talking to that old man?' kind of spitting out those last words. I told her you was Levi Carter's son. A *Cataloochee* Carter.

"Sir, her face looked same as if I'd said the moon was purple. I'll never forget what she said: 'Well, some Carters are all right, but some's pretty bad likker sots.' I vowed you weren't that kind. Then she cried, and I put my arm around her, and she said I wouldn't understand till I had a girl of my own. It was days before she said I could see you. Never was so nervous in my life."

Hiram nodded. "My heart's true love."

"She sat me down. 'You still want to see that Hiram Carter?' I bit my lip and gave a little nod. 'Yes, ma'am,' I said. 'Will you promise one thing?' she asked. I said, 'Yes.' 'Always remember your mother.' Well, I gave a little laugh. 'How could I forget my own dear mother?' I said. 'Listen, child,' she said, 'your mother is with you, unto death and past, so if this man doesn't suit you, stay with me—if you marry and he no longer takes care of you, come back. I am your constant friend.' We hugged and had a good cry. Then I was about to bust to tell you."

"Climbed we the hill together."

"That we did."

. . .

Manson, sharpening his hoe, turned toward the noise of the preacher's Model A. Reverend Will Smith liked to come to Cataloochee before a Sunday service and visit. Years ago he'd arrive Wednesdays, but lately so few parishioners were left he drove in Saturdays. Manson leaned the hoe against the fence and wiped his forehead.

"Preacher, good to see you," he said as they shook hands. "Mama'll be proud you're here. Thomas's checking livestock at Levi Marion's old place."

"Yes, I visited on the way up. I hope you're doing as well as your brother. By the way, he said your mother's not as . . . good as she has been."

"Her wits is woolgathering, Preacher. She talks to herself, but her kind's not normal. I mean, heck, I do it all the time myself. It's just that . . ."

"What, son?"

He made sure no one was within earshot. "She acts for the world like she's talking to *somebody*. And, don't let on I said it, but it's Papa. I've heard her. Gives me the willies."

"Is she otherwise all right?"

"I reckon. She doesn't complain any more than the rest of us."

"How old is she?"

"Let's see, this is 1931, so she'll be seventy come October."

"I'm no physician, but hardening of the arteries can cut off blood to your brain. Have you asked Dr. Bennett?"

"Me and Thomas has mentioned it, but we haven't done anything."

"I'd suggest that, and soon. Is she inside?"

"Sure, Preacher. She'd love to see you."

When the porch boards creaked, Manson stopped and put up his hand like he was riding point. "Look, Preacher, she's pulled him up a chair," he whispered.

Through the screen door they saw Mary, talking softly to some unseen presence, tuck a red scarf into a newspaper. She looked straight at the spot Hiram's face would have occupied had he sat there. She smiled, spoke, and pulled out a paper with the headline: FLOOD KILLS MANY IN WNC. Manson coughed and began to open the screen door.

Startled, her face ran from tender smile through confusion to hospitality in about two seconds. She finally said, "Law, me, it's Reverend Smith!" in a perfectly normal tone. "I was about to tell," she said, and stopped to scratch the side of her nose, "the Cataloochee news the very day this paper came out. I'll never forget it—the day Henry Sutton's mule turned up dead. But it'll keep. It's mighty fine to see you, Preacher. I'll fix you a glass of milk and a piece of cake."

"Who were you about to tell, Mama?"

She looked at the empty chair. "Why, did I say 'tell'? I meant 'remember.' Don't pay no attention to a foolish old woman."

"Mama, who's that other chair for?"

"Nobody, silly. It's in case I want to keep these things off the floor."

Smith put his hand on Aunt Mary's shoulder. "Cake and milk sounds just right."

"You men go in the front room and I'll rustle it up." When they left, she put her hand out to Hiram, gone like a ghost. But the chair seat felt as warm as a husband's love.

Dr. Lucius Bennett, second son of Old Man Bennett and brother to Old Man Bennett junior, doctored like Will Smith preached—kept an office in Waynesville, but every other week set up shop in a different precinct Thursdays and Fridays, prescribing, setting bones, suturing elbows.

He seemed not to care whether he was paid, as long as his appetite was satisfied. Folks gave him money if they had it, chickens or butter when they did not. He was welcome at any table in the county—and gained a considerable belly therefrom.

Bennett came to Cataloochee on Thursday, June 6, to set up a makeshift office at Aunt Mary's. Manson pulled him aside before dinner and outlined his concerns about his mother, emphasizing Preacher Smith's suggestion.

"What do you think, Doc?"

"You know, Manson, I heard Will Smith preach once, and wasn't impressed. But from what you say, he might be a better doctor than preacher. Hardening of the arteries is a big umbrella, but it's been known to make old people daffy. See, arteries begin pliable and soft, but when they ossify, whatever organ they supply is shortchanged."

"What's that word, Doc?"

"What word—oh, 'ossify,' it means 'harden.' Sometimes blood vessels age to a texture like cartilage. When that happens, especially in the carotids—they're here in your neck—that restricts oxygen to the brain. That can make you forgetful, or take to wandering." He rolled down his sleeves. "Of course, it could be something else. I'll look at her, if she'll let me, and we'll see."

"Then you don't think she's losing her mind?"

"I didn't say that, Manson, but don't worry—if she isn't about to set the house on fire or walk up the middle of the creek, we've time to figure this out."

Dinner with the family was a feast featuring bear roast and rhubarb and strawberry pie. No one showed up after dinner with a medical complaint, so the doctor sat on the porch until Aunt Mary finished the dishes and came out, fanning herself with her apron.

They rocked, watching crows follow the ridge. Finally Bennett broke the silence.

"Mary, why don't you let me examine you? It stays this quiet, I might lose my touch."

She stopped rocking and looked at him sideways. "You want to examine somebody, try Jim Hawkins's wife, Nell."

"What's wrong with her?"

"You tell me. Got a handsome husband and two pretty young'uns. Lives for free in a big house in the prettiest place in the world. Yet she's broody as an old hen."

"I generally need permission before I check people's health."

"I saw you talking to Manson. Did he give you my permission?"

"Oh, Mary, we were just talking. You know, you get to a certain age, you ought to have your blood pressure taken often enough to get a jump on potential problems."

"Have my sons told you the old woman's losing her mind?"

"Haven't said a thing. I just like you, and don't want to do without your good cooking."

"Well, long as I don't have to take clothes off in front of God and everybody, it's all right."

"Good. Let's read your blood pressure." After a thorough questioning, he slid his instruments into the bag. "Do you take any aspirin, patent medicine, whatever?"

She shook her head. "Once in a blue moon I'll get a headache and reach for an aspirin. I don't too often—a body can get addicted to such. Never have gone in for Dr. Grove's tonic or any of that for the same reason. But I do have a confession."

"What's that, Mary?"

"Sometimes I sup a dram of whiskey."

"There's nothing wrong with that, unless 'sometimes' means every hour or two."

"It don't."

"Then you're in pretty good health for your age—going on seventy, did you say?"

"You must have got that from Manson."

"Sorry, Mary. I won't spread it around."

"Law, I don't care if folks know my age. I'm just glad to be here, most days, and for the most part enjoy myself. I've known people this old who were downright miserable. I'd hate that. Well, Dr. Bennett, are you through with me?"

"Yes, ma'am. Thank you for your time and good dinner."

"You're very welcome. I'll see you in a little while." She stood. "I've got work to do."

"Guess I'll wait for the hordes of sick and infirm."

"Hmp. Ain't any hordes left, Dr. Bennett. Ain't far from looking like the county home around here." She cleared a column of ants with her finger.

"You plan on staying?"

She turned to look at him. "I used to think as long as my family's buried on yonder green hillside I'd stay. A body was to leave, Lord knows what the government might do with the cemetery. But anymore I'm tired of fighting the park. I don't know. I'm going to trust God for an answer."

"That's always best."

As she went inside, the clock struck two. The rosebuds Hiram had carved for the clock's front panel still looked to her like sweet peas. Their spruce had mellowed into a color altogether blonder than the reds and browns of cherry and walnut. She thought to ask Hiram if she needed to put some kind of oil on them, and while she was at it, if he'd ever found out for sure his grandmother's first name.

CHAPTER 21

The Sweat of Illness

Maude and Silas clopped down the road, her rider straight in the saddle, watching for signs of life. He had journeyed from his house to the post office hundreds of times, paying little attention to his surroundings, but lately every little change shouted at him—the creak of a gate opening into an empty field, a pile of feathers where a hawk had devoured a jaybird, a fence strand broken by a deadfall limb.

Years ago he could count on stopping a dozen times along the two or three miles to chat with neighbors about anything from the weather (usually too hot, cold, wet, or dry) to the world situation (always dire). A round trip might take three hours. Sometimes he rode in rain so he wouldn't have to be sociable. Now, however, he could count on seeing people only at Mary Carter's place, unless you counted the shadowy presence of Willie McPeters. *How long will it be before I'm the only sane soul left this side of Cataloochee Mountain?*

He dismounted in the churchyard and lit his pipe. "Maude, remember when we found Harrogate, the summer of 1916. Wonder where he is. Likely carousing in some dirty old city. Don't mind saying, I miss the boy." He gave Maude a sugar cube, remounted, and let the horse walk beside the creek toward Nellie, which these days resembled a ghost town.

Very few people, except his kid sister in Atlanta—herself now sixty-seven—sent Silas mail, but he counted on an envelope from her every other Thursday or Friday.

Silas loved the "funny papers." The first thing he opened to in the Asheville daily was "Bringing Up Father," with Jiggs and Maggie, and "Mutt and Jeff." Sundays he used to keep up with "Maude the Mule," and "Happy Hooligan," lately dropped in favor of brand-new strips with irritating names like "Belles and Wedding Bells" and "The Van Swaggers," to his mind another mark of how far civilization had crumbled.

But one bright spot remained. In 1920 his sister had sent "Krazy Kat," a George Herriman cartoon altogether different from his usual fare. Simple plot: mouse bonks back of cat's head with brick. Silas immediately wrote to say it tickled him to death and keep them coming. She had done so for a decade.

The first strip he saw began with Krazy observing, to a dog working with hoe and mortar box, "I see you are quite a li'l 'mixer.' " The dog replied, "Bum pun." Ignatz Mouse, never a fan of wordplay, beaned Krazy with a brick, which knocked him into the mess, an experience Krazy deemed "mortarfying." Ignatz tossed another brick. Krazy's reaction: "Plastered again!" Besides the humor, Silas was delighted to see a cartoon bold enough to ridicule the Volstead Act, and a paper with the gumption to print it.

Eleven years later Silas still loved "Krazy," and the "Probation," as Cataloochans called it, was, everyone hoped, about to end.

He dismounted at the little post office with its sign, NELLIE, NC, both Ns backward. It needed paint. *How long has it hung there? Since Nelse's daughter was born, and she's every day of forty. Horseflies, houseflies, time flies.*

Nelse usually greeted patrons promptly, but he did not appear. His apron hung on a peg beside the entrance to the back room. Silas hollered—silence answered. He riffled through the pieces scattered on the sorting table and found a fat envelope from his sister. The outbound box was empty, so Hub Carter might make a trip for nothing tomorrow.

He shrugged and opened his mail as he walked to the porch. Folded around a note, which he put in his pocket to read later, were a half dozen Sunday strips. Silas chuckled, fished for his pipe, and looked down the road toward the sound of a horse. "Look here, Maude, it's getting crowded again." He packed his pipe with Prince Albert, another concession to age. He no longer grew tobacco.

Jim Hawkins reined up his mare and tied her beside Maude. His brass buttons and shiny leather gleamed in the sun. "Afternoon, Silas. You all right?"

Silas nodded. "Fine, Jim. You doing good?"

"Yep. Pretty day."

Silas lit his pipe and looked to the sky. "It's a mite dry. We could use a shower."

"Fire lookout said falling weather's in west Tennessee, so it might rain tomorrow. Nelse in there? I'm expecting mail from headquarters."

"Didn't see him, but he might have been out back."

Jim went inside while Silas unhitched his horse. As he started to mount, he heard Jim yell his name. "In here," said Jim, in a tone Silas construed as urgent. He tied the horse and ran inside. In the back room he doffed his hat and turned his head away. Nelse, slumped to the floor in the north corner beside a stack of empty drink crates, held a pistol in his lap. His head hung at an odd angle, opposite his tie. Blood congealed on his left shoulder, and his trousers were dark with urine. Jim squatted and laid a finger under Nelse's nose. "He's dead. You didn't hear anything?"

"No, son, I didn't even think to look back here. Didn't hear a shot on the way down, either. I guess he killed himself?"

"Don't know. Was he right- or left-handed? I don't remember."

Silas hesitated. "Right-handed, I'm pretty sure. Which hand's the gun in?"

"The right."

"There a note?"

"I haven't looked."

Silas tried to relight his pipe, but his hands were too shaky. "Damn it, Jim, why would a man do such a thing?"

Jim stood and shook his head. "Silas, I don't know. I've seen some pretty dark days, but never anything to make me kill myself."

"We've come to a pretty pass if living here's enough to make you want to do this. I'll get Doc Bennett."

"Good. I'll make sure nobody bothers nothing."

Silas put his hat back on and hurried out. He returned in ten minutes, arms braced on the dash, feet mashing the floor of Bennett's dark green Chevrolet. They raised a great cloud of dust.

"I'd a lot rather ride a horse, Doc," said Silas.

"It'd take a big one to haul me around now."

Jim came out to the porch. "Thanks for coming, Doc."

Bennett snorted. "Jim, I'd say 'you're welcome' if this were a social call, but this is duty." He absently hefted his bag, then set it behind the seat. "On second thought, not much in here'll help. You call Sheriff Leatherwood?"

"No, I didn't want to leave this mess unattended."

"Good. Let's have a look."

The men entered the back room, Bennett first, then Jim. Silas stood Janus-like in the door frame. Bennett squatted and looked at his watch. He felt for a pulse, then evidence of body heat. "He's been dead since about two or three, I'd say." He looked at the entry wound, just under the hatband at the right temple. "He right-handed?"

"We think so," said Jim.

"We need more than just thinking." He removed Nelse's hat. "Looky here, boys." His fat fingers pulled a gore-covered bullet from the hatband. "Here's the cause of death. Old Mister Thirty-two Caliber Lead. Delivered by our friends, Smith and Wesson. Had it been a .38 we'd have had to dig it out of yonder wall." He stood, kneecaps popping, and stretched his legs. "Knees aren't what they used to be." He wiped the bullet with a handkerchief. "You'd think someone would have heard it. But I was on the Carters' porch and didn't. How far's that? Half a mile, anyway. A .32 going off indoors wouldn't carry that far, even on a humid day. Silas, you didn't hear anything?"

"Nope, but I was horseback. Only time a rider hears a little gun is in the horse operas."

Bennett looked around the little room. "What have we here?" He picked up a penny postcard, no address save "To Whom It May Concern." "This might tell us something," Bennett said, turning it over. His brow wrinkled. "What kind of sense does this make?"

He showed the note to Jim and Silas. All it said was "Like Elbert Hubbard said" in block letters. "This his handwriting?"

Jim nodded. "Nelse always wrote block print like a schoolboy. What you reckon that means?"

"Ain't Hubbard that writer that talked about building a better mousetrap?" asked Silas.

"What would that have to do with killing yourself?" asked Bennett.

"Hey, I remember that name. We read "A Message to Garcia" in history class," said Jim.

The doctor grinned. "Silas, education sticks to some folks. Yes, time was, you couldn't go anywhere without seeing a copy of that. Hell, even I gave away a stack at my office. Companies printed them for advertising. But, again, what would that have to do with killing yourself?"

"The bullet's the message to Garcia?" said Jim.

"Pretty final one, I'd say," said Silas.

"Jim, I think this qualifies as an emergency. Call Leatherwood. He'll probably let me wrap this up, but I don't want to without permission."

"Yes, sir. Be back in a bit." He brushed by Silas and left.

"I never figured Nelson Howell to kill hisself. Never was what you call jolly, but always had a good word. Now he's laying here dead," said Silas. "I've seen dead folks all my life, but never a suicide. It's a mystery to me."

"Nothing surprises me anymore. The only mystery here is this Hubbard business."

"Wasn't he on the *Lusitania*?"

"You know, you're right. He and his wife went down with the ship. Voluntarily, as I remember. They could have jumped, but instead went into a stateroom and closed the door." He chuckled. "Wonder if they drowned *in coitu*?"

"If that means what I think it does, he died with a smile on his face."

. . .

That evening Bennett called Nelse's brother and learned Nelse had been right-handed, but the men had quarreled so many decades ago that the brother could not recall why they no longer spoke to each other. Nelse's sister recalled seeing Nelse coming out of Dr. Alexander's office in Waynesville a week before but could add nothing else. Alexander would not speak of the matter over the telephone because he feared nosy operators, so Bennett arranged to see him at eight the next morning.

Bennett woke at three-thirty to hear rain falling. He didn't like to drive all those switchbacks in rain but headed to Waynesville, wipers barely fast enough to clear the windshield. "At least there's no traffic," he muttered.

When Bennett knocked, he heard Alexander shout. "That you, Coroner? Come on back." He opened the pebble-glass door into a waiting room empty of patients, two *Progressive Farmer* magazines lying on the floor. The room smelled of the sweat of illness cut by rubbing alcohol and pine oil. Through the door to the left he saw Alexander's shadow and leaned on the door frame.

Alexander was a gaunt man upward of eighty, who, when he started practice in the 1870s had had to convince folks he delivered babies more safely than granny women did. He was changing a bulb in the swing-arm lamp over his examination table. "Coroner, come on in." He tightened the bulb and held out his hand.

Bennett shook the old man's hand. It was cold but dry, and its grip was strong. "Good to see you, Doctor. Are you well?"

"Well enough for a worn-out pill peddler. Come back and have a chair."

Alexander's private office overlooked the alleyway behind the two-story building. The room contained a battle-scarred oak desk with a swivel chair, a leather-covered wing chair in the corner, and a glass-doored case full of well-used books. Alexander sat behind the desk and pointed Bennett to the chair.

"I'll be brief, Coroner. Your suicide had carcinoma of the pancreas. I noticed it a month or two ago—the exact date isn't important, is it?"

Bennett shook his head. "No, Doctor, that diagnosis is enough for me. Not much to be done."

"No, and last Tuesday I felt sure he was metastatic—enlarged lymph nodes, a slight fever, and a very elevated white count. I told him I was going to level with him." He stood, looked out the window, and took a deep breath. "I said he had six months, maybe more, probably less. I said they would be painful. I advised him to get his affairs in order, make a will, that sort of thing."

"How did he take it?"

Alexander turned to Bennett. "About like I'd have thought. He asked me if I was sure, and when I nodded, he looked at me kind of puzzled-like, then said, really slow, 'Doc, Elbert Hubbard was right.' I asked him what he meant. 'He said life's just one damned thing after another.' Then he cried. Slow at first, then bawled like a dying calf in a hailstorm. I gave him that very box of tissues over there. When he pulled himself together, he shook my hand and asked me how much he owed me." The swivel chair squeaked as Alexander sat and put his elbows on the desk. "I told him, and he paid me. He stood, put his hat on, and said good-bye. I didn't know he was spelling it with capital letters."

Bennett barely returned in time to tell Jim and Silas what he had learned before Nelse Howell was to be buried. As the men trudged up the steep hillside to the cemetery, a pair of crows, dark against an overcast sky, watched them intently. Manson and Thomas led a mule and sled bearing a pine coffin. Aunt Mary, Nell and her children, half a dozen Waynesville Howells, and two Cove Creek Johnsons followed. Nelse's daughter was in California so did not show up.

The cemetery had been terraced in the last century from the first fairly flat ground halfway up the mountain behind the Methodist church. It held four store-bought tombstones, one shaped like an obelisk, under which lay old Levi Carter, Hiram's father. Next to it was Hiram's gravestone, a flat affair with a sun rising through heavenly gates carved at the top. A hemlock grew at the center of the yard. Scattered here and there, fieldstones poked out of the ground like toadstools, marking infants mostly, stillborn or dead from various fevers. Even Aunt Mary could not identify all of them, although her first had rested under one until Hiram had scared up money to buy a child's stone capped with a carved lamb.

The men hobbled the mule, untied the casket, and set it on woven straps bridging the open grave. The crows began squalling. Jim thought of his shotgun, then wondered what kind of fellow had such thoughts at a burial. He walked over to Nell, smiled, and patted his children on their heads.

Preacher Will Smith was in Henderson County, so Silas turned to the little congregation and opened his Bible. He read the twenty-third and hundred and twenty-first psalms, then said, "Folks, Nelson Howell was a good neighbor. When he said he'd do something, he'd do it. If you needed something, he'd give it without question or complaint. He was a good man.

"I wish I could comfort this family. To do what he did, a man has to be of a different mind than I've ever had. I can't judge that. I don't think Jesus will, either.

"I've never had a doctor tell me I had only a little time left. I don't know if facing months of pain would make me pick up a pistol like Nelse. But today his troubles are over. He ain't hurting no more. He's at peace.

"Sure as there's a world around us, there's a heaven above us, and that's where Nelson Howell is this minute. He's all right now. He's with Jesus. I have to believe it. Because to believe anything else would make life not worth the living of it. Amen."

After the grave was covered, the townspeople wandered around the little cemetery, pointing and whispering. Jim showed gravestones to Nell and the kids, reminiscing about bygone folks. Aunt Mary's sons and Bennett watched her gaze at Hiram's stone and wondered if she saw him standing beside it.

Bennett put his hand on Mary's shoulder. "Reckon he's with Hiram now?"

She looked startled. "You mean here in the cemetery?"

"Silas was talking about heaven, I believe."

"Their bodies are here. Their spirits are in heaven. Ain't that the way it's supposed to be?" She dabbed at her eyes with a handkerchief. "Poor soul."

The men were nearly finished covering the grave. Mary put her handkerchief into her purse and looked around. She crooked her finger for the doctor to follow. Under the hemlock she asked, "Doctor Bennett, would you level with me?"

"Certainly."

"How many years do I have left?"

Bennett laughed. "Last year, I saw no reason you couldn't be kicking around another twenty years. Maybe more. That's not to say you might have an aneurism tomorrow. One never knows. But, God willing, you'll live a good while."

Manson and Thomas, cleaning their hands with a piece of towel, joined them. "Boys, I was just telling your mother she might have twenty or more years left in her."

"That's mighty good, Mama," said Thomas.

"Don't know so well about that," she said. "It's getting too hard to live here, and I don't know if I want to keep it up."

"Mama, are you talking about dying, or moving?" asked Manson.

"Sometimes I wonder what's the difference. You stay here, it just gets harder and harder, and lonesomer and lonesomer. You move, you have to start all the hardships again. I don't know if I'm strong enough for that."

Silas had been talking to the Johnsons and Howells, who in a group were now holding to each other, trying not to fall down the hillside. He approached Mary about the same time as Jim and Nell did. "Somebody say something about moving?" Silas asked.

Mary took Silas by the arm. "My Hiram's best friend," she said. "Did you tell those nice people to stop for dinner at our house?"

"I did." They watched the town folks in their slick-soled shoes inch down the mountain. "If they don't break their necks first."

"Silas, we were just saying how hard it's getting to live here anymore."

"Tell me about it," said Nell under her breath. Jim put his arm around her, but she did not respond to his hug.

Silas cocked his head toward the couple, then embraced Aunt Mary.

"Well, you got a point, Mary. You know, I was thinking, looking at that pitiful crowd, twenty years ago the postmaster's death would have drawn hundreds. Now Cataloochee's near about in the history books. Jim and Nell and these young'uns are the first new blood in years. But you know what I saw the other day? Two of them big old woodpeckers working dinner out of that old maple by the barn. Hollering, knocking on them old limbs, having a big time. As long as I can see such as that, I'm not going anywhere. And when it's over for me, they can lay me right here."

"You'd spend now till the last trump close to Hiram," said Mary.

"My body would. Like Nelse here. But I'd see Hiram in heaven."

"You really think that's where he is, Silas?"

"I don't think it, Mary, I know it."

"I wish I could be that certain."

"Don't give it no more consideration. He's in heaven, period."

"Thanks, Silas. Mama needed to hear that," said Manson.

Mary bristled at her son. "Young man, I'll judge what I need to hear and what I don't."

Manson led the mule down the mountain. Thomas took his mother's left arm and Silas her right as they eased down the mountain, talking of weather and anything besides death, burial, and resurrection. Jim and his family followed a dozen paces behind, too far to hear the details but close enough to know it was small talk. Jim held Little Elizabeth's hand with his left and kept the right steadily behind Mack. Nell focused on the ground, wondering if they closed the post office how she would get her mail orders.

CHAPTER 22

All by Himself

Willie McPeters owned no toothbrush, nor would have known what to do with one save perhaps to dip it in coal oil before scrubbing rust off an ax head. A bearlike omnivore, he paid little attention to what he ate. The only thing that kept teeth in his head was eating lots of raw apples— peel, core, seeds, and all.

He set the Big Creek fire in the summer of 1931 just to watch it burn. He brought with him his Marlin model 94, and a tow sack, in which lay two boxes of kitchen matches, half a pair of binoculars, a box of ammunition, and two Prince Albert tins. He added a dozen apples from an abandoned orchard halfway to the top of Mount Sterling. He set the fire with no particular haste, using the large lens to focus sunlight on leaf piles. Then he climbed to the summit of Old Sterling, stretched his legs in front of him, and munched an apple. The fire smoldered for a while, then caught in earnest on a crosswind, and he grinned as with one hand he glassed the ridge for spreading smoke and flame and with the other pulled at himself like a deranged pirate spotting a boatload of whores.

McPeters watched for the better part of two days, content with fire, self-abuse, and apples. He moved occasionally to crush an ant or spider unlucky enough to venture onto his leg but otherwise watched the fire line devour the remnant of woods. The timber companies had left slash where it had fallen, fine kindling to light stunted trees for which they'd had no use.

It was a fine, clear night. Save for bowels and bladder he did not move off the peak. It was fascinating to watch the fire at night as it crept toward the creek from several directions. He rose the second afternoon and headed back, after ratting through an old shack, the remains of a camp used by men checking their summer pastures. He found nothing worth keeping among the bones of small creatures, nut hulls, and mica-flecked pebbles. Strangely, he did not torch it.

He met no one between Sterling's top and Long Bunk, a descent of a thousand feet, and saw few animals—a wormy-looking rabbit that bounded across the road too quickly for him to shoot, a squirrel he briefly regarded as food until he thought what his rifle would do to such a rodent. No songbirds greeted him. He spooked a pair of pileated woodpeckers, which undulated deeper into the woods. He'd never heard of eating a woodpecker, but those would be big enough if a man were careful to get a shot at the shy varmints.

He walked into the deserted settlement at Ola at suppertime like a silent movie villain, rifle on right shoulder, arm over the stock as counterbalance, left hand holding the sack, eyes shifting to see neither opposition nor greeting. At the creek behind the post office he set the Marlin against a rock. After opening one tobacco tin, he rolled and lit a cigarette, then removed fish line and hook from the other tin. He turned over rocks beside the creek until he found a hellgrammite with a nearly devilish design on its carapace. He hooked it and threw it downstream. On his third cast he landed a pretty trout, gutted it, and spitted it on a wild cherry limb.

McPeters built a fire beside a lean-to shed attached to the post office, cooked the fish, and ate it slowly, staring into the flames. Picking his teeth with one of the ribs, he threw the rest of the bones into the fire, which hissed and smoked far out of proportion to their size. He ate an apple. Not bothering to put the fire out, he resacked his belongings, picked up the rifle, and ambled toward the top of the next rise, where the Baptist church perched over the valley like a sentinel.

He'd never entered such a building, but this one seemed unthreatening as to either hellfire or salvation. The door opened easily to a pitch-dark interior. He lit a match that revealed a coal oil lantern in a windowsill. It held a little fuel yet so he lit it, trimmed the wick, and looked around.

In the center of the room stood a cast-iron heater, stovepipe vented straight through the ceiling. He cracked the legs off a broken-down chair and laid them inside. Then he scratched himself and shook his head. Going outside, he found small sticks for kindling. He relaid the fire, and pissed in the back corner. Gathering more firewood against impending chill, he noticed smoke and flames coming from Ola. "Aaaa," he said.

Running down the mountain, he arrived in time to see the post office roof collapse and send thousands of sparks into the night sky. He masturbated to the rhythm of the fire, then walked back up to the church, lit the fire, lay down on an adjacent pew, and immediately slept.

Next morning he woke to the shrill chatter of a house wren, which wanted him gone from her territory. He had one stick of firewood left, which he flung at the bird left-handed. It was wide of the bird and broke a window. She continued to protest until he gathered his truck and left.

It took him most of the day to get back to Nellie, where he sidled behind the post office and banged on the clapboard with his rifle butt, then quickly went around front. Hub Carter, who had driven mail in and out of Cataloochee for years, had acquired Nelse Howell's job by default. When he went out back to see who had disturbed his nap, McPeters quickly lifted two tins of potted meat and a bottle of Coke, and ran into the woods. He emerged past the church, eating and drinking as he went, like a pilgrim bound for glory. He threw the bottle into the creek, where it shattered into bright pieces. A meat tin he crushed with his boot and put in his shirt pocket for no other reason than he liked the picture of the devil on the label.

He was resting in Henry Sutton's barn, eating the other tin's worth, when Jim Hawkins rode into the yard. Jim was the first human he had seen in three days, and McPeters did not care to be found. He pointed the rifle toward Jim and mouthed an explosion. Grinning, he saw Jim lead his horse toward the back porch, so he headed for the woods behind the barn. He squatted fifty yards in and watched the warden eat dinner and talk to his horse.

When McPeters moved, the horse spooked. He watched Jim steady the horse, draw his weapon, and slowly walk to the barn. When he heard Jim say "Who's in there?" McPeters could easily have put a slug through the man's forehead. Instead he mouthed another explosion as if to remember this face for later. Following Deadfall Branch a ways, he then sidetracked to the main road and silently headed southeast, over the mountain into Carter Fork.

In less than a half mile he peered down toward his homeplace, a sprawling structure covered by a roof that was some places sheet metal, others wooden shakes, tarpaper, thatch. Some surfaces had no covering, the rafters bleached chicken-bone white.

Something didn't smell right. The sun came briefly from behind a cloud, and a winged shadow the size of a bushel basket skimmed the ground. He looked up at two soaring turkey buzzards.

He threw the rifle's safety off and walked into the yard. Neither chickens nor dogs milled to greet or warn him. The barn was empty, the ancient milk cow having been butchered at the beginning of the past winter, and the mule having wandered off the summer before. He found no small mammals or reptiles that could cause such a stink. On the porch his father's empty chair sat in front of a wide-open front door. He grunted, but no one answered. The front room was empty.

A pot sat on the kitchen stove. He picked it up as though it might be the source of the stench, but after sniffing it, he propped the rifle against the wall, raked some of the contents onto his finger, and ate. It had been peas or beans a week or more ago. McPeters did not notice the mold. He ate until the pot was clean as it ever would be, chewing slowly, without enthusiasm, swallowing without water.

He retrieved his Marlin and looked through the first story, empty of life, or, for that matter, death. Whatever the source of the odor, it was upstairs, underneath, or outside. Stairs squeaked as he mounted. Halfway up, his shoulder brushed by a silver star pinned to a tacked-up squirrel hide. He searched the three rooms in that wing and found a dead mouse in the corner of the last bedroom, but it was too dry to stink, and anyway too small to cause the present trouble.

Something scraped and popped sheet metal not attached to the main structure. He looked out the glassless window at a buzzard atop the outhouse, with an awkward purchase on the front roof edge, trying to stick its red head in the door below, like an outsize parakeet beginning a somersault.

On the back porch he rubbed his eyes against the sharp odor. He walked down the steps and flapped his arms at the vulture. "Haaah," he yelled, but the bird only kept at the door. Another lit in the yard twenty feet from the privy. McPeters yelled "Yaaah" but neither bird moved.

He threw a stick of firewood at the one on the ground. Raising its wings, it began to run, whether to build momentum for takeoff, or to attack, McPeters did not know. He shot it head-on, at which noise the privy-perching buzzard righted itself, flapped twice, and headed for the barn roof, where it folded its wings, waiting for McPeters to leave. After McPeters shot it, the bird rolled off the barn and hit the yard like a sack of soft potatoes. McPeters walked over and touched it with his boot toe. He had shot its head clean off. He grunted.

At the outhouse door he knew he was at the source of the trouble. He went to the creek, taking off his shirt on the way. It was a question whether odor from the shirt or the outhouse was worse. The garment ripped halfway up the back, but he dipped it into the creek and tied it around his face like a bandit's mask. At the outhouse door he took a breath, then pulled.

The door did not yield immediately, so he yanked it harder. It creaked and popped as he pushed it wide open. Inside sat his father. His overalls were below his knees, and he looked like he had leaned against the back wall for one final push to empty his ancient, costive bowels, or perhaps had simply gone to sleep. His skin sagged and his color was as putrid as the smell. He hosted a multitude of ants, flies, and beetles, and even McPeters had no desire to see what feasted on his father from below.

McPeters went to the shed for a sledge, a tool they had used so seldom that it still boasted the handle the blacksmith had mated to it a generation ago. It was a nine-pound hammer, and the jakes was a two-hole affair. McPeters began busting the bench beside his father, and at a particularly hard stroke the old man's body moved enough to begin to fall sideways. McPeters heard and saw a cloud of gases erupt from the body before the reek hit his nose. By the time he had destroyed the bench, his father's body rested in three feet of sludge and splinters. The stench made McPeters reel for a couple of seconds, but he did not throw up. Instead he staggered to the shed for a can of coal oil.

After hammering the door into splinters, he threw them into the hole, doused the pit with kerosene, and threw a lit match with no more ceremony or regret than he would have used drowning a sack of kittens. When the building caught, he threw in the avian corpses. The huge birds nearly put the fire out, but he got it roaring again with barn hay and the remains of the chicken house. McPeters's fire sent a smell heavenward composed of death rot, shit from various species, feathers, flesh, and whatever else had ever been tossed into the outhouse. The afternoon was humid and the aroma commanded Jim Hawkins's attention in Big Cataloochee when it settled later that evening.

When the fire died, McPeters headed for the porch and sat heavily in his father's rocker. He had masturbated only once around the old man, who had enjoyed such things himself but who had been particularly disgusted by such behavior in others, and had nearly knocked his son's head off. But now McPeters could do what he damn well pleased. He built another small fire in the yard, took down his overalls, and had a big time all by himself.

CHAPTER 23

Uncle Silas

Silas Wright's first morning labor, after scratching himself as he took a sup of whiskey, was to start a fire in the Home Comfort, a fancy contraption, heavy, decorated with lacy cast iron, a thermometer in the oven door. On its right stood a water jacket and atop sat a dual-compartment warmer.

Rhetta had regarded its best feature to be the iron gingerbread on the front, but Silas admired its efficiency and output. Only in coldest weather did he have to build a morning fire from scratch—riddling the grates nearly always exposed enough embers to start a fire.

When he meditated about change—lately, in the spring of 1932, a frequent activity—he wondered why people were in a sweat for electricity. His niece, for example, told him of the great boon of moving out of Cataloochee—power, run from a roadside pole to his new house. "You'll turn a dial, and it'll perk coffee in less than a minute. Think about that." He did, and wondered why such an arrangement might be of any appreciable benefit.

He enjoyed building fires: first laying tinder on coals, then kindling, splits, and what he called "tree wood"—unsplit limb rounds—as well as cutting, splitting, stacking, and carrying firewood. He even liked to clean out ashes, nutrients for the kitchen garden. And electric ranges gave no aromatic nose of cast iron and smoke.

Besides, power cost money. They sent you a bill every month. *They can call me old-fashioned as long as I can bootleg enough firewood to keep warm, cook, and keep healthy.*

A fire made the Home Comfort pop and expand with the rising sun. At the kitchen window Silas watched the barn emerge from the mists of dawn. *That's it. Same as preferring a horse over an automobile. Both get you where you want to go. But there's no satisfaction to this modern tomfoolery. It's no better—just faster. I like to see, feel, and smell where I'm going, which you can't do in a car. And a pot of soup beans and ham hocks cooked on an electric range can't have but a hint of flavor. Half the satisfaction of eating is smelling it simmer slow on the woodstove. I remember when I was a young'un sniffing dinner—we didn't have no kitchen then, but we'd stick our heads in the cabin and smell that stuff cooking, almost as good as the eating itself. Still love it, old as I am.*

You know, that's what's wrong with this country. We want everything, and now. Especially young people. Won't wait to build a fire, they got to have an electric stove. Won't wait for beans to grow in the garden, they got to buy them in a tin can that sucks flavor right out of them. Won't enjoy a journey, they got to be there today. Next thing you know they'll come up with something that'll get you there day before yesterday. And anymore the there they're getting to is a damn national park.

He walked into the front room. On the hearth sat a fire screen. He bent to pluck a piece of straw from its wire mesh. *That's more'n half the problem with Jim Hawkins and that wife of his. Jim's like me—rather ride than drive. She was born to run, and you can't run in Cataloochee.*

It ain't any of my business, but if I was him, I'd lay down the law. Listen here, this is where my job is, and you belong with me. Period.

Silas laughed and shook his head. *Yeah, sure, just like I put my foot down when Rhetta had to have that buggy.* "You don't need that a bit more'n I need another hole in my head," *I said. Lot of difference it made. She ran it so much there ain't an original part left on it. A wonder I ever done any farming, just keeping her on the road. But a man's a fool over a woman more times than not. I know I was.*

Reckon I'm about ready for this evening. Can't believe Jim Hawkins talked me into this. I got as much business keeping young'uns as I do growing sugar beets.

Jim had shown up the previous afternoon wearing a worried look. His voice crackled as he asked a favor. Silas looked at him in pure disbelief. "Now let me get this straight, Warden Hawkins. You want me to keep your young'uns all weekend?"

"Yes, sir."

"That's a load of bunkum. I'm an old man, Jim. My heart was racy the other day. What if I was to up and die? What would they do with a dead man until Sunday afternoon?"

"Silas, you're too tough to die."

"Son, I ain't been around young'uns in ages. Mary Carter'll mind them for you."

"Aunt Mary's not in her right mind, Nell says."

"But there's Manson and Thomas."

"What do those old bachelors know about young'uns?" The look on Jim's face made Silas fear he might drop to his knees.

"Listen, Silas," said Jim. "I know this is strange territory for you. It is for me, too."

"What in thunder do you mean?"

"Nell's unhappy. I have to do something."

"What do you aim to do?"

"We're going to Asheville. To the George Vanderbilt hotel."

"So how's a spree in a fancy hotel going to help? No, let me rework that. I ain't so old I don't know how you think it'll help *you*. But how would it do any good for *her and you*?"

"We need time by ourselves. No kids. Lots of loving. If we're not back in love by Monday . . ." Jim's voice choked.

"Catchy line. A man could build a song around that, maybe even get on the Opry." Silas shrugged his shoulders and grinned. "Well, I'll help this once."

He'd put the fire screen away after his children had grown up. He and Rhetta had used it when bedding sick children at the hearth. All childhood diseases demanded the same remedy—boiling water, brown sugar, and whiskey in equal proportions, with lemon or dried mint. The afflicted youngster drank hot tea as fast as his or her swollen throat would tolerate, then burrowed under a pile of quilts in front of the fireplace. By morning the crud would either be gone or preferable to the hangover.

Silas had fetched the screen, along with a box of dusty wooden toys, from the barn. He figured if Jim brought the children after supper, he'd soon bed them before the fireplace. Then he'd have only Saturday and the first part of Sunday not to lose, sicken, or injure them.

Friday evening Jim and Nell brought Mack and Little Elizabeth to Silas's porch and knocked. When Silas answered, Jim shook his hand and Nell stood on tiptoe and hugged him—which did not hurt his feelings, for she smelled delicious.

"I'll just leave their bedrolls on the porch," said Jim. He had shaved again that afternoon, leaving a small cut on his left jaw. When Nell patted Little Elizabeth's head nervously, Silas caught the glint of a bracelet in the car lights.

"Come on in," he said.

"We'll go," said Jim. "It's getting dark, so we'll play hell on that road. I thank you, Silas."

"You lovebirds get on. The rest of us'll figure out what we're up to, won't we?" He winked at Mack, who wore a short jacket and an earflap cap the color of fried liver. Mack smiled and nodded. Little Elizabeth, nearly three, didn't know so well about this. She held a cloth rabbit by its ears over a navy-blue pea coat, a sailor cap perched on her head. Silas opened his arms. "Come to Uncle Silas, little lady."

She looked uncertainly at her mother, who nodded. "Go with Uncle Silas, sweetie."

She sidled shyly toward the old man, who picked her up with a hug. "Me and you's going to be fine," he said. "You'uns go on before we decide to go with you."

After Jim cranked the car and drove out of sight, the children looked at Silas, who pointed toward the fireplace. "Want to bed down by the fire?"

Mack nodded vigorously. Jim and Nell had never allowed the children to sleep by themselves before a fireplace. Mack had been sorely tempted to move his bed near the fire after Nell tucked them in, to watch closely the fire's comforting journey from flame to coal to ember.

Silas helped Mack lay out two bedrolls, built up the fire, then read the story of David and Goliath to them. Mack and Little Elizabeth knelt as Silas prayed over them: "Lord, watch over these children, tonight and forever. Let their folks come to their senses. And help me this weekend, while you're at it. In Christ's name, Amen." He banked the fire, tucked them in, and blew out the lamp.

He meant to stay awake most of the night, so he figured to reheat the morning's coffee to counteract the dram of whiskey he deserved. Besides, a kitchen fire would help calm the fantods. Again he resurrected a fire and started the pot to boil. He sat at the table. No untoward noise from the front room. A picture of Rhetta, made at least thirty years ago, grinned like she thought she might be about to hear a good story.

Me and her was married sixty-odd years, and never once thought of parting. "Till death do us part" was as natural to say as "granite is rock." Young people today don't think like that. Flighty, like skittish birds. I even heard of a preacher about to marry a couple, asked what if they had trouble. One said, "If it don't work out, we can go our separate ways." Don't that beat all?

As he listened to fires pop and the house settle, he sipped coffee laced with a liberal amount of whiskey. *I'll be up all night keeping this little flock. Not my first sleepless night. A few when I tended livestock, or watched after fever and sickness, or sat with corpses. Some nights of hard, senseless drinking, but those countable on no more than one hand's worth of fingers. Coon hunts, I'd return with the sun, smelling like campfire and wild moonlight. A few nights courting Rhetta, when I came home wired like I was hooked to a battery, moonstruck so deep it hurt to breathe. One of those nights*—here he smiled—*I lit a dozen rich pine torches and split a winter's worth of stove wood before sunup. Mama said, "What in the world," but Papa just said, "The boy's got it bad." And he was right. I sure understand Jim's need. God help them tonight.*

· · ·

Silas's eyes opened to Mack, standing beside the kitchen table, gazing at his host with a worried air about him. "What, boy?" Silas said. "What time is it?" When he raised his head from the table, he immediately knew an old man should neither drink more than a dram of a night nor sleep sitting at a table. Neck stiff as a heart pine board.

Mack's hair was flat on one side, and a white knot of sleep rested in the inside corner of his right eye. "It's morning, Uncle Silas."

"So 'tis, child." Silas figured he'd be unkinked by dinnertime. "Is little sis all right?"

Mack nodded. "I need to pee."

"They ain't moved the outhouse. Need your coat?"

Mack shook his head as he bounded down the back steps. Silas poked up the kitchen fire and went into the front room. Little Elizabeth still slept, thumb laid across her mouth. Silas was torn between staring at an advertisement for pure innocence and starting breakfast.

The back door slammed and Mack bounced into the room. "Wake up, sleepyhead," he cried at his sister. "You're going to fritter this day away."

"Who says that, son? Your papa or mama?"

"Papa."

"I thought so. What would you say to some ham and eggs?" Silas welcomed Little Elizabeth to a new day by rubbing her head gently. "You young'uns get ready. I'll put something on the table."

By noon they had worked up another appetite. Silas had cleaned the wooden toys—a locomotive, a set of blocks that long ago had been painted bright colors, a three-legged horse, two carts with wheels made of thread spools, and a race car. He had also found a rag doll he figured Little Elizabeth would like, but she cradled it for only a few minutes before stacking blocks, aiming to build a house.

Silas was creaky, but if he sat on the floor and pushed toys to Mack, they soon had a rousing back-and-forth game. Little Elizabeth joined them, so they triangled toys back and forth. By the time Silas needed to fix dinner, they were all laughing so hard their faces hurt.

Dinner was cornbread, string beans, boiled Irish potatoes (which Silas pronounced "arsh"), leftover ham, baked sweet potatoes saturated with butter and brown sugar—pie without a crust. Mack wolfed it down while Little Elizabeth ignored all but the sweet potatoes, of which she ate two.

Afterward the sky, lifting all morning, shone as blue as lapis, and Silas asked his charges if they wanted to try their luck fishing. Both children cheered for Uncle Silas, who made sure they wore their coats and caps. "Daddy took me fishing," said Mack, "but we didn't catch anything."

"What did you use for bait?"

"Arty-fissil flies."

"Young'uns, I'll show you how to fish."

Silas found an empty pint jar and headed outside. He asked Mack to lift some sticks of wood outside the shed, and plucked from underneath some sowbugs and two or three redworms. "Let's see what's out back," he said, and handed the jar to Little Elizabeth. "Now, don't drop it, sweetheart," he said. "When I say so, hand it here."

In the hog pen a shovelful of wet dirt rewarded them with half a dozen fat nightcrawlers. "We'll catch us some fish with these, yessir. Now let's wet a hook or two."

He cleaned spiderwebs from two short cane poles pulled from the shed, then restrung them from a spool of heavy cotton thread and tied a hook to each. At the creek bend he baited up and handed one pole to Mack, the other to Little Elizabeth. "Now throw it out there. When you feel it pull, set the hook and bring it on in," he said.

Little Elizabeth's first strike so excited her she threw the pole into the water. Silas laughed and fished it out, complete with a trout the size of his hand. "Good girl," he said. "Want to try again?" She jumped up and down and giggled. Mack's pole bent about that time, and he pulled in a fish a couple of inches longer than the first.

For the better part of the afternoon they ranged the creek, relieving its hidey-holes of trout. Little Elizabeth's hands would have looked proper on a mud baby. Mack could barely drag the stringer Silas had cut from a maple branch. Trout for supper and breakfast. On their way back they heard the Ford cross the rocky creek bed.

It hadn't occurred to Silas to worry about possessing enough illegal trout to put him under the jail, for Jim and Nell weren't due for twenty-four hours. Whose automobile? As they turned toward the whine of four cylinders and gearbox, Silas put his hands on the children's shoulders.

Mack broke silence first. "Daddy! Lookit! Lookit!" He held the fish high, but tails still mopped the ground.

Silas figured he was about as caught as the fish. He could not tell if Jim was alone, because of glare on the windshield. The automobile slowed and pulled even with the miscreants. The window rolled down to reveal Jim, hatless, wifeless, a lollipop stick dangling from his mouth. "What in the world?" he said, slow as Christmas. "Silas, you've led my young'uns astray."

"With all due respect," said Silas, "I didn't catch none of these here fish."

"Little Mack Truck, did you and Lizzy catch *all* those?"

"Yes, sir," Mack said proudly.

"Lizzy, your momma's going to keel over dead when she sees that coat." He tried to look stern but couldn't quite pull it off.

"Daddy, I love you," Little Elizabeth said. "Where's Mommy?"

"Back at the house. Having a headache." He looked at Silas. "Mind if I stay a little bit?"

"Be my guest. We'll have us a fish fry. You young'uns want to learn how to clean fish?"

"Are they dirty?" asked Little Elizabeth.

Silas laughed. "You just wait, little miss."

Later, as Mack and Little Elizabeth napped on their bedrolls, Jim and Silas shared a little whiskey. "I knew something wasn't right when that Ford showed up a day early."

"I think maybe we were trying too hard," said Jim. "Kind of like when two people knock heads when they bend over to pick up something."

"So—let me guess—she's not staying."

Jim looked into his whiskey glass as if his future lay in the bottom of it. "Silas, I don't know." He glanced into the front room. "You know what hurts?"

"You mean besides the general hurt of being a human?"

Jim nodded. "I asked her to stay, if not for me, for the young'uns."

When Silas figured the woodstove was hot enough, he set a large cast-iron skillet loaded with congealed grease on top. He began rolling fillets in cornmeal. "Don't tell me," he said. "She's taking them with her. So they won't grow up here."

Jim sipped his liquor. "How'd you know?"

"She's a town girl. Ain't no amount of here's going to change that. First time I laid eyes on Nell, I thought it was a shame you and her got hitched. Because she wasn't never going to like it here, and you were literally born to your job. And there's considerable stubborn in both of you."

The first fillet popped like it had come alive, threatening to spatter both men with hot grease. "A woman like that don't want her offspring talking like a hillbilly. Get an education. Make a name for theirselves. That ain't going to happen here, much as I love it." A dozen fillets in the pan somehow calmed the noise considerably. "How about you?"

"What about me?"

"You going to stay, or go with her?"

Jim downed the rest of his whiskey. "Sometimes I'm staying. Others I'm going. I don't know, Silas. Any advice?"

"Follow your heart, son. That's about all I could ever say about such as that."

"It's torn in three pieces, Silas. My job. My woman. My children." He stood and looked into the front room. "I'd sure hate to give any of them up."

"A job's just a job," Silas said. "You could do that in Asheville and keep the rest."

Jim looked out the window. "It isn't just a job to me, Silas. It's where I came from. It's where I need to stay."

"Can't argue," said Silas, turning fish. "These'll be done in a minute. Fetch me that plate."

In a few minutes enough fish to feed a small congregation graced the table. "This look good enough to help a man with a heartache?" asked Silas, spreading his arms wide. "Especially when the cornbread's done?"

"Nearly. Want me to scare up a crowd? I'll see if Nell's feeling better, and ask Aunt Mary."

"Fine. Care for another snort?"

"Nope. I'd hate to have to arrest myself for driving drunk. And then I couldn't haul you in for having all these fish." He picked up a piece of fish and ate it slowly. "I'll have to say, though, if they don't fry trout in heaven, I don't much want to go."

"They don't have them this good in Asheville, either."

"Good point. Nell says I don't ever think with anything except my pecker. But sometimes my belly trumps it. I might just stay."

"Like I said, follow your heart. That's a bit north of both of them organs."

"I'll be back, Silas. Save me a few bites."

From the kitchen window Silas watched Jim. A man with a lot to lose, either way he went.

CHAPTER 24

Hen Upstairs

"Never used to talk to myself," Silas Wright said, running a file across the blade of his reaphook. "Never needed to—Rhetta, rest her soul, said enough for the both of us." He extracted a red handkerchief and wiped his brow. Sweat beaded at the end of his nose. "Hotter'n a hen upstairs in a wool basket," he muttered.

His file smoothed two nicks, then he switched to a whetstone until he was satisfied with the edge. He mopped his brow again. "Might as well get on with it," he said. "It ain't going to cut its ownself down."

Spring had been dry. May's hay cut had yielded only three ricks, and he despaired of a second cut worth messing with. But now, in late June, on the creek bank tall bearded grasses shot up among stands of poke-weed, rattletop, and fleabane. Silas meant to mow them by dark.

Poke stalks sliced easily in any weather, but drought only toughened grass. He held grass tops with his left hand and swung the reaphook with his right. As he bent to his work, his back began to look like someone had doused him with a bucket of water. "Damn," he said, and straightened. "This is too much like work. Specially for an old man."

A poplar on the opposite bank shaded a goodly spot ten yards away, a goal he reached before a break. He dipped his hand into the creek and drank. Taking off his boots and socks, he eased tired feet into the creek. The water was nowhere near bone-chilling, but its cold felt so good he did not notice nearby maple leaves turning silver side up. He looked at his twisted toes and thought how he'd look in a cartoon—squiggly steam rising from his scorching feet, sweat drops leaping from his head. His wiggling toes dislodged a baseball-size flat rock, from under which a crawfish drifted backward. "Better not pinch me, old feller."

Across the creek a mass of hairy vines on the terraced slope bore buds nearly ready to produce yellow flowers. *Let's see now, it was the year of the cloudburst, right about this time of year in 1916, me and Harrogate and them Hawkins boys cleaned and terraced this bank after that. Harrogate figured it for a dandy melon patch, and damned if it hasn't turned out so. Too good, really—last year we sold two wagonloads, and still had so many that my niece pickled the dern rinds, and I hate such a sweet pickle. Might as well eat a spoonful of Karo syrup.*

We won't have that many this dry season. And look at the field behind the house—dry as last year's bird nest. He laughed to himself as clouds collected, unnoticed, over Spruce Mountain.

Wonder where the old people are. I imagine Rhetta and her mother's setting around in heaven talking ninety-leven miles a minute to anybody flying by, but my momma was one to set in the chimney corner and sew. I bet there's different rooms there like Jesus said.

To be fair, I hope heaven ain't like some say, where all a man would do is sing praises around the throne. First place, I can't sing. Second, that would be about as captivating as watching a bunch of snails hightail it to town.

Folks say you'll meet all them that's gone before. Now, it'll be fine to see Rhetta, and I'd love a reunion with our boys that died, but her old man and I got along about like hard-shells and Catholics, and I think we'd both just as soon heaven not be a dern family reunion.

Saint Paul says we'll be changed, in the twinkling of an eye, so maybe we'll look like stars, or comets, or vapors or something. It'd have to be like that to get me to want to spend eternity with her father. She'd of course never imagine him in hell, where I wished him many a time.

Don't much believe in hell. There's enough on earth without having to suffer for eternity. But sometimes I'm hopeful there is one, where they put really mean folks, so not to worry the rest of us. Of course, that assumes I get to heaven. If at the gates there's poison oak, I'm a goner.

Silt-laden eddies coiled downstream from his right foot. Silas had stopped sweating. Stowing his handkerchief, he wiped his feet with his socks, picked up his boots, and headed for the shed. A bird cooed once long, three times short. "Damn, look at them clouds, and streaks going to the sun. Ain't seen that in a while. And I believe I heard a rain crow." After hanging the reaphook on the back wall, he shuffled through the yard to the back porch.

He sat in a cane-bottom chair and lit his pipe. "Reckon I'll rest awhile," he said, closed his eyes, and kept smoking.

Bud Harrogate had been putting a new handle on a corn sheller. He came out of the barn and squinted toward the heavens. He had shed his plaid flannel shirt, tying its sleeves around his waist, shirttail flapping in a sudden breeze. His torso was fish-belly white, his body tan only at neck and hands. Ambling to the far side of the porch, he stopped, a line of sweat dripping through dark chest hair. He grinned. "Silas, you got a snake on the porch," he said, as flatly as if he'd observed a pea pod.

Silas grabbed his pipe and looked around. "Where?"

Harrogate pointed to a dark, slowly moving foot-and-a-half long *S*. "Want me to kill it?"

"Naw, that's just a baby blacksnake. He'll fatten up on mice and such. I'd take it kindly if he wouldn't climb my leg, though."

When Harrogate came closer, the reptile edged under the porch. "You'd sung a different tune if his daddy'd showed up."

"I've known them big'uns to be mean," Silas admitted. "One about chased me out of the cornfield one time. But, hell, dry weather puts a kink in my tail, too. Even snakes need water."

Distant thunder split the afternoon silence. Silas's bluetick beelined under the porch. Harrogate nodded. "It's God's judgment."

"What do you mean, Bud? That sound?"

"No, that's a blessing. I mean the drought. It's God punishing the federal government."

Silas cut his eye toward Harrogate and relit his pipe.

"You been slipping off to Holiness meetings?"

"Silas, you know better'n that. Long as church don't bother me, I'll leave it be, and we'll both be happy. What I'm talking about is I remember my grandmother's opinion of Yankees. She was one of the few in our neck of Tennessee who came out for secession. Said the weather borne her out."

Silas knocked out his pipe on the porch rail. "You're going to have to explain that one."

"Granny said it was plain as the nose on her face, and that was saying something. Her nose looked like somebody'd hit her in the face with an anvil when she was a baby. Anyway, she'd noticed when the Yankees held sway it didn't rain, cows didn't give milk, crops failed. But when the Rebs had the upper hand, it rained, we had food. God's judgment, she called it."

"So this park business is the same thing?"

"I'd take it so."

Silas looked to the woods across the field. "Bud, we might have us a storm. Thunder's getting closer. Wind's from the southwest." He scratched the back of his shoulder. "More I think about it, you might be right about that judgment business." The men stood and eyeballed the sky. Lightning snicked atop Mount Sterling—wind swirled dust devils in the yard.

"That flash was a mile off," Harrogate said.

"Coming this way."

Drops pocked the yard, creating marble-size craters.

"Must be ten degrees cooler," said Harrogate.

"We might take to killing hogs."

Harrogate sniggered. "It'll be a while before that, Silas. Here it comes."

At the first close lightning Silas moved to the opposite end of the porch. Thunder was almost instantaneous, rattling windows and causing the hound under the porch to moan. "I bet Roscoe's shit hisself," yelled Silas, but wind blew his words far from Harrogate. Silas watched yard dust turn to mud and skitter before windblown sheets of water. Confused songbirds flew in search of shelter. Wasps dodged under the eaves and settled like boats to a marina.

With the next crash of thunder rain began in earnest. Little red clay yard freshets became branches that made creeks, which combined in a general river after a minute or two. Silas didn't know which was worse, drought or storm, famine or feast. Harrogate did not flinch as lightning and thunder seemed simultaneous. The storm paused for a second, as if taking a short breath. Then hail the size of spring peas bounced like marbles in the yard. The men watched in fascination, as though they had never seen a thunderstorm.

Over on Carter Fork, Willie McPeters was passed out beneath a huge hemlock when the storm hit. He had neither money nor much desire to earn any, but knew the stills thereabout and lurked in the woods until the lookout fell asleep or was caught short, or some errand called him home. Then McPeters stole what he could carry.

The afternoon found him facedown on prickly needles, small ants wandering into his ears. He had pissed his overalls sometime around dawn, and yellow jackets and butterflies alike had found his front tempting fare. The first riffs of thunder did not faze him, and the coming wind bothered only a wisp of hair on the back of his head. A solitary crow jeered from the top of the hemlock.

He likely would not have started awake even at the onset of rain, but an ant mining in his nose did the job. He sneezed, and the force of it nearly made him retch. Digging brought a fair-size black ant entangled in a wad of dried snot. He ate it slowly, looking over the ground beneath him as if he had no idea who or where he was.

He stared at the broken jar beside him with no recognition. He picked up a shard, sniffed it, licked it carefully, then threw it as far as a sitting toss would carry. Closer thunder made him look to the top of the tree and decide perhaps he needed to move with the crow, which headed for whatever shelter a bird could find.

Standing made him woozy, but he stepped into the path and looked up the hill and down, turning finally downhill and stumbling from the hemlock. A crash of thunder frightened him into a run, and he made it past the second bend in the trail before he tripped on a tree root and flipped ass over kettle. He hit on his belly with a *Whuf!* and for about ten seconds could not inhale. When simultaneous lightning and thunderclap restored his breathing, he crawled to his knees.

Rain began to pock the dry trail as he stood and looked up the mountain. Again he saw lightning and heard thunder at the same time, and began to run back downhill.

It was pouring by the time he tumbled onto his porch like some windblown weed. Sheets of wind-borne water washed that side of the house. When hail came, he went to the yard and held out his hands like he could prevent such phenomena. Wet to the bone to begin with, he shivered, and came into the porch's shelter when his scalp began to bleed.

He went inside, shuffling from room to room like he was looking for some solution to this storm. He finally stopped in what had been the kitchen when there had been enough people there to prepare and eat a meal. In a cabinet all he found were mouse turds and dead spiders. He remembered a bucket of springwater on the back porch.

He took up the dipper and was about to have a long drink when lightning hit the top of a dead chestnut uphill of the house. He dropped the gourd and opened his mouth in a silent *Oh, shit* as the tree split at the top. Electricity traveled its length and plowed a beeline to his house. Every hair on McPeters's body stood as stiff as a porcupine quill as something traveled under or through or over the house. The smell of scorched hair blended with the crash of the chestnut top as it hit the room that used to be his father's.

McPeters rubbed his bleeding head, which had considerably less hair than a minute before. He went inside and stared, transfixed at flame in his own house. The fire caught quickly, but with it came heavy rain through the opening in the roof. Soon McPeters, coughing, rubbing his crotch, and dancing like a kid needing to piss, found it too smoky to stay inside. He grabbed his rifle from over the back door. On the porch he looked around the corner at the fire, which put out as much smoke as a Shay locomotive heading upgrade.

Within fifteen minutes the fire seemed dead. His father's bedroom was full of chestnut timber, broken joists, and mangled tin. He tried, but the tree would not move, jammed somehow into the corner where a chiffarobe used to sit. The bed had not held a mattress in years. If anyone had been lying there, he would have been impaled by a limb.

The outside wall consisted of snaggled studs over which two layers of wallboard had been nailed. The insulation was a layer of newspapers, which had disappeared in the fire along with most of the wallboard. McPeters could have thrown a cat through the wall, had he had one willing to be caught. The only unscathed piece of furniture was the washstand in the opposite corner—washstand in name only, having never held a basin or pitcher. Old Rafe used to keep a pistol and a box of shells in the drawer, but McPeters found only a mouse nest and half a black walnut hull.

When the rain slacked, he went to the yard and decided moving the tree was not something he needed to do that day. Smoke had ceased to rise from that end of the house, and the sky showed no sign of clearing. Thunder rolled in the distance as if warning folks not to follow.

He felt oddly calm. Something about flames in his own house subdued him. He needed a drink. He had a headache. His eyes were scratchy. Having neither drink nor aspirin, he decided to finish sleeping off his hangover. He lay in his bed, rifle beside him like a child's stuffed toy.

He woke about suppertime to the stench of burning house. He kept his eyes closed for a minute, listening to fire crackle. When something fell and shook the bed, he opened them and saw a wall of smoke. He grabbed the rifle, rolled out of bed onto the floor, and wormed his way outside.

By dark there was nothing left of the ramshackle house. It had caught from an unnoticed smoldering coal, and finally collapsed onto itself, cracking and roaring like giant popcorn bursting, before the fire petered out in waning shades of orange and red.

McPeters shrugged. He still had a barn.

· · ·

The storm passed over Jim Hawkins's place quickly and did little damage. He was in the yard, offering thanks for the rain, when he saw smoke from Carter Fork. He saddled his horse and headed that way, hoping this was not a lightning-set fire he'd take days to put out, or a fire at his homeplace. He crossed where Carter Fork entered Cataloochee Creek and headed up the little road beside the branch. A mile up the road he saw that the smoke likely came from either his homeplace or the McPeters compound. He spurred the horse as his heart raced. Halfway up the hill he stopped to rest, since he could see it was McPeters, not Hawkins, whose patrimony was ablaze. He looked to the left up a trail where he knew there to be two graves. Who was buried there no one absolutely knew, except they were Confederate deserters killed by Kirk's Yankee raiders at the end of the war—or Confederate outliers killed by Teague's home guard—or Union soldiers killed by God knew who. At least, Jim thought, it had something to do with the end of that awful war and could have been some of his ancestors.

When he got to the McPeters place, it was too far gone for him to do anything but sit his horse and watch the pile smolder. No sign of Willie. He tied the horse and poked around. He yelled "McPeters," but no one answered. "Wonder where he is," Jim muttered. "Dare I hope he was home and couldn't get out?" He decided that was an un-Christian thought, then reflected he nonetheless hoped it to be true. He did not see McPeters, who scuttled silently up the ridge behind, occasionally pausing to sight the rifle at Jim's back and make a little firing noise with dry lips.

CHAPTER 25

Bucket of Balls

In the late spring of 1932 Mary Carter and her sons decided they'd had enough of park regulations and bought a small farm with a fair-size house and large barn close to Zeb and Mattie. Mary hadn't moved in decades, and dreaded it like the plague.

As a girl she had picked up stakes she didn't remember how many times. Her father had been a good man, but that had been the trouble. He'd give a man not only his cloak and coat but the rent money if the man had a sad enough story. Before they settled in Suttontown, she had lived in any number of little Tennessee settlements, Ellejoy and Prospect, Chilhowee and Nails Creek, Sandsuck and Big Pine. One particularly penurious year, the household knew the rent was due by a certain sheepish rake to her father's gait when he walked down the lane. Women and children started packing, dogs ceased to bark and ran to their kennels, while chickens lay down and crossed their legs to be yanked up into coops. Moving required cooperation.

They didn't own much back then—but it all seemed heavy. They carried a cookstove from place to place, and Mary would cringe every time she looked at the mass of iron and steel—a white porcelain scratched and scarred Knox Mealmaster with water jacket and warmers. Her father made a dolly from a knocked-down packing crate and four crazy wooden wheels to move it from house to wagon, but when they pushed it on rough ground, the range slid onto whoever pulled in front, so they made kindling out of the dolly and wheels alike.

They always packed the stove first, its weight over the front axle. Behind it came whatever furniture they happened to own, which varied from move to move. Kitchen table, bottom to the range, legs disassembled and stowed next to the side panels. If they had a mirror, it came next, padded with a ratty quilt, against the tabletop. Dresser base backed to the mirror. Bed rails slid underneath to the front of the wagon. Beds next, headboards, footboards, and mattresses, along with anything else flat, secured by hemp rope. They crammed baskets of potatoes and onions, chicken coops, canine enclosures, crates of blankets and quilts and clothing, jars of preserves and pickles, crocks, and tools against the furniture so it would not move. Last came chairs, facing backward, some with splint bottoms, others upholstered and patched, still more seatless, backless, or both, destined for kindling wood or repair.

They left Grindstone one afternoon just a step before the landlord. They didn't even remove the warmers from the cookstove—in fact, a few coals remained, so the stovepipe pointing at Mary's grandmother's head smoked like a cannon barrel. When the mules pulled, the load made an ominous, shifty racket, but her father did not stop to rearrange. They careered down the mountain, and amidst a left-hand curve the right-hand forward wheel ran over a fair-size rock. The next thing Mary knew, the cookstove headed warmers first toward the stakes, which cracked upon impact. She jumped off the back ahead of a crate of poultry. The wagon turned over and the cookstove landed upside down on the roadside, along with the flutter and chaos of chickens and turkeys, her father having decided to diversify. They did without warmers that winter.

Hiram Carter had begun life as poor as Job's turkey, but ended up owning at least one of everything. His wife, Mary, was also acquisitive, and when he died, even though their closets bulged, she could not bear to throw or give away even a necktie. Manson and Thomas inherited their father's penchant for hoarding against a rainy day, and had broadened it to include such items as a canoe, for which Thomas had traded a horse collar, two pocketknives, and a dollar. No matter that Cataloochee Creek was too skinny to navigate, no pond graced the valley, or that the vessel leaked. Just as Thomas could not pass up a bargain, his brother saw no sense in buying one can of coffee when he had room for three, and was delighted that the empties made convenient containers for rusty nuts, stripped-thread bolts, and bent nails.

So Aunt Mary and her sons fretted about moving. It was one thing to accumulate a life's worth of truck when you knew the life would be lived in one place. But to move it all? And when?

Hiram—or at least Mary's remembrance of him—had some advice. "I'd move before bad hot weather," he told her. "It makes you crazy."

"How in the world will we manage all this?"

"Put one foot in front of the other and don't think, just do. It'll go by before you know it."

"Can't we leave some of this?"

"Like what?"

"That rusted plow yonder."

"Honey, my brother John made that. You can't get shed of something like that."

"The boys never use it. They bought a new one five or six years ago."

"It's still a good plow."

"There's that basketful of rusted pipes in the shed."

"Honey, grandmother Carter made that basket. As for them fittings, sure to goodness when you throw them away, you'll need them the next day. Besides, if they have another big war, they'll be good for scrap."

"Hiram, I declare. I can't talk you out of nothing."

"Now, sweetheart, next thing you know you'll want to ditch your clock."

"Hiram Carter, you made that for me. I'd sooner leave myself behind."

"Glad to hear that. Now, Mary, if you want to get shed of something, what about that string you've been saving? It's the size of a medicine ball. Or all them empty jars?"

"That's different. A body could need that soon enough."

So they stopped arguing about what and began to plan how. Thomas and Manson wrote to Hugh Carter, Levi Marion's oldest boy, to see if he and his brother Rass might help.

Thomas and Manson and Mary boxed and bagged and otherwise corralled their stuff. Mary had wanted to learn piano not long after they'd built the big house, so Hiram had traded for one in Georgia. How a Yankee piano by Hallett & Davis had made its way to Elberton, Georgia, was beyond him, but he traded right for it. Now, under the square grand with rosewood top and ebony legs, sat boxes stacked with sheet music, more or less arranged by genre—at least they had attempted to put Saturday night in one place and Sunday morning in another.

Mary's two large quilting frames and many embroidery hoops and a collection of all colors of thread had to be moved. Bags of rags to make hooked rugs, stashes of scraps and batting for quilts. Dyestuff. Pictures of Jesus. Jellies and preserves, pickles and chowchow, beans and corn. A smokehouse full of hams.

She saved calendars for reasons known only to herself, but if anyone happened to wonder exactly when the blizzard of '03 had started, she could show them. Only trouble, they now came to be packed away, and she forgot which quadrant of which room of which building they were in. Boxes of *The Progressive Farmer* and *Good Housekeeping* and *The Saturday Evening Post,* what Sears catalogs they had not consigned to the outhouse, and newspapers. Boxes of home remedies and patent medicine. Sunday school quarterlies. And a file of obituaries clipped from newspapers going back to the last century, as if to prove to Saint Peter she had outlived everyone. She had kept every letter or postcard anyone had written to her, and store circulars if she thought she might be interested in ordering something in the future. "Mama, why don't we burn all this?" asked Manson. "Paper adds up. Gets heavy on you."

"One day I'll be old," she said. "And these will be a comfort. I'll read them and remember where I was when they came."

"You was mostly in the front room, weren't you?" he said, and it was true enough. Hiram had been a wanderer, but Mary had rarely left Cataloochee.

"You know what I mean," she said. "This is my life."

Manson and Thomas could not part with tools or fasteners, whether rusted, worn out, or new. A shed held everything from buggy springs to a posthole digger with only one blade. Baskets were crammed with grease fittings, plow points, and rings from long since dry-rotted harnesses. Thomas found a bucket of balls, four or five round creek rocks wrapped with string and black tape—their childhood baseballs. They debated whether to keep or toss, and finally decided it stayed with the shed. The new farm had no spacious outbuilding except the barn, and Manson figured they might dismantle the shed, in which case they would move it, balls and all.

Had they stopped to think, they would have walked away with only the clothes on their backs and begun anew (for they had at least three cents of every nickel Hiram had ever made), or killed themselves on the spot rather than attempt such a Herculean task. But they unreflectively sorted and piled stuff in corners. After a few weeks, though, they debated whether to leave a few things behind, or at least give them away. Jim Hawkins turned down such offers as a scythe with half a blade, and a broken grindstone.

A cattleman came in a stake-bed truck for their last eleven head of livestock. He gave them two dollars apiece, figuring to resell them in Asheville for four. The next day Hugh Carter showed up in a faded green Studebaker ton-and-a-half. Four boys rode in the cab—Hugh, Rass, and two of Rass's dorm rat friends. Rass had just finished his freshman year at Chapel Hill, and his eastern North Carolina buddies thought it a lark to come to the mountains, help the hillbillies, and maybe catch a trout while they were at it.

Hugh emerged and lit a Camel. "Boys, looks like we got a job of work," he said, eyeing what he feared was only the beginning of an avalanche of stuff. Thomas and Manson came to the porch. "You boys make yourselves at home," Manson yelled. "We'll get you some water."

By dinnertime Silas and Jim had shown up. "By God, that's a stout truck," Silas said. "Hugh, is it yours?"

"Nah, I borrowed it from the man who owns it. I put a new Bendix on it at the garage I work at, and he said if I'd not charge him labor, he'd let me borrow it two or three days."

"Them high round fenders put me in mind of a big old praying mantis."

Mary rang the dinner bell. She put a feast on the table—ham and fried chicken, mashed potatoes and gravy, soup beans, turnip greens, and biscuits. They washed it down with plenty of iced tea and sweet milk. Dessert was hot apple pie.

"You expect us to work after that dinner?" asked Jim.

"Can't take a nap," said Thomas. "Except for Mama's bedstead, they're all apart. Rest of us'll sleep on a cot or the floor till we get moved."

"Jim, lead us off," said Manson. "You got experience."

"Take the heaviest first. That'd be the cookstove."

"You hadn't had such a good dinner, it'd be cold enough to move by now. It'll have to go in the next truck," said Mary.

"Then let's clear this table and take it apart. Here. You boys get a pair of pliers from my toolbox. Come on, college boy, it won't hurt," Jim said to Rass with a grin. "I'll be in back of the truck when you get it outside."

So they loaded the truck. Mostly furniture—tables and beds and chairs, and Mary's fancy davenport, and the black walnut corner china Hiram had made. Trunks full of quilts and blankets. Into each hollow Jim directed something be jammed—a towel, or a runner, or a basket. He pointed and they lifted and grunted, and by mid-afternoon their burden was secure.

Jim figured to give them this one day, then back to his job. Thomas and Manson were tired, but willing to head to Saunook. Hugh and Rass were sweaty but figured they might as well get it over with. Rass's buddies looked half-dead. "How can three people have so much stuff?" one asked.

"It's not the quantity," Rass said. "It's the quality. All this furniture was built to last, not like they make it now."

Hugh laughed. "Listen to my twerpy kid brother, will you? An expert on everything."

"I know more'n you, big man."

"Maybe about some things. I know more'n you about how to keep this old baby running."

"Let's go," said Manson. "Quicker we get going, the quicker we get back."

So they piled in and headed to Saunook, a journey that took nearly till dark. They unloaded, set up beds, ate a snack, and spent the night in deep, dreamless sleep.

They were up well before daylight and back to Cataloochee by nine. Two loads that day, two the next. Hugh had to have the Studebaker back in Waynesville the next afternoon, so they returned for one last fling. The rest could be moved with pickup and team and wagon.

This time they loaded the cookstove, Aunt Mary having cooked her last meal at the homeplace. It had not been moved in thirty years. Several hundred pounds of ornate porcelain enameled steel and cast iron, it had cooked countless bushels of beans and had fried enough chickens to overpopulate poultry heaven. Jim swore it had taken root, but they finally budged it. The warmers were off, the eyes and grates out, and the oven and ash and fire doors removed, but it still weighed more than a thing that size had any right to.

They saved two pieces of furniture to ride behind the stove. One was an upholstered chair perfect for Aunt Mary to ride in. The other was the hall clock, which, after they padded it, reminded Rass of a coffin. He thought it wise not to say that out loud.

Mary emerged from the house, head held as high as she could manage on that cloudy morning. She wore the black dress and veiled hat she had worn to church since her husband had died in 1926. Her right hand held an ash bucket containing coals from their last fire, covered with a metal lid.

"Mama, what's that?" Thomas asked.

She looked at him with the tenderness a mother reserves for a sweet but dumb child. "Why, Thomas, that's right, you never moved before."

"No, ma'am."

"Well, this is what the old people did. When they got married, they built a fire and never let it go out. When they moved, they took coals to start a fire in the new place. Me and Hiram moved this fire from the old cabin. I reckon his daddy and mama did, too. No telling how old it is."

"What if it sets your chair on fire?"

"It'll ride in the cab with you all. If anybody don't care to set with it, they can come back with me. Or walk. But hit's a-going."

Thomas and Manson tenderly helped their mother into the back of the truck, where she looked around as if momentarily confused, then smiled. "There you be," she said, to no one seen by anyone else. She sat primly in the easy chair and leaned to touch the clock strapped beside her.

Hugh started the truck after the rest found their places. Rass climbed aboard beside his great-aunt, who, when they began to roll out, took what she feared was her last look at the house where she and Hiram had spent so long together. Something caught in her throat, and she bit the back of her hand to keep from crying out. Rass balanced himself on the chair and put his arm around her shoulders. The last thing anyone saw of them was Rass handing a white handkerchief to Aunt Mary, who by then bawled like a baby.

CHAPTER 26

Real Mountaineers

The Cataloochans who had moved to Saunook—Jake and Rachel, Mattie and Zeb—were tired of farming. Seemed the ground there wasn't as fertile, and, besides, they were getting to an age where they wanted to sit instead of work. They approached the owner of a defunct Pure Oil station to see if he would lease it to them. "I'm not getting a thing now," he said, "so if we, say, rent on tenths, a tenth of something's better'n a tenth of nothing."

So M&R Pure Mountain Mercantile opened, rushing the spring of 1931 with two dozen quilts Mattie had made, a similar number of Rachel's paintings, a scattering of tablecloths and pillowcases and other embroidered goods, a collection of peach-pit figurines Jake had carved, and miscellaneous items from the stockholders' homes. They opened of a morning, built a fire, and looked at one another until dinner. After eating, they watched no one enter the little gravel parking lot until they locked up and went home. After a week or two they posted a sign telling customers how to find them, but no one did until the first of March.

They reopened on a daily basis on April first, and by summer were actually selling a few things.

Over the winter they held on, and by the beginning of tourist season had recruited other craftspeople. The 1932 season added canned food, along with baskets and bedspreads, jams and jellies, slingshots and carved fish, bittersweet wreaths and dried corn arrangements, wooden back scratchers and birdhouses.

One day Mattie found one of Hannah's old bonnets, and thought it might be fun to wear it to the store. A tourist from South Carolina that day bought five dollars' worth of goods. The man tried his best to buy the bonnet for his wife, but Mattie—not having learned that when a customer offers cash money for something not actually nailed to the building, you sell it—refused to part with something that had belonged to her mother-in-law.

That evening Zeb suggested she wear full regalia—bonnet, one of Hannah's old dresses, an apron, old-timey shoes—and maybe even affect a cob pipe. "Bet you'll be our top salesman," he said.

Before the next day was over she had sold fifty dollars' worth and would have been ecstatic had not the shoes rubbed blisters on her left heel. A particularly loud individual from the north took Jake aside as he and his family were leaving. "You know why I bought all this here? You're the real thing. I can find a salesgirl in a skirt and blouse anywhere. You're real mountaineers."

"I think we've struck oil," said Jake. "If they want real mountaineers, we'll give it to them."

"Yeah," said Mattie. "Remember when Lige and Penny put a spinning wheel at their boardinghouse? Nary a one of them remembered how to run it, but it brought in the business." Next day they moved Hannah's old spinning wheel into the entryway. "Anybody know how to work this thing?" asked Mattie. Before dinnertime Mattie, dressed in one of Hannah's old outfits, made a passable run at carding and spinning flax. Rachel sketched her profile in silhouette for a series of roadside signs to plant in both directions. The cash register was noisy.

Jake proved a hit with customers, sitting in a rocker beside the fireplace, carving and telling stories. His more outlandish yarns came to be known as Jake Tales, and one day a newfangled folklorist showed up with a tape recorder.

Drummers stood in line to try to sell them salves and yardsticks, souvenirs and flyswatters, patent medicine and yard ornaments. The cracker companies also noticed, and soon M&R Pure Mountain Mercantile sold Nabs, and soft drinks from a cooler on the back wall. Penny candy and hoop cheese followed like inevitabilities.

One morning a man entered the store. His face was square, like in the Can You Draw This? ads in *Grit* and *The Saturday Evening Post*. Pleasant enough smile to go with bushy eyebrows and horn-rimmed glasses. A flattop haircut finished the cube that was his head. He smelled of pomade and toilet water.

His suit showed every wrinkle known to mankind, and was the luster and color of his face. His carrying case bulged as if it were about to explode.

Mattie removed her corncob pipe from her mouth. "Kin I hep ye?"

"Just looking at your wares," the man said, putting down his case. "Here's my card." Raised print announced that Preston G. Offhaus represented the Galax Import Company. He walked the three aisles, occasionally stopping to pick up an item.

"Howdy, stranger," said Jake from the rocker near the potbellied stove, although it held no fire, and outside was hot for April. "Nice we're having weather."

"Yes," said the man, after a moment's hesitation. He shook Jake's hand. "You work here?"

Jake's overalls bore multicolored patches, and he had cut the brim of his straw hat with a coffee can to look like a mule had bitten a hunk from it. "I'd not call this working. I just set here and talk and every now and again carve me up a bird or something."

"But you are connected with the business?"

"I'm one of the stockholders."

"Do you do any buying?" He produced another card.

"You walked past our head buyer, Mr. Offhaus. That a German name?"

"Yes, originally."

"Where are you from?"

"Near Harrisburg, Pennsylvania."

"That so. What do you sell?"

"Imported goods of all sorts. Great prices. High quality. You can make a killing on it."

"You could talk to Mattie. Me, I think we should only stock mountain goods."

"Come hear about a golden opportunity."

They gathered around the sales counter with coffee. His valise contained several catalogs—baskets, hooked rugs, pieces of small furniture, ironware, stoneware, lamps, and light fixtures. He even carried hearth brooms. All made overseas.

"Mr. Offhaus, we sell a lot of this already," Mattie said.

"I saw that," he said. "But let me show you prices. That three-legged stool you stock has a six-dollar price tag. The same identical item I will sell you for two. You can retail it for four, doubling your money. Or for the six it's selling for now, triple it. Your stack of rugs over there? You retail that little one for eight. I'll sell you one for three."

Mattie scratched her head. "How can you do that?"

"Quantity, madam. Plus cheap labor."

"Are they as sturdy as what we carry?"

"Absolutely. I'd pit my merchandise against anything in the country. How many of those stools will you sell in a season?"

"I'd guess two dozen," Mattie said.

"So—follow me—you're currently grossing a hundred forty-four dollars on that item. I'm guessing you pay three for it."

"Four," said Jake.

"Hm. So that's ninety-six dollars cost of goods—leaving you forty-eight dollars in profit. Sir and madam, I suggest that's not enough. Price my stool at five instead of six, gross a hundred and twenty dollars, net seventy-two. You have made twenty-four extra dollars while lowering the retail price, which will increase your volume. Or you could sell it for six like you're doing now, and pocket ninety-six dollars. You can't lose!"

The odor of hair oil and stale Luckies was getting to Jake. "What about what I said before, Mr. Offhaus?"

"You mean about mountain merchandise, Mr. Carter?"

"Yes, sir."

"There are mountains in Japan, Mr. Carter."

Jake finished his coffee and turned to the salesman. "Sir, am I to understand that you would propose that we pass this off as real North Carolina merchandise?"

"Why not?"

"Well, in the first place, it's *not*."

"Virtually indistinguishable, I assure you."

"Mr. Offhaus, I've never lied to a customer—at least not about what they're buying. I might tell a stretcher every now and then, but I won't tell a man a stool's made over the mountain when it comes from Japan."

"Jake, we could sample some of these," said Mattie. "Maybe a dozen hooked rugs. Put up a sign saying they're imports. See what happens."

"There's the ticket," said Offhaus, producing an order book from an inner pocket. "I'm ready."

"Hold on, Mattie," said Jake. "Looks like we need to have a meeting of the minds."

"If I might interject," said Offhaus, "you also need to know that your competitors buy these items like hotcakes. You don't want to be left behind in the profit race."

"Are they selling them as mountain-made?" asked Mattie.

"You betcha."

Jake took Offhaus by his arm. "Sir, you best let us hash this out. Come back in a few days."

The salesman repacked his bag. "Let me leave you a few matches. I'll call on you again the next time through—about a month."

Jake picked up an embossed matchbook. "These made overseas, too?"

"Heavens, no. Those are the world's best. Made in Pennsylvania."

Jake smiled like he had just laid a straight over two pairs.

That night the stockholders met, and did not take long to decide not to order from Offhaus. "You know," said Rachel, "if we bought that imported stuff, it would take money out of a local man's hand. I bet Galax Imports doesn't pay those Japanese or whoever more'n a nickel for something they sell for two dollars. That isn't Christian."

"Well, ordering from this company might be good business," Mattie said. "But I'll bow to you men on that."

Zeb scratched his ear and stretched. "The man made a good argument about profit, but Rachel's right. If we do right by our suppliers and customers, we aren't going out of business. Even if we did, we could still hold our heads up."

Jake smiled. "Going out of business wouldn't be the worst thing by far. We've all been run out of our homes. That's a sight worse."

So they agreed to reconcentrate on cider and honey, blankets and bedspreads, back scratchers and walking sticks. Local stuff. They added craftsmen and -women to their stable of suppliers. M&R Pure Mountain Mercantile seemed on its way, if not to prosperity, at least to stability. As Jake said, "It keeps beans on the table."

It was warm for the first of June. Aunt Mary Carter stood on the porch of their new house—new to them, anyway—and listened to the Studebaker's transmission whine down the mountain like it was holding back a landslide. She pulled a wisp of hair from the back of her neck and fanned herself. "Where in the world are we going to put all this?"

They had moved everything from the big house in the valley. Boxes and barrels and crates full of more than fifty years of married life cluttered the hallway. Every porch was laden. The hall clock could barely be heard for the piles of stuff. The barn loft was full. Manson had even parked boxes in the outhouse, a two-holer with room on either side.

Mary unpiled a chair and plumped down. "Lord have mercy, Hiram, what will we do?"

"You'll think of something," he said, leaning against a stack of boxes and tamping his pipe with a nail head. "I have an idea things will work out." He blew smoke toward the ceiling. "They always do. Who's that coming?"

Mary stood and saw a woman walking purposefully down the road. She wore a gingham shirt and dungarees with rolled cuffs. A straw hat with a red feather in its band angled toward the back of her head. She waved. "Good day, Aunt Mary."

"Lord, it's Mattie Banks," Mary said to Hiram, who disappeared with his pipe smoke. The women embraced in the yard.

"Child, how are you? It's been a coon's age."

"I'm happy as if I had good sense," said Mattie. "You look well."

"I'm tuckered out. Too old to move."

Mattie looked around. "Aunt Mary, you do have a God's plenty. I know what to do with a lot of this stuff."

"Lord, child, I'd be tickled to hear what."

"You know me and Zeb and Jake and Rachel opened a store?"

"I've heard that."

"We're trying to stock mountain-made goods. Quilts, bedspreads, doilies, that kind of thing. Honest mountain products. So the money will stay here instead of going off."

"Sounds like a good idea. How are you doing with it?"

"Very well, Aunt Mary, but we need something extra. I think you might be that something."

"What in the world do you mean?"

"Look at you. The essence of a mountain woman—stout, straight, determined. Rachel couldn't paint a better picture than you in the flesh. You know how to spin and embroider and quilt and I don't know what all. Churn, can, weave. And look at all this stuff you have brought! Quilts, hooked rugs, furniture, geegaws of all kinds. It's perfect. Tourists will buy anything."

"Child, I don't know what you're getting at."

"Aunt Mary, don't you see? You come to the store whenever you want to—every day if you do, every now and then if you don't. Just be yourself. Talk to the customers, do a little embroidery, quilt a little, just be everybody's favorite aunt. Zeb and Jake'll help sort all this stuff out for you. Keep what's really valuable for yourself. Sell the rest at the store. It'll boost us up and give you something to do. Make you a little money. You can be a stockholder. What do you say?"

"Child, I don't know nothing about business."

"What makes you think any of the rest of us do? Or did, until we started in? Oh, Aunt Mary, it's perfect. All this stuff, and you're the real thing."

"I've never had a job."

Mattie took Mary's hands in hers. "Look at these. How old are you, Aunt Mary?"

"I'll be seventy-one this fall, if the Lord lets me live."

"Have these hands ever been idle in those seventy-one years?"

"I'd have to say not much, that's a fact."

"Then it's not a job. What would you do if you were here? You'd be working at something. Even if you were sitting, you'd be embroidering or something. Do it at the store is the only difference. Just because you call it a job doesn't mean it's drudgery."

"I'll have to talk about it."

"To Manson and Thomas? Well, of course. They could help, too."

"Oh. Them. Yes. Of course."

"It'll be great fun. I'll come back tomorrow and we'll talk it over some more."

"If I can find my kitchen stuff, I'll bake us a cake."

"Oh, see—we could sell that, too. You bake as good a pound cake as there is in creation. I bet we could get a nickel a slice for it."

"Pshaw, child. Who's going to pay that kind of money for an old woman's cake?"

"You'll see, Aunt Mary. You'll see."

By summer Mary Carter came to the store every day. She found enough bonnets and Mother Hubbards and button-up shoes to outfit Mattie and Rachel for long careers, and Zeb and Jake enjoyed wearing Hiram's old-fashioned suits every now and then. Mary was well on her way to becoming everyone's favorite Haywood County aunt. And Hiram smiled at her from behind Jake's rocker, as if the whole thing had been his idea.

CHAPTER 27

Hearthstones

Levi Marion spent the winter of 1932 as busy as any farmer in the county. He sharpened his edged tools, restrung straps, oiled, polished, and greased. New ground, new beginning. He might have lost his money, and he might be living off the charity of relatives—he and his brood lived in a tenant house on Zeb Banks's land—but he would prove he was still able to farm.

But his soil wasn't fertile, at least not to his standards, and spring was late, unpredictable. His father, Levi, had always planted beans on Good Friday, and in 1933, April the fourteenth seemed late enough to be safe. A May frost, however, dogwood winter, forced him to replant. Radishes and greens delighted the whistlepigs, which gathered in numbers sufficient to nibble every green shoot. Blackberry winter bit his apple trees. He took to his bed after another influx of groundhogs ate what little corn the crows hadn't stolen. It wasn't even the middle of June.

His oldest son, Hugh, visited often, and one weekday afternoon found his father in bed. He tried to talk him into getting up, but Levi Marion shrugged. "I ain't worth nothing," he said.

The rest of the family was out back stringing a pan of beans Mattie had brought. Hugh walked outside and sat beside Valerie. "Mama, we got to do something," he said, picking up a handful of beans. Ada was fourteen and as freckledy as a redhead despite her dark hair. She kicked George after he poked her in the ribs. "Quit that," said Hugh. "Papa's sick."

"Get a doctor," said Ruth Elizabeth, a ten-year-old with pigtails. Her mischievous smile usually brightened the gloomiest days, but today her lip stuck out.

"Honey," said her mother, "it isn't the kind of sick a doctor can help."

"What kind is it, Mama?" asked Mary, three years younger, a gingham ribbon in her hair.

"Homesick. He misses Catalooch real bad."

"So do we, Mama."

"We can't live there again," Valerie said, with a drawn-out sigh.

Hugh threw a handful of broken beans into the pan. "Here's an idea. Remember when we moved, you and Papa brought a bucket of coals from the old hearth?"

"I sure do. I was never so sad as when we found them dead and cold."

"Papa said that was a bad omen. Remember, he leaned on the mantel and cried."

Ada looked at her brother like he could barely remember to come in out of the rain. "What kind of idea is that?"

"That's not my idea, Miss Priss. Here it is. Why don't we steal our old hearthstones? And get some genuine Cataloochee firewood?"

Valerie's eyes brightened.

"Stealing's against the law," said Ruth Elizabeth.

"Ruth Elizabeth Carter, who laid those stones?" asked Valerie.

"Papa?"

"No, it was his papa, your grandpa."

"The one the tree killed?"

"That's right. Marion Carter."

"So those stones were his?"

"First his, then ours. But then the park came."

"We can't steal from the park."

Valerie brushed bean strings from her lap and stood. "I want you'uns to hear something. There's different kinds of stealing. The kind the Bible talks about, when you take something somebody needs. Like food, or cattle. That's stealing, and you'll go to hell for it sure as I'm standing here. But what Hugh's talking about is what you might call resurrecting hearthstones taken from folks that needed them—us—by something— the park—that don't have a bit of use for them. In fact, we might as well lift them before they burn down the house."

Hugh smiled at his mother. "When does Rass get home?"

"Thursday."

"Okay, here's the plan. Mama, make us a picnic. First thing Saturday we'll go to Catalooch. We'll take the truck, and stow our tools under a tarp. We'll let the fish poles show. If Hawkins is off somewhere, we'll— what was your word, Mama?—resurrect the hearthstones. If he's around, some of us can divert him so me and Rass and George can lay them in the truck."

Ruth Elizabeth frowned. "If we get caught, do we go to jail?"

Hugh grinned at her. "We ain't going to get caught, Miss Worrywart."

Little Mary put up her hand. "I want to go to jail."

"Why, child?" asked her mother.

"They feed you light bread with ketchup."

Hugh rubbed his knuckles on her forehead. "Then I hope you get to go."

Rass arrived Thursday afternoon with a load of books in his cardboard suitcase and clothes in a duffel bag. Finished with sophomore year at Chapel Hill, all of seventeen years old in a month, still lost in the wonder of what to a Harvard man was a backwoods academy but to Rass was Greece and Rome and Renaissance all at once. He wanted to be a writer.

All crowded to see his books. A Latin primer. A dog-eared English grammar. A *Complete Works of Shakespeare*. *The College Book of Prose*, its cover decorated with Pan piping atop an Ionic column. A red-bound algebra text. H. Rider Haggard's *Swallow*. A well-worn *Camping and Wood-craft* to show his father what Horace Kephart did for a living.

Kep, as his friends called him, had boarded at Silas's house, and had impressed most of the Cataloochans except his host. "You can't tell he's a writer to listen to him," Levi Marion said. He opened the book to "Camp Making," read for a minute, and laid it back on the table. "Don't know why a body would need a book for that. I've known you need water and firewood and a level place to lay a bedroll since forever. But, you know, son, if he can make a living writing about building a dern fire, you can, too."

Hugh arrived Friday afternoon, and the family shifted into high gear. He gave their old pickup the once-over and pronounced it ready for the trip. Valerie and the girls killed, plucked, scalded, cut up, and fried chickens. They boiled eggs and potatoes and cut up onions for potato salad and deviled eggs. They made a gallon of tea and packed a basket with sweet pickles, blackberry jelly, apple butter, and chowchow. In the morning they planned to pack another with butter and cheese and sweet milk from the springhouse. By dinnertime the house smelled like Christmas.

They all slept like it was Christmas Eve that night, wakeful and anxious. On the road by five-thirty, crowded into the Model T, they made way slowly toward Cove Creek. Levi Marion stretched out in the truck bed with his brood, watching receding stars and wondering what the day would bring.

At the gap Hugh passed the new sign for the park and let the truck freewheel down the mountain long enough for his mother to scream, then shoved it into second gear. They had not seen this road in nearly a year, and no one said a word as they looked at abandoned houses, poison oak, thistles, tulip saplings, sumac. Future wilderness.

At Jim and Nell's place Hugh cut the motor and blew the horn. Mary scurried from Levi Marion's lap as he looked at the house like it was the prettiest thing he'd seen in a while.

Nell came out on the dogtrot, Little Elizabeth shyly holding her leg. Mack came running from the barn. "What are you all doing here?" Nell asked. "It's so good to see you."

"Nell, we're here for a picnic, just like tourists," said Valerie. "We'd love for you and the family to come, too. We've enough food for Pharaoh's army."

"Jim's off at Mount Sterling, but we'd love to join you."

The male Carters met in front of the truck. "Hear that?" asked Hugh. "Hawkins is off at Sterling, so we'll have time."

Levi Marion wrung his hands. "We need to be careful. We get caught . . ."

"Papa, let us worry about that. If we spread out by the creek for a picnic, we need an excuse to get the truck to the house. How about you hurt your foot a week or two ago?"

Levi Marion grabbed a snake stick. "Here's my cane. I can limp with the best of them."

Nell dressed Little Elizabeth in a yellow Sunday frock. She had given up on dressing Mack in anything but denim and flannel. He bounded out proudly wearing his duckbill cap. Nell carried a basket with bread and a jar of peaches. Everyone piled into and onto the truck and headed up the road.

At the corner of Lucky Bottom the road bent west with the creek. The motor was too loud for all to hear the collective gasp when they spied the homeplace crowded against the mountain two hundred yards away. It was intact, but that was about the only good anyone could say. Levi Marion had never let grass grow in the yard, but vegetation threatened to hide the porch. Someone had nailed a strip of siding across the front door, and windowpanes were broken. The building looked like an injured man with a bandage across his mouth.

The creek had not changed, making a sudden right bend by some huge rocks, creating a perfect wading and swimming hole. Years ago Levi Marion had terraced the bank with rocks so small feet might easily reach water. The group stopped and laid out a tarpaulin beside the bank and secured it with baskets. The women sat on its edge with the little ones.

"Mr. Carter, is your foot giving you trouble?" asked Nell.

"I just turned my ankle," Levi Marion said, winking at Valerie. "You ladies mind if we drive to the house? I oughtn't to be putting weight on it."

Valerie beamed at her husband. "Go ahead. We'll play with the young'uns until dinner."

A game of hide-and-seek broke out among the girls. Levi Marion, Hugh, Rass, and George headed to the house and backed the truck to the porch. "Here goes, boys," said Hugh, fetching tools from under the tarp. Rass removed the batten with a claw hammer and let his suddenly lame father enter first.

Their shoes shuffled on the pine floors thick with dust, ashes, bits of straw, nut hulls, droppings. At the doorsill into the kitchen, where they had measured the offspring every Christmas day, marking their heights with initials and year, Levi Marion rubbed the pencil marks with his stubby fingers, biting the inside of his cheek.

They turned to the fireplace. Marion had laid the hearth—three flat, beveled river stones three inches thick and not quite two feet wide. On either side rested brick pilasters. "Okay, let's work," said Hugh. "George, keep a lookout for Hawkins. Rass and me will knock out these bricks."

They made considerable racket with sledgehammer and pry bar, but the women at the creek did not seem to hear. Two people could not pick up one stone, but three could turn it over, and four could set it on the tarp and slide it to the truck.

The women were nowhere to be seen. "Two to go," said Levi Marion.

When they emerged with the third, the women sat on the creek bank while Ada, Ruth Elizabeth, and Little Mary headed their way, skipping like storybook girls. Ada turned her nose up at Rass. "You're sweaty. Shoo."

"You'd been working like this, you'd sweat, too."

"Girls perspire."

"Bull hockey."

"Get to work," said Hugh. "We got to cover this."

They stowed tools beside the rocks and covered it all. Levi Marion decided it looked suspicious, so he sent Rass to the barn for straw. Levi Marion went inside with the claw hammer and came out with the family doorsill. Rass returned with straw, and news that firewood aplenty lay in the shed. When all was loaded and covered, one might have guessed any number of things were underneath the tarp besides hearthstones.

At the creek, if Nell noticed anything strange, she offered no comment. All the children milled about, hungry, boys skipping rocks in the creek, girls picking flowers for the picnic.

When dinner was laid out, Levi Marion blessed it as they held hands. Then they fell to eating. Nothing but teeth and elbows for a quarter hour. Nell heard Jim's horse before the rest. "He'll want some dinner," she said, standing. Levi Marion prayed that he wouldn't examine their load.

Jim let the mare drink, then tied her. He hugged Valerie and shook hands with Levi Marion and the boys. Nell gave a slight smile to his glance at her, so he put his arm around her shoulders and kissed her cheek. "Mind if I take a bite of nourishment with you all?" he asked.

Jim gnawed a chicken leg and looked their truck over. "How old is that thing, anyway?"

"It's a 1916 model. It's about seventeen year old, now."

"Fords last forever, seems like. Hope mine goes that long. Or at least long enough to use the new road."

"What new road?" asked Hugh.

"You know Hell's Half Acre?"

They nodded.

"And you know where the road bends with the creek coming toward my house? Well, they plan to bridge the creek there and send a macadam road straight to Sal's Patch."

"Jim, that's steeper'n a mule's face. Nothing but a bear ever goes there."

"They say they're going to do it anyhow. Since Congress passed the Civilian Conservation Corps, they've been talking about having a camp full of those men in Catalooch. Already got a bunch working at Sugarlands. Trails, roads, the works."

"Roosevelt's doing good for a Yankee," said Levi Marion. "Folks pay attention to him."

"You bet." Jim picked up a thigh and walked to the old truck. "What you hauling?"

"Hay for folks to set on." Levi Marion's heart raced.

"She's going to drown!" shrieked Nell.

Rass and George and Mack had rolled up britches legs and waded in to look for crawdads. Little Elizabeth had decided to follow but had stumbled into the deepest bend, where her dress tail had caught on a rock. The water was nearly over her head, but the boys fished her out quickly. When Jim and Levi Marion rushed up, she was crying, but safe. While she swaddled the crying girl in a blanket, Nell fussed at Jim for not paying attention.

On the way to the creek Levi Marion left his limp behind, but still held his makeshift cane. He had forgotten which ankle he'd said he'd hurt. "I believe that scared the hurting out of it," he said.

Valerie had brought extra clothes, so Little Elizabeth soon wore a pair of trousers with the legs rolled up and a blue gingham shirt. "That's my Lizzie," Jim said, swinging her as she giggled. "You look great."

"She's a pretty one, all right," said Levi Marion. "Like her mother."

"Can you stay the night?" asked Jim. "Gets lonesome here. We could play and sing a little."

"Thanks, but we need to get back," said Levi Marion. "And I promised George he could fish that hole by the bend in the road before we leave."

"Suit yourself. But promise you'll bring this gang back. Make a week of it. Nell would love the company."

"Sure thing," said Levi Marion. "The women can arrange it."

After Jim left, they took Nell and her children back home. The Carters stopped on the way out to let George fish. "That was close," said Levi Marion. "I thought sure we was cotched."

Valerie hugged him. "You know, I doubt he'd have said a word. And I bet he'll look in the house before dark, just out of curiosity."

"We'll be long gone by then," said Levi Marion. "What's wrong? You look like something's on your mind."

"I'm worried about Jim and Nell."

"How come?"

"You didn't notice?"

"What?"

"You men wouldn't notice some things if they walked up and said hello. It's plain as day they ain't getting along."

"I ain't surprised."

"Why not?"

"First time I heard Jim Hawkins married a town gal, I thought to myself he might as well kiss Cataloochee good-bye. Stay in town with her and get civilized. When we heard she was moving over here with him, didn't I say it wouldn't last?"

"Not that I remember," she said with a grin.

"Well, I at least thought it."

"You were right. But the big question is about you. You feel all right about this load we're taking back?"

"Can't hurt. Thank you for thinking this up."

"It was Hugh's idea."

"I'll not hug him, but I'll give you one." As he held her, he looked over her shoulder at the contraband and wondered what the world was coming to. He didn't much like the direction it was going, but had to admit he felt some better.

BOOK 4

The Hardest Part

August 1933–August 1934

CHAPTER 28

Emergencies

One night, after they put the children to bed, Jim laid out a section of newspaper on the kitchen table. On it he set a bottle of Hoppe's number nine, three rags, and a short dogwood rod worn as smooth as soapstone. He unholstered his revolver and laid it on the table.

Nell, sitting opposite, glared at her husband. "Do you have to do that in the house?"

"It's windy out." He picked up the weapon and spun the cylinder.

"What if it goes off, Jim?"

He smiled, ejected the bullets, and held it toward her. "See, it's un-loaded. Relax, okay? You know as much about a gun as I do by now." He poured solvent on a strip of cloth and guided it into the barrel with the dogwood. An odor as distinctive as the flash of a cardinal in a cedar lingered over the table.

"I know. I'm just nervous tonight. A little stir-crazy, I think." She twisted a lock of hair with her right hand. "What was in that package in today's mail?"

"Word from headquarters. Evans sent a bunch of draft regulations to look over, sketches for a campground, that kind of thing. He wants me there next Wednesday."

"How do you plan to go?"

"I'll drive the car, unless you have another idea."

"Couldn't we go home first?"

He began cleaning the cylinder, pushing the extractor in and out and anointing it with solvent. "I thought this was home."

"You know what I mean. I haven't seen Mother and Father in a month. And they haven't seen the children."

"Ain't that kind of out of the way? I mean, *really* out of the way?"

"Not to me. You know I hate it here by myself. We could make it a family outing. We'll stay with my parents, you can drive to headquarters from there—and we'll return Sunday after church."

He wiped the weapon with a clean rag, then began to oil its mechanism. "I'll ride, then. You're talking a good four-hour drive from Asheville." The little chip of diamond on her hand glinted in the lamplight. "Besides, we'd have to leave Tuesday. That'd mean I'd be AWOL nearly a week."

"Take a little vacation, honey. You haven't had one since you started."

As he reloaded the revolver, he frowned as if in great pain. "Nell, after I see Evans, he'll want me back immediately. I can't take that kind of time."

"Do you mind if I go to Asheville anyway?"

"Suit yourself. Sounds like we'll be going in opposite directions." He reholstered the pistol and began to clean the table. While he worked, she thumbed through a *Good Housekeeping,* pausing at an ad for a Sunbeam toaster. He stood behind her chair and began to rub her shoulders. "When we get electricity, you can have one if you like."

"Do you really think so?" she asked, patting his left hand with her right.

"One of these days."

"Can't be too soon for me."

"Let's go to bed," he said, and slipped a hand into her blouse.

"Wash those hands first," she said, and squeezed his other hand.

. . .

A hard day's ride brought Jim over Balsam Mountain to the Cherokee nation, and from Smokemont a long, fairly straight haul to what seemed the crest of the world at Newfound Gap. He rested and ate, peering over thousands of acres of cut-over mountain range pointing skyward through clouds, like promises that God would one day heal the land. He figured to be five thousand feet above sea level, or more, and wondered if these ground squirrels were the same species as ones in the valley. After dinner he rode down to a brand-new campground on the Little Pigeon River, where he spent the night.

He walked into the park office promptly at eight Wednesday morning. Ray Bradley, hunched over a typewriter and frazzled like he had been working all night, jumped up and grinned. "Morning, Warden. Hope all is well with you."

They shook hands. "I'm fine, Ray. Just a little saddle-sore."

"You rode over here?"

"Nell took the auto to Asheville."

"I believe I'd have gone with her. Then you could have driven over."

"But I'd have had to stay with my in-laws."

"Point. You want coffee?"

"Sure."

"How do you take it?"

"Like I like my women. Hot and strong."

"Coming right up."

Two cubes of sugar made the coffee palatable. Jim headed toward Evans's office with a cup. "Boss in a good humor today?" he asked.

"Reasonable. Just don't say anything about the game."

"Wasn't that Saturday?"

"His Wildcats lost. He won't get over it until they win again."

Evans sat behind his desk looking out a picture window at a pair of squirrels tearing through the hemlocks. When Ray knocked, Evans swiveled and motioned them inside. "Morning, Hawkins. Have a seat. Ray, is that report ready?"

"No, sir."

"Damn it all, then, what are you doing in here? I need that report by ten."

"Yes, sir." Bradley closed the door as he left.

Evans's desk was clean of everything except a miniature brass top hat, upside down and full of paper clips, a brass nameplate, and his riding crop. He gave Jim a pointed once-over. "Well, Hawkins, I see you have not polished your boots."

"Sir, I forgot to pack my kit."

"Where did you stay last night?"

"At the campground."

"That would explain the lack of crease in your trousers. Why would you bunk there?"

"Anymore they don't appreciate a horse at a hotel, sir."

"I suppose not." He tapped the desktop with the crop. "It's a new era, Hawkins. Within a generation there won't be one person in a hundred who will know which is the business end of a horse. How does it feel to be part of a dying breed?"

Jim smiled. "Not bad. Give me a minute, though, and I might could feel sorry for folks who don't know a good horse."

Evans's eyebrows arched. "What are you implying, Hawkins?"

"Nothing, sir."

"Hawkins, you're a study. Are you as transparent as you seem?"

"Transparent, sir?"

Evans stood and looked out the window. "Guileless. There's a certain veneer of innocence about you that I don't know whether to trust or not."

"You know you can trust me, sir."

"I wouldn't have kept you otherwise. Tell me about your post. Are things going well?"

"Yes, sir. The leaseholders aren't giving me any trouble. Got into a brawl last weekend with a visitor, though."

"Describe the situation."

"I was patrolling Mount Sterling. Found a car with a couple in the backseat going at it like a house afire."

Evans's grin threatened to burst his face. "Did you try to arrest them? Or, better still, ask for sloppy seconds?" He tapped his leg with the crop.

"Sir, I didn't know what to do. I couldn't think of any law against open-air sex, except the Mann Act, but the car had North Carolina plates, and, if the woman was a minor, she sure had a lot of experience. Then I noticed a couple of buckets and a shovel next to the front bumper."

"Neither a poacher nor a pussy-hound be, the Bard almost said." Evans's crop switched an insistent rhythm on his thigh.

"Yes, sir. I waited to show myself until they had smoked a cigarette. When I made it clear I was going to charge them, he pulled a gun on me, but I wrestled it out of his hand. Ended up citing them for possession of a firearm and two flame azaleas."

"Amazing, isn't it—people all over think public land belongs to them, enough so to pull a weapon on a uniformed officer."

"Yes, sir." Jim shifted in his chair. "Actually, the woman was a class-mate of mine. She was just lonesome for flowers that used to grow at the homeplace."

"Sentiment is no excuse for stealing. Tell me about your fire situation."

"About the same, sir. Sporadic small fires. I can't quite figure it out."

Evans turned to face Jim. "It's a combination of things. Some folks are angry because they think the government stole their land. So they say, 'If I can't own it anymore, I'll just burn it down.' Then you have folks who start fires, then show up hoping we'll hire them—pay them actual cash money—to help put them out. Damnedest thing I ever heard. And then there's your common firebug, who simply likes to watch stuff burn."

"I expect I've got some of all of them, sir."

"Any suspects?"

"One. A man named McPeters. He's a strange one."

"How so?"

"He ain't right. Never has been. My daddy said he used to set fires when he was not much more than a baby. Like you said, he enjoys watch-ing things burn."

"If you catch him starting a fire, we will prosecute him to the fullest."

"Sir, I hope not to get that close to him. He'd just as soon shoot me as look at me."

"Then shoot him first."

"For no particular reason?"

"Self-defense is always justified, Hawkins. If you cross paths with a homicidal firebug, and always carry your weapon, sooner or later you can kill him with impunity. Enough of that. What did you think of the campground plans?"

"It's laid out nicely, sir. But there's one problem."

"And what would that be?"

"It's too close to the creek. What if it were to flood?"

"Damn, Hawkins, haven't you noticed that people want to get close to water? Hear it, see it, touch it. Folks would sleep *in* the damn creeks if they could figure out how. No, that campground will be at the water's brink. If it floods, they'll either get wet or be swept away, depending on the severity. How's the house we put you into?"

"Fine, sir."

"And your wife—Nell, isn't it?—by the way, a very good-looking piece, you lucky dog. Does she like her situation any better?"

"Can't say she does, sir."

"Is there anything we can provide that will help?"

"She sure would like to use the telephone."

"Impossible. I have told you, that is for emergency communications only."

"I know, sir. It's just that in the house she can't help but look at it every day. It'd be better if I put it in the barn."

"Then put it there, as long as you can figure out how to hear it ring." He sat at his desk and eyed Jim. "Hawkins, does your wife go to church?"

"Yes, sir. It's about all there is to do besides stay home and work."

"Do you?"

"Not always."

Evans laid down the crop and folded his hands under his chin as if in prayer. "Hawkins, you need to get your ass in church with that young woman. For two reasons. One, she's liable to meet some man."

Jim opened his mouth, but Evans shushed him quickly. "Listen, and that's an order. Even if she didn't meet a man, you need to be there to make sure she hears Jesus telling her to be content with her lot. It's God's will that she stand with you. And how in the hell is she going to hear that if you're not sitting beside her, you nincompoop?"

"I guess you have a point," said Jim.

"Of course. Now, look here. I want your opinion of these proposed trails."

Two hours later Jim was on his way home. He felt as if he'd given Evans a week's worth of entertainment and maybe even earned himself a raise.

On the late afternoon when Nell returned to Cataloochee, she met two cars on the way in. She refused to budge for the first, which finally reversed to let her by. The second driver would have none of that, so Nell backed into a tree, which shook her and the children but, upon reflection, was much preferable to tumbling off the mountain. The driver squeezed by her, at first lifting hand and finger signals, then spewing advice not to get out again until she learned some manners. To top things off, she had also spent much of the trip yelling at two children full of grandparental indulgence and a substantial amount of sugar.

When she pulled into the yard, stopped the Ford, and laid her forehead on the steering wheel, the children piled out and ran around the maple like wild Indians. Nell could neither control them nor nap, so collapsed in the bedroom, cool washcloth over her eyes, oblivious to the golden dying sunlight.

When Jim arrived, Mack had a bellyache, and Little Elizabeth's forehead was seriously warm.

Jim had put up vegetable soup—beef stock, plus tomatoes and beans and okra and potatoes and carrots and whatever had been left over after his kitchen garden had rioted with abundance. He heated a quart and found no one wanted to share. He ate quickly, sopped his bowl with bread, and then began to tend his invalids.

He fixed Nell a dollop of peanut butter on toast and a glass of sweet milk and took it to the bedroom. Mack had gone to bed, too, but when Jim checked, he said he was hungry. Jim scrambled two eggs with ham and ensconced his son at the kitchen table with milk. "I'll be right back, buddy. I want to see your sister."

Little Elizabeth lay outside quilt and sheet, knees drawn up, hair pasted to her pillow. Jim put a finger to her forehead. "Wow," he whispered. When he turned up the wick, he saw a red-faced girl dredging oxygen in shallow, rapid breaths.

When he smoothed her hair, she turned, moaning. "Darling, do you want some water?" he whispered. Eyes shut tightly, she frowned.

He carried a wet washrag and a glass of water when he returned. He held her upright, but she barely opened her mouth. Her dress was wet with sweat. He laid her bed gown on the back of a chair and turned her to unbutton her dress and peel it from her feverish, red-splotched body. He pulled her gown over her head and laid the washrag over her forehead, covering her lightly with a sheet.

He opened their bedroom door slowly, trying without success to avoid its high-pitched squeak. "Nell, honey, are you okay?" he asked softly.

"What is it?"

"Little Elizabeth has a fever."

"Oh my God. Let me see!" She bounded into the kids' room, Jim close behind. She felt Little Elizabeth's forehead and picked her up. "Oh, sweet baby, it's going to be all right. Mommy promises," she cooed. She leveled that look at Jim. "Right now, call the doctor."

"Honey, that telephone's for emergencies."

She clenched her jaw and grabbed Little Elizabeth a little tighter. "What in blue blazes do you think this is?"

"Let me fix some spicebush tea, best thing in the world for a fever. It'll give her relief way before we could get to town."

"Tea," Nell said. She wiped her daughter's forehead and mouth with the damp washrag. "My precious could die in my arms and you want to make tea. TEA? What kind of hillbilly hick are you, anyway?"

"Nell, I'm just trying to do what's best. This stuff'll sweat that fever out of her, I swear." He started to fill the teakettle.

"Jim Hawkins, call the doctor. *Now*."

Considerable heft to her words made him lift the receiver. After a half minute someone picked up. Jim arranged to be connected with Doc Bennett's office, but no one answered. Jim rubbed his eyes and asked for the hospital. They said Bennett was at Ironduff but a new doctor was there. "My daughter is sick," Jim said.

"Where are you?"

"Cataloochee. This is Warden Hawkins. My little girl has a high fever."

"Can you get her here by ten?"

"I'll try. Can you at least tell me what not to give her, or what to let her have? I see. Okay. Please tell the doctor to stay." He hung up.

"What did they say?"

"You heard my end of it. There's a Dr. McGuire there. The nurse said it could be one of any number of diseases. No way to tell over the phone. I'll get the car."

The hospital was a new three-story brick building with a stone-stepped portico. They walked up the steps a bit before eleven, shoes echoing in the night air. Jim had driven like a bat out of hell. Nell's hat was skewed, revealing frizz above her right ear. Her dress was spattered from car sickness. Jim had no idea if his hat had blown out the window or lodged somewhere in the car. His tie hung at half-mast and his forehead was sore from hitting the bouncing car's windshield frame. Mack looked confused and scared.

Dr. McGuire, just out of Chapel Hill's medical school, was not yet used to people whispering about his youth. "Don't want him cutting on me," folks said. "He ain't dry behind the ears." At the exterior door's whoosh, he looked up at a tall, angular man wearing half a uniform and holding a young boy's hand. A pretty but disheveled woman stood at his side, holding a gangly girl in her arms who looked—he could think of no other term—dead. One leg swung lazily in odd time with her head, which hung at an angle to reveal an unblemished lily-white neck. Her face was cold and as white as marble. So was her mother's.

"You are the Hawkins family," McGuire said quietly. "Come this way, please." As they followed him down the hall, their shadows alternately lengthened and shortened under the yellow glare of ceiling bulbs.

Nell laid Little Elizabeth on an examining table, white paper crin-
kling loudly under her limp body. "She's going to be all right, isn't she,
Doctor?" Nell asked, smoothing her daughter's hair.

"I have to diagnose her," said McGuire. He looked at Jim. "Sir, please
take your family to the lobby. I'll be out soon."

"I'm not leaving my little girl," said Nell. "Not for a million dollars."

"Ma'am, I'm sorry, but you must. Hospital regulations. Please, there's
no time to waste."

Jim put his arm around Nell. "Honey, let the doctor work."

Nell pointed Mack door-ward. "Okay, Son, your father's right." She
kissed Little Elizabeth's cheek. "See you soon, dearest. Be sweet, hear?"

McGuire found a pulse and decent blood pressure, for which he lifted
thanksgivings. Her temperature was 103.8. He checked eyes, ears, nose,
and throat. After listening to lungs and heart he wrote on a form and
walked down the hall. He returned with a nurse and an IV setup.

Within two minutes the girl's cheeks bloomed and her breathing
slowed and deepened. He gave her aspirin by mouth, and she drank a little water through parched lips. Her fever soon dropped two degrees. He
left her with the nurse.

Nell jumped from the chair when she heard the doctor's footsteps.
"How is she?" she cried. Jim stood beside her while Mack slept in a chair.

"She's going to be fine," he said.

"What has she got?"

"Could be one of a number of things. Fever and rash suggest scarlet
fever, although it could be meningitis or the initial stage of whooping
cough. But she responds to aspirin and I'm giving her a bottle of saline.
We'll need tests, of course."

"Can we see her?"

"Certainly. This way."

Dr. McGuire studied religious art avidly, like some men fished or
hunted. When he left Little Elizabeth's family, he felt he had viewed a
new Nativity—light focusing on the mother adoringly brushing her
sleeping child's hair, father and brother shadowy except for expectant
faces reflecting the female glow. Missing were the traditional cattle and

sheep, shepherds and magi, but the IV and its stand somehow served as a modern savior.

Nell used to keep her mother's letters in a small box, but had lately taken to burning them, because Elizabeth Johnson had escalated her campaign to convince Nell to leave Jim.

The letter Nell received after she told her mother of her granddaughter's illness—three weeks after the fact—was what Jim would have called (if he had seen it) a son of a bitch's son of a bitch. She read it the night it arrived:

My Dear Daughter Nell,

It is a beautiful summer day, but one can barely keep windows open here lately for the haze in the air. I have been SO miserable, nose running and eyes scratchy, it's enough to make me want to live in Arizona. How have YOU been? You used to be such a dear baby, but I thought you'd never learn to blow your nose.

Pastor King preached this morning on that horrid passage about Moses lifting up a snake. Seems to me we have enough as it is without having to hear about them in church. It's nice when they talk about Jesus without dragging in all that unseemly ancient stuff.

How is my Precious Little Elizabeth? I hope very well by now and that medicine has worked. It is a miracle what they can do these days. When I was little, there was nothing to be really done for fever except horrid hot tea to sweat the fever out. Barbaric, don't you agree?

How is Henry? I hope he is not suffering from not being around children his age. I worry about him being around men so much—they can be such Beasts.

Now, Nell, I must tell you—not ASK, TELL you—that if you will not leave Cataloochee for my sake, or your father's sake, or even your own— please leave for the sake of your dear, precious children!!!! Next time you might not get a sick one to the hospital in time. A child with a high fever can be severely damaged so quickly. I know you love your Husband, but, *really, dear, he has <u>done his work</u>. He has given you two wonderful lives. Whether he considers that a sacred trust is one thing, but as a MOTHER you certainly do, and must act upon it. If that means leaving him in that dreadful place, SO BE IT!*

Your father and I have prepared a place for you and will welcome you when you come to your senses. We would happily make that awful journey once more to get you and our grandchildren, so they can grow up in a safe place that will give them a good education and all the benefits of a caring church and loving community. Let us know when you are ready and we'll be <u>Johnny-on-the-Spot!!!!</u>

Nell sighed, laid the letter in the fireplace, and lit a match to it. Walking to the window, she looked at her reflection in the crazed glass, held herself, and wept.

CHAPTER 29

Wash Day

Nell had never fully mastered kitchen chemistry, nor did she enjoy gardening, even after Aunt Mary showed her the difference between radishes and pigweed. The one household chore she perfectly understood was washing clothes. Not that she ever came to love it, but it got her out of the house, gave her some exercise, and made her feel as though she had accomplished something.

She had not grown up with a washing machine—in fact, until she was six there had been no indoor plumbing—but after that her father bought appliances as long as he had credit. In 1924 he replaced an old machine with an Allen from Sears with a punishing wringer atop and a *Good Housekeeping* seal of approval. Then Nell married Jim and left for Cataloochee.

When Nell first asked Jim where the laundry room was, he laughed. "Out here," he said, and led her to the creek, where an ancient iron pot sat beside a fire pit. Her eyes popped. "You're joshing. I am supposed to wash *here*? Jim Hawkins, this is the twentieth century."

The pot was surely as old as its original owner, Lige Howell's wife Penny's mother—at least a century. Jim told Nell to build a fire under it, but not before filling it, lest the old iron crack. "Treat it nice, it'll last another generation or two," he said, and it sounded to her like he meant her to be using it that long herself.

The beetling block—a wooden bench upon which boiled clothes were paddled clean—was the fourth or fifth copy of the original Lige Howell had built about the time of the Civil War. "It's got nothing to do with beetles," Jim explained. "It's because you beat the clothes half to death to get the dirt out. Up some coves they're called 'battling blocks.'"

Jim, in a concession to modernity, had bought her two galvanized tubs. Her routine was to fetch firewood—after once being frightened nearly to death by a weasel in the wood stack, she had learned to knock on it with an ax handle before picking up a load of firewood—then fill both tubs with creek water and throw clothes in one. She fetched in turn overalls, shirts, and dresses, laid them atop the block, beat them with a paddle, then rinsed them in the other tub. When her pot boiled, she laid in clothes and soap, and stirred them. She refilled the tubs while the clothes boiled, then rinsed them twice, Jim's really messy things thrice. The children loved to help, holding pins while she hung the wash on the line at first, then doing all the hanging and a great deal of the beetling.

"Nell, I don't think it's a good idea to wash today," Jim said on an August Monday in 1933.

"Why, Jim?"

"I've lost Willie McPeters."

"What's that got to do with laundry?"

He sat at the kitchen table. "I hadn't wanted to worry you, honey, but McPeters sets these dern fires around here. He's not dangerous, I don't think—anyhow, I haven't known him to bother women." He examined the salt shaker like he'd never seen one before. "But he carries a Marlin, and they say he killed a revenue man back in 1916. I was chasing him the other day and lost the trail. Unless I have an idea where he is, I don't want you or the young'uns outside." He dusted his palm with salt and licked it.

"What does he look like?"

"Three inches shorter'n me, about one eighty, I'd guess. Kind of stooped, with these black eyebrows jammed together. Mean look to him. Not mean like the old grinning devil, but kind of vacant, like he would kill you same's he'd swat a fly, and maybe for less reason."

"Is he a native?"

Jim laughed. "You make folks from here sound like aborigines. He was born, if that's the right word for such a critter, up Carter Fork, close to my homeplace. Always was quare, never talked much. Don't think he's done a lick of honest work in his life. So, dear, I'd appreciate it if you'd keep the doors locked."

Monday folded into Tuesday. Jim came home both days with no news of McPeters. Nell washed the insides of the windows with vinegar and newspaper and scrubbed the floors. Wednesday morning she decided to get out of the house long enough to wash the curtains, which the half-clean windows made look shabby. After checking on Mack and Little Elizabeth, who—despite their father's objections—were allowed to sleep late in summer, she filled the pot, lit the fire, and looked around. Nothing seemed amiss, but she was aware of her heartbeat. Rearranging a curl, and wiping perspiration from her upper lip, she noticed nothing moving except chickens and a solitary towhee scratching at the base of the big maple. A jaybird screamed but seemed only to warn of the barn cat to Nell's left.

Suddenly the cat skittered behind the outhouse. Nell laid two more sticks under the pot and folded arms over her chest. Still. No breeze, no crows. Nell slowly walked toward the house. Her footsteps in the yard seemed as loud as Chinese gongs.

Indoors it seemed no more threatening than normal life in such a place. But she nearly jumped when Jim's dogs barked, tentatively at first, then earnestly, not the music of chase but a chorus of "I'll rip its guts out."

She ran from the kitchen across the dogtrot to the children's room. "Mama, want me to make them be quiet?" asked Mack, who had crawled out of bed to look out the window. Little Elizabeth thrashed groggily in her bed.

"Hush, Son. Stay in here."

She went to the porch and crossed the dogtrot again. Parting the gauze curtains in the kitchen, she peered toward the road. Across it, in a patch of incipient woods, mostly tulip trees and scrub hemlocks, was a tree, walking. *No,* she thought. *Look again.* It floated fog-like to the edge, then stood as still as a cigar store Indian. No tree, but a man, intently watching something to her left. The dogs raised holy hell.

Nell returned to the kitchen and locked the door, hoping the man would not hear the click that seemed to her as loud as hammer on anvil. At the window she saw the figure had moved toward the road. He held a rifle in his left hand like a suitcase and rubbed his crotch rhythmically with his right, eyes focused toward the creek.

Good God, that's nasty. What kind of wickedness ruts after a wash pot? Oh, my God, what if he decides to come in here?

She ran to the pantry. Jim had given her a .32 Smith & Wesson not long after they'd moved. He had had in mind protection, but Nell had thought it fun. They had practiced with paper targets nailed to the barn, and she had aptitude and soon learned not to recoil at the noise. The pistol's four-inch barrel gave a small chance of hitting what she aimed at.

It stayed wrapped in a dish towel behind the pickles. She pushed the latch with her right thumb and with her left index finger persuaded the cylinder to open. Six cartridge ends stared at her like fish eyes. She snapped the cylinder shut and tiptoed to the window. McPeters rubbed his swollen, filthy overalls more quickly. He seemed not to hear dogs or have an eye for anything save the dwindling fire. She cocked the pistol and looked at it. Its hammer reminded her of some odd, running animal. She wondered if she had the nerve to open the door and kill a man.

Then she uncocked the weapon. *If I miss . . . he'd kill me . . . or worse. . . . Better keep it, though. He might try to break in.*

Little Elizabeth squalled for her mother from her room. "Oh, shoot," Nell whispered. "Please, God, don't let him hear." She unlocked the door as slowly as she could and glanced outside. McPeters did not seem to notice. She whisked across the dogtrot into the children's room and shut the door as gently as her shaking hand would allow. When she put finger to mouth to shush Mack and Little Elizabeth, she realized she still held the Smith.

"Mama, why the gun?" asked Mack.

Little Elizabeth ran to her mother and embraced her waist. "Mama, I'm scared," she said.

"Both of you please be very quiet. There's something unpleasant on the place."

"What is it?" asked Mack.

"A man. A bad, bad man. He mustn't hear us."

McPeters did not change expression when Nell's fire burned itself out. He eyeballed the place, walked toward the house, then stopped. A dark spot bloomed a few inches down his left inseam. He sniffed the air behind him and put his hand to his midsection. He held his breath and closed his eyes for a moment, then turned and stalked toward the barn.

The dogs quieted after a time, and Nell wondered if McPeters had wandered out the back of the barn for other places. She did not want to risk a kitchen fire so figured to serve the children peanut butter and bread for dinner.

At about eleven the dogs started again, but in their "Here comes the guy who feeds us" bark. Nell had grown up with cats, so was always amazed at the sensitivity of dog ears. She did not relax, however, until Jim rode in.

The horse would not enter the barn, where a vile odor in the shape of a man hung like a mist. *McPeters*. Jim pulled his revolver while trying to calm the mare, which he tied beside the maple.

The tracks were clear—the boot heel with the cross had come from the road, stood for some time facing the creek, then started toward his house, then turned toward the barn. Torn between finding McPeters and checking on his family, he looked first one direction, then the other, then ran to the house when Nell waved frantically from the kitchen.

Nell did not remark Jim's hugging her with a pistol in his hand, nor did he chide her for a similar offense. "Did you see him?"

"That was the most disgusting thing I have ever seen. Oh, I'm sooo glad to see you."

"Which way did he go?"

"He went into the barn, then I never saw him again."

"How long ago?"

"Maybe a half hour, I don't know. Jim, I'm so rattled I can hardly think."

He holstered his pistol and took hers. "Never show this unless you mean to use it, honey. Never."

"I know. You've told me that. I just thought, if he tried to break in, I'd . . . Oh, Mack, Little Elizabeth, honey, don't listen."

Jim squatted for a hug from his children. "Don't worry. Things are fine now. I'll take care of that bad man."

"Promise?" Mack blubbered into his father's shoulder.

"Promise."

Jim spent that day's remaining light searching for McPeters, who had quit the barn by the side opposite the house. Instead of following the road, he had ascended the mountain northward, taking a rest at the cemetery. The boot heel had paused beside each marked stone as if the wearer were taking inventory. McPeters seemed not to have paid attention to unlettered fieldstones marking infant graves. It was almost as if he could read.

The tracks headed east from the cemetery. Jim wanted to find them wandering away from his home, but soon they began to descend on a trail made by small night-journeying animals. Possums, coons maybe. *If this trail leads straight down, it'll come out at our springhouse.*

Years before, Lige Howell had figured he'd not haul drinking water from a spring halfway up the mountain. He built a reservoir of some hundred gallons and connected it to the springhouse first with poplar pipe, then with cedar to sweeten the water. What liquid they did not drink cooled butter and perishable foodstuffs. Lige used to sell water by the quart to fishermen, claiming it cured anything from the addle-pate to the epizootic.

McPeters had stopped at the spring to drink. An orange salamander with a back that looked to have been peppered liberally scuttled away from Jim. *I hope you'll be alive tomorrow. That man'd evil up water just by breathing beside it, much less dipping hands in it. Nell'll need to boil water for a few days.*

McPeters kept to that elevation until he was even with the new CCC camp, where Jim lost the trail. No one seemed to have seen, or smelled, an interloper, but there were only a dozen men in camp, the rest out planting pines or cutting trails. Jim figured the twelve had been left so they couldn't interfere with real work.

After three circles of the camp, each one fifty or so yards farther out, he picked up McPeters's trail, heading toward the Bennett place. He followed until he found on the roadside what, were he tracking a bear, he'd call "sign." Copious amounts of shit, bloody, with remnants of things man was never meant to eat. *Damn, that must have hurt. Reckon they call this the bloody flux? Maybe I won't have to kill him after all.*

The Bennett place had been boarded up since the CCC had begun to build their camp. Jim knew the place well, both from stories of the night the Yankees had burned it and from spending long Sunday afternoons there when Old Man Bennett junior, who had rebuilt the structure, had held open house.

It was a two-story frame house of unremarkable architecture except for the upper story on the north side. Old Man Bennett had died regretting he hadn't seen the federals coming—said he would have killed them one by one if he'd had the foresight and time. So junior, a devoted reader of Walter Scott, and who remained convinced until his death that the Yankees would return, had built a small platform and parapet in front of the north window, complete with crenels and merlons, behind which a man could hide and spy and shoot. He had finally left Cataloochee valley in a straitjacket a couple of years ago.

Jim rounded the last bend and immediately dove behind a roadside tree. A glance had shown him the boards were off the front door and north window. He unholstered his revolver and wished for binoculars. Nothing showed in the window. He was pretty sure all had been secure the last time he had ridden this direction. *How much hot water am I in right now?*

If McPeters were in the house, Jim would be a fool to rush forward like Tom Mix. He could not turn right or left without revealing himself. But giving up and going home didn't feel right, either. Somehow knowing McPeters was over in Little Cataloochee or even up Carter Fork was enough distance for him to sleep at night. But this was another thing entirely.

He peered around the tree again. A wisp of smoke rose tentatively, like it wasn't sure where to go, from the north chimney. *What in hell is he doing in there? Not cooking, at least not in the kitchen. Upstairs fireplace or down? Is he living here now? Can't have that.*

He decided to get out of sight of the house and figure what to do. Pistol in hand, he stood and walked slowly backward until he tripped on a rock and fell on his butt. His Stetson fell to the ground. As he scrambled, a bullet pierced the hat and zinged off the ground behind. "Jesus, Mary, and Joseph," Jim yelled, and ran for the bend in the road.

When he stopped running, he realized if McPeters had wanted to kill him, he would be as dead as a doornail. *Just a warning. Keep the hell away. Denned in there like a critter of some kind. How to roust him out. How to roust him out.*

CHAPTER 30

The Afterward of Love

Jim Hawkins often said a man couldn't think straight unless he was fishing, and he did not mean in a creek. He referred rather to lying on a lake bank in the shade. Or, better still, in a boat, where, as Jesus knew, or at least hoped, the chances of anyone bothering you for a light or a spare worm were slim to none.

Some twenty-five years before, God had led the Methodists to build a conference center halfway between Clyde and Waynesville. That would have been of no interest to Jim, except they had dammed Richland Creek, creating a nearly two-hundred-acre lake, called Junaluska after a Cherokee chief. With this grand gesture they'd outdone every cold-water Baptist in the region.

God had also told them to build a boat, which they called the *Oonagusta*. It carried conferees and sightseers from the train station on the south shore to the inn. When after a dozen seasons it wore out, they called its successor *Cherokee*. Despite this distraction, Jim adopted Junaluska as home water.

He had fished there when debating whether to attend college or work at the paper mill. A glorious afternoon catching bluegills after his first year at Cullowhee had helped him decide to stay in school. And after Nell told him she was pregnant, he had caught catfish all weekend, wondering what manner of mess he was stepping into.

He hadn't been lake fishing since Little Elizabeth had been born, but on a fine September day in 1933—he was reasonably certain McPeters had vacated the Bennett house for Carter Fork—he found himself shelling out a quarter to rent a jon boat constructed of well-oiled maple and birch. He left the dock with two paddles, a paper bag full of lunch and fishbait, a thermos, and a rod and reel. No creel, for he hoped not to return with fish.

He dug into the lake's placid surface and paddled to the far side. After dropping anchor, he shook a wasp nest from his sack, baited with a grub, and cast the line.

A beautiful late morning sun reflected like a spray of jewels, and he smiled at three mallards paddling over to check the human for signs of generosity. "You can have a crust in a while," he said. A peanut butter and jelly sandwich, a tin of potted meat, and a pack of crackers lay in the brown paper bag. The line jerked, rod tip dancing toward the transom. "Here goes," he said, and reeled in a bluegill blazing silver, green, and yellow. "Hey, little fellow. You're lucky. I'm not taking prisoners." He backed the hook out and laid the fish just under the surface, where it zipped into the dull green depths.

He rinsed and sniffed his hands. "Well, at least something's still right with the world. Fish still smell fishy." He baited again and within twenty seconds hooked another. "Damn it all. I don't have time for this." After releasing it, he flung a bare hook. "Now, then. I have to think."

He laid the pole over the forward bench, settled his hat against the sunshine, put his elbows on his thighs, and stared at the floor. A former occupant had crammed a yellow Mary Jane wrapper underneath the seat. *Who had eaten the candy? Did he have a troubled mind? Was his girl too refined to throw it into the lake? Where had they been going?*

For that matter, where am I going? Likely up Shit Creek without a paddle. The big problem's my woman. The hardest damn dilemma I've ever faced. Now, it isn't that I don't love Nell. Hell, she still doubles me over with the lovesick. I love making spoons with her early of a cold morning. She used to make me feel on top of the world. But lately . . .

When did the slide start? We got along fine in Scratch Ankle, me working and her having Mack. I reckon it was when I landed the Cataloochee job. No, that wasn't it, because she was hot to go. "Jim, honey, living anywhere with you would be keen, and Cataloochee will be an adventure. I can't wait." I think she really meant it.

Of course, she hadn't actually seen our house yet. I told many times of the groaning tables and lively dances and long Sunday afternoons visiting neighbors, all true enough. When I was coming up, we ate well, and we worked and played hard.

Can't remember if I told her about waking in winter to snow on the quilts. And I expect I never let on how much time and work it takes to keep warm. You hang blankets on the windows so it's dark as the inside of a coal mine all winter. Nell hates dark as much as cold. She'd love to live in Florida.

But I got to admit, she's done well, for a girl raised in a house with central heat and a grocery nearby.

He nodded at the bottom of the boat. *It was that first night here. Damn in-laws. I thought Elizabeth Johnson was going to die before Henry put her in the truck and headed home. That woman can purr, and bark, and for damn sure roar. That night her voice was something between a cat in heat and a screech owl, and I was afraid Nell would head home with her, if nothing else but to keep her from exploding.*

But she stood by me. Cleaving to her husband, like God said to do. I was mighty thankful. We put the young'uns down, slid the beds together, and did some cleaving of our own. We could have won a prize.

The afterward of love puts me to sleep, so I turned over, thinking, What could be wrong with loving a pretty woman, living half a hundred miles from her parents, and sleeping in the valley I was born in?

Later I reached for her, but her place was cold, and I heard her in the front room, crying.

I really do think men and women are about as similar as goats and chickens. They think different. I didn't have sense enough to get up and lay my hand on Nell's shoulder, like, really, any woman would have done. "There's something wrong," a woman would say. "Let's make it right, and now's as good a time as any."

Like a dumb son of a bitch, I turned over, pulled up the covers, and figured things would look better in the morning. I mean, loving was so good three hours before, why should I worry?

He gazed toward the assembly grounds, where conventioneers swarmed. Halfway across the lake the *Cherokee's* passengers broke out with "Love Divine, All Loves Excelling," but by the time it reached his ears, the last phrase sounded like they were "lost in thunder, guns, and haze." Then silence, and the hollow knock of water from their wake.

Wonder how many of these good Christians have marriage problems. You know, Christ said a passel of fine things, but, hell, He wasn't married. Can you imagine if He was? She'd up and say, "Jesus, Nazareth's the world's armpit. I'm going home to Mama." What in hell would He say to that? "I am the bread of life"?

A green dragonfly perched on the end of his rod. *A snake feeder's supposed to be good luck when it visits your tackle. I could use some. But maybe that's just fishing luck. What to do?*

My mama would have said, "Read the Bible and pray about this mess." But what was Jesus' word about family? Something like you had to love Him more than mother or brothers and sisters. I take that to mean wife and children, too. Somewhere else He outright said to leave family and follow Him. Now, I know Nell would raise holy hell if I said, "I love Jesus more than you." And she might want out of Cataloochee, but she'd not stand for me becoming a preacher.

Maybe it all comes down to what, or who, you love. And you go with who you love the most.

Here's the rub, though. I might not love Jesus more'n Nell. In fact, I don't love Jesus half as much—excuse me, Lord, but it's the truth. But—and here's the big question—do I love Cataloochee more than her?

He unwrapped wax paper from his sandwich. As he ate and drank coffee, his mind raced. *No question. I love home. I was born there, and I hope to die there. And I'm getting paid cash money to live there. And lately, I love my work more than being at home. Her moods make it hard to come home evenings. She won't want to hear about my day, and I don't want to lis-*

ten about hers, so we don't talk, and I go to bed with supper still in the pit of my stomach. Yeah, there are times I don't love being with Nell anymore. When she's silent, or when she bitches instead of talking.

The rope squeaked when a bit of breeze blew the boat slowly toward the north end of the anchor. A water snake, looking like a copperhead except for its sharp nose, swam lazily toward shore. Jim picked up his rod and cast toward it. "Here, old devil, try this for size," he muttered. It swam with no more regard for Jim's hook than the man in the moon.

We've been happy. Least I have. But something's got to give. I thought I'd double over with pain the other night. She might as well have told me she was seeing somebody else. Hell, that would have been better. I could just shoot the son of a bitch and be done with it. This other, though, it's eating at me like acid on glass.

She's leaving if I mean to stay in Cataloochee. I could have died when she said that. The part about me not knowing her, not being sensitive to her needs, being selfish, that's my mother-in-law talking. But the leaving? Is that Elizabeth, or Nell?

She said she'll never adjust, nor learn to like it one little bit. When I ask her to try, she says she's sick of it. What's scary is, she's stubborn, and if she makes up her mind to go—or if her damn mother makes it up for her—only way she'll stay is if I bury her here.

When *Cherokee* was out of sight, he stood, unzipped his pants, and pissed over the side of the boat, scattering a half dozen hopeful ducks. The boat tried to rock, but he corrected his stance mid-piss.

He zipped, sat, and took up the rod and tackle. *God, there it is. I have to decide. Stay with Nell, leave the service. Stay in Cataloochee, lose Nell and the young'uns. About simple as that.*

He swore aloud. "God damn. Does she have the right to paint me into that kind of corner?" He threw his hat onto the floor of the boat. "To think—she's going to make me decide. So whatever happens will be my damn fault. *My* God-damned fault. I can't win."

That evening he pulled up beside the house, cut the motor, and stepped into the yard. Mack jumped off the dogtrot, his index finger crossing his lips. "Mommy's got a sick headache," he whispered. "She's in the bed."

"How about your sister?"

"She's asleep with her. I'm bored."

"Well, let's think up something to do."

"We could cook your fish, Daddy."

"Didn't bring any."

"Why not?"

"I was catching bigger things than fish, Son. Let's play in the woodpile, what do you say?"

"Okay, Daddy."

They spent nearly an hour sorting and stacking firewood, Jim slamming billets around with some vigor and Mack gathering kindling chips into a basket, and stacking his father's splits when he took a break. Jim did not know whether he wanted to face Nell or not. Maybe not just yet. But she woke and came outside, hugging a shawl around her shoulders and shaking her head.

"Where's your fish?" she asked in a sleepy voice.

"Didn't bring any," Jim said.

"Good. I don't like fish very much."

"What's for supper?"

She smiled. "Whatever you want to fix," she said. "I'm not over this headache yet."

"Then, little man," he said to Mack, "let's raid the springhouse. If there's nothing there, I'll bake cornbread for crumble-in."

After the children were asleep, Nell began to prepare for bed. Brushing her hair, she looked in the mirror at her husband, staring into the fireplace. "Penny for your thoughts," she said quietly.

He put his hands on her shoulders. "My head's empty as a tin barn," he said.

"I thought you went fishing."

"I did."

"You didn't bring back fish, so you must have occupied yourself somehow."

"Just sat in the boat and thought."

"About us?"

"Some." As he rubbed her shoulders, she leaned up to him like a cat. "That feels good. Did you make any progress?"

"What do you mean?"

"Did you make up your mind about us?"

"No."

She stopped his hands and turned toward him. "Until you decide, you best not touch me."

The feel of her flesh and the sight of shadows playing on her face had been nearly enough to make him promise her anything, but her voice unmanned him suddenly, like a candle snuffed by a sharp wind. "You don't want me anymore?"

"Not until I know about our future."

"Then I'm going to take a walk."

He banged the screen door and kicked violently at the ground, but went no farther than the side yard. Beside the outhouse he looked at the sky for sign of encouragement or guidance but found none. He swayed a little, not having lost his sea legs. He went inside the outhouse but left the door open.

While he was in there, she set a piece of luggage on the bed. She opened it slowly, then turned to the chest of drawers. She took out a slip and laid it inside the suitcase, then brought the back of her hand to her mouth in an attempt not to cry. She stamped her foot, then sat on the bed and cried, hard, for a good three minutes.

When Jim emerged from the jakes, he looked toward the house. He had missed his wife's sorrow. All he saw was Nell, blotting her eyes with a handkerchief, looking blankly out the window. He waved before he realized she did not see him. When she turned, he saw the suitcase. He had forgotten they owned such baggage. His chest tightened when she threw the contents of the top drawer into the case, closed and stowed it, and stomped out of the room.

He stood numbly long enough for her to return and stare out the window. She seemed not to be looking for anything in particular. *She ain't looking for me. Best I can tell she's set her face in a direction from which it won't be turned.* She blew out the lantern.

After his eyes were used to dark again, he looked to the zenith, but saw only evidence of the unceasing revolution of the heavens. No billboards. No guideposts. No comfort save that life would continue. He stood unsteadily in the yard a long, long time.

CHAPTER 31

Say It Isn't So

Twelve years out of high school, Nell Hawkins was stumped by a subjunctive. She should not have been. After what had seemed months of her teacher's drill and lecture, Nell had understood the rules surrounding the contrary-to-fact statement. Her colleagues, however, scratched their heads and wondered, Why not say "If it was," instead of "If it were"? Why did a simple "if" demand a plural verb follow a singular subject?

Mrs. Kramer, a tall woman with hair like a hornet's nest, demanded both exemplary conduct and impeccable grammar. Her best example of proper subjunctive was biblical. "In the good book," she said, clasping a grammar to her breast like a shield against interloping sin, "in the fourteenth chapter of John, Jesus told His disciples He was going to prepare a place for them. His very words, His ipsissima verba: 'If it *were* not so, I would have told you.' Jesus, dear students, was perfect. He *could* not say 'If it *was* not so.' We must emulate the Savior in all ways, including grammar."

Nell had been a good grammarian and had even loved to diagram sentences. She never split infinitives, dangled participles, or spliced sentences with commas. But, a dozen years past high school and eight into the rocky rapids of marriage, she was no longer sure about rules. *"If you weren't so stubborn" sounds better than "if you wasn't," but I've listened to these people so long I swear I don't remember which is proper.*

For weeks she had been composing a letter to Jim. She figured she would need paper to anchor her thoughts, but so far the effort had failed. She'd write a page or two, then put them in her drawer and stew about what she had scribbled. Throw them into the fireplace and start anew. After wearing out two nibs, she started drafts in pencil, figuring to make a fair copy in pen when it was perfect.

Jim had taken the children to Silas's house to help clean out a shed, so she had time to herself. She wrote a few minutes, consigned another page to the fire, and went to the window. Leaves blew through the yard like wraiths bound for a rendezvous. The cold creekside wash pot reminded her that Monday, like a drunken relative, would soon come reeling home from the weekend. She hugged herself and sighed.

Why can't I simply tell him? Sit down like civilized people in the front room, then be done with it, get up, walk out, go home. Home, that has electricity and telephones and doctors. Home, where there are motion picture shows and soda fountains. Home, where my children and I belong.

A long time since we sang about the big rock candy mountain. It was going to be such a picnic here, but he never told me how much work it would be.

He never said how much work it would be to love him, either. Oh, at first it was heavenly, the loving, I mean, the physical kind. I blush to think how many times and ways we've made whoopie.

That kind of loving is the easiest thing in the world, and those first months flew by, days with sunshine, nights with too many stars to begin to count. We'd lie on a blanket in the hay field, little Mack asleep on one corner, Jim snuggling me. He'd tell me names of constellations and show me planets and stars and rub my tightening tummy and tell me everything was going to be great. A summer to remember.

But the other kind of loving—the being in love, not the making of love—is tested when things aren't going right. Especially when one party doesn't see that's the case. Jim's so stubborn. He really thinks he's living in some Garden of Eden, Shangri-La, fairy-tale country. He can't see through his rose-colored glasses what this godforsaken place does to me. I feel myself getting older every day. He tells me, "Honey, give it a chance. You'll see." I have. And I never will.

I stayed the first night because I felt I was doing my duty. The right thing. After all, Jim was *my husband, and we* were *set on making a good life together. I'd never seen such a desolate place nor such a ramshackle house except in the poorest parts. But I really thought I could stand anything so long as I was with him. When you're first in love, you don't have the sense God gave a goose, Mother says.*

I mean, look at me. Never built a fire. Never cooked a whole meal by myself. Hadn't used an outhouse in years. Home held a wringer washer, telephone, central heat, an icebox. Here I was young, pregnant, the soul of optimism. I thought I had strength and savvy to, initially, live here and be Jim's wife forever. When I despaired of that, I had to make him see we must leave.

That night, God, I remember like it was yesterday, the first time I really defied Mother, which, to tell the truth, felt pretty good. Somehow the combination of being itchy crazy for a man and wanting to live on my own, away from Mother's special lunacy, was powerful. I felt like a heroine on the moor, a rebel, free, being someone.

That was before I knew the difference between potato plants and pokeweed. I admit I have learned much in the last few years, thanks to Jim and Aunt Mary. When to plant beans, where to find guinea eggs, how to make bread. The difference between green locust and dry poplar, poison oak and creeper, garter snakes and copperheads, trout and hornyheads.

What a great big deal. I also know how to lie awake and grind my teeth. How to be lonesome when people are around. How to hide it from the children. And the ache in my heart! I miss nearly everything. Even Mother. Especially her. I see now how deeply I hurt her. For that I am sorry. Mother is, as she says, "too delicate for the slings and arrows of this world." Sure, that's her big Elizabeth-an drama, but she is *china doll fragile. I should not have wronged her.*

Jim says I'm just like her sometimes—not only my looks but how I talk, the way I walk. One time he said he should have run the other way the first time he saw us together. Maybe he should have. . . . I'm between a rock and a hard place. On one hand, I am scared, because I don't want to inherit her nervous breakdowns. But she is my mother, and deep down she has nothing but good intentions for us. Bless her heart. She will forgive me for hurting her.

I have told Jim how I feel. Pled with him to find another job. He's selective in his hearing, and I'm like a radio he can turn down, or off. He'll not suddenly understand, come to his senses, and take us away. I'm going to have to leave. It will hurt him. Perhaps given enough time he can forgive me.

Wait. What about my *hurt,* my *anger? I mean, he* will not *bring me safe and sound to a place where I can be comfortable and loved. He* will not *see he owes me that to save his soul. So I suppose forgiving's for us both.*

I wonder what "forgive" means. Not "forget," for I will never forget these lonely days of mindless work, nor, for that matter, our good times. Something like "to pardon." Just say "It's okay" and never bring it up again. Or as Preacher Smith said a few weeks ago, losing your anger in the pardoning of the wrong.

Mrs. Kramer's highest authorities were Pope, Shakespeare, and Jesus. Let's see. Pope said, "To err is human, to forgive, divine." So maybe it's not for me to do.

I memorized King Lear's last speech to Cordelia:

When thou dost ask me blessing, I'll kneel down,
And ask of thee forgiveness: so we'll live,
And pray, and sing, and tell old tales, and laugh
At gilded butterflies . . .

Rats, I have forgotten the rest. Poetry is pretty, but I don't know it helps, except to say all will be well if we both *ask. I've asked the right questions until I'm blue in the face. He hasn't. It's enough to make you scream.*

Jesus is a whole 'nother kind of authority. Best I remember, He didn't say much about forgiving, but sure did a lot of it, even for the soldiers and thieves. I know one thing, I'm not Jesus.

She laid another stick of wood in the range and sat at the table. Had she seen the mouse run the baseboard behind the wood box, she would have shrieked. Removing a sheaf of folded paper from her apron pocket, she smoothed it on the tabletop. The paper sounded as soft as vellum, but in the silent house even that was too much racket. She wanted the chatter of company to drown her thoughts.

A year ago Jim had bought a record player, a Sears contraption standing on squat cabriole legs. She went to the front room and lifted its lid. Jim had left "Papa's Billy Goat" on the turntable, but Nell had never warmed to that. She decided to play instead "I'm Looking over a Four-Leaf Clover."

When tinny clarinets and saxophones blared from the cabinet, she tried to dance, but fox-trot by herself was no fun. Searching through her odd collection of records, she saw she was in no mood for Cole Porter or the Carter family. In the distance she heard a crow. She decided to try Rudy Vallee.

She cranked the phonograph and set the needle on the seventy-eight. An oscillating scratch led into a song that made her shake her head and smile at the same time. Hugging herself and swaying, she tried not to pay attention to the lyrics.

> People say that you found somebody new
> and it won't be long before you leave me.
> Say it isn't true.

Suddenly she wept as if she might turn inside out. Before she found her lace-trimmed handkerchief, tears wet her dress front. Blowing her nose and wiping her eyes, she walked back to the kitchen and put her hand on the counter as if it might sweep her to a place free from pain.

As her vision cleared, she noticed something stood as still as a stone beside the barn. Nell strained to focus on a doe staring intently at the house, as if trying to decide whether to cross the yard or head back up the mountain. Neither sleek nor fat, she carried her head as high and as proud as a lion.

A smaller, spindly, spotted version of its mother, not nearly as still as its parent, appeared. Nell thought she saw the doe snort disapproval. *He's*

*so cute! And she's—"regal" is a word I never would have associated with deer,
but there is a noble cast to her countenance. I wonder—there's a bag of field
corn in the shed. I wonder if I dare see if they'll come to me? Maybe if I go out
front, I can reach the shed without spooking them.*

She tiptoed through the house, afraid every squeak would frighten
them. The front door hinge for once did not squeal, but the screen door
spring stretched loud enough to wake the dead. She shut the door as
slowly and quietly as she knew how.

It took her what she thought was forever to descend the steps without
racket. When her feet hit the ground, she hurried to the corner of the
house and peered toward the barn. The animals still stood.

When Nell stepped toward the shed, the creatures looked at her for
what seemed two or three seconds, then turned and with flashes of white
made for the top of the mountain as if pursued by a bear.

In the shed she found four ears of corn. She laid them in what she sur-
mised to be the animals' path to the creek. *If I'm going to stay a few more
days, I want to see those beautiful animals again.*

She ambled back and looked toward the mountaintop. *They're so cam-
ouflaged I could stare for hours and never see them. They know how. I don't.
I've always stuck out here, like a sore thumb.* She walked to the porch and
turned toward the mountainside, hugging the thin porch column. She
sighed. *They're coming home. And, you know, so am I.* She brightened as if
lit by a phosphorous match. *So am I. Those creatures are a sign. So am I.*

Inside, her letter lay on the kitchen table like an accusation. She read
it in silence, occasionally biting her lower lip. Sighing, she laid it down
and poured a glass of water. She twisted her wedding band with her right
hand, then sat and absently curled a strand of hair. *I think it's finished. In
fact, I know it is. Question is, am I going to leave it for him? It likely won't
do any good. He'll read "when I go home" in that first paragraph and go off
like a Roman candle. Home. I'm going to take my precious angels home in a
few days. Make the arrangements with Mother and let them take us all in.*

She stacked the paper, threw it into the firebox, replaced the eye, and
carried in enough stove wood to finish supper. In fifteen minutes she was
startled by Mack and Little Elizabeth running into the kitchen.

"Mommy, Mommy, lookit what Uncle Silas gave us!" shouted Mack.

Her son held a piece of a singletree, and her daughter shyly carried a red tomato-shaped pincushion. Jim arrived behind them with a narrow smile.

"That's nice, Mack," she said. "What is it?" She knelt to examine the broken implement, a piece of chain dangling from one end.

"Uncle Silas says it's a bonker," said Mack. "I can bonk things with it."

"Not Mommy or Daddy or Sister. Little Elizabeth, that's a pretty pincushion. Did Uncle Silas take out the sharp pins and needles?"

Little Elizabeth nodded and handed it to Nell, who rubbed it to make sure.

"What's with the corn?" asked Jim.

"I saw a doe and a fawn. I thought they might come back."

Jim laughed quietly. "Only thing that'll come back for that is a possum or a coon. I'll put it back after awhile."

"Jim, I'd really love to see those deer again."

"About the only time you see them is when they want you to. I've hunted for days without seeing one, although I knew they were all around me. What's for supper?"

"Chicken, potatoes. I think there's beans. You all need to help me get it ready. Children, wash your hands and faces. Little Elizabeth, you look like the Little Match Girl. Jim, hand me some potatoes to peel and build up the fire."

When Jim lifted the stove lid, he saw ghosts of penciled words in the center of a charred stack of paper. "Home," in capital letters, underlined. Likely another plea from Elizabeth for Nell to leave. He said nothing, but hoped Nell was standing up to her mother again.

CHAPTER 32

Holocaust

Jim had not seen hide nor hair of McPeters in a month. No fires, no footprints, nothing. When Nell ventured outside, she kept the .32 in her apron pocket, so Mack and Little Elizabeth played under the eye of an armed guard. Stray noises spooked the children, and Mack had several times awakened screaming about a mean old booger man with a gun. Even the dogs seemed jumpy.

When Jim left the place, he felt antsy, uneasy. For that matter, he felt that way at home. A testy peace had settled there, but he had about as much use for it as a lace doily. Nell had grown moody and irritable, and he had begun almost to wish she would do whatever she needed to do.

One afternoon he rode home and put the horse in the barn. He walked out to see Nell, suitcase in hand, step off the dogtrot toward the car. Something caught in his throat. "Well, hell, it's finally here," he said. Leaning against the barn entrance, he watched Nell carry another satchel to the Ford. He spat in the dirt and shook his head. "No sense in putting it off, I reckon," he said, and started a slow stride toward the house. Nell emerged with another bag. "Where you going, sweetheart?" he asked.

Her green eyes broadcast a humor halfway between choler and melancholy. "Home."

"Daddy's here," yelled Mack as he ran out the front room door and leapt off the step.

"Little Mack Truck," shouted Jim, who caught and swung his son around. "Man, you're growing. Soon I won't even be able to pick you up." He looked at Nell. "Home," he said flatly.

Her gaze fell. "Don't, Jim. Please, not now."

"When?"

"I don't know. Just not now."

Jim set Mack on the porch. "Tell you what, little man. Where's your sister?"

Mack frowned. "She's inside playing house or something stupid."

Jim smiled at his son. "Why don't you help your sister so me and Mama can talk?"

"Okay, Daddy," he sighed. They ritually touched hands like prize-fighters before a bout. "Twenty-three skiddoo."

Jim stood as Mack closed the door. A mockingbird trilled somewhere behind him. He looked at his wife, who, despite seeming to have been asleep when he went to bed the night before, looked like she had not rested at all. His voice was calm. "Not where, then. When?"

"First thing in the morning."

"Okay. Now I know when and where. One thing still troubles me."

She looked toward the road and twisted a curl at the back of her neck with her left hand, a mannerism that still drove him wild. "What?"

"Why?"

She stared at him. "Jim, we've been down this road a thousand times. Why can't you accept it? I don't belong here. Neither do the kids."

He stepped toward her. "Don't you love me anymore?"

She exhaled sharply. "Don't, Jim. It isn't fair."

He took off his hat and scratched his forehead. "Fair. Like it's fair to haul off and leave?"

"Like it's fair to make me stay here without anybody to talk to except little old ladies so buggy they think their dead husbands follow them around? Like it's fair to tend a sick kid half a day from a doctor? Or fair for us to dread that monster out there somewhere?"

"What about our vows, Nell?" He reached for her hands, but she hid them behind her back as quick as lightning. "Something about richer and poorer—sickness and health—from this day forward, till death do us part. That don't mean from this day eight years. It means forever."

She looked at the door behind which she imagined the children listening intently. "Come over here," she said softly, covering her chest with her arms and walking toward the kitchen door, head lowered. She leaned on the door frame and looked him in the eye. "Jim, I'm not going to say this again. That language you use, about death? I die every day I'm here. Not just a day's worth at a time, either. More like a year for every day." Jim opened his mouth, but she laid a finger against his lips. "Let me finish. I love you. I used to love you like I couldn't ever get enough of you. Now I love you different. Differently, I mean. See, I'm beginning to talk like you. Them.

"Anyway, my love's for my children, too, and I want them to have a future. A *future*, Jim, that doesn't include living in this rat hole, carrying water, cowering from feebs, chopping kindling wood. Things that are making me old before my time. Look at these hands, Jim Hawkins. I'm ashamed of them. I look like I'm fifty.

"This love business cuts two ways. If you loved me, you'd find a real job. You'd put a decent roof over our heads—in Buncombe County. Hell, Jim, I wouldn't mind if you took a third-shift job. Oh, Jim, if only you'd understand." It was all she could do to keep her eyes from flooding.

He stared at the dimple above her elbow like he could dive into it. "Nell, I don't know what else to say. I can't just up and quit. This place . . ." He looked toward the ridgetop, then eyed the creek in the opposite direction. "Nell, I was born here."

"I was born in West Asheville. So what?"

"Cataloochee's different. I don't know, there's something about taking care of this land that fits me like my favorite shirt. If I was to leave here now, it'd pull me back inside of a month. This place needs me."

"And I don't?"

"That's different."

"How, Jim? How can you say you love this godforsaken place more than me?"

"You know it's not that, Nell." He took off his Stetson and fingered the brass NPS insignia.

"Then, what is it? Why can't you just come with me?"

He took a deep breath. "Duty. And if I quit, I'd always have a question in the back of my mind. 'Did I do my best by them?' Both the 'them' that stayed, like Silas, and the 'them' that come in here to fish and hike and such. I'd not look at myself when I'm fifty and say I let 'them' down."

She sighed. "This is like arguing with a signpost. I'm leaving in the morning. With the kids. Mother is expecting us. If you want to join us, I'd be happy as a clam. If not tomorrow, then soon. But don't wait too long."

"What does that mean, Nell?"

"Exactly what I said. And since you seem to prefer your horse's company to mine, you can sleep with her tonight." Eyes brimming, she went into the front room and slammed the door.

Jim, not much of a drinker, carried the jug to the barn. At about ten he ended up in the loft, swaddled by a pile of hay. Sometime in the middle of the night he started to the outhouse and would have stepped out of the loft into thin air had he not tripped beforehand on a loose board and passed out two inches from the entrance.

He was up at gray dawn—"first thing" to Nell meant eight-thirty—feeding, milking, and wondering what the morning would bring besides a crackling headache. He made breakfast and brought it to their bedroom. Nell came to the door wearing her beige traveling suit and a look that made him abandon all hope.

He kissed and hugged his children and promised to see them soon. When he turned to Nell, she hugged him so quickly he wondered if she were afraid he might scald her. "Think about it," she whispered into his ear. "Good-bye, sweetheart," she said as airily as possible.

Woe danced in the dust the auto raised. He shook his head, put his hat on, and looked at the house. "I'm not staying here today," he said. "I got to be moving. I think I'll go to Little Cataloochee. That means going by the Bennett place. I might as well see if McPeters is there."

Jim had taken to carrying his Winchester .30-30, which he called his "Equalizer." He knew the only way it would impress McPeters was if he killed him with it, but it at least made fishermen respectful when he checked licenses and creels. A canteen of cool springwater hung from the left side of his saddle, and a pair of binoculars went into the right saddlebag. His horse snorted and seemed amenable to a day out.

He set out slowly, walking her creekside, tall and somber in the bright morning light and shadow. Usually the horse's rhythm put him almost to sleep, but he was alert, watchful, a tight feeling in his chest. Thirsty. As close to a hangover as he'd been in a long time.

He tied the mare at creek's edge near the CCC camp entrance. He knelt for a few handfuls of water himself, then pulled his binoculars, checked his rifle, and felt for cartridges in his pocket. If McPeters was still at the Bennett place, he wanted to give him neither warning nor opportunity. A CCC boy pointed toward himself, then toward Jim, then house-ward, as if to invite himself along. Jim, distrustful of what he called the "Peckerwood Army," waved him off and waited for him to return to the camp.

Halfway to the turn a toad had been flattened in the right-hand rut. Jim squatted to examine it. Flat and dry, its arms bent upward like some bizarre votive holder. It was surrounded by ants only slightly larger than pissants, circling the body at the head and doubling back under the concave body and ant-lining to their hill with whatever they plucked from underneath. "Poor old boy," Jim whispered. "But he's still doing some good, long as these ants are working. Probably more good than I'm likely to do today."

Knees popping, he stood, light-headed, spots swimming before his eyes. "I've known water to get a man drunk again after a hard night. I ain't going on such a toot again, women be damned." A hawk keened toward the eastern ridge as Jim began to step quietly toward the bend.

At least McPeters hadn't burned the house down. Jim stopped behind a tulip tree and studied the building for a while. Still close to the creek's murmur, he strained to hear other than natural sounds. The breeze was from behind. No motion in or around the building.

No curtains helped him read the windows. A ground squirrel skittered from a woodpile back of the house and raced under the underpinning. The second story commanded most of Jim's attention. A small bird hopped on the railing behind which McPeters had fired. When he glassed it he saw a finch, which he took for a good sign.

Save for the sweat on his upper lip, he felt as dry as Ezekiel's bones. He imagined a quart of iced tea, then figured he'd about trade his soul for just a cube from the pitcher.

He didn't want to take all day figuring out whether his nemesis was there, but equally did not want to be shot between the eyes. He figured to be no hero. As a stripling he had read about Alvin York but saw nothing in his mettle to compare. "Might as well get this over with," he muttered. "He shoots me, wonder if Nell'll care at all." He thought about throwing rocks on the porch, but decided the Winchester would either frighten or challenge McPeters if he were there, and either prospect seemed better than dying of thirst this close to a creek.

The first shot sounded like the crack of doom and took out a pane in the second-story window just above the absent finch. Jim waited a couple of minutes, but no return fire came. He disturbed silence with three more shots over ten minutes, listening hard when the ringing in his ears subsided.

He remembered a trick from the moving pictures, and hung out his hat on his rifle barrel. It attracted no fire. "Guess the only way to find out is to go in."

Putting his hat back on, he stepped from behind the tree, scanning all windows for glint of weapon or any movement. Running in a crouch, he gained the front porch and stood with his back to the wall. He made himself stay until his heart calmed down, eyeing a wasp nest the size of his palm for signs of hostility. He heard nothing save the creek. He would have felt the floor shake if someone were walking inside.

He opened the door and stepped inside carefully. McPeters had been there by the look of the dusty boards, but not lately. Jim heard nothing moving upstairs. Some animal had scattered hickory hulls over the floor, and for some strange reason a glass inkwell sat in the corner. Something smelled sweet and musty, like a small creature had died some weeks before.

He'd about decided he was safe when he heard a thump upstairs. *What in hell was that?* Something blown off a windowsill? McPeters? Had he shot him? A fine string of dust descended from where he thought he'd heard the noise. Dusty spiderwebs moved in the breeze.

He stood as still as a fence post until his neck hurt and his left hand shook. No more racket from upstairs. He walked slowly to the stairs, floor creaking, and put his weight on the first step. This journey would be loud and slow.

At the top he wheeled with his weapon and nearly fired into a wad of blankets that had hosted generations of mice. Something in the front room cast a lurking shadow. He swallowed, took a deep breath, and sidled to the door.

Later he couldn't figure why he'd noticed no odor until he'd entered the room, rifle first. McPeters was slumped against the eastern wall, naked as the day he was born. Clothes piled beside were covered in blood, shit, and blowflies. His legs were splayed quite unnaturally. Between them on the floor sat an empty glass jar, beside which lay a few wooden matches, one of which had been struck.

Between his legs hung something charred, nothing recognizable. His face was bloated and fly-covered, but just before Jim turned to throw up, he thought an incipient smile lurked behind the body's black tongue.

Before he left, Jim looked for a wound but found none save whatever had happened to the man's crotch. The jar on the floor smelled of kerosene. *How in the world did the building not catch? And am I reading this right? He about shit himself to death, then set his pecker on fire? Damned if that ain't the awfulest thing I ever saw.*

McPeters's rifle proved the only thing worth taking from the house. *Damned if this house ain't full of ghosts. The first house got burned by the Yankees—reckon I've heard that story a thousand times. Now here I am— Old Man Bennett would say I work for the Yankee government, too—about to burn the new place down, with a secret that this time I hope will stay dead a long time.* He came downstairs and stopped.

Behind the screen door stood the boy who had signaled him from the CCC camp, peering in like he was watching a baseball game through a knothole. He might have been twenty. Jim knew he wasn't a mountaineer. He had black curly hair, thick eyeglasses, and nearly lobe-less ears. "What are you looking for?" Jim asked.

"Just looking," he said.

Jim stepped outside. The boy was generally innocent of soap, by the smell of him. "Do me a favor," said Jim.

"What?"

"That's 'What, *sir*.' "

"Oh. Since when did you boss the CCC?"

"Since right now. You peckerwood army boys are in my territory. Do me a favor."

"Maybe." He paused. "Sir."

"Get a can of gasoline. And a rake or broom or two."

"Why, sir?"

"We're about to burn a house."

The young man brightened considerably. "Yes, *sir!*"

He reappeared in five minutes with a can and two companions with rakes over their shoulders. These boys looked no better than the first. Jim wondered how dumb you had to be to be camp-bound while your colleagues were out cutting trails, but figured some help was better than none. "Okay, men. Give me that gasoline. I'll douse inside. You'uns soak the porch. Then we'll see if we can keep from starting a brush fire."

He dashed inside and soaked what was left of McPeters, then trailed the liquid down the stairs and out to the porch. The boys used the rest of the can on the exterior. Jim lit one of McPeters's matches and threw it at the porch.

The initial whoosh nearly sucked all the oxygen from their lungs. All four retreated from the blaze with singed eyebrows. The house required a full hour to crumple in on itself and its dirty secret, a body Jim hoped might be a holocaust, somehow putting his world back into kilter.

CHAPTER 33

Good-Luck Birds

Jim woke with what he would have called a hangover, except he had drunk nothing to cause it. Headache, dry mouth, a slight disorientation as if he had slept in unfamiliar territory. He looked the bed over but found himself, as always, these days, alone. By himself with a cotton-filled head and a yearning for sex. On the one hand, he'd love a tumble, but on the other, that required a woman, and he didn't want life to be any more complicated.

It was the first of December 1933, a Friday, his mother's birthday. She had been gone two years—longer than that, really, for hardening of the arteries had claimed her mind well before she'd died. Jim sat on the bed's edge and remembered how she'd abhorred any fuss over her birthday. She wanted neither presents nor party, and chided people for spending hard-earned money on a card.

Besides his wife, the women he knew best were his mother and sister, both retiring, shy. In a room full of people you might not notice them. Nell was their pluperfect opposite, so what he knew of them helped him not at all to understand his—what exactly was she now? Wife? Estranged wife? His "ex"? Words he knew very little about.

He had not seen Nell and the children since they'd left in September, the day he'd burned the Bennett house and its awful mystery. He had sent penny postcards in care of her mother, two to Nell and three to Mack and Little Elizabeth, but gave up when Nell didn't reply. He knew Nell's mother waited for the sound of the postman's shoes on the porch, and usually visited with him while looking through the mail. So she could have intercepted and destroyed those cards.

She would not have found them very revealing one way or the other. His notes held no begging—in fact, he tried to sound as happy as possible without making Nell think he was better off without her. Which, despite the pain, some days he thought he was. Life was, however lonesome, simpler. When he was honest with himself—something that happened fairly seldom—except in bed, he missed his children more sharply than he did her.

He dressed quickly. Poking at the front room fireplace, he found enough coals to rekindle a blaze. Firewood was low, but the weather promised to be sunny enough not to require a fire all day. He meant finally to get things ready for winter, something he should have taken care of in August, when life had become too crowded.

He had yet to knock last season's creosote from the chimneys, and needed to order a couple of bags of coal. And firewood. He would not do anything the residents of the valley could not do, so he cut no green wood but snaked what deadfall he could find. Last season he had bought a load of green wood from a miller who'd hauled it into Cataloochee at what Jim considered to be highway robbery.

He had to laugh. *Silas Wright's got a world of green firewood behind his house—that little trail to and from his woodlot wasn't made by possums—but can I ask him to let me buy some of it? I can hear him now. "Jim Hawkins, I bet you'd need one of them fancy permits just to ask me about it."* And the prospect of a resident finding a warden cutting firewood was too ironic to think about.

The outside thermometer read forty-two degrees. He backed to the fireplace. As the hinder parts of his wool trousers warmed, he saw dust blow across the floor. *Nell was right about one thing—this is a drafty old house. This year I'm a good mind to bunk in the kitchen. Just shut up the rest of the place. Maybe I'll do that today.*

Chimneys were his first concern, for a chimney fire could set the whole house ablaze. His father had advocated periodic chimney burns to clean his flues. He would build a big fire, then make a newspaper torch, light it, and shove it up the flue. Within seconds the chimney would roar as the creosote burned, a whooshing in-suck and out-blow that would put Jim in mind of a giant fairy-tale dragon. His father would then throw water on the fire, which, at least in theory, would send steam up the flue and put out the conflagration.

Jim was hardly that adventuresome. He hauled a rope and a rock the size of a small cabbage to the roof over the kitchen, tied the rock securely, and lowered it into the chimney, swinging it east to west, north and south, up and down, over and over, beating the inside until he was certain he'd dislodged all the accretion.

Inside the kitchen he set a bucket on the range's warmer and slowly removed the pipe between stove and flue. He had knocked a gallon of shiny creosote from the chimney itself, which he swept into the bucket. The stuff reminded him of obsidian, and he wondered if a man could sharpen the bigger chunks. When he held the stovepipe over the bucket and knocked it sharply with a screwdriver handle, the black flakes sounded like dry raindrops. He replaced the stovepipe and stowed the bucket. Next time he had a roaring fire, he'd feed the contents to it.

Before dinner he was atop the high part of the roof, cleaning the front room chimney. The fire beneath had gone out, but the chimney's breath felt warm and smelled ashy. Sunshine also warmed him, and there was no breeze. He peeled off his denim jacket and hung it on the comb of the roof. He started the rock on its downward journey. Looking up, he saw a soft, gray motion in the creek, whether imagined or real he couldn't decide. The presence seemed suspended in a patch of shade in the bend, its outline deckle-edged, fuzzy.

It was maybe a yard tall and as thin as a hoe handle. Jim quietly brought the rock out of the chimney and tiptoed down the ladder. The still shape turned slightly to align perfectly with Jim's vision, shrinking to the thickness of a galax bloom. It might have been a vertical line drawn by an unseen hand.

Jim smiled. *I can be as still as he can. If it's what I think it is, I mean to see it up close.*

After a minute or two the creature turned slowly, as if on creaky joints. Two steps upstream it was not quite broadside to Jim but enough for him to make out a great blue heron's question mark of head and neck.

Herons rarely visited Cataloochee, a place with nothing save skinny water in which to fish. *Perhaps it's on its way to the big lake and decided to find a snack.* The bird stood in the creek bend and peered patiently into shallows, where water dashed around rocks. It stretched its neck toward the boiling surface and soon speared an unfortunate crayfish, which in a trice disappeared down the long neck.

Don't know why they call them blue. This one's Confederate gray. Don't ever see one without it reminds me of Papa. He thought they were good-luck birds.

I'm not superstitious, least not like him. Thought a hat on a bed was bad luck. Wouldn't let you give gloves, said that was bad luck. He'd always go out the same door he came in at. If you'd have nailed the door shut, he'd have sat there until doomsday, or you unnailed the door, one.

I don't know where these ideas come from. Why would it be good luck to see a heron and bad luck to see a hawk? I guess because a heron won't kill chickens. Anyway, I'm not as bad as Papa, but there's still something in me that would be obliged if this bird changed my luck.

Jim watched a good twenty minutes while it found a dinner's worth of prey, then turned as if to see whether the man were worth further concern. Wings unfolding, it pushed itself forward, like a man might heave himself from a diving board. It unleashed a wad of yellowish waste and flew parallel to the ground until it got a good purchase, lofting toward Nellie Ridge.

Doubling back a quarter mile up the creek, it was as graceful in mid-flight as it was awkward on takeoff. Dark legs tucked and folded, it soared over the house heading downstream. *Reminds me of a machine, the way they unfold themselves. Like something you'd need to oil ever now and then. I swear, I hope Papa was right.*

He went back to the roof and finished the chimney. The rest of the day he weather-stripped kitchen door and windows, and moved his things into the little room. A cot on the south wall. A stove for heat and cooking, a place to sit, a place to eat, a place to sleep. Outside, food was buried or in springhouse or smokehouse, and inside, canned tomatoes and beans stocked the pantry. He'd get by.

He'd mail order a coal and firewood delivery in the morning. He would have picked it up himself but had no car, and he had not yet built a wagon his horse might pull.

He slept like a man with a clear conscience. After tending to livestock and feeding chickens, he ate breakfast, then headed to the post office. The creek to his left sparkled in the sun like diamond lacework. No heron. He stopped to examine fresh deer prints and wondered if the animals were still nearby. They had come from the ridge to drink but had not returned, at least not there. They might be standing in the bend of the creek, just out of sight, watching him for signs of danger. Probably the doe and fawn Nell had seen.

A hundred yards up the road someone had thrown a soft drink bottle and a paper bag onto the roadside. The shattered bottle's neck looked sharp enough to hobble horse or human for a long time. The bag held wax paper, pieces of light bread crust, and several hundred red ants, which Jim brushed off his hand. *Biting little bastards.* He protected his fingers with the bag as he painstakingly put glass shards into his saddle-bag.

Wonder why folks think a car window's something to throw trash out of. I've told Evans we need receptacles, but he says there's no money. They can build that damn road, and a campground. Seems they could afford a couple of trash cans.

At Nellie, Hub Carter's beat-up Essex was not yet in evidence. It had started life dark brown but was now faded to the color of an elderly camel. Hub's habit was to leave Waynesville early with mail bound for Cataloochee, spend the day in the post office jawing with whoever might pass through, or napping if no one showed up, then carry outgoing mail to Waynesville. A routine broken only by Sunday.

Jim emptied his saddlebag in the canister on the porch. He looked inside. Empty shelves testified this had once been a thriving store, but Hub carried only bare necessities these days—matches, coffee, shotgun shells. A few camping tools, fishhooks, line, leader.

The mail sorting table was nearly bare. Five years ago Jim would have had to rat through at least a hundred pieces, but this morning there were only three, including one that made him flinch—a letter to him, wrapped in a pink square envelope smelling of Nell's perfume, a purple three-cent stamp in the upper right-hand corner, aligned perfectly with the envelope's edge.

It was cold in the little building, but it was this find that made him shudder all over. Sniffing the envelope again, he put it into his jacket pocket and walked outside.

On the porch he saw no reason to think anyone but he was in Cataloochee. Sign of neither automobile nor horse save his in any direction. He smelled no wood smoke, and nothing but breeze tickled his ears. "Lonesome Valley" came to mind, which he hummed and sang on his way home. He'd know after reading Nell's letter whether he'd have to keep walking it by himself.

Stirring up the fire, he sighed, then sat at his hermit's table. When he slit the envelope and turned it over, two pictures slid out, his children smiling like life was perfectly happy. School pictures, except Little Elizabeth was not yet a pupil. He wondered about that for a minute, then propped the pictures against the base of the lamp. He'd give a hundred dollars to catch them running off the porch, then swing them as he had done so many times.

He took a deep breath and unfolded the letter.

Dear Jim,

I hardly know how to put words on this paper. Or rather I don't really know what to say that will do either of us any good. I do hope you are well, and taking care of yourself. And I assure you Little Elizabeth and Henry Mack are just fine, growing like weeds. They miss their daddy.

Jim, I had hoped you would follow me, if not for my sake, for theirs.

But, sadly, I suppose it was not to be. I had thought you cared enough for me to leave that place where I could never ever be happy.

It hurts that you have chosen not to come. And it hurts even more that I must ask for a <u>divorce</u>, so I can get on with whatever life is left me.

Jim stood and looked out the window. *Divorce.* The word slapped his mind, same as if she had called him a vile name. Made him out to be sinful. A thousand things flurried in his head, but chief among them were anger and astonishment, so much that at first he didn't notice the melodrama in her last phrase.

He finished reading the letter at the window.

No, I haven't found a beau. I want to have nothing to do with <u>men</u> for a while. You have numbed something inside of me. I hear music on the radio but don't want to dance just yet. Maybe someday. But not yet.

I really have no hard feelings, Jim. At least none to make me want to hurt you, or myself. I trust you have none toward me, either. We can still be <u>friends</u>.

Mother and Father are well. They asked me to tell you to send money for our children's support, and I think that is reasonable.

I would appreciate hearing from you soon, as this is tiring and vexing to us all. We need to get it behind us.

Jim, I will always remember our first days together, and hold you warmly in my heart, always.

She signed it, simply, *Nell.*

After rereading it a few times he consigned it to the fireplace and threw another stick of wood atop. "Last heat I'll get out of her," he muttered. He put on his jacket and went to the porch.

And wept. For his marriage. For his children. For all Cataloochee. For all good people who found themselves in sorrow. But mostly for his children.

He finally sat on the step and blew his nose. Through red eyes he looked toward the barn and knew she was right, she could never have been happy there. He was a dumb son of a bitch not to have realized that off the bat. The more he thought about it the more he realized that staying in the valley was right for him. If he could see Mack and Little Elizabeth fairly often, it might be all right.

That night he sat at the table with a couple of sheets of notebook paper. He meant to tell her of his feelings, but after several false starts he knew he could no more do that than crochet. He threw the sheets into the cookstove and found a postcard. On its back he wrote:

Dear Nell,

I am fine. I don't know how to get a divorce, but I'm sure your mother can figure what to tell me to do. If Henry could pay for it, that would be good. I will send money, but I want to see my kids as often as I can. Keep the car. I loved you the best I knew how.

Jim

After he banked the fire for the night, he drank a stout toast to Cataloochee and rolled instantly into a dreamless land.

His luck did not change one way or the other over the winter. He signed separation papers drawn up by Henry Johnson's attorney. He visited Silas Wright on one pretense or another every couple of weeks. They both needed company, although neither would admit it. Keeping warm occupied much of his time, and he looked forward to spring, when he would plant a garden. The big bed in the main part of the house stayed empty except for a family of field mice, which found it a dandy place to spend the winter.

CHAPTER 34

Directive

Superintendent Evans's first directive about structures, issued back in 1931, was vague enough for Jim to be a literalist about it. He had been enjoined "to destroy all useless shacks which might serve as fire hazards." In the first place, burning down a fire hazard was an act fraught with irony. In Jim's view, there were few "shacks" in Cataloochee, and "useless" was a relative term. A man might be caught in a tempest and find, even in an abandoned hog pen, shelter from the storm.

Evans had, however, been specific about Uncle Andy's farm. Jim had to admit the place was dilapidated. Jonquils and hyacinths still graced the grounds in spring, just before apple trees rioted full white. But years ago—about the time the big chestnut died—things started downhill. Uncle Andy went to his reward during the bad winter of 1892, and as children moved away and Aunt Charlotte aged, neglect began to strangle the house. Humans had not lived there in a decade or more.

Jim set the can of coal oil on the front porch and sighed. He fingered a box of wooden matches. *A house needs to be lived in, same as a person. If the spirit's gone, the body dies. When a family leaves, a house never feels a hearth fire or hears happy stories or smells beans cooking or sees young'uns learn to walk. That means peeling paint and stove-in steps and leaky roof, and it soon dies. You might say I'm getting ready to cremate a body that's been dead awhile.*

He decided to start with an outbuilding or two. He looked all over for signs of life. The dog they had spooked was long gone, and no sign of her pups remained. A lone brown bat slept in a corner of an eave on the barn shed. Inside was a broom handle. *Gosh, Uncle Andy left firewood. But he died sudden, so didn't get to choose the leaving of it. When I was a young'un, Mama kept a picture of his corpse on the mantel next to a picture of my daddy. He was laid out in the front room, everything a little out of focus except his nose, thin and sharp as a hatchet. Gave me the creeps.*

He knocked wasp nests into a basket for fishbait when he might get away to Lake Junaluska. A groundhog had burrowed beneath the back side of the barn, something Uncle Andy never would have put up with. *Reckon a little warmth overhead'll bring him out of there. Wonder what all else lives here. Ground squirrels, birds, snakes, lizards, rats. Ain't seen a sign of a house cat.*

Papa used to tell of mink, otter, and beaver, but they're long since trapped out. As a young'un I hunted plenty of small animals, but now about all you see is possums and mice. A mole or two. Coons and skunks are uncommon. Ain't seen a bobcat in years, unless you count that shadow on the trail a couple of weeks ago. Foxes are gone. But look here.

His boot toe scattered a fair quantity of rabbit pellets. *Used to call these things smartness pills. Feed them to a kid, he'll smarten up quick. So rabbits are coming back. Foxes will follow. And big cats. Maybe this place will change for the good, who knows. I know once you light a match, you can't go back.*

He sloshed coal oil on the corncrib and fished a match from his pocket. The little structure roared like a locomotive for a few minutes, giving off an inordinate amount of smoke, fed by corncobs and dusty leaves. Jim looked around for Uncle Andy, halfway expecting the old man to point a bony finger at him and make him stop.

Each successive structure was larger, but practice did not quiet his shaky fingers. As the smokehouse went up, he remembered helping hang meat many a fall. *When we finished working up the hogs, Aunt Charlotte put out a feed, and Uncle Andy set the furniture against the walls and broke out a mandolin. I fiddled and we danced till way after midnight. We was having fun. No honky-tonk to it, just something joyful, even worshipful, thanks for another year, thanks for the meat, thanks for a gal to smile at and touch. Sure wish Nell could have seen such as that.*

A dance anymore's just for the hell of it, drinking and carrying on. Not a bit of joy. Like it was a job almost. Times have changed.

After burning this farm, he reported to Evans and hoped to wait a long while before burning others. Horace Wakefield had not yet given up on a museum in the park, and when he heard Jim had destroyed the Andy Carter house, he renewed his campaign. Everyone from Superintendent Evans to Secretary Ickes to President Roosevelt was asked to help preserve something of the mountain way of life. To no avail.

It took the wheels of government a while, but Jim finally received a new directive. Evans was this time specific to a fault. Jim was to supervise burning "all houses, barns, and any and all outbuildings associated with abandoned properties." Jim was standing in his kitchen with the document but had to sit halfway through the reading of it. He was to begin by meeting a party of CCC enrollees at the Mack Hawkins place on Carter Fork, Cataloochee, North Carolina, on Wednesday, June 20, 1934, at nine in the morning. Evans, moreover, had contracted with a man named Thad Carter to help destroy structures. Evans trusted Jim would give Carter "any help, aid, and assistance" necessary to carry out his orders, and reminded Jim that if he couldn't fulfill his duties, hundreds of men needed work. And the closing, instead of Evans's normal "Very truly yours," read "Cordially." A handwritten note said he would come "to personally inspect" Thursday.

"That son of a bitch," Jim muttered. Orders to burn his own homeplace. Tomorrow. And to get along with Thad Carter. "That son of a bitch."

Jim had last seen Thad Carter in the mid 1920s, loafing at the train depot in Waynesville, swinging a long silver chain attached to pleated trousers, and hinting of easy money up north. Rumor had it that he went to Dearborn, Michigan, to work for Ford, but could not keep a job and spent time in jail for some petty crime or other. In Jim's opinion the boy had not been worth shooting then, and likely was perfectly worthless now.

Jim had not slept well since Nell had left, nearly a year before. That night he gave up trying at about four and fixed a breakfast he could not eat. He had his mother's habit of showing up early for anything— church, funeral, doctor's appointment, wedding. So he rode slowly up Carter Fork a little after eight, nervous, creaky, like a man bound for his own execution.

Hitching his horse, Jim saw a man of middle height with graying, un-parted hair and a pronounced slouch emerge from the front room, lean against the column, and light a cigarette. Eyebrows like gray woolly bears. His crooked, shit-eating grin made Jim want to puke. Prepared as he was to dislike this man, Jim was nevertheless surprised at how intensely and quickly he did so.

"Hot enough for you?" Thad drawled as Jim approached.

"Maybe. You must be Thad Carter."

He blew smoke in Jim's direction and held out his hand. "The same. You're Hawkins. I remember your daddy was bad to lay out of a night."

"I believe you're confusing him with some of your people."

The eyebrows undulated like snakes. "Oh, a little tetchious, are we?"

"Listen, Carter. Ain't nothing I like about this. Especially you. So let's get something straight. I'm in charge here. You stink like a brewery. There'll be no drinking on the job, and if that's last night I smell, you're too drunk to work. Show up like that again and you're gone. Under-stand?"

Thad lit a fresh cigarette off the old one and grinned. "Yup, Mr. Ranger, sir."

"Do you have tools?"

"Matches."

"I brought rakes and shovels to the barn last night. Maybe by the time you get them the CCC will be here. Move it."

Thad saluted, sloppily, left-handed, and headed to the barn. Jim stared at him and fingered his revolver.

The CCC supervisor left a half dozen enrollees with Jim and headed off toward Rabbit Ridge with nine more for a day of hard labor. Jim's bunch looked at the same time cocky and relaxed, like they would have a lark this workday. Jim looked them over and figured he could do worse, but not much. The six of them plus Thad promised to be about as intelligent as three normal Haywood County men.

"All right, boys, you're mine for eight hours," he said. "Carter yonder and I are to make sure these structures are destroyed today. Nothing left except ashes, and all fire extinguished. Understand?"

Holding rakes and a mattock, they nodded and shifted from foot to foot. Two carried tow sacks folded over their belts.

"Those sacks for anything in particular?" Jim asked.

"Naw, sir, they was just handy." This boy was a Yankee of some description.

"Okay. I want every inch of this place searched. Put anything of value in these bags."

"Is it evidence?" Thad asked.

"What do you mean?"

"Evidence somebody worth a tinker's damn used to live in this falling-down house."

Jim wheeled on Thad. "You know good and well I grew up here, and I'll thank you to keep your damn opinions to yourself." He looked at the boys and pointed. "I tended cattle and horses, milked and fed and castrated stock here. I shucked corn from that crib and slopped hogs in that sty. Played a lot of music and danced here. Mourned some kinfolks here. So if anybody has any objection to policing this place, let me know and I'll send you the hell home." The CCC straightened up considerably.

An hour later they assembled in the yard. Slim pickings. Castoffs like a broken stove lifter and some hairpins, half a pair of ice tongs, a zinc circle with BALL stamped in the middle. Stuff Harrogate had missed.

"Didn't leave many valuables, did we?" asked Jim.

"Except this, sir." The one redheaded man handed Jim a penknife.

"Where was this?"

"In the room over the kitchen, shoved under the baseboard."

Mack had traded for the knife years ago and given it to his wife. It boasted inlaid mother-of-pearl handles, one of which had a silver shield engraved with her initials.

"Momma lost this when I was about eight. She fretted for days. Said she'd give whoever found it a Yankee dime."

The tall one with the Adam's apple asked him what a Yankee dime might be.

"It's what Mama used to call a quick peck on the cheek."

"Sir, I don't understand."

"Where are you from?"

"New Jersey."

"No wonder. Let's get on with it."

They started small, successively burning the corncrib, hog pen, outhouse, springhouse. The barn had not held hay in years but contained plenty of tinder and fuel. They doused the interior supports with coal oil, lit them, and ran outside. Once established, the fire chimneyed through a hole in the roof, which cracked like cannon fire. The building turned upon itself, a mass of yellow and orange and red with dark spaces representing the chestnut framing. The building threatened to smoke for days, and Jim wondered if Evans, the prick, would smell it in Sugarlands in a day or two. *One of the points they sold this damn park with was that it would "save the American public's heritage." Bull feathers. Here I am burning my own.*

Jim had so far helped light all the structures but handed off to Thad when it was the house's turn. Jim walked fifty yards down the lane, listening intently but not daring to look. When he heard the building catch, he looked toward the heavens, then turned. The CCC had stationed themselves on the perimeter like sentinels. Fire raged like the blood in Jim's temples, and he stood with tears streaming. Witnessing a vile sacrilege.

Destroying the place where as a baby he had padded in knitted booties. The place he'd learned fire burns and ice is cold, and that nothing is better for the sniffles than a mother's love and warm VapoRub. The place he'd broken windows with homemade baseballs. The place that had kept him dry during storms and wet in the tub on Saturday nights. The place where his father had read the Bible out loud every night, and where

Jim had learned about alcohol when he was caught sneaking from Mack's jug, and where his punishment had been to keep drinking until he retched. His place.

Two boxwoods beside the front porch exploded into flame and almost as quickly turned into skinny fire bushes. As Jim wiped his eyes, the yard maple too caught fire. Jim hoped it would survive. His childhood friend. He'd used its keys for helicopters and its dead branches for kindling, watched many an ant on its errands up and down the gray bark, learned during rainstorms that tree bark is designed to nudge water to go where it is needed.

By three the CCC patrolled each site, raking ashes to make sure they would be dead by dark. A desultory drizzle started, raindrops sibilant when they hit hot ash. Water from the creek created smoke and steam in short gray columns, hissing like miscreant snakes. Jim hoped his hands would stop shaking.

Two chimneys seemed to rise phoenix-like, bracketing the ashes on the east and west sides. Two river rock columns, four hearthstones never again to know warmth. If he kept this up, there would be hundreds of these snaggletoothed monuments to progress. But he also knew Evans would never let them stand, for such a thing could kill a tourist stupid enough to try to climb one of them.

Slow hoofbeats announced Silas Wright heading toward the scene like some ancient bearer of bad news. He pulled up and sat his black mare, packed his pipe, and lit it to augment what was lifting toward heaven. Raising a batwing from his coat, he drank, dismounted, and slowly walked to Jim's side.

The men stood there for ten minutes, the old man seeming to stoop with age as he watched, the young man holding himself as if he might pop. Silas finally put a hand on Jim's shoulder. "Mean sumbitch, ain't it?"

Jim drew in about a gallon of air. "Silas, this hurts like hell. Worse than Nell leaving."

"I smelled it all the way over the mountain. Didn't smell right. A brush fire's a clean smell, but this had the devil in it. Had to see what you were up to."

"I wouldn't be doing this except my job kind of depends on it. Like I said, it hurts, but you know what's the hardest part?"

"What?"

"Today I realized it's all going to be gone. My homeplace is gone. My wife is gone. My children. Soon everybody'll be gone. And the hard thing is, I'll stay, and survive, damn it to hell."

"Same way I felt when Rhetta died, son. And, by the way, I ain't going nowhere."

"You mean you aren't going to die?"

"No time soon. Want a drink?"

"Silas, if I took one, I'd not quit until I killed myself."

"I'll have yours, then." He turned up the bottle. "Who in hell is that? He don't look right."

"He ain't. That's Thad Carter."

"Jacob's boy?"

Jim nodded.

"Ain't seen him in forever. Didn't he burn a barn one time?"

"I don't know. When?"

"Eight, ten years ago. He'd been up north. Best I remember he showed up in Waynesville, kind of down and out. He took up with that son of Bill Howell's. You remember him, a fat man named Jesse. He'd been feuding with his cousin Joe, lived down the creek from me. You likely don't remember it because you was in school. Anyhow, Jesse and Thad showed up one day. Next thing you knowed, Joe Howell's barn was a pile of cinders. I heard whoever done it done it with gasoline. Throwed it on two mules and a cow that had the bad luck to be in the way, too. And come to find that Thad soon got considerably better off, enough to go plumb to Asheville and get hisself thrown in the drunk tank."

"Evans sent him. To help destroy structures."

Silas drew on his pipe and nodded. "So now the government's paying him to burn houses down. I'm beginning to think the damn government has good sense every now and then."

"Why?"

"At least they've hired somebody with experience. I wouldn't let that boy out of my sight. You know what? I believe I'd just as soon have McPeters running around loose."

Jim was silent.

"What happened to him, anyhow?"

"I couldn't say."

"Can't, or won't?"

"Let's just say I'm not worried about him anymore."

"I'd sure as hell put this Carter in his place. Andy Carter's spinning in his grave, that's for sure. If he'd known a grandson of his was burning houses in Cataloochee, he'd jump up and kill him his own self. A Carter that would burn down a house is lower than a snake's belly." Silas stretched and looked around. "Now, then. Here's a question."

"What's that?"

"Are you going to be all right?"

"I hope so, Silas."

"Good. Because it's plumb stupid for two growed men to stand in the damn rain and watch folks spread ashes around. If you won't have a drink with me, I'm going home. But if you need anything, let me know."

"Thanks for showing up, Silas."

"Keep that damn firebug away from my end of the valley, hear?"

Silas unhitched his horse and led her down the lane as if he were walking his sweetheart home from school. Jim did not guess that Silas no longer cared for people to watch him mount a horse. Jim just knew he finally appreciated hell out of this old man, his neighbor.

CHAPTER 35

No Farming

Silas woke to rain's rhythm on the shake roof and a steady southern breeze through his open window. He turned from back to side and closed his eyes but within a minute raised up like Lazarus. "Who in hell *was* Miss Agnes?"

He had dreamed about his brother, dead sixty or more years from a gunshot through the head. What they never knew was who pulled the trigger or why. A right-handed man, Paul had lain dead on the bedroom floor with a Forehand .32 pistol in his left. His wife and mother-in-law had both been in the building but neither had admitted to having seen a thing. Silas had been at the barn when he'd heard the shot. When he'd torn into the front room, Paul's wife had knelt beside the body, cradling her husband's right arm in her lap and wailing. Her mother had stood in the front doorway, arms akimbo, expressionless. Coroner's inquest had ruled a suicide, but they never knew what really had happened.

Paul had been a happy-go-lucky man who could double you over in laughter with a particular turn of phrase. Whenever he'd heard something extraordinary, he'd whistle and say, in a high-pitched, nasal voice, "Well, kiss my ass, Miss Agnes," with a strong iambic beat.

Silas sat on the edge of the bed and shook the cobwebs from his head. "Well, kiss my ass, Miss Agnes," he said, and smiled. How long had it been since he had heard that? *I was barely twenty when they found Paul, over sixty years ago. I'm eighty-four. Nearly sixty-five years. I'll be damned. I'm about to get old.*

He lit the lamp and dressed by its flickering light. He almost never looked in the mirror over the washstand but this morning lingered at a scarecrow of a man, lined like a bad road. If he thought of himself at all, it was as a man of thirty, a full head of brown hair, ears unlike an elephant. He shook his head as he raked a wet comb through his hair, covering bald patches as big as tomatoes. "Some old son of a bitch the government's about to evict," he said, frowning.

In the kitchen he lit lamps, built a fire, and checked on a funnel spider beside the wood box. "I won't kick you out, old man," he said, peering into a silken cone in which legs were poised to grab breakfast. "If they send me out, I'll take you with me."

He sighed, poured a drink, and sat at the table, upon which lay a letter.

August 25, 1934
Mr. Silas Wright
Cataloochee, NC

Dear Mr. Wright:
Replying to your letter of the 22nd, I regret to advise you that all lease fees both state and federal are cash in advance and I cannot make exceptions to this rule. Indeed, I might add, no farming will be permitted until the fees have been paid.

Regretting my inability to give you more time on this, and, trusting that you will give the matter your prompt attention, I am,

Yours very truly,
J. R. Evans, Supt.

The letter Silas had written that had occasioned this reply had asked for leniency. He had mentioned the hard times and had asked permission to make his annual lease payment, sixty dollars, in September, after he sold his cattle. Until then he did not expect to lay hands on two bit's worth of cash. He had posted the letter with some optimism. Where that had found a source, he could not now say.

He put on a pot of coffee. He'd seen worse times, during the war, when neither salt nor coffee were to be had. This depression, as folks were calling it, hurt everyone, but he had plenty to eat and drink, unlike back then, when a month's rations might have been a peck of potatoes. Folks now were hollering, but mostly because they weren't old enough to know real deprivation. Salt and coffee and meat and potatoes were still for sale. Only trouble was, people now thought good times should go on forever, and had not squirreled away even a buffalo nickel.

Silas's father, Jonathan, had always said a man needed to keep a little something put by, the whereabouts of which were known only to himself and God. Jonathan had followed his own advice but had had the bad judgment to salt bills away in a pasteboard box. During the depression of the 1880s he'd discovered that mice and mold had spent it long before he'd unearthed it.

Silas kept a few hundred dollars in a mason jar under a bedroom floorboard. He counted it every now and then, pleased by the ring of coin in glass and the musty smell of wrinkled dollars. He could pay the government—but it was the principle of the thing. He had asked nicely, without sarcasm or bad humor. Evans's reply had been curt and officious, and to Silas's mind, deserved a reprimand.

He looked out the kitchen window. Rain echoed his mood as he scratched his chin. *Hair falls out like October leaves, but this damn beard won't quit growing.* After Rhetta had died, he had briefly let it sprout, but his whiskers came in as white as a dogwood flower. This morning he said, "To hell with it. If folks think I'm old as Methusalem, that's their problem." He did not reach for razor and strop.

Over coffee he decided to talk to somebody about the letter, but who? Harrogate had slipped away again amidst talk that a woman might have finally latched on to him. His closest neighbor, Mary Carter, had been gone quite awhile. Really, the only person left with any sense was Jim Hawkins, who worked for the service. But maybe that was exactly why he needed to talk to him.

Perhaps a half dozen families still lived between his place and Jim's. When a thousand or more people had lived in Cataloochee, Silas could have wished them all gone. No longer.

He saw nothing amiss in the mile between his house and Uncle Andy's place. No poison oak to speak of, the creek making music by the roadside, an occasional bird flitting in the rain. The ruins of Uncle Andy's place, overgrown with grass and scrub trees, showed what the valley was becoming.

Aunt Mary's porch was empty except for a forlorn rag hanging on a clothesline like some orphan had left it behind. At the church house he dismounted. Somehow he needed to see the door shut against the dampness. He stumbled at the steps and caught himself on the railing. "Damned if I don't hate getting old," he muttered, and sat on the step. *Wonder where Harrogate's got off to. I first saw him right here, when—sixteen, eighteen years ago. Wonder if there's any truth to that rumor he's got caught by a woman.*

Rain settled into something like mist. *It's how I see things anymore. Through a cloud.* At Nellie he saw no one awake or, for that matter, alive, although by the footprints, folks had come through recently. As he rounded the turn into Lucky Bottom, the horse snorted and flicked her ears. Wood smoke curled a yard off the ground like a blue-white snake. Silas would not have been more surprised to see a gypsy caravan.

Three tents had sprouted in the field like mushrooms. Two men tended a campfire before the largest tent. One of the smaller tents bulged occasionally as if someone inside were trying to subdue a small animal. Whoever had left boots outside the third tent would have sodden feet that day.

Silas sat the horse and stared at the vagabonds, who apparently had not heard his approach. Either they were trying to cook with green wood or everything in reach was too wet to burn. The men, determined to make coffee if nothing else, fanned the meager fire with floppy hats.

When Silas urged his horse close, one of the men stood and waved.

Silas nodded. They looked friendly but wore enough clothes to stuff a freight car. He dismounted and greeted them.

The two were maybe thirty, and had not seen soap in a while. Stale armpits, wet wool, cigarette smoke. Silas held out his hand. "Morning, stranger."

"Good morning, sir," said the balder of the two. Gangly, an inch over six feet, with an engaging grin. "I'm Spee." He shook Silas's hand.

"If you don't care," Silas said, "tell me what kind of name that might be."

The man laughed. "A nickname, sir. My name's James Pettigrew. Folks started calling me S.P. in college, I guess because of the *s* and *p* together. It stuck."

"Okay, Mr. Spee, I'm Silas Wright. Where you boys from?"

One of the tents opened suddenly, as if birthing two men in succession, brothers by their looks, dressed in as much weather gear as they could extract from their knapsacks.

"We're from the central part of the state," said Spee. "I'm from Davidson County. This is Robert. These that just got up are Wendell and his brother George. There's two more in that other tent, I guess they're getting some beauty sleep."

"Some of us need more of that than others. What brings you to Catalooch?"

"We're hiking the Smokies," said Spee.

"Why?"

Spee looked at the old man curiously. "Just because," he said. "It's beautiful here—and we mean to see as much of it as we can this vacation. Started at Soco. We thought we were heading to Clingmans Dome but were sidetracked. Hope to end up in Cades Cove."

"At this rate you'll be there in about two years. So you're on vacation. What from?"

"A furniture plant," said Spee.

"I thought you said you was a college man."

"I am—or was. We're management. I'm a designer. They're bookkeepers, idea men, owners."

"Do tell. I take it you ain't too inconvenienced by this Wall Street panic we've had?"

"We have some savings, and closed the plant for a month. We'll see what happens."

"Well, son, I'd say everybody will pretty well stay home until this is over. Which means they'll wear out their furniture. If you can make it until better times, you'll do well."

"That's what we figure."

Two more emerged, one with spiky hair and the other wearing a clipped mustache and long sideburns. "Mr. Wright, this is Bob and Joe. Sir, can I ask you a question?"

Silas nodded.

"Do you actually *live* here?"

Silas wasn't sure whether to laugh or hit the boy. "About two mile up the road. In an actual house. With a roof. I slept dry last night."

"Remarkable, just remarkable. How many people live here?"

"Oh, I don't know. A few dozen in Big Catalooch. Don't think anybody's left on Little Catalooch."

"May I ask if you plan to stay?"

"You're right nosy."

"Sorry, Mr. Wright. It's just that we've not talked to a real mountaineer before. Except the warden, I guess."

"Do I measure up to what you was expecting?"

"Yes, sir, I believe you do."

"Then keep very still. I'm a-going to kill you."

The boys stared at one another. "Excuse me?" said Spee.

"Hain't you heered? We et flatlanders for breakfast yere, and I ain't had me none this morning."

Joe looked for a weapon, but all he saw were trout rods. Bob turned as if to bolt.

Silas laughed. "Ain't you boys got enough sense to know a joke? Oh. I forgot. You slept out in the rain."

Spee reached into the corner of his tent for a black box. "Mr. Wright, do you mind if I snap your picture?"

Silas noticed the boy was missing a thumb tip. "Do I look like a critter in a zoo?"

"No, sir. I didn't mean to offend. I'd just like to remember you."

"You can't remember this old mug, there's something wrong. But, yes, make my picture."

Spee posed his five friends and Silas across the fire and snapped a few photos. Silas suggested some more from the other side. "You wouldn't want to remember this sorry fire," he said.

"Thank you, Mr. Wright. If you give me an address, I'll mail you copies."

"Cataloochee, North Carolina, is all you need."

"You mean you get mail back in here?"

"Every day, son. It might not look like where you boys is from, but it's still North Carolina."

Rain stopped as Silas reined Maude up at Jim's porch. He had been afraid the warden would be gone, but Jim raised his hand in greeting at the kitchen door. "Morning, Silas." He wore the uniform less jacket, tie, and hat. "What brings you so early?"

"Hello, Jim." He dismounted and tied the horse. "It ain't early. I been up three hours."

"True. I'm having trouble getting started. Didn't sleep good."

"You have a dram before bed?"

"I've never been much to drink."

"Me neither. But a dram of a morning and another at night keep a man going. Kind of like cutting the switch on and off. You ought to try it."

Jim nodded. "How about some coffee?"

"Don't mind if I do."

Jim held the door for Silas, who stooped as he entered the warm room. As he stood by the cookstove, his clothes began to steam. "Kindly damp," he said.

"We need the rain," said Jim, pouring two cups. "How about a biscuit and jelly?"

"Is that what you're getting by on, Jim Hawkins?"

"You want a load of breakfast? I'll be happy to cook it up."

Silas laid his hat on the scarred trestle table and sat. "No, Jim. I didn't mean it that way. Looks like me and you are bachelors hunkered at the ends of the valley."

Jim sat opposite. "I appreciate your asking. Looks like I'll be by myself for a long while. But I'll not starve. I'm a lot like you, Silas. I can get along fine."

Silas sipped his coffee. "What's fine at seven in the morning can be awful at midnight. Seven in the morning, a man's got some small reason to hope he'll have a good day. Come dark, he knows he ain't had one, and he's got eight more hours to put up with whatever ghosts his mind might care to entertain."

Jim nodded and drank. "God, that's the truth." He stood and looked out the window.

"Jim, you got to keep busy."

He turned and smiled. "I do. I'm really doing pretty good, neighbor. And I appreciate your words. But you didn't ride all the way down here just to hold my hand."

Silas nodded. "I crave a little advice."

"What's the problem?"

Silas took Evans's letter from his inside pocket and spread it on the table. "I don't know how serious to take this."

Jim read the letter and laid it faceup, like the last card in a game of stud poker. "I'd have to study about that, Silas. He means what he says, of course. Will you send the money?"

"Not inclined to."

"I know that. I asked if you will."

"What if I didn't?"

"I assume you have it."

"Of course I do. I also have principles."

Jim chuckled. "So you ask me, who makes his living with the service, whether you ought to disobey it?"

"Who better to ask?"

"I have principles, too."

"Jim, we all got them. Question is, do we have loyalties?"

"What do you mean?"

"I need to know if I'm asking somebody who's first a human being and my Christian neighbor, or a man who's a dad-jim government employee before he's a human being."

"Let me put it this way. You can trust me. If I need to tell you something you don't care to hear, I'll do it. Fair enough?"

"Okay. So what does he mean by 'no farming'? How do you not farm? Does that mean I can't milk until I pay up?"

Jim smiled. "I'd milk, just to keep the cow quiet. Of course, the only way to enforce that is for him to catch you farming, whatever that means. And he's pretty busy."

"So I could sow corn, and go ahead like last year and send money after I sell my cattle?"

"I didn't say that. All I meant was you could likely get away with it. Unless, of course, Evans told me to enforce it."

"Now we get down to it. Say you got orders to get that sixty dollars from old Wright up there. What then?"

"I'd be obliged to ask for it. By mail, because I wouldn't want to catch you farming."

"But you'd eventually come see me."

Jim sat and rubbed his forehead. In a minute he leveled his gaze at Silas. "Yes, if Evans ordered me to. Then I'd need that sixty dollars."

"What if I didn't fork it over?"

"I'd have to report, then wait on Evans's reply. That'd take another week or two."

"But eventually you'd nail my ass to the wall."

"I wouldn't exactly put it that way, Silas. Let's say I'd have to enforce the law."

"You'd evict me?"

Jim shook his head slowly. "I don't know if I could, Silas. I don't know if I could. But listen here. Why don't you write another letter. Tell Evans you'll do your best to send the money. Keep doing that every couple of weeks. That might keep us off your porch."

Silas folded the letter and put it away. "Good advice. But, truth to tell, I don't know if I want to stay, after what I saw this morning."

"What was that?"

"Bunch of boys camping smack in the middle of Lucky Bottom. Beat anything I ever laid eyes on."

"Yeah, I saw them yesterday. Nice guys."

"They don't know no better'n to try to start a fire with wet wood. You think there'll be more critters like that in here?"

"Sure. But we'll restrict them to the permanent campground. That way we can keep them to one place. Less risk of setting the woods on fire."

"Ain't no danger of that from those boys. So I'm seeing the start of something, eh?"

"Yep. Afraid so."

"Well, I reckon I'll go on home, if you don't think the government will come for me."

"It'll be a while, Silas. More coffee?"

"No, Jim, I'll need to stop six times to piss as it is."

The men stood. "Hope I didn't make you mad, Silas."

"No, son, I ain't mad. I just needed to know if you was still a man I could deal with. This is more important than that fishing business we agreed on a few years ago."

"Take care of yourself, Silas. If you were to happen to find sixty dollars laying around, bring it down. I'll send it to Evans."

"Not likely. I'd just as soon write them letters."

Jim watched the old man struggle to get his foot into the stirrup for a few seconds, then turned away. The whole world was growing old and lonesome.

Requiem

January 22, 1935

CHAPTER 36

His Solitary Way

Silas Wright, dreaming.

Ahead of him railroad tracks laddered until they converged at the eastern horizon, while behind him they splayed whorishly toward the west. Hunkered beside a thicket of white-blooming roses, Silas pointed his aquiline nose eastward, as if preferring to smell fire and hot metal instead of fragrant blossoms.

He moved an errant briar cane, pricking his finger. Muttering to himself, he dislodged the point with his hawksbill. At his age even slight punctures bade fair to bleed him dry, but this wound healed immediately. His skin was no longer papery, nor were the backs of his hands spotted with troubles or time. A young man of quickening spirit.

After whetting the knife on his boot, he dropped it into his pocket. The eastern sky was intense, impasto, blue, like an ancient Florentine pot. He felt in his fob and pulled out a scrap of newspaper from May 1873, then found a filigreed gold watch with red hands that indicated a quarter after twelve.

Time usually shadowed him, hurling headlong insults, but this afternoon he felt no urgency, as if nearly nine decades had not diminished his body. He clicked the watch closed and glanced to his left.

His friend Hiram, wearing a broad-brimmed black hat and chewing a stalk of orchard grass, touched his hat brim and winked. "She's a-coming," he said quietly. Silas nodded and reviewed the horizon. Their mounts, tied to a pair of tulip trees close to a ravine dropping sharply westward, nickered nervously.

Hiram removed his hat and wiped his forehead with the back of his arm. His dark hair shone above his brow, unlined, like Silas's. He wore no ring on his left hand. Both men scanned the east intently, like train jumpers, desperadoes.

Hiram pointed. Silas barely made out gradually approaching smoke past the Padgett farm. There was no station where they crouched, but they stood and hitched their trousers like the train would stop simply because two whippersnappers wanted to study it.

They watched the machine toil closer through a shimmering curtain of heat. Then through tremulous light burst a thoroughly old-fashioned locomotive, huge, a wood burner guaranteed to cover both passengers and freight with a downfall of ash and live coals. Smoke poured from an oversize diamond-shaped stack, on the front of which hung a cyclopean lantern. Ground vibrated under Silas's boots. Their mounts, bridles and all, vanished.

The iron horse screeched and clanked and hissed like a threshing machine separating nuts from bolts in hell. It pulled no cars save the tender. On it rode three soot-blackened men flinging wood into the firebox as fast as they could pitch. Every fifth log seemed to shoot straight out the smokestack, like thick flaming arrow shafts spreading destruction. Silas turned to run from the apparition, but his legs would not obey. When he looked at Hiram, the stalk of grass in his friend's teeth incinerated. Hiram's hat burned on the ground behind him. The train was by then behind them, spitting brimstone, while fire ate everything in its path. Hiram himself caught fire, and just as Silas braced to be engulfed, he awoke.

Even from dreamless sleep, these days it took a while for Silas to figure out who—and when—and where he was. Over a quarter of an hour he changed from the young man in his nightmare to an old man, in the winter of 1935, in an even older bed, in a frame house, the last occupied dwelling save one in Cataloochee. Cataloochee, itself no more, everything except Silas's time-harried soul engulfed and digested by the Great Smoky Mountains National Park.

He sat shivering on the side of the bed. A few inadequate fireplace coals glowed. He stood at the edge of the hearthstone and stirred them with a shiny-handled poker. Adding a stick of dry deadfall, he muttered. "How in hell do them bastards expect a man to keep fire all night with one stick of green wood?" The piece caught.

His shaky hand threw in another stick. He sat on the bed and stared at the flames. "Hiram Carter. My Lord. How long's he been gone? Let's see . . . he died spring of '26, and it's winter of '35. Near about nine years. God, time flies."

Yawning, stretching, he stood again and banked a larger stick in front of the first two, and wondered how long that would heat the room. "Wasn't so damn much trouble I'd heat with coal," he said. "But I ain't got nobody to fetch it from town. Guess I'll stay cold."

He padded to the kitchen for a drink of springwater, cold enough to hurt his teeth. Outside dry snowflakes fell from an iron sky. He had no hope of further sleep, but on the other hand found no enthusiasm to begin a day that augured to be disagreeable. He went back to bed and pulled quilts about his chin. An inventory of aches and rasping joints uncovered a new pain toward the back of his head. Closing his eyes against it, he was asleep within ten minutes, breathing shallowly.

Silas Wright, dreaming, again.

The fire started in the schoolhouse he and Hiram and George had burned years ago, and although a brigade arrived, they could not bail enough creek water to do any good. People Silas had not seen in decades battled with buckets and hats and brooms, but they simply spread flame from tree to tree. Soon the church erupted in tongues of fire—all rushed there to no avail. The big field Hiram used to sow in oats itself blazed and threatened the sky. Animals bawled and brayed and barked as when an eclipse obscures the sun.

Silas wondered why he didn't feel warm as he walked slowly through the conflagration. A burning yellow-eyed mongrel dog seven hands high brushed his leg as it howled out of sight. The road simmered in front of him, and the only place not aflame was the creek. As Silas walked toward the water, it moved away from him, snakelike through the flames. Jumping trout incinerated immediately. His head hurt sharply.

Out of his barn loomed Rhetta's buggy pulled by four flaming draft horses. The driver, a woman who resembled his dead wife, wore a fiery dress. Like an opera character, she held a silver-strawed broom like a spear in her right hand and gentled a smoldering three-legged fice with her left.

The roof of his house exploded in flames. He walked to the front porch, sat, and looked back toward the valley. All Cataloochee—a burnt offering. He leaned against the skinny porch column to think. *My father's house. Built as a one-room cabin. I finished framing it.* The structure collapsed behind him. He saw a flaming chariot, whether lowering or riding atop a whirlwind, he could not tell, nor did he much care, for whatever was in the back of his head claimed his ultimate attention.

Jim Hawkins woke to a fine dusting of snow, weather that always made him want to hunt rabbits. Upon reflection, he had no desire to kill and dress a mess of them just for himself. Yesterday's mail had included two postcards for Silas, so he figured to tote his shotgun on the way in case he jumped a couple. If he did, he'd fix him and the old man some dinner.

After breakfast Jim saddled his horse and headed up the valley, thinking of what he had seen in the last six or seven years. Lots of beauty, from the white of potato blooms in his kitchen garden to the black fire of the big woodpeckers hunting ants in dead trees. Senseless destruction, not only of perfectly good houses and barns but also of rich lives uprooted like barren trees cast into the fire. Lots of misery on the faces of the old men and women leaving to spend their last years in cold, fireless exile.

The CCC had at least built a campground, but regulations decreed this time of year no one could use it. It seemed snatched from underground—boulders strewn like some giant's child had been playing. Levi Marion had laid his head there that past summer, sleeping by the creek because he couldn't rest in his new home. The Yankee tourists made fun of his stories and brogue, but he did not mind as long as he slept to the music of living water. Now he was buried near the church, and Jim wondered if he could hear the creek from there.

At the road to Carter Fork, Jim did not turn left, nor even look that direction. The last time he'd gone there was to burn his homeplace, and that scab was still anchored to the quick.

Empty store. Nelse a suicide. Vacant church, door nailed shut for the winter and maybe longer. Schoolhouse open to any firebug. Aunt Mary's house and outbuildings empty of anything save hopeful snakes and dry corncobs. A hairy poison oak vine spreading hydra-like over a fence post, from which depended rusty, sagging barbwire.

Nobody but the government would let poison oak get that rank. But Silas's fence is still tight, so there's hope left in the world. Haven't seen a fool rabbit, so I reckon me and him'll just have some coffee.

At the edge of the yard he sat his horse. No smoke from Silas's kitchen—very little from the main chimney. Tracks in the snow told of one lone fox loping through the yard in the night. Jim left his mount at the hitching post and came onto the porch, his boots leaving white images of his soles. He knocked several times.

The door had a lock, but Jim had never known it to be used. He strode into the front room, and heard only the muffled pop of the floor underneath the hooked rug. "Silas," Jim called. "You there?" He stomped, hoping to awaken a deep sleeper. Something rattled in the corner cabinet. He called again and shook his head, fingering the mail in his jacket pocket.

In the back bedroom he found Silas, still, unbreathing, covers to his chin, mouth open as if he had started to speak to whatever his closed eyes had seen.

"Damn," Jim muttered. Taking off his hat, he put a hand on Silas's shoulder. He moved it enough to know the old man was dead.

He poked at the fire, which responded with sparks and, after a few seconds, a piddling flame. A withy basket, its floor littered with crumbs of bark and slivers of wood, yielded enough tinder to bring a fair blaze. Jim picked up a stick of green oak, hefted it as if it were something for sale at a market, and smiled. He rejected it in favor of cured locust, which popped and spit and began to throw warmth into the room.

He pulled up a straight chair, and sat by the bed. "I'm going to have to write you up for that firewood." He stared at Silas like the old man might nod his head. "You know I'm kidding, Silas. Rest, brother. Just rest. You don't need any more firewood."

Let's see. I'll get in touch with his family. I think I have Ethel's phone number. If I can't find a casket—there might be one in his barn—I'll call Maney's Furniture. I'll have to take Maude to my place. Reckon this might be emergency enough to call Evans for a PSSUP so we can bury him.

He pulled two postcards from his pocket. "I'll read you your mail, anyway. You got one from the service. It's a receipt for that sixty dollars you said you weren't going to send. And here's one from Knoxville." He turned it over like it was some runic oracle. "It's from Bud."

Dear Silas,
Little Gene Silas Harrogate is cute like his mama but he's kinda stubborn like you. Don't let the d—n govmint run you off. Tell em I said ever body works for them'll burn in h—l fire.

  Your friend, Bud

Jim turned the card over and stared at the address, then read the message several times to himself. He stood, laid the card atop Silas's stiff fingers, and prayed, "Lord have mercy on us all." He sobbed the better part of five minutes, whether for Silas or himself he could not have told. Blowing his nose, he turned away from his neighbor and went to the porch. He looked eastward, then made his solitary way to his horse.

Acknowledgments

To colleagues, friends, and family who put up with my scribbling, I offer heartfelt thanks.

Special thanks:

to Stephen Woody, who told me tales of his grandfather;

to Leigh Feldman, who kept me focused;

to Laura Ford, who, I was told, was the best of editors, and I wholeheartedly agree;

to Jerry Leath (Jake) Mills, my "old perfesser," who has saved me from egregious errors, particularly about firearms;

to the Holden Beach Writers' Conference—Mary, Guy, Anita, fine listeners who helped discern the shape of this story;

and most especially to Mary, my muse and boon companion.

Notice: Persons attempting to find history in this narrative will be disappointed. It is not, nor has it ever pretended to be, history. But it's a pretty darn good story.